CAT WINTERS

AMULET BOOKS
NEW YORK

Library of Congress Cataloging-in-Publication Data

Names: Winters, Cat.
Title: The steep and thorny way / by Cat Winters.
Description: New York : Amulet Books, 2016. | Summary: "A sixteen-year-old biracial girl in rural Oregon in the 1920s searches for the truth about her father's death while avoiding trouble from the Ku Klux Klan in this YA historical novel inspired by Shakespeare's 'Hamlet'" — Provided by publisher.
Identifiers: LCCN 2015022705 | ISBN 9781419719158 (hardback)
Subjects: | CYAC: Prejudices—Fiction. | Murder—Fiction. | Ghosts—Fiction. | Racially mixed people—Fiction. | Oregon—History—20th century—Fiction. | BISAC: JUVENILE FICTION / Historical / United States / 20th Century. | JUVENILE FICTION / Horror & Ghost Stories. | JUVENILE FICTION / Social Issues / Prejudice & Racism.
Classification: LCC PZ7.W76673 St 2016 | DDC [Fic]—dc23
LC record available at http://lccn.loc.gov/2015022705

Text copyright © 2016 Catherine Karp
Jacket and title page photography © 2016 Symon Chow
Book design by Maria T. Middleton

For image credits, see page 337.

Printed and bound in U.S.A.
10 9 8 7 6 5 4 3 2 1

ABRAMS
THE ART OF BOOKS SINCE 1949

115 West 18th Street
New York, NY 10011
www.abramsbooks.com

IN LOVING
MEMORY OF
MY COUSIN
JIMMY
HACKER

DO NOT, AS SOME
UNGRACIOUS
PASTORS DO,

SHOW ME **THE
STEEP AND
THORNY
WAY** TO
HEAVEN,

WHILES, LIKE
A PUFFED AND
RECKLESS
LIBERTINE,
HIMSELF THE
PRIMROSE PATH
OF DALLIANCE
TREADS . . .

— HAMLET

DRAMATIS PERSONAE

HANALEE DENNEY, *daughter to the late Hank Denney, and stepdaughter to Clyde Koning*

GRETA KONING, *mother to Hanalee, and wife to Clyde Koning*

GHOST *of Hank Denney*

CLYDE KONING, *physician*

FLEUR PAULISSEN, *friend to Hanalee, and sister to Laurence*

LAURENCE PAULISSEN, *brother to Fleur*

POLLY PAULISSEN, *widow, and mother to Fleur and Laurence*

JOE ADDER, *accused of the murder of Hank Denney*

REVEREND AND MRS. ADDER, *parents to Joe and six other children*

MILDRED MARKS, *a neighbor*

BERNICE MARKS, *younger sister to Mildred*

MRS. MARKS, *widow, and mother to Mildred, Bernice, and seven other children*

SHERIFF RINK, *head law enforcer*

DEPUTY FORTAINE, *assistant to Sheriff Rink*

ROBBIE AND GIL WITTEN, *twin brothers, and friends to Laurence*

MR. AND MRS. FRANKLIN, *restaurateurs*

OPAL RICKERT, *sweetheart to Laurence*

HARRY CORNELIUS, AL VOLTMAN, OSCAR AND CHESTER KLEIN, *local boys*

SCENE: *Elston, Oregon*

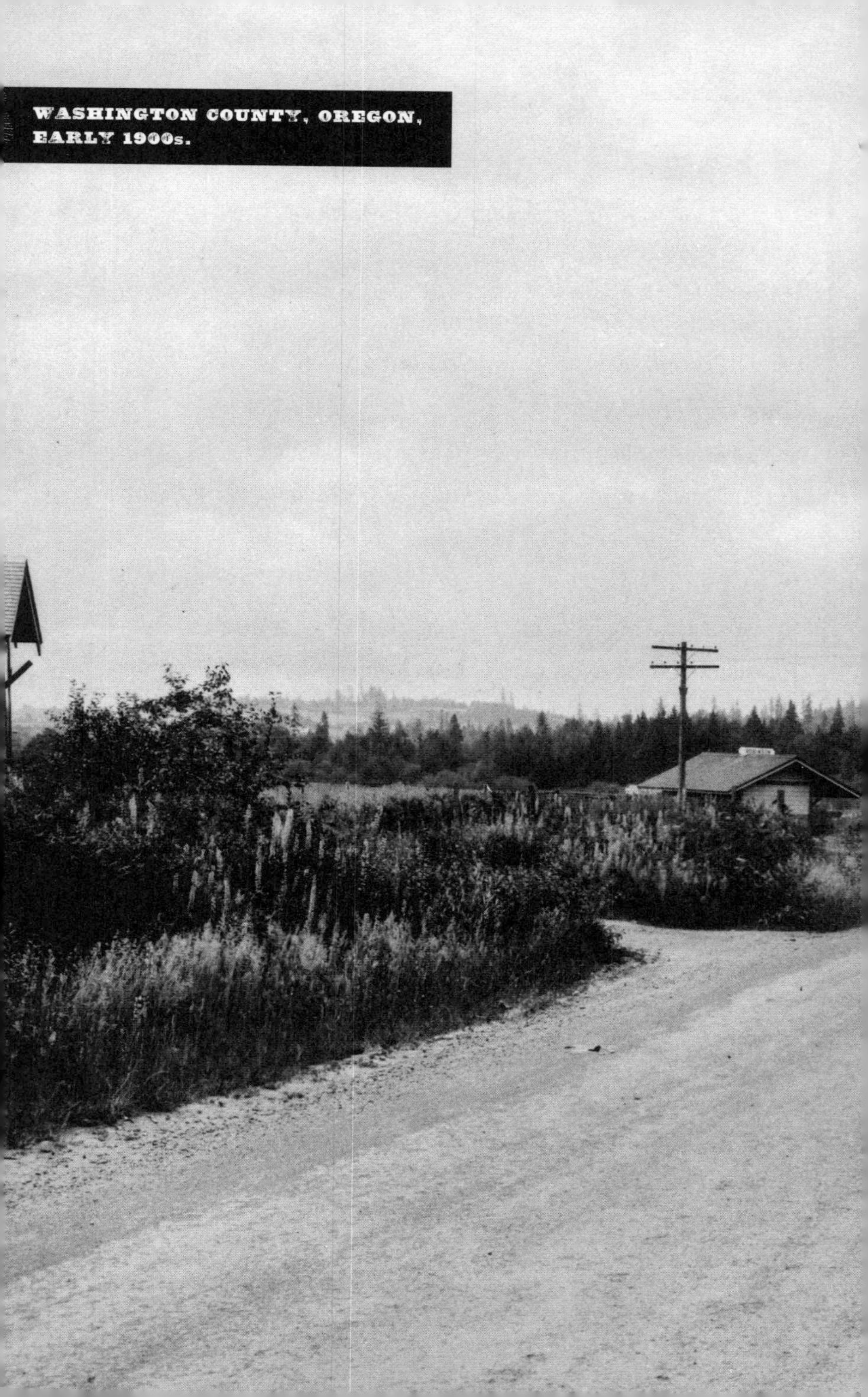

WASHINGTON COUNTY, OREGON, EARLY 1900s.

CHAPTER 1

MURDER MOST FOUL

═══JULY 1, 1923═══

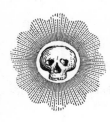 I DREW A DEEP BREATH AND MARCHED into the woods behind my house with a two-barreled pistol hidden beneath my blue cotton skirt. The pocket-size derringer rode against my outer right thigh, tucked inside a holster that had, according to the boy who'd given it to me, once belonged to a lady bootlegger who'd been arrested with three different guns strapped to her legs. Twigs snapped beneath my shoes. My eyes watered and burned. The air tasted of damp earth and metal.

Several yards ahead, amid a cluster of maples blanketed in scaly green lichen, stood a fir tree blackened by lightning. If I turned right on the deer trail next to that tree and followed a line of ferns,

I'd find myself amid rows of shriveled grapevines in the shut-down vineyard belonging to my closest friend, Fleur, her older brother, Laurence, and their war-widowed mama.

But I didn't turn.

I kept trekking toward the little white shed that hid the murderer Joe Adder.

Fleur's whispers from church that morning ran through my head, nearly tipping me off balance during my clamber across moss-slick rocks in the creek. "Reverend Adder doesn't even want his boy around anymore," she had told me before the sermon, her face bent close to mine, fine blond hair brushing across her cheeks. "He won't let Joe back in the house with the rest of the kids. Laurence is hiding him in our old shed. And Joe wants to talk to you. He's got something to say about the night his car hit your father."

I broke away from the creek and hiked up a short embankment covered in sedges and rushes that tickled my bare shins. At the top of the bank, about twenty-five feet away, sat a little white structure built of plaster and wood. Before he left for the Great War, Fleur's father used to store his fishing gear and liquor in the place, and he sometimes invited my father over for a glass of whiskey, even after Oregon went bone-dry in 1916. Bigleaf maples hugged the rain-beaten shingles with arms covered in leaves as bright green as under-ripe apples. A stovepipe poked out from the roof, and I smelled the sharp scent of leftover ashes—the ghost of a fire Joe must have lit the night before, when the temperature dropped into the fifties.

I came to a stop in front of the shed, my pulse pounding in the side of my throat. My scalp sweltered beneath my knitted blue hat, along with the long brown curls I'd stuffed and pinned inside. I

2

leaned over and drew the hem of my skirt above my right knee, exposing the worn leather of the holster. I took another deep breath and wiggled the little derringer out of its hiding place.

With my legs spread apart, I stood up straight and pointed the pistol at the shed's closed door. "Are you in there, Joe?"

A hawk screeched from high above the trees, and some sort of animal splashed in the pond that lay beyond the shed and the foliage. But I didn't hear one single peep out of Joe Adder.

"Joe?" I asked again, this time in as loud and deep a voice as I could muster. Tree-trunk strong, I sounded. Sticky sweat rolled down my cheeks, and my legs refused to stop rocking back and forth. "Are you in there?"

"Who's there?"

I gripped the pistol with both my hands. The voice I heard was a husky growl that couldn't have belonged to clean-cut, preacher's-boy Joe, from what I remembered of him. It and a splashing sound seemed to come from the pond, not the shed.

"Who's there?" he asked again. I heard another splash.

I lowered the pistol to my side and crept around to the back of the shed, feeling my tongue dry up from panting. I pushed past a tangle of blackberry bushes, pricking a thumb on a thorn, and came to a stop on the edge of the bank. My feet teetered on the gnarled white root of a birch.

In the pond, submerged up to his navel in the murky green water, stood a tanned and naked Joe Adder, arms akimbo, a lock of dark brown hair hanging over his right eye. His shoulders were broad and sturdy, his biceps surprisingly muscular, as though prison had worked that scrawny little white boy hard.

My mouth fell open, and my stomach gave an odd jump. The last time I'd seen Joe, back in February 1921, seventeen months earlier, he'd been a slick-haired, sixteen-year-old kid in a fancy black suit, blubbering on a courthouse bench between his mama and daddy.

This new version of my father's killer—now just a few months shy of his eighteenth birthday, almost brawny, his hair tousled and wild—peered at me without blinking. Drops of water plunked to the pond's surface from his elbows.

"You don't want to shoot me, Hanalee," he said in that husky voice of his. "I don't recommend prison to anyone but the devils who threw me in there."

I pointed the pistol at his bare chest, my right fingers wrapped around the grip. "If you had run over and killed a white man with your daddy's Model T," I said, "you'd still be behind bars, serving your full two years . . . and more."

"I didn't kill anyone."

"I bet you don't know this"—I shifted my weight from one leg to the other—"but people tell ghost stories about my father wandering the road where you ran him down, and I hate those tales with a powerful passion."

"I'm sorry, but—"

"But those stories don't make me half as sick as you standing there, saying you didn't kill anyone. If you didn't kill him, you no-good liar, then why didn't you defend yourself at your trial?"

Joe sank down into the water and let his chin graze the surface. Long, thick lashes framed his brown eyes, and he seemed to know precisely how to tilt his head and peek up at a girl to use those lashes to his advantage. "They never gave me a chance to speak on

4

the witness stand," he said. "They hurried me into that trial, and then they rushed me off to prison by the first week of February. And I didn't get to say a goddamn word."

I pulled the hammer into a half-cocked position with a click that echoed across the pond. Joe's eyes widened, and he sucked in his breath.

"You lied to your family about delivering food to the poor that Christmas Eve," I said, "and you crashed into my father because you were drunk on booze from some damn party. My new stepfather witnessed him die from injuries caused by *you*, so don't you dare fib to me."

"Don't you dare shoot me before I talk to you about that stepdaddy of yours."

"I don't want to hear what you have to say about Uncle Clyde. I'm not happy he married my mama, but he's a decent man."

"Stop pointing that gun at me and let me talk."

"Give me one good reason why I should listen to you." I aimed the pistol at the skin between Joe's eyebrows. "Give me one good reason why I shouldn't squeeze this trigger and sh—"

"You should listen to me, Hanalee, because you're living with your father's murderer."

A shallow breath fluttered through my lips. All the doubts and fears I'd harbored about Dr. Koning since he married my grieving mama last winter squirmed around in my gut. I stared Joe down, and he stared me down, and the gun quaked in my hand until the metal blurred before my eyes.

"For Christ's sake, Hanalee, stop pointing that gun at me and let me talk to you."

"Clyde Koning did not kill my father."

"Your father was alive when I helped him into my house. He even joked with me—he said he thought he'd been hit by Santa's sleigh as punishment for misbehaving on Christmas Eve."

I shook my head. "My father wouldn't have said any such thing. The only thing he did wrong that night was to walk down the dark highway to try to join us at church. He wasn't feeling well, and—"

"His leg was bleeding and maybe broken," continued Joe, ignoring me, rattling off words as if he had them memorized from a script. "So I let him lean his weight against me while I helped him inside. My family was running the Christmas Eve service, so I laid your father on my bed and telephoned Dr. Koning."

"I don't—"

"The last thing your father said to me before I opened the door for the doctor was 'The doc's going to be the death of me. I just know it.'"

I stepped off the gnarled root, landing so hard I jarred my neck. "That's a lie."

"And when I asked, 'Do you want me to send Dr. Koning away?' he told me, 'No, just make sure no one ever hurts my Hanalee.'"

My eyes itched and moistened. I blinked and rocked back and forth. "You don't know what you're talking about."

"When Dr. Koning arrived, he shut my bedroom door behind him and left me to wait in the living room." Joe rose back up to a standing position. Water rained off his body and splattered into the pond, and a wave lapped at his stomach, just above his hip bones. "The next time that bedroom door opened, your father was dead. He wasn't hardly even bleeding before that point—he seemed to have only suffered a busted leg and a sore arm from the crash. But suddenly he was dead, as if someone had just shot a poisonous dose of morphine through his veins."

I shook my head. "That's not true."

"People shut me up at my trial. No one, not even my own lawyer, let me speak, as if they'd all gotten paid to keep me quiet, and I suffered for it." His voice cracked. "I can't . . . do you know . . ." He pushed his hair out of his eyes and exposed a C-shaped scar above his right eyebrow. "Do you know how badly I fared as a sixteen-year-old kid in that godforsaken prison, Hanalee?"

My hand sweated against the gun. "I don't feel a shred of pity for you."

"Just one week before the accident, someone—my father wouldn't say who—came by the church and tried to recruit him into the local chapter of the Ku Klux Klan, which I'm certain had something—"

"No!" I marched right into the pond's shallow edge with the pistol still aimed at Joe's head, and I pulled the hammer into the full-cock position. "I know full well there's a Klan church up the highway in Bentley. I know they host baseball games and print anti-Catholic pamphlets, but they never once gave a damn that my black Christian father lived in this measly spit stain of a town."

"I'm not the one you should be shooting, Hanalee." Joe backed away in the water. "I'm not the one who deserves to die."

"I've never even heard about a single Klan-provoked killing in this state, Joe. You can try to scare me all you want, but I know you're just switching your guilt onto other people because you—"

"No, I'm not. Look in your stepfather's bedroom." He stopped backing up. "I bet you'll find a robe and a hood stashed among his clothing somewhere. I bet he married your white mother just to piss on the memory of your father. And I bet the Klan promoted him to a powerful position for killing the last full-blooded Negro in Elston, Ore—"

I squeezed the trigger with an explosion of gunpowder and fired a bullet straight past Joe's ear—not close enough to hit him, but enough to make his face go as white as those hooded robes he talked about. I staggered backward from the kick, and my ears rang with a horrendous screeching that sounded like a crowd of keening mourners wailing inside my head.

Beyond the cloud of dissipating smoke, Joe thrashed his arms about in the water and struggled to stay upright, but I didn't wait to see if he'd recover from the shock. Instead, I tucked that gun back into my holster and hightailed it out of the woods.

CHAPTER 2

LESS THAN KIND

"HANALEE?" CALLED MAMA FROM our backyard, beyond the Douglas firs that shot up to the clear July sky on the edge of our property.

I stopped in my tracks. My black-and-white Keds sloshed and squeaked with pond water.

"Hanalee?"

I shoved the derringer—still tucked inside the holster, still holding one remaining bullet—into the depths of a hollow log ten feet from the opening in the woods. I wrapped the leather in an oilcloth that I kept hidden in that spot specifically for times when I couldn't sneak the pistol back into the house, and I scattered leaves over the lump. Dirt clogged my fingernails; mold from the leaves tickled my nose. I sneezed so hard, my ribs hurt.

"Hanalee?" called Mama again, her voice high and panicky.

"I'm coming," I called back, and I kicked off my wet shoes and moseyed out of the woods with my best attempt at a casual strut. Mama hated guns. She didn't know that my former friend Laurence—once my staunchest protector—had given me a pistol when I was just fourteen.

My mother relaxed her shoulders when she saw me coming her way, but her face looked paler than usual.

"I heard a gunshot," she said.

I shrugged. "It was probably just Laurence, shooting squirrels again."

"Where were you? I thought you said you were going to pick raspberries for our Sunday dinner."

"I remembered something I forgot to tell Fleur at church this morning." I picked up the wicker basket I was supposed to be using for berrying. "I'm sorry if I scared you."

She put her hands on her hips and scowled at the woods. Loose strands of honey-blond hair fluttered around her eyes, which she narrowed into slits. "I don't want you going over there if Laurence is shooting his father's guns again," she said. "I don't know why his mother allows him to do that."

"It's his way of grieving for his father."

"That war killed Mr. Paulissen five years ago."

"Sometimes it takes a while to recover from a father's death, Mama."

She swallowed and averted her gaze, her lips squeezed together.

People told me that she and I had the same mouth, especially when we looked as vexed as she did at that moment. "A white girl's lips," the older ladies in church would say when sizing me up like a county-fair squash, debating the degree of my whiteness. I'd also inherited my mother's hazel eyes and long, slender neck, but my nose, my brown curls, and the shape of my eyes "derived from that Negro father," the ladies often added in their bored-old-biddy evaluations. My skin—a medium shade of golden brown—was a few shades lighter than my father's had been, but it caused all my troubles.

"Did you hear that the prison let Joe Adder out early?" I asked Mama.

"Yes." She fussed with a lock of hair that had fallen out of its pin and coiled down the nape of her neck. "I overheard all the whispered rumors at church."

"His parents won't let him live with them anymore."

"I heard that, too. I understand they're ashamed of what he did, but I hope to God they can learn to forgive him."

"Forgive him?"

"Yes." Her eyes met mine. "That accident that killed your father was just a stupid mistake made by an intoxicated sixteen-year-old boy. He served seventeen months in the state penitentiary. That's a lot for a person that young."

"But—"

"You've got to learn to forgive Joe, too, Hanalee. Otherwise, that hatred will eat you up."

I dug my teeth into my lower lip. "Does Uncle Clyde know he's out?"

"I don't know." She tightened her apron strings behind her back. "He's been at the Everses' house since church, checking on the children's measles. Mrs. Evers planned to serve him a little lunch to thank him."

"Hmm." I tapped the basket against the side of my right leg where the holster had so recently hung. Joe's tale snaked around inside my brain, unsettling regions of my mind already perturbed, churning up a hundred different questions. I pressed a hand to my stomach to curb a queasy feeling.

"What's the matter?" Mama cocked her head. "Are you worried about seeing Joe?"

"No." I hooked the handle of the basket in the crook of my arm. "He's the one who should be terrified of seeing me."

Mama tensed. "Go pick those raspberries for me." She nodded toward the bushes. "Go on. I need to prepare dinner."

"Yes, ma'am." I sauntered away.

"And watch that harsh tone of yours," she added. "It's not like you."

I sighed and wandered to the rows of ripe red berries on the eastern side of the twenty acres of farmland Mama had inherited from her father. Over my shoulder, I saw Mama heading to the back door of our yellow farmhouse with her hands on her hips—her tired walk, her *Don't bother me anymore, Hanalee* walk. My ears still rang from shooting the bullet next to Joe Adder's skull, and I wondered if I'd been talking louder than usual over the commotion in my head. I wondered if Mama suspected that the gunshot had something to do with me.

....

IN THE LATE AFTERNOON, MY MOTHER AND STEPFA-
ther took their seats at opposite ends of our dining room table,
across Uncle Clyde's late mother's tablecloth, which was embroidered in cobalt-blue tulips. I sat down between the two of them
without a word or a smile. The spices in my stepfather's shaving
soap clogged up my sinuses so badly, I had to squeeze the bridge of
my nose to keep my head from erupting. Joe's tale of murder was
also boring a hole through my brain. The sickening combination
made the food look and smell unpalatable.

Uncle Clyde, a six-foot-tall white man with trim brown hair and
Dutch-blue eyes, spread his napkin across his lap and licked his
pale pink lips. He wasn't an actual blood uncle, just an old family
friend I'd called "uncle" all my life.

"The ham smells delicious, Greta," he said.

"Thank you, darling." Mama smiled and waited for him to take
his first bite before lifting a forkful of potatoes to her mouth.

I just sat there without touching my silverware, facing the dining
room window and the stretch of woods that hid Joe deep within.
The curtains billowed on a hot July breeze that dried out the skin
on the backs of my fingers and elbows. The dreamlike dance of
the lace—the shimmying of fabric possessed by an unseen force—
turned my thoughts toward all those disquieting rumors of my
father's spirit wandering the main highway late at night.

"Did you hear the news, Uncle Clyde?" I asked, still massaging
the bridge of my nose.

My stepfather regarded me through the wide lenses of his spectacles, those large blue eyes of his betraying nothing but curiosity.
"What news might that be?"

My mother shook her head. "No, Hanalee. Let's not discuss that subject at the dinner table."

"The state pen let Joe Adder out early on good behavior," I said.

Uncle Clyde switched his attention to his plate and used his fork to poke at a fatty piece of ham—a morsel shaped like the state of California, with brown sugar encrusted on the ends.

I sat up straight and dropped my hands to my lap. "Did you hear what I—?"

"I heard the rumors this morning," he said in his calm, physician's voice that used to assure me he could mend anybody's woes and take care of everyone's troubles, including mine.

"What do you think of his release?" I asked.

"Hanalee," said Mama. "What does it matter? Joe's out, and there's nothing we can do about it."

"I worry a little bit about—" Uncle Clyde stopped himself from speaking by slipping the fatty sliver into his mouth. He chewed like a gentleman—lips closed, jaw moving up and down with delicate little movements, not a tooth or a crumb exposed—and his clean-shaven tidiness and upper-middle-class politeness irked me no end that afternoon. I wanted to shake him by the lapels of his gray coat and scream at him to tell me whether Joe had lied to me.

"What do you worry about?" I asked, my stomach tightening.

He dabbed at the corners of his mouth with his napkin. "I don't mean to offend either of you by saying this, but I have to wonder how Joe is doing—physically. I'd like to be able to examine him. Prison isn't known for its hygiene or freedom from diseases." He spread the ivory cloth back across his lap. "Do you know where he's staying, Hanalee?"

My heart stopped. "Why would I know that?"

"I just wondered, since you brought him up."

Mama took a sip of water without a sound.

"He might be armed," I said, just to see how Uncle Clyde would react.

He gave a start, and I'd swear, his pupils swelled.

"Why do you say that?" he asked.

"He's a jailbird. A wayward youth prone to drinking and reck-lessness in this noble age of Prohibition." I kept an eye on his every blink and facial twitch. "It just seems like he might be armed. And angry."

Uncle Clyde shifted in his seat and made something pop in his back. "Well . . . let's"—he downed a gulp of water, then dabbed at his face again—"let's end the subject of Joe Adder for the rest of the meal, if you don't mind. I'd like to enjoy this delicious ham."

I did mind, but I kept my mouth shut.

AROUND SEVEN O'CLOCK THAT SAME EVENING, WITH Mama and Uncle Clyde's somewhat hesitant permission, I packed the old brown canvas valise Mama had purchased when she worked as a telephone operator in downtown Portland and Daddy served food at the swanky Portland Hotel. My father had lived near the hotel with other Negroes, and my mother resided in a Salmon Street boardinghouse for young, unmarried white women. They met while crossing paths to their respective places of employment, even though everyone around them told them that the paths of a black man and a white woman should never, *ever* cross.

With the valise swinging by my side and my feet squelching

inside my damp Keds, which I'd fetched from the edge of the woods after dinner, I walked up the highway to Fleur's house. I puckered my lips and whistled "Toot, Toot, Tootsie, Goo'Bye" in a desperate attempt to forget Uncle Clyde's squirmy dinnertime behavior. The sun wouldn't set until close to ten o'clock, but I opted not to travel by forest trail.

Up ahead, Mildred Marks, a girl my age—just turned sixteen— with thick red hair shoved beneath a gray fedora, pedaled toward me on a squeaky green bicycle. She rode at such a snail's pace, I could have ducked into the trees to avoid her if I had wanted to. She and her eight younger siblings, along with their widowed mama, lived in a farmhouse less than a mile west of mine. They were known for pumping out large batches of moonshine and reaping quite a profit, while the sheriff looked the other way.

"Hanalee! I've been wanting to talk to you all day," called Mildred, bicycling closer, her vehicle chirping and groaning with each labored pedal. "How serendipitous that I decided to take a ride this evening." Mildred used words like *serendipitous* to show off the brain sitting inside that big old head of hers, even though she'd had to quit school after the seventh grade to help her mama.

I clutched the handle of my valise. "Hello, Mildred."

She slowed to a stop and planted the soles of her brown boots on the road. "I saw your father in our house last night."

My stomach dropped. I nearly bent over and threw up on the road, right in front of her.

"He walked through the front door," she continued, her pale brown eyes expanding, "and just stared at me, as clearly as I'm looking at you."

"You . . ." I swallowed down a foul taste that reminded me of coffee grounds. "You must be talking about my stepfather, Dr. Koning."

"I'm talking about your real father—Hank Denney." She leaned her freckled face forward. "He seemed confused and upset, as if he were trying to reach you but couldn't find his way. I saw urgency in those big dark eyes of his."

I shrank back, my skin cold.

She rolled her bicycle closer, crunching stones beneath her wheels. "I think he's trying to find you. I've seen his spirit roaming the road before, but I—"

"No, you haven't seen my father." I inched backward. "It's bad enough I hear little kids telling ghost tales about him, but a girl my own age . . ."

"He wouldn't speak to me, but if he's got something on his mind, I'm sure he'd say it to his own child, especially if she was equipped with a tonic that would allow for spirit communication."

"I need to go." I turned and continued up the road.

"'Necromancer's Nectar' is what we call the concoction. Our patented elixir would allow you to talk to him this very night."

"'Screwy Ladies' Moonshine' is more like it." I trekked onward, toward Fleur's. "I'm not buying any of your whiskey water and giving Sheriff Rink another reason to ask me what I'm up to. It's bad enough I tried your disgusting hair-straightening tonic that turned my curls carrot-orange."

"I wouldn't even charge you for the elixir. You can have it for free."

I stopped and swung my face toward her.

Mildred never offered anything for free.

"If you don't speak with him," she said, "he'll just keep searching for you, every single night. I wonder if . . ." She closed her mouth and squeezed her fingers around the bicycle's black handle grips.

"Go on," I said. "What do you wonder?"

"If his frantic state . . . has anything to do with . . ." She averted her eyes from mine. "With . . . J-J-Joe. Joe Adder."

I stared at her and tried not to appear fazed, but gooseflesh rose across my arms. "My father isn't a ghost, Mildred. Please don't ever make such a claim again." I turned and broke into a trot.

"If I see him again, Hanalee," she called after me, "I'm coming to your house and forcing that elixir upon you. I'd normally charge three dollars for it, but I don't want him haunting me."

"Good-bye, Mildred."

"Hanalee . . ."

"Good-bye!"

In the distance behind me, Mildred's bicycle slowly squeaked away.

Chirp. Chirp. Chirp.

POLICE OFFICER WITH WRECKED CAR AND CASES OF ILLEGAL LIQUOR, 1922.

CHAPTER 3

DESPERATE WITH IMAGINATION

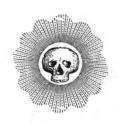 MR. PAULISSEN'S FORD TRUCK SAT IN the gravel drive in front of Fleur's house, a pretty white structure with forest-green shutters and geraniums blasting bright red fireworks of color from boxes in front of each window. Laurence Paulissen—almost eighteen years old, close to two years older than his sister and I—stood next to the hood of the truck, raking his hand through his short blond hair. He nudged the toe of his shoe against a front tire and spat as though he hadn't noticed a female wandering into his company. Behind him, the Witten twins, Robbie and Gil, took off their coats and slung them over the slats of the truck's wooden siding.

I walked through the shade of an apple tree that Fleur, Laurence, and I used to call "Jack's beanstalk" when we climbed into its branches as little kids. I slowed my pace the closer I got to the boys, for I didn't completely trust those twins, with their slick, tawny hair, their teasing green eyes, and the comfortable way they chatted with me, as though we were old chums who'd shared years of laughs, even though we hadn't. Their faces were identical, with broad foreheads and square chins—a really rugged sort of appearance. Their father had come to Elston to fill our pharmacist vacancy in 1921, and they dressed a little nicer than the rest of us.

"Hanalee!" said Robbie, the louder of the twins, with a clap of his hands. He removed his cap and swaggered my way with a grin that stretched to his ears. "I see you have a bag all packed, darling. Are we eloping tonight?"

His brother, Gil, brayed a laugh that made his chewing gum fall out of his mouth and splat against his left shoe. Laurence frowned and turned his attention back to the truck's tires, testing out a back one with a solid kick of his foot.

I stepped past Robbie, smelling cigarette smoke from his clothing. "I'm just here to visit Fleur."

"Here"—Robbie grabbed the valise from my hands—"I'll carry that for you."

"All right. Thank you." I proceeded up to the porch with Robbie close to my side.

At the top of the steps, he shot me a sidelong glance and said, "You seem tense tonight, Hanalee. What's wrong?"

I rubbed the back of my neck. "Nothing."

"You sure?"

"Yes."

"Come on, we need to get going, Robbie," said Laurence. He bent down in front of the truck's grille and turned the starter crank. The congested old vehicle coughed and shuddered to life, and Laurence circled around to the driver's side of the cab. "Quit chatting with Hanalee."

"Quit flirting with her is more like it," said Gil with a laugh that carried a bite, and he climbed over the back slats of the rumbling truck.

Robbie set my bag on the steps by my feet. "Is it Joe's return that's bothering you?"

I picked up the valise without answering.

"Joe Adder's not right in the head, Hanalee." Robbie leaned his left hand against the wall beside the Paulissens' screen door, above the brass doorbell. "He's dangerous."

"H-h-how . . ." I swallowed. "How do you mean, 'not right in the head'?"

"He's immoral. Depraved. Disgusting." Robbie sniffed and wrinkled his nose. "If you see him, telephone Sheriff Rink immediately."

"Come on, Robbie," called Laurence from behind the steering wheel. "You're gonna make us late."

"I'm coming, I'm coming." Robbie fitted his cap back over his hair and galloped down the steps. "Just protecting our womenfolk, unlike you two useless boobs."

"She's not our womenfolk," said Laurence, the boy who used to race me into the woods on hot summer days—the first boy I'd ever kissed. With his face tipped toward the steering wheel, Laurence peeked up at me from the tops of his sky-blue eyes, and, without a trace of feeling in his voice, he added, "It's just Hanalee. You know what I mean."

I shifted my bag to my other hand and lifted my chin, as though his words hadn't hurled a dagger into my chest.

Robbie climbed into the passenger side. Laurence broke his gaze from mine and backed the truck down the driveway. In the truck bed behind them, Gil gripped the wooden slats and whooped with the cry of a coyote embarking upon a hunt.

I swung open the screen door and ducked inside the Paulissens' front room, a modest-size space filled with doilies and potted plants and butterscotch-colored furniture. The house always smelled like cinnamon and Christmas, no matter the time of year, and it immediately made me feel better.

"Fleur?" I called across the empty room.

From the kitchen, in the back of the house, came muffled adult voices and laughter. To my right, a clock made of blue and white delft ticked away the seconds on the mantel above the brick fireplace.

"Are you here, Fleur?" I asked, strengthening my grip on the suitcase.

"I'm upstairs," she called. Her footsteps hurried across the floorboards above. "Hello!"

She emerged at the top of the stairs and scampered down the steps with a copy of *Motion Picture* magazine tucked beneath her left arm, the white lace of her hem swishing against the curves of her legs, a smile brightening her eyes, which were as blue as her brother's. She was one of those blondes so fair that even her eyebrows and lashes looked as yellow as morning sunshine, and she was prettier than all the motion-picture stars in the magazine she carried—all of them combined.

"Hanalee . . ." Her smile faded, and she slowed to a stop on the last step. "Why do you look so upset? Did the boys say something to you out there?"

"Would your mother mind if I stayed here tonight?"

"What did they say?"

I peeked over my shoulder at the empty driveway. "Are we able to talk privately without anyone overhearing?"

"Mama's in the dining room with Deputy Fortaine."

"She is? Why?"

"He ate Sunday dinner with us. She invited him. Come here." Fleur backed down the hallway next to the stairs and beckoned with a wiggle of her right index finger. "I'll show you, so you can see what you think of this little tête-à-tête."

I lowered my valise to the floor, and we tiptoed past Mrs. Paulissen's framed needlepoint meadowlarks and chickadees, which were hung on flowery red and yellow wallpaper that also reminded me of Christmas. At the far end of the hall hung a photograph of my family and theirs picnicking in the woods, back when we children hadn't yet grown old enough to start at the schoolhouse on the edge of town. My father held us girls on his lap, and Laurence sat between our mothers, wearing a crown of leaves I'd made for him. Mr. Paulissen had taken the picture with his Kodak camera.

Fleur nudged open the dining room door with the tips of her fingers. "Hanalee's here," she called inside.

I poked my head around the corner and saw Deputy Fortaine, dressed in his Sunday-best suit and a smart striped tie, sitting at the oval table with Mrs. Paulissen. He was the most handsome law enforcer we had around—Hollywood handsome, to be honest. Yet his dark eyes and wavy coal-black hair made everyone whisper that he hid a secret life as a Jew or an Italian Catholic. Some people claimed his real last name was Fishstein.

"Hello, Hanalee," said Mrs. Paulissen, tucking a golden-blond curl behind her ear. She crossed her legs beneath the lace tablecloth, swinging the right one over the left. "How are your mother and Dr. Koning?"

"They're well, thank you."

"We're planning to listen to some records, if that's all right," said Fleur.

"That sounds fine, darling." Mrs. Paulissen caressed the stem of her water goblet with a flirty little finger, as though she imagined the crystal to be Deputy Fortaine's neck.

"You two girls have a swell time," said the deputy with his motion-picture-star smile.

I bit my bottom lip to avoid laughing. Fleur shut the door, and we skedaddled back down the hallway to the living room.

"You see? Those two lovebirds won't pay any attention to us." Fleur slipped a shiny black record out of a paper sleeve that crinkled in her hands. "And the music will muffle our conversation." She placed the record on the Victrola and wound the crank on the side of the machine until Henry Burr's sentimental "Faded Love Letters" drifted out of the horn-shaped speaker.

I glanced at the window behind me, half expecting to find Joe Adder standing on the other side of the glass.

"Come down here." On the braided blue rug, Fleur laid open

her copy of *Motion Picture* and flipped the pages to an article titled "The Vogue of Valentino."

"Look"—she turned another page—"an eminent psychologist claims that women have fallen passionately in love with Rudolph Valentino because American businessmen aren't meeting their needs as lovers. Isn't that a hoot?" She giggled in her rich, Fleur way that always quelled the worries inside my brain.

I crouched down beside her, my knees digging into the braided rug, and I leveled my head next to hers. Henry Burr's voice filled the room with music, and Valentino's suave Italian face and figure arrested our eyes. I couldn't even watch motion pictures. The next town over had a nickelodeon theater, but the manager had posted a sign on the door that said, NO NEGROES, JEWS, CATHOLICS, CHINESE, OR JAPANESE.

"I saw Joe," I said.

Fleur's face sobered. "And . . . ? Is everything all right?"

"Well, I didn't kill him, if that's what you're wondering." My glance flitted toward the hallway. "Are you sure Deputy Fortaine can't hear us? Uncle Clyde is chummy with him . . ."

"The music is loud, and he and Mama are too busy holding hands under the table. I think she's worried that Deputy Fortaine will find out what Laurie is doing for money. He doesn't look the other way as much as Sheriff Rinky-Dink does."

"You sure Laurence is a bootlegger?"

"Shh." Fleur held a finger to her lips. "Don't say that word. But, yes. Have you seen the nighttime sky? It positively glows with the fire of all the moonshine distilleries in these woods. Local restaurants—the Dry Dock and Ginger's—and Portland establishments, they're all paying good money for home-brewed hooch, and Laurence has Daddy's truck to deliver it to them."

"I thought the Dry Dock was genuinely dry."

Fleur rolled her eyes. "They claim to be, so the good people of Elston will dine there, but the owners keep bottles on hand for certain patrons with money."

"Is that where Laurence was going with those Witten boys just now? Out delivering?"

Fleur nodded with loose locks of her hair swaying against her face.

"And Joe Adder?" I pushed myself up higher on my elbows. "Is he going with them, too?"

"I don't think so. He can't risk jail again. He's just hiding out until he figures out what to do with his life."

"Fleur . . ."

"Hmm?"

I scratched my left arm. "Robbie just told me Joe's not right in the head. Do you know anything about that?"

She shrugged. "I'm sure prison doesn't make a person very sane. It's certainly not going to make people believe you're upright and sweet."

"Why is Laurence letting him hide in the shed, then? I didn't even know they were friends. Didn't they once get into a fistfight when they were younger?"

She shrugged again. "Laurence doesn't talk to me about much of anything anymore. He just mutters about taking the 'moral high road in life' all the time." She stroked a photograph of Valentino dressed in some sort of exotic costume with a vest and long white pants. "Maybe Laurie sees Joe as a charity opportunity. A chance to repent for his sin of bootlegging. Church has become important to him."

"Hmm . . ." I readjusted my weight on my knees, unconvinced that God would forgive Laurence of anything just because he snuck a few slices of bread out to the likes of Joe Adder. "Why'd you go see Joe in the shed in the first place?"

"I'm sorry." She nestled her shoulder against mine. "I knew it would upset you, but Laurence told me Joe cut up his legs pretty badly when he hopped a fence to steal eggs. I made him a poultice and brewed him some tea. But I wasn't nice to him at all—I swear."

I leaned away so that her shoulder no longer touched mine.

She lowered her head. "Maybe I shouldn't have told you about him, but there was something in his eyes that made me feel his message was important. I thought he might want to make peace with you."

I pressed a hand over my forehead and drew a long breath through my nose. "He didn't make peace with me at all, Fleur."

"Then what did he say?"

"He told me Uncle Clyde killed my father."

The record stopped. Fleur jumped up, the scent of lilacs breezing away with her, and set the phonograph needle back to the beginning of the song. The fanfare of trumpets recommenced, and Henry Burr again warbled "Faded Love Letters." Fleur crouched back down beside me, hanging her head next to mine over a new article, one that explored the shape of ten film stars' noses in relationship to their personalities. *Good Lord*, I thought, *I sure hope my nose doesn't reveal what's going on inside me.*

"He didn't really say that, did he?" asked Fleur.

"He claimed that Daddy's arm and leg hurt badly after he crashed into him with that damned Model T but that Daddy didn't seem like a man about to die. After Uncle Clyde went in to see my father, however . . ." I cleared my throat, experiencing an ache that felt like the stab of a fork into my tonsils. "That's . . . that's when Daddy suddenly died, 'as if someone had just shot a poisonous dose of morphine through his veins,' Joe told me."

"And you believe Joe?"

I clenched my teeth and stared at the "backward dip" of Mary Pickford's right nostril, which supposedly demonstrated her "great affection and sympathy."

Fleur nudged me with her arm. "Do you believe him?"

"No. Of course not. I think I would know if I were living under the same roof as my father's murderer. If Clyde Koning hates Negroes, I'd be long gone, too, wouldn't I?"

"Hanalee!" Fleur grabbed my hand. "Dr. Koning does not hate Negroes. Did Joe try to convince you he did?"

"He hinted that Uncle Clyde's involved with the Klan."

At that, Fleur sputtered a laugh. "This isn't the old South. Do you know what the Oregon KKK is like?"

"I know, I know—they're pushing to fix roads and improve public education."

"And they have ridiculous names for their ranks. 'Imperial Wizard,' 'Exalted Cyclops,' 'Great Titan.'"

I shuddered, not liking such names. "How do you know?"

"Mama once received an invitation to join the Women of the Ku Klux Klan in Bentley, and they included all sorts of pamphlets." Fleur flipped the magazine to an advertisement for Mulsified Cocoanut Oil Shampoo. "But she didn't join them. She heard that the organization's mainly a big business venture out to collect money from people still scared of immigrants from the war years."

I held my forehead in my hand and sighed from deep within my lungs.

"Hanalee . . ." Fleur squeezed my right shoulder. "You're safe here in Elston, despite a few prejudiced folks out there who might imply otherwise. And you're safe in your house with Dr. Koning. You've told me yourself that he saved your mother when she was sick with grief and drugging herself with nerve pills. How could a kind man like that commit murder?"

"He did marry her awfully quickly—just thirteen short months after we put my poor father in the ground."

"Hanalee, don't—"

"Uncle Clyde was always friendly with her"—I picked at one of the magazine's curled-up corners—"even before Daddy died. They've known each other as long as your mama has known her, since childhood."

"Your mother's a likable person."

"She is. She'd be worth killing for, wouldn't she?"

"Stop it, Hanalee."

"Especially if your target was a man with no rights and no respect—only a pretty white wife who wasn't even considered his legal spouse within this state. Oh, Jesus, Fleur"—I gave a start, for the music came to an abrupt halt again—"I hate that I'm tempted to believe that jailbird. I hate that he planted these sickening seeds inside my brain."

"Shh." She cupped her warm fingers over my hand. "Stop thinking about him tonight. Stay here with me, have a calming cup of tea, and push all your worries off to another time. I'll take care of you, Hana-Honey." She kissed my cheek with lips butterfly soft. "Like always."

WE LISTENED TO FIVE MORE PHONOGRAPH RECORDS and skimmed at least ten additional *Motion Picture* articles. After those diversions failed to assuage me, Fleur brewed a pot of tea in the kitchen, and then we trooped upstairs to her bedroom with our beverages and my bag.

I fetched my drawing pad from the valise, sank onto Fleur's bed, and rested my back against the rosebud-papered walls of her bedroom with a charcoal pencil in hand. A teacup steamed by my side, smelling of chamomile.

I sketched a portrait of Fleur, who sat across the way in her window seat, half hidden behind the tendrils of two creeping Charlies that dangled from pots hanging above her. Fleur's favorite grandmother had died when Fleur was ten and bequeathed to her a stack of Gertrude Jekyll gardening books and a journal of handwritten herbal folk remedies. So Fleur lived in the Garden of Eden and served as mother to dozens of potted children.

"You always sketch when you're nervous," she said from behind those lanky vines that brushed at her right shoulder, for she sat half-turned toward the window.

"What are you talking about?" I lowered my left knee and, with it, the pad of paper. "I sketch whenever I feel like sketching."

"But you always seem to be pulling out a pad of paper whenever something's troubling you."

"Hmm. Well"—I adjusted the arch of her eyebrows on the paper to mimic her worried expression—"at least it's not as bad as you biting your stubby little nails whenever you're nervous."

She peeked over the brim of her teacup, her eyes smiling. "Just drink your tea."

"Yes, dahling," I said in a poor imitation of a British-born woman named Mrs. Hathaway, who attended our church—a woman who liked to ask Mama if she'd consider bleaching my skin. "Quite right."

I set my paper aside and took a sip of my chamomile tea, fragranced with a hint of lavender, tempered with a splash of hot milk. Warmth spread through my insides.

Downstairs, Deputy Fortaine's muffled voice still accompanied Mrs. Paulissen's titters. I cradled the cup against my chest and wondered if I could trust the deputy enough to tell him Joe's story.

Fleur pulled her pale pink curtains open, inviting the moonlight inside with us. "You see it out there?" she asked.

I craned my neck forward. "See what? The moon?"

"The brightness from all the whiskey stills lighting up."

"No." I shook my head. "I don't see anything but stars and evergreens."

"It's an orange glow that hovers over the trees. I overheard Laurence tell Robbie it's even brighter in Oregon's eastern outback, where the land is flat and you don't have pines and firs hiding everything."

I took another sip and let the heat travel down to my toes. "I'm afraid to look out my window at night."

Fleur turned her face toward mine, her eyebrows raised. "Why?"

"You've heard the stories"—another sip, more of a gulp—"about his ghost."

"Oh." She nodded. "Well, but . . . wouldn't you want to see him, though, if he were out there?"

"No. He'd be a ghost, not my father. That's not the same at all."

She squirmed on the window seat and tucked her legs beneath her in the nest of pillows.

"Mildred Marks claims she saw him in her house last night," I decided to add, even though the thought of Mildred and her devil's moonshine made the tea taste sour. "She said Daddy wouldn't speak to her, but she told me if I drank some concoction she brewed up, I'd be able to talk to him. 'Necromancer's Nectar,' I think she called it."

"Hmm." Fleur frowned. "It sounds like something that might make you hallucinate."

"Do you know of any local plants that would allow a person to speak with the dead?"

"Not at all."

"That's what I thought." I clanked my cup onto the ivory saucer sitting on the bedside table and grabbed my sketch pad again. "I just wish people would keep those ghost stories to themselves."

Fleur's face crumpled, as though she might cry. She shifted back toward the window and squeaked the tips of her right fingers down the glass.

"What's all that about?" I asked. "You look like you're about to burst into tears."

She sniffed.

"Oh." I shrank back against the wall and remembered Mr. Paulissen, killed overseas in the war, just like Mildred's father. "I'm sorry no one ever talks about your father still existing somewhere out there. But, honestly, Fleur, it's for the best."

"I think I saw him, too."

I shuddered. "You saw . . . who?"

"Your father." She ran her fingertips down the windowpane again. "Just last night. After I helped Joe with his scrapes from that fence, Laurence took Mama and me to the Dry Dock to celebrate Mama's birthday. On the way back home in the truck, just for a fleeting moment"—she pushed aside one of the vines and met my gaze—"I saw your father in the moonlight, walking down the road, toward our houses."

The tip of my pencil quivered against the paper and made an ugly, dark smudge. I couldn't formulate a single word in response.

Fleur twisted a clump of her hair between her fingers. "I'm sorry, Hanalee. Maybe telling you about it only makes things worse . . ."

"Well, there's nothing we can do about it." I scratched out my drawing, disappointed with the results. "I'd have to be a fool to wander out on the road at night, all alone, looking for him, so there's no use dwelling on ghost stories. I'm sure you just saw moonlight and shadows."

She nodded, and we closed that chapter for the night, sitting in

34

silence for a good long while before unpinning our hair, changing into nightclothes, and climbing beneath the covers of her bed.

I squirmed around under the blankets for about a minute or so, digging my shoulder blades into the mattress, bumping into Fleur, until I formed a nice groove that fit the shape of my spine. With my eyes closed, I heaved a sigh that came out as a wheeze.

"Are you all right?" asked Fleur from the darkness beside me.

"You talked about Joe hiding out until he figures out what to do with his life, but what about us?"

"What do you mean?"

I shifted about again. "What are we supposed to do with *our* lives? Should we even bother starting the eleventh grade in September if we're to be trapped here in Elston until we're old and dead?"

Fleur wound one of my spiraling curls around her right index finger, gently tugging at my roots in a way that felt nice. "I thought we were going to move to New York City and become artists."

I gave another sigh. "I wonder if there's ever been a black female lawyer. I should look in that book Mrs. York gave me. *Noted Negro Women.*"

"You want to become a lawyer?"

"Maybe." I rubbed my lips together and contemplated that potential plan. "To keep from feeling so helpless . . . maybe."

Fleur released my curl and let it spring against the side of my left arm. "Mama hopes I'll find a fiancé soon, probably so I'm one less mouth to feed. She says I'm getting too old for that little one-room schoolhouse."

I grunted. "I wouldn't allow you to marry any of the goofs here in Elston if my life depended on it. Can you imagine, always having to pretend to like all those terrible farm jokes?"

Fleur laughed so hard, she shook the bed.

I smiled, but the expression was so forced, it made the muscles in my cheeks hurt. "I mean it. I'm scared to death we'll get stuck here."

"We won't get stuck. I won't let us."

"I'll be trapped with my mother and a potential murderer."

Fleur grabbed my shoulder. "Dr. Koning didn't kill your father, Hanalee. Don't let that terrible thought cross your mind ever again."

"But—"

"Ignore Joe. Naturally, he's going to put the blame on someone besides himself."

I shifted onto my right side, away from her, and the mattress whined and rocked us about as if we were afloat on a raft at sea.

"If Joe doesn't genuinely possess a need to avenge himself"—I wiggled my right arm and shoulder into the spine-shaped space I'd made—"then why is he here? If his family doesn't even want him, why doesn't he simply run off to some other place?"

Fleur didn't answer, although I strained my ears to hear a response.

"Fleur? Why else would he be here, living like a rat in a shed, if he didn't genuinely believe he suffered in jail for someone else's crime? If he wasn't furiously seeking justice?"

"Go to sleep—and stop worrying," she said in a voice so quiet, it sounded like the wind whispering through the curtains of that open window that looked out at the stills and the empty highway.

CHAPTER 4

SOMETHING
IS ROTTEN

 WITH MY VALISE STILL IN HAND FROM MY stay at Fleur's, I wandered up the brick front path that led to Mildred Marks's house, a brown bedraggled thing that seemed to have nudged its way out of the ground alongside the weeds and wildflowers that shot from the earth around it. Vines of bloodred roses curled around the porch rails, clinging tightly, as if prepared to yank the structure straight back into the earth if anything inside those walls ever required concealment. A plain white cross stood among the dandelions and the browning tufts of grasses in the front yard, although no actual body rested in that unhallowed ground, as far as I knew. Mrs. Marks's husband lay in a grave in a field in France, buried with other fallen Great War soldiers.

I climbed up the steps to the front porch and smelled fresh bacon in the air, a scent that reminded me that I had ventured out of Fleur's house before most people sat down for breakfast. The brightening sun warmed away the chill that hung close to the ground.

I set my valise beside me on the whining boards of the porch, where the wood looked cracked from the sun and black with winter mold. Before I could even raise my hand to knock, one of Mildred's younger sisters, Bernice—another redhead, just like all the girls in the family—swung open the door.

Her shoulders fell when she saw me. "It's not the sheriff," she called behind her, and she flipped one of her braids onto her back, as if her hair disappointed her as much as the sight of me had.

Behind her, in the shadows of the long front hall, Mrs. Marks and Mildred tucked wads of money into their apron pockets and plodded toward the doorway. Poor Mildred's hair, despite all the pins holding it down, stuck out all over the place, like an explosion of fire.

I smelled something sour and peculiar beneath the whiffs of bacon.

"What do you want, Hanalee?" asked scrawny Mrs. Marks, her hair more cinnamon-brown than red. She massaged the side of her neck and rose to her toes to see over my shoulder.

I glanced behind me. "Are you expecting Sheriff Rink for breakfast, ma'am?"

"I beg your pardon?"

"Never mind Hanalee." Mildred yanked me inside by my wrist. "I know what she's here for."

"Her daddy's ghost?" asked Bernice.

"What?" asked Mrs. Marks, the color draining from her cheeks.

"Nothing, Mama." Mildred wrapped her arm around my shoulders and ushered me farther inside the house. "I've got a book in the library that I told Hanalee she could borrow. I'll just be a moment before helping with breakfast."

"Don't scare that poor girl with talk of her father," her mother called after us. "No ghost stories in this house, you hear?"

"I hear, Mama."

Mildred guided me toward the back of the house, in the direction of some sort of machine that produced an obnoxious thumping commotion behind a closed door, down on the right. The sour aroma grew so powerful, my entire mouth tasted fermented. I covered my nose and was about to ask if the thumps and the smell came from their whiskey still, but then Mildred steered me to the left, into some sort of library or study, lined from floor to ceiling with shelves of books that reeked of age and dust.

On the right-hand side of the room, beneath the sole window, stood a wide mahogany desk smothered in envelopes and official-looking papers stamped with black seals. A stuffed crow watched over the mess from its perch upon a stack of ledgers, its beady glass eyes glinting in the sunlight that slipped through the sheer curtains. The coldness in the air, the neck-prickling silence, gave the impression that I'd just stepped into a mausoleum that held the remains of the Markses' prewar prosperity.

Mildred closed the door behind us, muffling the ruckus of the still and the chatter and footsteps of the other children. She turned toward me and smoothed out the wrinkles in her apron. Brown stains—food maybe, or blood, or some other foul fluid—speckled the white linen of the garment.

"Mama hasn't seen your father's ghost," she said, "as you might have guessed by her befuddled expression when Bernice flapped her mouth about him."

I swallowed and nodded and didn't really know what to say other than a meager "Oh."

"She believes in spirits; she sees them." Mildred headed over to the desk and that beady-eyed crow. "She just doesn't like to hear about them wandering around inside our house. Neither do I."

I shivered and rubbed my bare arms. "What's in that Necromancer's Nectar you told me about?"

She pulled out the chair from the desk. "I had a feeling that's what you were here for."

"What's in it?"

"Can't tell you," she said. "All our elixirs are family secrets."

I folded my arms across my chest. "Fleur says there's no such thing as any herb or flower that would allow a person to see the dead."

"Fleur doesn't know anything about black magic, does she?" Mildred scooted the chair toward me, the legs scraping and screeching against the floorboards. "Her granny might have been a healer, but mine was an occultist."

I shrank back. "An occultist?"

"That's right."

"I don't like the sound of that at all."

Mildred stopped pushing the chair. "And I don't like the sound of your father pacing the floorboards of my house when he should be resting in a grave."

My eyes stung at those words. I blinked and clenched my hands by my sides.

"You need to tell him to stop coming here, Hanalee," said Mildred. "He's making me feel as though I've done something wrong, and I don't like it one bit."

I squeezed my hands tighter. "*Did* you do something wrong?"

Mildred stepped back. "Of course not."

"Then why is my father able to find his way to your house and not mine? Why am I not the one seeing him?"

"B-b-because . . ." She straightened her apron so it didn't hang so cockeyed over her chest. "You're probably too busy looking for him in the church . . . or at all your favorite shared places. He's searching for you along the road, where all that trouble occurred, and it's high time you look for him there. Here"—she patted the back of the chair—"have a seat. I'll fetch you that bottle."

"I feel wrong about taking something for free," I said.

"This is a gift. An emergency."

"But . . ." I glanced at the room's faded elegance—the dust, the darkness, the bills scattered across the desk. My eyes dropped down to my right hand, where a gold band with an emerald stone glistened on my ring finger. The heirloom had belonged to my late grandmother in Georgia. My father gave it to me on my twelfth birthday.

Mildred's eyes also veered down to the jewel.

"I'm wearing a pink satin step-in my mama made me," I offered instead, tucking my right hand behind my back.

Mildred's eyes brightened. "Satin?"

Using my left hand, I raised the hem of my dress well past my knees for a peek at the pink lace of the undergarment's bottom edge. "It's made with lace on the bodice, one-inch-wide straps, and a small pearl button that fastens to create the closure between the legs." I dropped the skirt. "Makes a girl feel less like a backwoods bumpkin."

Mildred chewed her bottom lip and released a vibrating *Hmm* from the back of her throat. "I'd have to sell it after I wore it once or twice," she said. "You can't eat satin."

"No, I suppose you can't."

She gave a brusque nod. "All right. I'll make the trade."

"I'll slide off the undergarment while you go fetch the bottle— just as long as no one is about to barge in here."

"The door locks." She turned a built-in knob on the door to show me. "I'll knock when I'm back with the bottle."

"All right, then." I clenched my hands again.

"I'll be right back." Mildred swung the door closed with a force that rattled the bookshelves.

I heaved a sigh of regret for promising one of my nicest unmentionables for a wicked bottle of hope. I wasn't even supposed to wear the satin step-in on a day that wasn't the Sabbath. But my regular cotton one smelled too much of sweat after I shot at Joe's head in the woods, so I'd chosen to wear the pink one when I packed up for Fleur's.

I slid both my brown dress and the step-in over my head—a feat I accomplished with lightning-fast movements—and I kept thinking how fragile and terrorized Joe must have felt when I pulled the gun on him while he was naked. *Vulnerable* was the word that came to mind. A once-fine grape with the skin peeled off.

Mildred knocked on the door no more than three minutes after she'd left. "Are you decent?"

"Just a moment." I fastened up the white buttons of my bodice. Without that step-in between it and me, my dress felt like flimsy layers of leaves hugging my skin.

I unfastened the latch, and Mildred hustled inside and shut the door behind her. I handed her the undergarment, and in exchange she gave me a little brown medicine bottle with a dark liquid sloshing about inside it. NECROMANCER'S NECTAR, said the label on the side, penned in an elegant, cursive hand. Pentagrams and other diabolical symbols encircled the words.

I held the bottle an arm's length away. "What in blazes is a necromancer?"

"A person who raises the dead . . . or the spirits of the dead"—Mildred stroked the pink satin in her arms, as if the step-in were a long-lost cat—"to divine the future and explore unresolved matters. I wouldn't chat with Reverend Adder about this concoction, but there's nothing dangerous about it, I swear. It'll allow you to communicate with your father."

My arm slackened. "How do I use it?"

"Take one spoonful at midnight, and then head immediately out to the set of crossroads on the highway. Draw a circle in the dirt. Step inside."

I frowned. "You want me to wander down the highway on my own? After dark?"

"Going to him in the place where he's been spotted the most is the surest way to guarantee a strong connection."

My shoulders sank.

"He looks so lost, Hanalee." She took hold of my left elbow. "So goddamned desperate. Pardon my French, but there's no delicate way to phrase it."

"But—"

"I don't want to see him like that another night."

I nodded and tucked the bottle into my right pocket. "If this makes me sick—"

"It won't."

I chewed my bottom lip and fingered the smooth glass.

She glanced over her shoulder at the closed door. "Sheriff Rink'll be here soon."

"Why's he coming over?"

"Just a friendly visit."

"All right." I slipped my hand out of my pocket. "I'll get going. Thank you for trying to help."

"You're welcome." She opened the door and led me past the smells and the racket of the whiskey-production process, and she steered me through the traffic of children darting through the house with toys and breakfast dishes.

Out on the front porch, I leaned over and picked up the valise. "Hey, Mildred, did you know Joe Adder very well when he lived here?"

She snorted and pulled at her stained apron. "Do you honestly think he and I would have been chums?"

"I just—"

"Don't you remember how he looked in church, Hanalee? The slicked hair? The handsome suits? Those big brown eyes?"

I stood up straight. "He's also the snake who hit my father with a car, don't forget."

She hunched her shoulders. "Why do you ask?"

"He's back in the area."

"I've heard that." She peered down at her boots and scraped her right sole against one of the boards of the porch. "But w-w-why'd you ask that question? What's he got to do with me?"

"Robbie Witten told me he's not right in the head." I shifted my bag to my other hand. "He said Joe's dangerous."

"Dangerous to himself, maybe. Not to you or me."

My eyebrows shot up. "How do you mean?"

Before she could answer, I heard an automobile motor puttering in our direction. Mildred's eyes strayed to the drive in front of her house.

I turned and spotted the sheriff's black patrol car cruising toward us, rocking back and forth from all the dips and potholes in the Markses' dirt drive.

"Sheriff Rink's here," said Mildred. "Better go."

I nodded and scampered down the steps of the porch.

Now, it should be noted that Sheriff Rink, nicknamed "Sheriff Rinky-Dink" between Fleur and me, possessed the highest male voice known to mankind—a wheezy, breezy squeak of a tenor that matched his short stature but not his sturdy build.

"Good morning, Hanalee," he chirped in a decibel that I had never once reached in regular conversation. He stopped the car beside me with the motor still running. "Did you spend the night with the Markses?"

I glanced down at my bag. "Oh . . . Well, no. I stayed at Fleur's house and made a detour over here before I head back home."

"Why?" he asked. His tiny gray mouse eyes peered at me from beneath his blue cap.

"Why?" I repeated.

He smiled. "What were you doing at the Markses'?"

I peeked over my shoulder, but Mildred had gone from the porch. The distant thumping of the whiskey still chugged like a heartbeat behind the house's outer layers.

"Mildred told me . . ." I turned back toward him, hoping he wouldn't hear the brown bottle sloshing inside my valise. "She . . . offered me a book to borrow."

The sheriff readjusted his backside in his seat. "Well, just be careful wandering around on your own right now. The Oregon State Penitentiary released Joe Adder over the weekend"—he darted a quick glance over his right shoulder—"and he's currently hiding out somewhere nearby."

I cleared my throat. "Why do you suspect that he's hiding?"

"His father won't allow him back in his house. Keep an eye out for him, but don't speak to him."

"Why not?"

"Why not?" The sheriff crinkled his graying eyebrows. "He was a convicted man, Hanalee. He killed your poor father by violating Prohibition and driving around like a hellion. Why would you want to talk to him?"

"I don't. I just wondered if you thought he might be mentally unstable."

"That boy is *definitely* unstable. Don't ever let him near you, and don't listen to a word he says."

"Yes, sir."

"Good girl. Now go on home." Sheriff Rink released the brake and steered his car to a patch of dead grass directly in front of Mildred's house.

A second later, Mrs. Marks threw open the front door and called out, "Oh, hello, Sheriff Rink. So nice to see you this morning." She smiled and waved the sheriff up to the porch, and I saw a wad of cash poking out from her apron pocket. "Won't you come inside?"

"Don't mind if I do." The sheriff—a man twice divorced and not typically popular with the ladies—climbed out of his car and removed his blue cap to reveal his head of silvery-brown hair, cut close to his scalp, combed to the left like waves breaking over a riverbank. He swaggered up the porch steps and followed Mildred's mother inside.

Mrs. Marks leaned her face out the door. "Go on home, Hanalee. I'm sure you've got something better to do than to linger around here, gaping like a fish."

Without a word in response, I swung my bag and myself in the direction of the highway and meandered away from the little scene of illegal moonshine production and police bribery. I envisioned Sheriff Rink driving away from the house with a bundle of hush money stuffed inside a pocket and a jug of booze stashed in the backseat for himself.

Despite all the warnings, I didn't once come across Joe Adder on my walk back home.

Nor my father's spirit.

It was just me and the forest birds and the bottle of Necromancer's Nectar.

MEDICINE BOTTLE, EARLY 1900s.

CHAPTER 5

WHERE WILT THOU LEAD ME?

 BY THE TIME I RETURNED HOME, Uncle Clyde had already driven off to his office in downtown Elston, two miles away, which was fine by me. For the better part of the morning, the house belonged to just Mama and me. We scrubbed stains out of the laundry on a washboard in the kitchen, while out in the backyard a fire crackled and simmered beneath a large iron pot, stacked upon bricks, filled with water and Lux laundry soap. We rinsed and wrung out all the whites, and once the water outside bubbled to a boil, we carried the garments from the house and plunked them into the steaming pot.

I jabbed the laundry plunger into swirls of fabrics the colors of cream and snow, while bubbles popped and spat at my fingers, threatening to scald. Steam dampened my cheeks and made me feel a little feverish. A little dizzy.

"Everyone's warning me to watch out for Joe Adder," I said to Mama.

She lowered the tulip-embroidered tablecloth into the pot, keeping her eye on the task at hand.

"Did you hear what I said, Mama?"

"Who's 'everyone'?"

"Robbie. Mildred. Sheriff Rink."

She lifted her head. "You've spoken to the sheriff?"

"I saw him on my way back home this morning." I plunged the tablecloth down to the bottom of the pot, where the tangle of fabrics resembled a woman in a nightgown writhing in the blackness beneath the water. I wiped my forehead with the back of my hand. "Has Uncle Clyde ever said Joe was mentally unstable?"

Mama took the plunger from me and stirred the mass of laundry herself. "He doesn't want to talk about Joe Adder, which you should have known at the dinner table yesterday. Don't ever bring up unpleasant topics during meals, Hanalee."

"Why doesn't he want to talk about Joe?" I asked. "I thought you said we're supposed to be forgiving."

"You can forgive him, but don't dwell on him. He's still not easy to talk about."

I watched her agitate the cloths and the undergarments in the tub and remembered Joe's talk of white hoods and robes.

"What does Uncle Clyde say about my future here?" I asked.

Mama peeked up at me without lifting her head. "Why do you ask that?"

"I'm not sure if I can imagine him paying for me to receive further schooling after I graduate. And we all know I can't marry anyone around here, unless a nonwhite young man actually moves into the region. I'm not sure if anyone would hire me for work." I drummed my fingers against my sides. "What on earth am I supposed to do for the rest of my life?"

"Well"—she brushed a lock of hair out of her eyes with fingers red and cracked from the washing—"Uncle Clyde says you're welcome to live here with us as long as you please."

"Does he even like me?"

"Hanalee!" She jabbed at the wash with a force that splashed water over the edge. "The questions you're asking . . ."

"How does he feel about the Negro race in general?"

Mama's jaw dropped. "Why are you asking such things? Uncle Clyde is most certainly not a bigot, if that's what you're insinuating."

"If I'm going to be stuck in a house with him, I want to know precisely what type of man he is."

"He's a good man who wants you to have a decent future."

"I'm thinking of becoming a lawyer."

Mama wrinkled her forehead and placed a hand on a hip. "A lawyer?"

"Yes." I grabbed the plunger back from her. "I would love to one day open up a newspaper and read the words 'Hanalee Denney, a little lady lawyer descended from Georgia slaves, overturned Oregon's exclusion laws and interracial marriage laws—and fought hard to bring justice to people like her father. People killed by cowards who hide their guilt behind others.'"

"What did you just say?"

I plunged the laundry deep into the scalding water until my back hurt from bending and straining.

"What's going on, Hanalee?" She shaded her eyes from the sun. "Have you seen Joe?"

I gulped, but I didn't stop plunging.

"Have you?" she asked again. "Hanalee?"

I met her eyes. "If I saw Joe, wouldn't I tell you?" A simple question. Not an outright lie.

"I certainly hope you *would* tell me. I hope you always speak the truth to me. Why did you say such a thing about your father's death?"

"I'm just exhausted. I didn't sleep well last night." I bowed my head over the water. "I don't know what I'm saying."

Mama gave a sigh and wandered over to the clothesline with her tired walk, her shoulders lowered, hips swaying. I watched her fetch the pins we'd use for drying. A troubled frown darkened her face.

We finished boiling the whites and hung them on the line before boiling all the darks, and then the darkest darks. Warblers twittered in the nearby woods, and sunlight crept over the back of my neck with the tips of its burning fingers.

We didn't say another word about Joe.

We didn't say another word about much of anything.

I KEPT QUIET ALL THROUGHOUT SUPPER AND DURING our evening of silent reading with Uncle Clyde. I sat on the sofa and flipped through the pages of *Noted Negro Women: Their Triumphs and Activities*, by Monroe Alphus Majors, a book I'd received as a

Christmas present from our former reverend's late wife, Mrs. York, when I was ten. She even wrote an inscription to me in the front of the book:

Keep dreaming, Hanalee, just like all the brave and wonderful women inside these pages.
—*Mrs. Georgina York, December 1917*

I came upon a section that featured a woman named Charlotte E. Ray, the first black female lawyer, who was admitted to the District of Columbia Bar way back in 1872. My heart beat faster, and I sat up a little straighter.

Yet I didn't make one peep about laws or injustices or the death of my father.

No more than six feet across from me, Uncle Clyde read his own book—Sinclair Lewis's *Babbitt*—with a mug of coffee steaming by his side, as comfy as can be in my father's beloved maroon armchair. Worn spots on the arms marked the places where Daddy's elbows used to rest. On the wall behind Uncle Clyde hung my father's framed pencil sketches of the hickory trees that grew behind his family's home in Georgia, as well as his delicate line drawings of the brick and sandstone buildings of turn-of-the-century Portland.

"Is everything all right, Hanalee?" asked my stepfather with a tilt of his head. He pushed his specs farther up his narrow nose, which ended in a sharp point small enough to fit inside a pencil sharpener.

I turned the page of my book, and out of the corner of my eye I saw Mama glance up from her copy of *Good Housekeeping*.

"Hanalee?" said Uncle Clyde. "You've been quiet this evening. Is something troubling you?"

"No, everything's just dandy," I said, and I flipped another page.

In my peripheral vision, I saw my mother share a look of concern with her new husband. They both wrinkled their foreheads. They glowered.

Later that night, I lay in my bed, tucked beneath my sheet and my quilt, still in my brown day dress but with my feet bare and my hair unpinned for the night. On the bedside table a candle flickered. Beeswax wept down the yellowish sides and pooled onto the pewter rim of the candlestick, and the air smelled of fire and honey. I reached out and touched the hot puddle, just to experience a sensation aside from the sting of distrust. A soft sizzle met my ears. My fingertip smarted. I blew on the skin until it cooled, but my chest continued to burn.

"People shut me up at my trial," Joe had told me at the pond. "No one, not even my own lawyer, let me speak, as if they'd all gotten paid to keep me quiet."

I fetched my sketch pad and pencil from the floor below my bed, and without even thinking much about it, I drew a picture of Joe standing in a body of water with his chest exposed and his dark hair hanging over his right eye. His mouth emerged from the tip of my pencil as two parted lips, poised to tell me his tale of my stepfather.

SOMETIME AFTER ELEVEN O'CLOCK, MAMA'S AND Uncle Clyde's footsteps and muffled voices traveled upstairs and to their bedroom, down the hallway from mine. Their door shut, and I winced, trying not to imagine them together, naked. Uncle Clyde's voice rumbled through the walls, and Mama's softer tones replied to whatever he said.

A gust of wind blew through my window, snuffing out the candle's flame. Darkness engulfed the room and turned all my furniture into shadows. I rolled onto my side and struck another match, lighting the wick, smelling sulfur in the air.

I could have used the lamp sitting on my chest of drawers to light my room, but I chose not to. Uncle Clyde had brought electricity to our house after his marriage to Mama last January, but I felt that electric light—that unnatural burst of blinding energy—possessed no heart. No passion. No joy. Candlelight cast such a delicate beauty. It flickered with emotions and warmed one's skin and soul.

Beyond the foot of my bed, the window beckoned. I slid my bare feet out from under the sheet and padded over to the half-shut pane. Fleur was right. A golden glow hovered in the sky above the treetops. I raised the sash to its full height, and a breeze fingered its way through my hair, carrying with it the odor of burning wood—the smell of all the illegal stills, perhaps. Or the scent of the stove in the Paulissens' old shed. Or even the flames of hell, waiting for me, should I choose to scheme with Joe Adder. I could see a stretch of the main highway to my left, through a cluster of trees with summer leaves the deep purplish-red of forbidden wine. I poked my head out the window and strained my ears for the sound of restless feet shuffling down the road toward our house.

Nothing.

Not even a single dog barked from any of the nearby farmhouses.

Next to my window, on top of the writing desk that Daddy had built and painted bright strawberry-red when I was five, sat two framed photographs of my father. The first was of my parents' wedding day, back in September 1901. They had to cross the Columbia River to Washington to find a preacher who would marry them, and it took them five tries before they found a man of the cloth willing to conduct the ceremony. Mama wore a high-collared white dress and a veil with a crown of plump rosettes. Daddy was as handsome as ever in his bow tie and suit, with a rose blossom pinned to the lapel of his coat. He had smiling brown eyes and a nose that was narrow on top and broad on the bottom, just like mine.

According to Mama, Fleur's father took the second photograph, a portrait of Mama, Daddy, and me, back when I was about two or three years old. Mama had put me in a dress with frills and lace that swallowed me whole, and a white hair bow devoured the top of my head of chin-length ringlets. I sat on our porch rail, and Daddy held me from behind, while Mama held on to him, all three of us interconnected.

I turned my head away from the photographs and cast my glance to the drawer of my bedside table. The bottle of Necromancer's Nectar was hidden within, as well as a teaspoon I had snuck upstairs earlier that evening, after cleaning up the supper dishes with my mother.

I crept across the room, and, without a sound, holding my breath, I slid open the drawer. The items lay before me.

A spoon and a brown bottle covered in symbols.

A spoon and a bottle and hope.

After a few swift twists, the cap came off in my fingers. My hands shook, but I managed to pour a spoonful of a liquid the color of rust and bitter in smell.

"Oh, dear Lord." I took a breath and eyed the potion sloshing about in the bowl of the spoon. "Please don't let this puddle of rust water kill me."

I slid the cold metal into my mouth and winced at the burn of fire and sin on my tongue. The tonic scorched my throat and sweated straight through my skin. My eyes watered; my hair thickened into a blanket made of wool that scratched at my neck and smothered my back. Perspiration trickled down my cheeks, my chest, my spine . . . I unfastened the top button of my bodice to keep from burning alive.

I shoved my feet into my shoes and left my bedroom, in search of cool air and answers. After every three steps, time seemed to hiccup forward, and I found myself five feet farther ahead than I expected to be.

The landing of the staircase.

The middle of the steps.

Halfway across the entry hall.

The front door.

The front yard.

Confidence surged through my blood, along with the flames of the potion. Before long I found myself marching up the highway, toward Reverend Adder's house, where Daddy had died almost nineteen months earlier. The light of the whiskey stills lingered in the air, practically begging to be discovered by federal agents, and the moon, waning in its last quarter, cocked a half smile in the black July sky.

Time kept skipping ahead. I moved a quarter mile. A half mile. Another highway—one that led to the farmlands of the south and the finer houses of the north—met up with the main road, and there I stood, in the crossroads, as crazy Mildred Marks had told me to do. Using the toe of one of my Keds, I drew a circle in the gravel, next to the southeastern points where the two streets met, and I stepped inside it. I waited with my arms hanging by my sides, my veins flowing with molten lava, all alone in the pitch-dark, near midnight, surrounded by a devil's circle.

"Lord, help me," I whispered.

The stink of manure was so sharp and ripe in the air, it woke me up a bit to my stupidity. I smelled stables and fields and the false sweetness of life in Elston, and I imagined someone like Robbie Witten driving by, finding me all alone, drunk on bottled moonshine.

I turned back to the east, ready to step out of my circle and dash back home, when a sound met my ears.

Footsteps.

Labored footsteps—like those of a man dragging a busted leg as he limped toward me across the macadamized road made of tar and broken rocks. I pivoted on my heels, facing west again, and peered into the stretch of darkness before me.

I saw him. A man my father's height, with long legs and a sturdy build. He wore a dark suit, a crimson bow tie, and a familiar black derby hat that Mama and I bought one Christmas during the war years, when our cornfields turned a fair profit and we waited for Daddy to return from the fighting overseas. He ambled closer, favoring his left leg, and I glimpsed the shine of his brown eyes—

eyes swimming with so much love, they just about melted me to the ground. I recognized his golden-brown skin, his strong jaw, his broad nose, his smooth complexion that always made him look much younger than a man who had endured forty-one years of hardships.

My father, Hank Denney, staggered toward me on that midnight road and stopped two yards away from the shoe-drawn circle in which I trembled.

"Daddy?" I asked, my voice catching in my throat.

He took off his hat and held it against his chest, and he peered straight at me, like a man who lived and breathed.

"I'm so sorry, Hanalee," he said, his voice gentle yet strong and deep enough to rumble inside the marrow of my bones. "I'm so terribly sorry. I should have gone to church with you."

"But . . ." I shook my head. My chin and nose quivered with spasms I couldn't control. "D-d-did you tell Joe—Joe Adder . . . Did you tell him that the doc would be—be the death of you?"

He lowered his face and wrinkled his brow. "My body just couldn't take what it was given that Christmas Eve, baby doll. I'm sorry I wasn't a stronger man and that hate won out that night." He heaved a sigh that made his shoulders rise and fall. "Hate is a powerful demon that worms its way into the hearts of fearful men."

"But . . . Joe . . . not the doc. J-J-Joe Adder killed you. Didn't he?"

"That Model T surely didn't feel good, I admit, but that boy was so scared"—Daddy raised his eyes to me, a sad smile on his face—"I worried more about him than about myself. No . . ." He placed his hat back on his head. "Joe Adder didn't kill me, Hanalee. I put full blame on the doc."

"But . . . Mama . . . she . . ." Tears swam in my eyes, blurring him from view. "Sh-sh-she remarried, just this past winter. Dr. Koning comforted her and—"

"Don't be harsh on your mama. I should have fought harder to survive that night. I should have taken better care of myself so my heart could've been stronger."

"How can you possibly blame yourself? You just said—"

An automobile engine growled our way from somewhere down the road.

Daddy glanced over his shoulder and stepped back with his good leg. "Go home. It's not safe to wander these roads late at night."

"Do you want revenge, Daddy?"

"Go home. And stay away from the doc."

"Do you want me to—?"

"For God's sake, girl, go home!"

Headlights swerved into view, and I thought of Sheriff Rink patrolling the streets, or Deputy Fortaine with his Hollywood smile and his ties to Uncle Clyde. I jumped out of my circle and dove onto my belly in a patch of dirt behind wild blackberries, and as soon as the car roared by, my father seeped away into the darkness, as if swallowed up by ink.

He was gone.

Again.

CHAPTER 6

WILD AND WHIRLING

 I TORE PAST TREES AND FERNS AND scraped my arms on berry thorns, twisting my ankle, not caring at all about the pain. The nighttime forest glowed in a strange haze of gold, and the fat trunks and green awnings soared high above, as if I were nothing more than a spider scampering through a window box. Branches and leaves pushed at my back, thrusting me forward, sending me on my way through the night to the Paulissens' little white shed.

I banged my fists on the door.

"Joe? Are you in there?"

Joe slammed his full weight against the door from within, as if to hold it closed.

"Wait!" I grabbed the knob. "It's Hanalee. I need to talk to you."

"Have you got a gun?" he called through the slats.

"No."

"You swear?"

I raised my hands in case he could see me through the cracks. "I swear. I left it behind. Let me in. I just spoke to someone. Someone who said you're innocent."

"What?"

"You heard me. Open up. I believe you."

The door opened, and I stumbled into the small space lit by a kerosene lantern, with just a cot, a potbelly stove, and some old fishing rods parked against a wall. My knees and elbows crashed against floorboards half sunken into the earth. I smelled and tasted dirt. And fish.

The door closed behind me, and Joe crouched down by my side, shining that foul lantern into my eyes. Bright light cut across my corneas. I hissed and shrank back.

"What's the matter with you?" He grabbed my arm and shoved the light even closer. "Your pupils are as large as dimes. What'd you take?"

"An elixir"—I pushed the lantern away—"from Mildred Marks."

"Jesus!" He set the light on the ground beside him. "You look like the dope fiends I met in prison."

"I don't know what the Markses put in there, but"—I clasped his left elbow—"I spoke to him, Joe."

"Who?"

"My father. My real father."

"You . . ." His face blanched, and I watched his own pupils dilate. "You mean—"

"He said he should have stayed away from the doc that night. He puts full blame on Dr. Koning."

Joe knelt so close to me, I smelled pond water in his hair and saw the C-shaped arc of the scar above his right eyebrow. His bottom lip looked as though it had once split open and tried to heal, with questionable success.

Without warning, the room swayed, and I had to cover my mouth to keep from retching. Kerosene smoke lodged in my lungs. I coughed and wheezed and curled onto my side, the heels of my palms pressed against my eye sockets.

"Hanalee." Joe nudged my arm. "Wake up. You can't go to sleep in here."

"We should talk to Sheriff Rink."

"I told the sheriff about Dr. Koning when he first threw me in jail. He didn't listen to a fucking word I said."

I flinched at his language. "There's got to be something we can do."

"There's only one way to get rid of a man who got away with murder, Hanalee."

I lowered my hands from my eyes and gaped at him. "He's my stepfather, Joe."

"He murdered your father." Joe pointed toward the door. "He took that man's life and robbed you of love and peace."

"I can't kill him."

"Where'd you get that gun? From Laurence?"

"I'm not shooting Clyde Koning."

"Talk to Fleur, then. She knows all about herbs and flowers, doesn't she? I'm sure she's aware of poisonous local plants and could—"

"No!" I sat back up. "I'm not tangling Fleur up in this mess. I'd kill myself before anything happens to her."

"I can't risk going back to that prison."

"Well, you're going to have to go back, because I'm not a killer."

"Neither am I."

I smacked his arm with the heel of my right palm. "You're an ex-convict with nothing to lose. You've got no family, no money, no house, no love—"

He snatched my wrist and squeezed my bones between his fingers. "They'll cut me up if I go back there."

I tried to wrench myself away from him, but he pulled me forward and tipped me off balance.

"I'm like you, Hanalee." His dark eyes glistened a few inches in front of mine. "I've got people who hate me and want to hurt me. There are doctors in that prison—barbarians with medical degrees who'll do unspeakable things to change me if I ever go back. There's no way in hell I'm going back there."

Lamplight wavered and rippled across the wall behind him, stretching and shaking his shadow above the bed. He smelled so much like the pond beyond the shed, I imagined him diving down into the murky green depths and hiding among the underwater grasses whenever I wasn't around.

"Are you sure murder is the only option?" I asked.

He nodded. "All you have to do is slip poisonous leaves into his tea or coffee—whatever he likes to drink. And I'll get you out of town directly afterward."

I squirmed. "Why don't you just stab Dr. Koning and run?"

"I just told you—I can't risk jail. Sheriff Rink would be after me the second I finished the job. He'd have the whole goddamned state searching for me with rifles and bloodhounds."

"They'd hunt you down even faster if your skin was as dark as mine."

"That's not necessarily true." He loosened his grip.

I lifted my chin. "I think you're a coward, Joe."

"If I murder Dr. Koning, I'd have to kill myself, too, just to make sure I don't end up in that pen again. If it comes to that"—he turned his face away and swallowed, hard—"I'll do it. But I think, if we're careful, and you get to him from within that house, we can both end up safe and free in some other place that doesn't want to get rid of us."

I breathed through my mouth. My tongue went so dry, my throat turned raw.

"Will you consider it, Hanalee?" He peeked back at me. "You just said yourself that your father blames the doc. You have your proof. And I know for certain you have a vengeful side."

I swallowed. "I wasn't ever truly going to kill you. I sent that bullet straight past your ear on purpose, so you'd feel exactly what I felt when Sheriff Rink told me my father was dead."

He didn't respond. He simply stared without blinking.

I rubbed the sides of my face and groaned from deep within my belly. "I'm not making any promises until morning. This might all feel like a bad dream by the time I wake up."

"Here . . ." He turned and reached for something under the cot, next to a couple of clothbound books with titles too hidden in the dark to read. I also saw a stack of playing cards, built into a triangular tower five cards high, constructed on the ground next to the foot of the bed. The crossword puzzle pages of a newspaper lay in a heap beside the tower, with half the squares still blank.

"I guess you're not so good at crossword puzzles," I said.

"Here, I've got a fountain pen." Joe reached toward me with the pen in hand. "Write down your father's words, exactly the way you remember them—somewhere on your body where Dr. Koning or your mother won't see."

I shrank back. "I don't know if the ink will show up on my skin."

He fetched one of the puzzle pages. "Then write the words here."

"What if Dr. Koning sees what I've written on the page?"

"I bet you've got a knack for hiding things from him." He tore a corner off the newspaper and laid it flat on the floor in front of me. "Like the gun . . . and the elixir you took tonight."

"All right." I snatched the pen from his hand. "Give me a second to make my brain slow down, and I'll write what I remember."

Joe spun back around toward the cot and grabbed a pair of beat-up brown shoes from underneath. We both remained seated on the shed's filthy old floorboards, which felt as hard as a rib cage against the backs of my thighs. Splinters needled their way into my left ankle.

I leaned forward, and, next to the ripped bottom of the crossword puzzle, I filled the newsprint with seven words:

I put full blame on the doc.

My hand shook so much, the letters formed as smudges and squiggles. My stomach twisted just from looking at them.

"There." I screwed the cap back into place and tossed the pen at Joe. "It's done. I gotta go home."

He shoved a shoe over his right foot and laced it. "I'll walk you back."

"There's no need for that." I crammed the piece of newsprint into my pocket.

"It's dark." He put on the other shoe. "You're on that tonic. And despite what my father and the state of Oregon claim, I am a gentleman." He tied the second lace and got to his feet.

I braced my hands against the floorboards and pushed myself up. "Why would doctors in prison want to perform surgery on you? What's wrong with you?"

He ran a hand through his hair and headed for the door. "Nothing."

"Are you sure about that, Joe? Everyone I've spoken to since yesterday warned me not to talk to you. They all told me you're crazy."

He stopped by the door. "Who said that?"

"Robbie Witten. Mildred Marks. Sheriff Rink."

A shaky breath rattled through his lips, and he averted his eyes from mine.

"Why would they say that?" I asked. "In fact, why should I listen to your plans to kill my stepfather if you're completely off your rocker?"

"I'm not crazy, Hanalee. Just . . ." He swung the door open. "Let's get you back home."

I didn't budge.

"Hanalee . . ." Joe sighed and shifted toward me. "Ignorant sons of bitches say terrible things about me because they don't understand my type of people."

I shifted my weight between my feet. "W-w-what do you mean, your 'type of people'? Are you part Indian or something?"

"No."

"Catholic?"

He rolled his eyes. "My father's a goddamned Methodist preacher, for Christ's sake. I'm not Catholic."

"Then what do you mean?"

He raked a hand through his hair once more and returned his gaze to the sunken floorboards in front of him. "It's none of your business."

"Tell me, Joe, or I won't conspire with you. I'll investigate my father's death on my own. I'll let the sheriff know where you're hiding . . ."

"Jesus."

"No secrets. Tell me the truth if you want me to believe everything you say."

"All right, if you're going to be so damn pushy about it, I'll tell you, but you can't breathe a word about it to another soul." He grabbed his stomach. "I'm a . . . what people call a . . ." His face made a wincing expression that reminded me of the way I'd felt when I first swallowed down the fire of Necromancer's Nectar. "Oh, Christ, just . . . I'm an Oscar Wilde."

I shook my head, confused. "You're a playwright?"

"No, I . . ." He dropped his arm to his side. "I'm a . . . what they call . . ." His chin quivered; every other part of his body tensed. "Queer." He swallowed. "A homosexual."

I merely blinked at him, not one hundred percent sure I knew what that latter term meant.

"I don't love girls in a romantic way," he explained. "I—I—I . . . it's boys." He clutched his stomach again and closed his eyes. "I'm attracted to boys."

"Oh." I gave a small nod.

A prickly silence fell between us. Outside, a frog belched a deep croak from the pond behind the shed. I slipped my right hand into my pocket and crinkled the newsprint that bore the accusation about my stepfather.

"Well, I should . . . I should get going." I sidled past Joe, careful not to touch him, and exited the shed.

He closed the door behind us, and I heard him following my lead through the clearing, his loud footsteps breaking up twigs.

We descended the short slope leading down to the creek, and I took extra caution crossing the rocks that jutted out of the water, for my feet felt cumbersome and unnatural. The nighttime world remained foggy and golden bright, and my head seemed stuffed full of cotton. Once I made it to the other side of the water, I pinched a fleshy part of my left arm to ensure I wasn't stuck in the middle of a dream. I pinched myself hard and flinched at the shock of pain.

Joe trailed behind me all the way back to the break in the trees that led to my house. His shoes crushed leaves and pine needles with a percussive rhythm that mimicked the sounds of my own feet.

I didn't know whether I should turn and say anything—or if the wrong words would tumble out of my mouth, or if he would suddenly look different, or if there *was* something different about his face or his body or his mannerisms, something I hadn't noticed before. I rubbed my arms and slowed my pace and felt the sudden urge to be cruel to him again.

"Is that why you want me to be the one who kills him?" I asked over my shoulder in the quietest voice I could muster. "Because you're not a true man?"

His feet came to an abrupt stop behind me.

My heart stopped, too. The words I'd spoken made my mouth taste rotten.

I turned around, parting my lips to apologize, but he was gone—a shadow slipping into the depths of the woods beyond the firs, leaving me all alone with a scrap of paper that burned inside my pocket.

CHAPTER 7

THOU HAST THY FATHER MUCH OFFENDED

 I AWOKE IN THE MORNING WITH A headache. Memories of the night before flared to life as scattered images: rust-colored liquid and candlelight. An empty road in the pitch-dark night. Trees illuminated in a haze of gold. The shed. Joe, running his hand through his hair. My father, standing right in front of me . . .

I covered my eyes with my palms and groaned through the sick feeling burbling in my stomach.

After a knock that scarcely counted as a knock, someone came into my room.

"Hanalee," said my mother, "Deputy Fortaine came over. He's waiting downstairs for you."

I rolled over in my sheets and faced her. The bottle of Necromancer's Nectar still sat on my bedside table, I realized, the cap unscrewed, the bottle wide open and smelling of booze and dope— or at least what I imagined dope to smell like. Bitter as molasses. Medicinal. Nauseating.

"Why is he waiting to see me?" I asked. I forced myself not to grab the bottle and hide it from sight.

"He wants to speak to you about Joe."

My skin simultaneously sweated and froze.

"Get dressed." Mama marched over and pulled the covers off me with a gust of air that blew hair against my face. Her eyes locked on to the dress I still wore from the day before. "You never changed into nightclothes?"

"I didn't feel well last night."

"Are you better now?"

I shrugged. "I don't know."

She lowered the covers to my knees. "Change into fresh clothes and come downstairs."

"I don't want to talk to Deputy Fortaine."

"He's here to help."

"To help whom?" I asked.

She creased her brow and put her hands on her hips. "To help us. All of us."

My glance flitted to the Necromancer's Nectar, which now seemed as large and conspicuous as a living creature, perched beside my bed.

Mama turned her face toward the bottle. "What's that?"

I sat up. "A tonic."

"For what?"

I grabbed the potion. "Straightening hair. Mildred gave it to me."

She grumbled. "Stop buying those horrible cure-alls from her. Your curls are beautiful."

I tried to screw the lid into place without appearing nervous, but my hands slipped and accidentally shook the liquid until it sloshed and foamed.

"Put that bottle away," said Mama. "Get yourself brushed and presentable. Deputy Fortaine is a busy man. We mustn't waste his time."

I nodded and pressed the bottle's black-magic symbols against my chest, finding the glass cold to the touch. The note from the night before rustled in my dress pocket, but my mother didn't seem to hear it.

She left the room and closed the door behind her.

I released the breath I'd been holding and concealed both the bottle and the note in the drawer of my bedside table. My clothing and hair smelled of smoke from Joe's lantern, I realized, so I changed into a fresh gray and white dress and sprinkled my hair with talcum powder before twisting it, tucking it under, and pinning it into the style of a faux bob.

A quick glance in the mirror revealed fear in the pupils of my hazel eyes.

WITH A FLASH OF HIS DOUGLAS FAIRBANKS SMILE, Deputy Fortaine stood up from his seat next to Uncle Clyde's at our dining room table.

"Good morn—" He bumped his thigh on the table's edge. Mugs of coffee jostled. "Good morning, Hanalee." His olive complexion reddened, but the smile stayed in place.

"Morning, Hanalee," said Uncle Clyde, bobbing up from his own chair for a swift moment.

Mama placed her hand against my back and urged me forward, while both men watched me with a kindness that tasted false. I stepped toward them with my hands clasped in front of me.

Deputy Fortaine pulled out a chair for me. "Please, have a seat."

Uncle Clyde clutched his own mug of coffee and nodded at me to obey the deputy's orders. The skin beneath his eyes bulged, as if he hadn't slept the night before.

I sat down with reluctance, and Mama plunked a glass of orange juice in front of me.

"Your breakfast will wait until after the chat," she said, her hand on my shoulder for a slip of a moment.

Deputy Fortaine sat back down, this time holding on to the table. Mama took the seat across from him.

I fidgeted and rubbed my hands over my skirt, and the cotton stuck to my palms.

"Hanalee"—the deputy cleared his throat and wrapped his fingers around his mug—"as I know you're well aware, Joe Adder is back in the area. The state penitentiary released him early on good behavior."

"Yes, I know." I summoned every ounce of restraint I possessed to keep my head from turning toward the window. Toward the woods.

The deputy took a sip of his beverage, and, after a smack of his lips, he lowered the mug back to the table. I smelled an off-putting potpourri of coffee, orange juice, and the deputy's musky cologne, the last of which Fleur's mother probably found arousing. Everything at that table made me sick to my stomach.

"Have you seen him?" asked the deputy, his head tilted to his right, his eyes narrowed.

All three of them—Mama, Uncle Clyde, and Deputy Fortaine—stared me down like buzzards.

I folded my hands on the table, and through gritted teeth I answered, "Why on earth would I be seeing the drunk who killed my father?"

"Hanalee . . ." Mama reached toward me across the table. "I'm worried about the questions you asked me yesterday. I feel your opinion of Uncle Clyde changed the day we learned Joe was back in town. I don't want any husband of mine feeling unwelcome in his own home."

I pulled my hand away from hers. "This isn't Dr. Koning's home."

"You see what I mean?" said Mama to the deputy, her voice desperate. "This is how she talks now. She seems suspicious of her own father—"

"He's my *step*father, Mama."

Uncle Clyde lowered his face toward his mug, and his knuckles whitened.

The deputy drummed his long fingers on the tabletop. "We need to know where the boy is, Hanalee."

"Why?" I asked.

"He's made far too many enemies in Elston, and some people aren't taking kindly to the idea of his returning."

I squeezed my lips together and remembered everything Joe had said about himself—his claim that people wanted to hurt him and get rid of him, his fear of surgeons in prison cutting him up and changing him.

I grabbed the sides of my chair. "Did Joe even kill my father?"

The deputy shifted his weight and exchanged a brief look of concern with my stepfather—a look I didn't care for in the slightest.

"Why do you ask that?" he said.

"Because people shut him up before and during his trial."

The deputy didn't blink.

"*How* did they shut him up?" I asked.

"Hanalee!" Mama grabbed my hand. "You're not the one who's supposed to be asking questions."

"How did they shut him up, Deputy Fortaine?" I asked again, shaking Mama's fingers off mine by flapping my wrist up and down. "Did you beat him?"

"No, I did not beat Joe Adder."

"Did Sheriff Rink?"

The deputy breathed a weighty sigh. "Joe was . . . caught in the act of another crime before he crashed into your father. His own actions were used against him. He knew that testifying on that witness stand wouldn't have done him any good."

"What other crime?" I asked.

The deputy grabbed the handle of his mug. "That's not for me to discuss."

"But—"

"I don't want that information slipping out into the public and triggering more trouble than it's already caused." The deputy took another sip, and I swore his hands shook.

"What trouble?" I asked.

"Hanalee," urged Mama, "stop badgering the deputy with questions."

Deputy Fortaine swallowed. "We need to know where he is, Hanalee. I have my suspicions that Joe intends to harm someone around here. I also believe that some people around here might hurt him—badly—even kill him, if they find him first."

I eyed the adults' silent stares and drawn faces. "What would you do with him if you found him?"

"What is he offering you, Hanalee?" asked Uncle Clyde. "I can tell by the way you're talking that he's communicated with you."

"How are you benefiting from helping him hide?" The deputy jabbed the tip of his right index finger against the table, as if he wanted me to lay my answer down on the white cloth before him. "Why would someone like you trust a person like him?"

I nudged my glass of orange juice away, for I couldn't stand to breathe its tangy scent a second longer.

"Hanalee," said Mama. "Answer the deputy. Why are you helping Joe hide?"

"I'm not. I don't even care if someone hurts him, and I wish everyone would stop looking to me for answers." I sprang out of my chair with a slam of my shoes on the floor.

"Where are you going?" asked Mama.

"Out for a walk." I pushed in my chair.

"You're not done speaking with Deputy Fortaine."

"I feel sick inside this house. I need fresh air."

Mama stood. "Sit back down, and tell the deputy—"

"Joe left town days ago," I said—an outright lie, but one uttered out of necessity. "Stop questioning me, and stop treating me like I'm the criminal, when all I've done is lose my father."

"Hanalee . . . ," said Mama, but I tore out of the room before anyone could say another word. I yanked open the front door to the blinding glare of daylight and ran eastward on the highway as fast as my legs could carry me.

BIRACIAL CHILD IN RURAL
AMERICA, EARLY TO MID-1900s.

CHAPTER 8

THE PLAY'S THE THING

 I SLOWED MY PACE AT THE ELM-lined driveway that led to Fleur's house, yet I pressed onward in a northeasterly direction, glancing over my shoulder every few moments to make sure Deputy Fortaine didn't follow me in his patrol car. The sun shone hot against my neck. I wished I'd remembered to grab a hat before flying out the door.

Overhead, a red-tailed hawk circled with outstretched wings in the bright blue sky. He cried out for his mate, a beautiful and haunting sound, and I found my eyes tearing up because of it. All around me, rolling fields of golden wheat smelled sweet and crisp and teased of a childhood long gone.

Fleur, Laurence, and I used to wander that same road on summer days past—careless days, aimless days—with our arms linked together. A blond-brunette-blond row of heads. Our fathers fought overseas in the war—in different regiments, due to the color of my father's skin—and our mamas hired workers to help with the farms. We grew crops for starving families thousands of miles away in Europe, and the government paid us kindly for our patriotism.

When we children were even younger, we'd play hide-and-seek in the middle of the woods. We'd also pretend we were characters in a fairy-tale forest, and I always got to play Snow White, on account of my hair color being only a few shades shy of "black as ebony." Both Fleur and Laurence would lean over and kiss my cheeks as I lay on the grass beneath the boughs of fir trees singing in the wind, and they'd try to see who could rouse me from my sleep of death. One time Laurence surprised me by kissing me on the lips, and when my eyes burst open, he grinned and said, "I won! I woke her in the fastest time of all."

After that day, he kissed my lips a few more times, always while playing amid the trees in our kingdom of pretend.

Until he outgrew such games.

Until he moved on to girls as white as snow.

I SNUCK INTO THE WOODS A BACK WAY, A HALF MILE or so north of Fleur's family's property. Goose pimples washed over my skin from the sprawling shadows of sky-high firs, despite the July heat cooking the rest of the world outside the forest. An entire choir of birds chattered in the web of branches surrounding

83

me; a woodpecker jackhammered one of the trunks to my right. A squirrel scampered across moss-covered boughs, rattling leaves overhead, giving me a start.

For breakfast I grazed on wild blackberries, and then I washed my face in the creek and made a quick detour to the stretch of the forest behind my house to check on my pistol, which I still needed to sneak back into my house. The weapon remained concealed inside the oilcloth beneath the leaf pile, untouched, loaded, minus the bullet that had whistled past Joe's ear. I left it there for the time being and trekked back into the heart of the woods, careful to keep my footsteps silent. The creek babbled and bubbled below the rocks that I crossed with my arms out-stretched, and loose soil from the embankment made my climb to the clearing feel like stepping up a ladder I had to carve with my own two feet. At the top of the slope, the little white shed came into sight. I knelt down in the tall stalks of horsetail grasses and listened for anyone following me.

"Just a couple more nights," said a voice up ahead.

I lifted my chin.

Laurence stepped out the front door of Joe's makeshift house with a red-and-white-checked napkin balled in his hand. His blond hair shone as brightly as fool's gold in the streaks of sunlight slicing through the trees. "I can't keep sneaking you food out here," he said, and he crammed the napkin into a back trouser pocket. "You're going to get me killed if anyone finds you here."

Joe exited the shed behind him and grabbed up a stick as long as one of his legs. "I don't plan to be here much longer."

"Another day at most," Laurence warned.

"Sure." Joe leaned over and picked up a pinecone, which he rolled around in his left hand.

Laurence shifted my way and scanned the woods, his blue eyes squinting into the sun. I ducked farther down in the grasses.

"You're lucky I'm a goddamned saint in this community, Joe," he said. "No one thinks to look for you back here, because I'm a pillar of respectability."

"Is that right?" asked Joe with a laugh.

"I'm dead serious. You're going to need to go soon. Real soon."

"Jesus Christ"—Joe tossed the pinecone into the air and whacked it with the stick, sending it whizzing over my head—"stop saying that, Laurie. I'll go as soon as I'm able. I've just got some business to finish."

"What business?"

"Never you mind. It's private."

Laurence's mouth tightened. He scanned the woods again, and the hardness of his face made him nearly unrecognizable to me. His chin jutted outward at an odd angle. Without another word, he marched into the thicket of firs, away from Joe and the shed.

I held my breath and stayed low to the ground. A black-and-yellow-striped honeybee landed on a knuckle of my right hand, and its little brown stinger bobbed up and down. I stilled my muscles and willed the thing away by blinking at it.

Joe kept his face directed toward the trees through which Laurence had disappeared. When he must have been assured that Laurence wasn't coming back, he hurriedly unbuttoned his gray cotton shirt and stripped down to his waist.

I aimed to stand up and say, *Joe! Wait!* Before I could spring upright, however, he unbuttoned his trousers and pulled both the pants and his drawers down his legs. I closed my eyes and turned my head, but not before catching sight of his naked white backside, as muscular as his arms but much paler than his top half. My stomach gave an odd squeeze.

I heard his legs brushing through the rushes and the ferns and couldn't help but wonder if the foliage tickled his bare flesh. I cracked my right eye open a sliver and couldn't see him any longer. I just crouched there in the grasses, an accidental Peeping Tom, not knowing what to do. The bee soared away, thank the Lord. At least I wouldn't make the situation worse by hollering from a sting.

A plunking sound and some splashes let me know that Joe had entered the pond. I debated whether I should leave him be while he bathed, yet no other obligation seemed as pressing as talking to him about Deputy Fortaine and what the hell we should do next.

I stood up and crept to the side of the shed, not yet seeing the pond beyond the trees.

"Hey, Joe," I called.

The splashes stopped. "Yeah?"

"I need to talk to you."

"Do you have a gun?"

"No. Stop worrying about that. I'm not going to shoot you."

"All right . . . I just . . ." He made a swishing sound in the water, as though turning away from me. "I'll be there soon. Just . . . go into the shed and wait. I want some privacy for a moment."

"Isn't that water awfully cold for bathing?"

"Go wait in the shed, Hanalee. I don't need you spying on me."

"I'm not . . ." I stood up straight; my face burned. "I'm not spying on you. I have no desire to see your"—I sidled back around the shed—"pale and naked fanny." With a nimble leap, I darted over his clothing and promptly made a loud to-do about shutting the shed door behind me, so he'd know I wasn't watching him.

The shed smelled terrible. Stale. Old. Fishy. Trace scents of ashes from the potbelly stove tried to break through the stench, but the fish stink proved too powerful. I leaned against the boards of the leftmost wall, across from the cot, and spotted a new playing-card structure built on the ground—a circular building with a flat roof positioned atop it. I tiptoed forward and knelt down in front of the construction with my mouth sealed closed, careful not to breathe wrong and topple the entire enterprise. The symmetry—the intricate complexity of all those perfectly angled cards—reminded me of a honeycomb.

Joe's footsteps padded toward the shed.

I jumped to my feet—and knocked over the structure.

"Oh . . . damn," I whispered, and I backed against the opposite wall, banging my right shoulder blade against it.

Joe hummed something outside the shed, perhaps to warn me of his approach. He gave two fake-sounding coughs outside the door, and I could see the shadows of his feet moving around beyond the space at the bottom. He hopped about a bit and slid his trousers back on, and I couldn't help but think of his naked backside again. Two firm loaves of uncooked dough.

He opened the door, still missing his shirt.

"Oh, Christ, Hanalee." He glared at the collapsed pile of cards. "Did you knock down my tower?"

"What criminal act did they catch you in before you hit my father with the Ford?" I asked.

He froze, his hand still on the doorknob.

"Well?" I said.

"Who told you I got caught for something else?"

"Deputy Fortaine."

Joe let go of the knob and sauntered into the shed, his gray shirt clutched in his right hand. The sleeves dangled down to his knees, like an upside-down person stretching toward the floor.

"Put your shirt on." I inched toward the door. "I'm not standing in a shed with a half-naked boy."

"Why did you talk to Deputy Fortaine?"

"Put your shirt on."

He raised his voice. "Why did you talk to Deputy Fortaine?"

"Dr. Koning brought him to our house this morning. They sat me down like I was a criminal on trial and questioned me about your whereabouts."

Joe rubbed his shirt over his wet hair, and I smelled the pond water all over him again. He reminded me of a river otter, drenched and slick and wild. His hair dripped rivulets of water down his bare shoulders. Old yellowed bruises marred the skin above his left ribs, as though someone had beat him up in recent weeks.

"If you committed another crime," I said, turning my eyes instead toward the wreckage of the card tower, "how in the world am I supposed to trust a word you said about your innocence?"

Joe plopped himself down on the cot and wiped his forehead with a shirtsleeve. "The deputy . . ." He sighed and leaned forward, his elbows digging into his thighs, the shirt hanging between his legs. "He caught me with another boy. Someone I met at a party that Christmas Eve."

I stood up straight.

"That sort of thing's illegal," he added, his voice quiet.

"I wondered if it might be." I glanced away from him again. "Now, put your shirt back on. I don't like talking to you like this."

"Well"—he tugged his right sleeve over his arm—"in any case, now you know why my father, the esteemed Reverend Ezekiel Joseph Adder, banned me from his house. I showed up at his door on the day I got back to town, scars on my face, tears of repentance in my eyes, and he called me—" His voice cracked. He shoved his left arm through the other sleeve. "My pop called me an abomination. I'm never setting eyes on that high-and-mighty son of a bitch ever again."

"He called you"—I swallowed down an ugly taste—"an 'abomination'?"

Joe nodded. "He told me he believed that surgically removing a part of my body would do me good."

My arms went cold. "What are you even talking about? What body parts are people in prisons removing?"

Joe bit down on his pink bottom lip until the skin turned white. "Castration." He shot me a stare that pierced straight through my heart. "Do you know what that is?"

"Yes." I nodded, my chest tightening. "I've lived in farm country all my life. I know what they do to bulls to tame them and keep them from mating with the cows."

"The government is taking it upon itself to do the same thing to certain inmates. 'Eugenics,' they're calling it. Forced sterilization."

"Why?"

"To cleanse America of sexual deviants, madmen, and the feeble-minded." He buttoned up his shirt, starting from the bottom, his fingers shaking as he went.

"I'm sorry," I said, and I truly meant it.

Joe finished with his shirt and leaned back on his hands. He sat with his legs flopped open, and he kept the top button of his shirt unfastened, exposing part of his chest.

"Does Laurence know what you're like?" I asked.

"I . . . I don't think so."

"Well, be careful of him." I smirked. "He is a 'pillar of respectability.'"

Joe snickered under his breath. "Did you hear him say that about himself?"

I nodded and swallowed. "I actually hate what he's become."

"Don't worry about him. He's all talk." Joe pushed himself off the cot and wandered the three steps it took to reach me on the other side of the shed. He leaned a hand against the wall near the left side of my head, and the wood creaked from the pressure. "Let's talk about what's important now."

I eyed the closed door. "They could be looking for me—Uncle Clyde and Deputy Fortaine. I left the house in a huff and ran away."

Our eyes met at that so-close distance, just a foot or so apart, and I could see a ring of gold encircling his pupils, right before the brown began.

"Are you sure killing him is our only option?" I asked.

"Aren't you furious at him, Hanalee? Don't you want justice for all the pain? A murderer and perjurer is walking free out there"—

he gestured with his thumb toward the door—"while we're suffering from his crimes and stuck with *nothing*."

"But . . ."

"But what?"

I gritted my teeth. "I need more proof. I can't just poison a man without being one hundred percent certain of his guilt."

"You got proof last night."

"A ghost?" I asked. "A hallucination? You said yourself I looked doped up."

"You were convinced last night. You were certain you spoke with your father."

"It's daytime now, and—"

"And what?"

I backed away, sliding my hand across splinters in the wall, for my knees weakened. "I don't know what to believe."

"You swore that he told you he blamed your stepfather."

"I need air. I can't breathe." I yanked open the door and tripped over the threshold, stumbling into sunlight that made my eyes sting.

Joe grabbed my left elbow from behind. "Think of everything you told me last night. Remember what it felt like to see him. What was he wearing?"

I pulled away, but my legs toppled like Joe's card house, and my knees slammed against dirt. The air thinned. A crow laughed from the roof of the shed. I knelt in the grasses and covered my face while remembering every small detail of my father's clothing from the night before—his crimson bow tie, the black derby, the ebony trousers and coat with gleaming glass buttons.

"Swear to God, Joe," I said. "Swear you're not lying to me."

"Hanalee"—one of his knees dropped to the ground beside me—"they threw me in the pen not because of your father, but because they wanted to arrest a boy like me without shaming my father and the town." He laid a hand on my back, right below my left shoulder, and I flinched at first, but then he spoke in a voice that reached deep into my insecurities. "Help me to set things right," he said, "and then we'll free ourselves of this godforsaken place. There's got to be somewhere better out there."

His hand felt warm against me, and I closed my eyes behind my fingers. I relaxed my muscles and rolled back my shoulders.

"Your father's dying words were a request to keep you safe," he said in a voice just a hair above a whisper, "and I intend to honor his wishes. I'm not the depraved sinner people around here make me out to be. I just want a murderer and a liar to get what he deserves—to pay for what he did to me. What he did to you."

I opened my eyes to the grasses rippling in a breeze. All around me, the wind whispered and murmured through the trees. A black garter snake slithered through the undergrowth no more than two feet away, and I didn't even wince. Joe stroked my back, and I arched my spine and leaned into his touch like a Siamese cat.

"I want to test him," I said.

"How?"

"I'll tell him a story that mirrors what we think might have happened. Observe his reactions." I rose to my feet and turned to face Joe, my left arm still slack from the comfort of his hand.

Joe scowled and stood up. "I'm not going to wait around while you tell your stepdaddy a damn bedtime story. Didn't you hear Laurence? He wants me out of here."

"I've got it." I straightened my posture. "David's murder of Uriah, to marry Bathsheba."

Joe squeezed his hands into fists by his sides. "I'm not going to wait while you read Bible passages, either."

"I need more proof before I do anything else, Joe. I'll test him tonight."

He wrapped his arms around his ribs and glanced at the wind rattling through the trees.

"Just give me tonight," I said, "and I'll have my decision by tomorrow. If he fails this test, I'll believe in that vision of my father. I'll believe you." I walked two steps toward him and lowered my voice to ensure no one else would hear. "I'll help you get revenge."

CHAPTER 9

SEE WHAT I SEE

MAMA FROWNED AT ME OVER A sheet of rolled-out dough when she caught me stealing in through the back kitchen door. Flour covered her hands and apron and made the air taste dry.

"Where were you?" she asked, setting down the rolling pin. "You had me worried sick when you ran off angry after talking about Joe."

"Is Deputy Fortaine gone?"

"He left shortly after you ran away. Where were you?"

"Just out for fresh air." I hustled across the kitchen and toward the main hallway.

"Hanalee," said Mama, stopping me dead in my tracks. Her

tone carried a strange calmness that worried me more than if she had shouted. "I know . . ." She tucked her chin against her chest and cleared her throat. "I know I've never told you this, but before you came along, your father and I tried for several years to conceive a baby, without success. We even lost two infants, just a few months into the pregnancies."

My mouth fell open. "Y-y-you did?"

She brushed flour off her palms and leaned the small of her back against the edge of the wooden countertop. "People around me, even well-meaning ones, hinted there might be something unnatural about your father and me having children together."

I pressed my lips closed.

"But," she continued, "instead of listening to prejudice and superstition, I educated myself about conception and birth. In fact, Uncle Clyde himself counseled your father and me on this matter. He even provided me with medical textbooks."

"I don't see what any of this—"

"I became well versed in the subject, you see." She wiped her hands on her apron, leaving behind streaks of white. "Science taught me that sometimes—no matter who might make up the members of a couple—it takes a while for a woman to become in the family way. Other times, it happens the moment a woman first lies with a man."

"Why are you telling me all of this right now?" I asked.

She walked over to the kitchen table and picked up my sketch pad. "I found this drawing in your room." She turned the pad toward me and showed me the picture I'd drawn of Joe, standing in an indistinct body of water as high as his hip bones.

I stepped back, fear prickling across my skin.

"It's Joe Adder, isn't it?" asked Mama. "Naked."

My face flushed. "It's just . . ."

Mama cocked an eyebrow and swung the sketch pad by the tips of her fingers. Flour snowed off her hands and speckled the empty white sky above Joe's head.

"It's just an imaginary young man," I said. "I made him up."

"He looks an awful lot like the way I remember Joe looking. Aside from the lack of clothing."

I put my hands on my hips. "Why were you snooping around in my room?"

"Were you with Joe just now?" Mama straightened her neck.

"I . . ." I couldn't look her in the face. My ears pulsed with a loudening beat.

"Why would you want to spend time with him?" she asked, her voice strained with hurt. "I don't understand why you're doing this, Hanalee."

"It's not . . ." I pulled at my collar. "You don't understand."

"You're no longer allowed to leave this house on your own."

"What?" I burst out laughing. "Oh, if you only knew how ridiculous you're being."

"Do you hear me?" she asked. "You've upset both your father and me by letting that boy whisper his lies into your ear and do God knows what else to you."

"Joe hasn't touched me."

"I want you to go sit in a hot bath."

I gasped. "Why?"

"Because I believe he has touched you, and I've always read that hot baths can impede a pregnancy."

"I'm not carrying Joe Adder's baby! That's the most absurd claim that anyone could—"

"Go!" She pointed to the hallway. "Draw yourself a bath."

"There's no reason—"

"You're staying inside this house from now on. No more journeying outside on your own. No more wandering in the woods. I'll lock you in your room if I have to."

"Mama—"

"I won't keep worrying about you. This will keep you safe."

"I'm not going to get—"

"Go!"

RELUCTANTLY, I FOLLOWED MAMA'S ORDERS AND plunked myself down in a scalding-hot bath in our little indoor bathroom, which was tiled in blue and white diamonds. My hair needed a washing, anyway. I leaned my head back in the water, my face sweating in the steam, and I soaked each curl from the roots to the spiraling tips. Then I scrubbed my scalp clean with Canthrox shampoo and dunked my head again.

Beneath the ripples in the water, my body seemed to waver back and forth like a reflection in a curved mirror I once saw at a church carnival. My breasts, my stomach, my navel, the dark triangle of hair between my thighs—all of me—shimmied back and forth, growing and shrinking; all the parts of me that no boy in my community would ever be allowed to see, unless his skin miraculously transformed into a shade of brown or black, or mine turned white. Unless we sinned and enjoyed each other outside the bonds of holy matrimony.

To think Mama believed that I would touch Joe Adder.

Or that Joe Adder would touch me . . .

To chase such thoughts away, I closed my eyes and nudged my mind back to the days when Daddy would take me out to the very pond in which I'd caught Joe bathing. The line between our property and that of the Paulissens blurred around the water, but our families never quarreled, and what was theirs was ours, and vice versa. Daddy would roll up the legs of his pants after hard work in the fields on a hot summer day, and we'd wade in far enough to cool our shins in water that reflected the greens and browns of the trees. My toes sank into the sludge below my feet, and I'd sometimes see crawdads resting on the banks, or the shadows of minnows darting around my legs. Daddy would tell me a story he once learned from a Creole fellow about a man who convinced a wizard to turn a prince into a fish as a punishment for loving his daughter. We'd sing "Wade in the Water," and Daddy's voice would rise up, deep and rich, into the boughs hanging over our heads. Sometimes he even sang so low, he sounded like the frogs croaking on springtime nights, and I'd laugh at the sound of it but would also feel filled up and get teary-eyed.

I rested the back of my head on the curved ridge of the bathtub and let myself stay in the pond for a while. Mama clanked her spoon against a bowl in the nearby kitchen, and the washroom walls darkened with shadows. But, for a moment, I stood within that swimming hole, next to my daddy, with the water lapping at my knees and my voice joining his on the wind.

MAMA HAD LAID OUT MY WASHED AND PRESSED BLUE cotton dress—the same dress I'd first worn into the woods to hunt down Joe—with wide pockets and a low waistline. After donning the clean clothing, I sat on the edge of my bed and brushed out the tangles in my hair, which soaked a damp spot across my back, but the curls were too wet to pin into my fake bob just yet. I didn't know how other brown-skinned girls with tight curls like mine combed and dried their hair, but I always begged my mother to allow me to buy one of the straightening combs I'd seen in the pharmacy. "Don't try to hide your pretty curls, Hanalee," she'd say every time I asked, even though she didn't know what to do with my hair, either. Daddy had never paid enough attention to his mother's and sister's grooming habits to pass along any beauty tips from them. He just said their curls were even tighter.

Down below me, between the mattress and the box spring, hid the sketch pad I'd grabbed back from Mama before my bath. And in the drawer of my bedside table, no more than two feet to my right, hid the sheet of newsprint from the night before, alongside the bottle of Necromancer's Nectar.

I could feel my words—*my father's words*—captured in black ink, beyond the table's wood. I squeaked open the drawer and stared at the phrase I'd scrawled across the paper.

I put full blame on the doc.

The longer I looked at the words, the more the ink seemed to bleed across the pores in the newsprint, growing thicker, blacker, stronger. The letters curled into vines that could strangle a neck— or serpents that could sting a body with a flick of a poisonous tongue and a bite of needle-sharp teeth. I saw my father staggering toward me on the highway in the dark with his busted leg, his eyes illuminated by moonlight.

"I'm sorry I wasn't a stronger man," he'd said, "and that hate won out that night."

I grabbed the bottle and the note and buried them in a box of old toys beneath my bed. A dented cardboard container of bullets also hid in the hiding spot, beneath a canister of Tinkertoys and my Raggedy Ann doll.

A knock came at my bedroom door. I started and shoved the box beneath the center of my bed with a clatter of blocks and bullets.

"Hanalee?" called Mama from behind the door.

"Yes?" I jumped back onto the mattress.

"Fleur came over to see you. Are you dressed?"

"Yes."

The door opened, and Fleur—lovely Fleur in pink cotton and a satin hair ribbon—slipped into the room with the look of a person encountering a wounded cat with blood matted in its fur. Her sky-blue eyes turned wide and dewy. She carried a small sprig of purple flowers.

"Keep the door open, Hanalee," said Mama from behind her.

"Why?" I asked.

"You know why. I'm worried about you." She set her hand on Fleur's left shoulder. "Stay with her as long as you'd like, Fleur. I think she could use your company right now."

"Yes, ma'am."

"I'll be down in the kitchen."

"Yes, Mama," I said.

I sat as still as a member of our church choir, my hands folded in my lap, my posture impeccable, so that Mama would wander away.

Fleur sat down beside me on the bed with the little floral bouquet nestled against the folds of her skirt. The staircase creaked during my mother's descent.

Once Mama reached the bottom floor, Fleur rested her chin against her right shoulder and looked at me. "How are you?" she asked.

I pushed my hands against the tops of my thighs and bent forward at the waist.

"Are you all right?" She laid her hand on my back, above my left shoulder blade, just as Joe had done in the woods.

I shook my head. "Not really."

"Are you still troubled by what Joe said about your father? Or what I said about"—she hesitated—"your father . . . on the road?"

"Well . . . to be most honest . . . I . . ." I took hold of Fleur's hand and squeezed it.

"What? What's happened?"

I swallowed and sat up straight. "I spoke to my father last night."

Fleur's hand grew still beneath mine.

Mama ran the sink down in the kitchen; I knew there'd be no

chance of her hearing the words I longed to say, so I continued in a whisper. "Don't ask me how I communicated with him, but he told me he blames Uncle Clyde for his death. He said his body couldn't take what it was given that Christmas Eve and that hate won out that night."

Fleur's fingers tightened around mine, and her eyes watered. "Are you positive you spoke with him? Or did—did you merely dream that you saw him?"

"I swear to God, Fleur, he talked to me. The more I think about the encounter, the more I remember how real it all felt—and what he looked like, standing just a few feet away from me in the moonlight. He said he doesn't blame Joe. He blames the doctor."

"Oh," she said—a small whimper of sound. She knitted her eyebrows and rocked a little. "I don't . . . Are you certain? Are you sure Joe isn't just planting wicked ideas in your head and tricking you into believing he's innocent?"

I slid my hand out of hers. "I don't think so."

"Joe seems in an awful hurry to accuse others of faults and crimes, when he was the one driving around blotto."

"'Blotto'?"

"That's what Laurence calls people when they're drunk." She gripped the edge of the mattress. "Joe's brought so much tension into this town over the past few days. It feels like an explosion's about to blast through the entire community because of him."

I cast a sidelong glance at her. "How do you mean?"

"Laurence keeps yelling at Mama and me, telling us to watch our behavior and spend more time with church groups, to mind how we look to the community. Deputy Fortaine and Mama had a spat, and now he's keeping an eye on Laurence, making sure he's not bootlegging. And those Wittens and some other boys are over all the time now, whispering about Joe, making accusations."

I stiffened. "What are the boys saying?"

"They call him"—her ears turned pink, and she hunched her shoulders—"a word I'm not going to say, but I know what it implies because of the shocking things they talk about him doing. They're planning what they'll do to him if they find him, and I have to wonder if Laurence is hiding him just to brag that he captured him for everyone. Just to impress them."

"Oh, Jesus." I dug my fingernails into the folds of my quilt.

Fleur transferred the sprig of purple flowers into my lap. "Please stay away from Joe. It's not safe to be around him. He's got . . . He's not . . ." She licked her lips. "The other boys say he—"

"I know Joe's secret, Fleur. I know the types of things those other boys are probably saying about him." I picked up the flowers by the stems and brushed the ball of my right thumb over the petals, which looked like wide-open mouths about to chomp down on my finger. "What is this for?" I asked.

"It's alfalfa . . . for luck." She cupped her hand around my hand and held the flowers along with me. "Please, promise me you'll keep safe. Don't go looking for your father's ghost anymore or hunting around for Joe."

I sucked in my breath. "Are *you* safe around those boys, Fleur?"

"Mama's always there. And Laurence wouldn't ever let any of them lay a finger on me."

"You see why I worry about the two of us getting stuck here in

Elston? That pack of hungry wolves you're talking about contains all your eligible picks for a husband."

Fleur nodded. "I know. Maybe I should just join a convent."

"No, the Klan is anti-Catholic, remember? They'll pass out pamphlets and host a baseball game to fund the demolition of your convent."

Our eyes met, and we both broke into nervous snickers with our heads bent close together.

"It's not really funny, is it?" she asked, still tittering. She leaned her head against my shoulder, and we both sighed at the same time, breathing the same air. "It's awfully unsettling."

I rested my head against hers and closed my eyes, absorbing the warmth of her body through the dampness of my hair. "It is unsettling. And it makes me want to get the two of us out of this place as soon as I can."

CHAPTER 10

THE MOUSETRAP

 FOR THE REST OF THE DAY, THROUGH-
out all my dusting and mending and other
household chores, I contemplated the loss
of Laurence in my life. I wondered if Uncle
Clyde was to blame for that particular heartache as well.

Looking back over the past two years, I could see all the influ-
ences that might have turned Fleur's brother against me. The
arrival of Robbie and Gil Witten in Elston. Daddy's death. Dr.
Koning's appearance on our doorstep to check on my grieving
mother, day after day after day. Somehow, all those incidents could
have interconnected. Little strings that, once pulled, unraveled the
world around them.

1921.

The year the KKK arrived in Oregon.

The summer Laurence wrapped his arms around me and taught me how to shoot that derringer.

The Christmas Eve Joe crashed the Model T into Daddy and witnessed Uncle Clyde take control of my father's fate.

The last time Laurence spoke to me with compassion.

Robbie. Gil. Clyde Koning. They must have banded together and persuaded Laurence that he needed to change his views—stuffed his mind full of prejudices against me.

Conformity.

Laurence quit our fairy tales and kissing games around the time he turned ten or eleven. He said he preferred playing ball games with other boys, and his face turned scarlet whenever my arm would accidentally bump against his or we touched some other way. When I got older—twelve, thirteen—he'd tickle my sides and make me squeal sometimes, if the mood suited him. If I said something that made him laugh, I'd see the same spark in his eyes from the days when we sat side by side by side, the three of us—Laurence, Fleur, and me—fishing in the creek with our bare shins dangling in the water.

Laurence danced with me at a wedding for two of our fellow church members the same week that I turned fourteen. He held my right hand and pressed the fingers of his other hand against the small of my back, and he squished his lips together as if he wanted to snicker—the same way he'd sometimes laugh and blush when we kissed as children. A week later, he taught me to shoot that gun so I would never end up on the floor of my house beneath white men crazed with power and hate, like what happened to Mrs. Downs in Bentley—a war widow, no less, with skin as black as pitch. He was just fifteen when he showed me how to use the weapon, and his chin, so close to mine, had grown fuzzy with the first sprouts of blond whiskers. He told me, with his breath warm against my ear, "Don't ever let them hurt you, Hanalee. Don't ever let them make you feel small."

Then, six months later, he left. He still lived beneath the Paulissens' roof. He physically remained with us. Yet after Christmas Eve, after Daddy's death, the Laurence I knew and loved abandoned us. I felt I'd lost my right arm, or something else equally vital to my existence.

I missed him.

And I now wondered if Uncle Clyde and the KKK were to blame.

BEFORE SUPPER, AFTER PINNING UP MY HAIR, WHICH finally felt dry, I snuck into the living room and pulled my grandfather's pipe-scented old copy of the family Bible off a middle shelf of the bookcase. I'd always loved the grainy feel of the black leather cover sliding against my fingertips and the crinkle of the gilt-edged pages, as thin as onion skin. I placed *Babbitt* down on the rug next to the armchair and put the Bible in its place on the end table. With the quietest of movements, I peeled back the cover and flipped through the fragile pages to the Second Book of Samuel. While holding my breath, I secured a pencil from my dress pocket and underlined one of the passages involving Bathsheba, the widow of the man whom David sent to his death.

And when the wife of Uriah heard that her husband was dead, she mourned for him.

After the time of the mourning was over, David had her brought to his house, and she became his wife . . .

Supper ended, and Mama and I washed dishes over the wide apron sink in the kitchen. Uncle Clyde wandered upstairs to replace his gray work suit with a tweed vest and comfortable trousers, and he gargled with hydrogen peroxide to clean his throat of bacteria. Our usual evening routines.

I dried a plate and poked the tip of my pinkie through a small hole I discovered in a bottom corner of the dishcloth.

"It's awfully quiet in the house this evening," said Mama, her hands submerged in water and bubbles.

I raised my head and listened. She was right: an unnatural hush had descended over the house. The hairs on the backs of my arms stood on end. My hands slipped and squeaked on the china.

"Are you all right, Hanalee?" asked Mama, her mouth taut.

"Of course." I nudged the plate onto the drying rack with a shakiness that rattled the rest of the dishes.

My stepfather reached the living room and the Bible before we did—I know, because I heard my mother's name cried out in a sudden roar that made me jump a foot in the air.

"*GRETA!*"

Mama and I exchanged panicky looks. Her face blanched to the color of death.

"What is it, dear?" she called back.

Uncle Clyde marched into the kitchen, slippers whooshing

against the floorboards, face boiling red, and he held up the opened pages of the Bible. "She replaced *Babbitt* with the story of David and Bathsheba."

Mama drew her eyebrows together. "I beg your pardon?"

"Hanalee laid out a passage in the Bible"—he turned his gaze toward me, skewering me with his clear blue eyes—"for me to see."

Mama handed me the last washed dish. "Is there something wrong with that? She and Hank often read Bible passages together."

Uncle Clyde's fingers whitened beneath the gold lettering on the cover. His chest heaved, and he glared at me through his spectacles.

I folded my dish towel over the edge of the sink. "I don't entirely remember the story of David and Bathsheba." I peeked up at the both of them from beneath my lashes, remembering the way Joe had employed that technique to soften me. "What's that one about again?"

"You know the story," said Mama. "David fell madly in love with Bathsheba, who was married to Uriah the Hittite. David seduced her and arranged for Uriah to get killed in battle, and then David took Bathsheba as his bride . . ." Her voice trailed off, and she froze in place, blinking at the empty space in front of her.

Uncle Clyde kept his eyes fixed upon me, staring and frowning as though he longed to dig beneath my skull and excavate the thoughts hiding away inside my head.

I untied my apron and laid it over the back of a nearby chair. "May I read the passage aloud?"

Mama turned her face toward me, hurt welling in her eyes.

I reached for the book. "May I? Shall we go out to the living room so you can get more comfortable?"

Uncle Clyde slammed the Bible shut and threw it onto the countertop.

I jumped. "What's the matter?"

"Stop it!" He clamped down on my left wrist and yanked me toward him. "Where is he, Hanalee? Is he in this house?"

"No. Let me go!"

"Where is he?"

"Clyde!" cried Mama.

My stepfather wrenched me out of the kitchen and half dragged me to the front door at the end of the entry hall.

"Where are you taking her?" asked Mama.

"Call Reverend Adder. Tell him to drive over here immediately."

"But—"

"Lock all the windows and doors. Make sure Joe can't get inside."

Uncle Clyde threw open the front door and tripped me down the porch stairs. My feet missed the last step, and my right ankle twisted with a shock of pain.

"Stop!" I said. "Stop—you're hurting me."

Uncle Clyde pulled me toward the darkening road in front of the house. "Joseph Adder!" he called out to the empty highway. "You come out here and face me yourself. Come out here and face me like a man, not a cowering little boy who hides behind girls."

"Clyde!" Mama ran up behind us. "Stop."

Uncle Clyde swung me around toward my mother. "I said, lock up the house, Greta! Go! Stay inside. Don't let him in."

"Hanalee, what have you done?" asked Mama, kneading her skirt between her hands. "Why did you have to go and align yourself with that boy?"

"Both of you, leave me alone." I pushed at Uncle Clyde.

"Where is he?" Uncle Clyde asked in my face, his breath sour, his lips pinched and chapped. "You tell me where he is right now. I know what he thinks of me."

"Oh, Hanalee," said Mama with a sob.

"Where is he? What is he offering you? What is he telling you about me?"

"The truth," I said. I kicked the doc in the shin and streaked like a bolt of lightning toward the trees on the edge of our property.

"Hanalee!" called Mama from behind me. "Clyde, don't chase her! You're making it worse."

I peeked over my shoulder and witnessed Uncle Clyde tearing after me, in his green tweed vest and house slippers. Catching him running after me like that, his teeth set, arms pumping, legs a blur, allowed me to see, for the first time, the devil lurking inside him. The killer.

I put full blame on the doc.

Mama yelled out both of our names. The woods drew nearer. My chest and my leg muscles burned, and I grunted through each stride.

Uncle Clyde cried out, "Damn!" and I looked back again to find him on the ground.

"I'm going to Fleur's," I hollered over my shoulder. "Don't you dare follow me, Dr. Koning. I don't want to see you ever again."

Tree trunks shrouded in lichen swallowed me up. I grabbed my holster from the oilcloth in the log and hid amid the trunks of the trees until I counted to sixty without anyone following me. In the distance, Mama and Uncle Clyde shouted. An automobile door slammed shut, as well as the door to our house.

I turned and took off again, past the lightning-blackened tree and the junction to Fleur's house, over the rocks poking out of the creek, and up the embankment to the little white shed.

CHAPTER 11

WITH FIERY QUICKNESS

 I DIDN'T EVEN KNOCK. I BURST straight into Joe's hiding spot and called out, "We've got to get you out of here!"

Joe bolted upright on the cot, a book in hand. The flame in his lantern sizzled.

"What the hell's happening?" he asked.

"Clyde failed the test. He's going to fetch your father and probably the deputy. I'm terrified Laurence will lead them here."

"Christ!" Joe bent down beneath the cot and stuffed his belongings—shirts, books, a toothbrush, a razor, a blue-plaid coat—into an old green carpetbag that looked faded and frayed and stained with mold.

"I'm so sorry." I lifted my skirt and strapped the holster around my right thigh. "We just need to get you out. Uncle Clyde started chasing me into the forest, but he tripped and fell."

Joe tossed me a brown blanket from the cot and fetched a pair of shoes. "He's following you?"

"He was." I tucked the bedding under my arm and grabbed a picnic basket that sat next to a brand-new card tower, a tall, rectangular one. "But he gave up. I've never seen him run before in my life. He knows what we think he did."

"Fuck!" Joe threw his shoes onto his feet.

I hustled outside with the basket and the blanket.

Joe ran out, as well, his laces untied and flopping about. He carried the carpetbag and the kerosene lantern by his sides.

"This way. Hurry!" He dove through a low set of branches that swished across his back.

I followed him, and we were off, shooting through the woods in a maze of trees and moss and feathered ferns that seemed to expand into primeval proportions. Firs stretched to the sky and blocked the waning daylight; leaves the size of my head scraped at my calves. We hurtled ourselves over poison oak and stinging nettles, logs, brooks, burrows, and even scampering chipmunks that eyed us with fear. Unseen creatures rustled through the bushes. Birds scattered overhead. The woods darkened. Our feet galloped onward, and my heart pounded until I worried it might explode.

"Where should we go?" I called from behind him.

"I don't know. Far." He launched himself over a narrow sliver of a creek and sprinted through a patch of mud that squished beneath his shoes and blackened his laces.

I followed, catching the water with my heel and splashing the hem of my dress.

Something howled.

"Oh, Lord! What was that?" I asked.

"Just run."

The forest brightened. Joe came to a sudden stop in front of me, and I crashed against his back.

"Damn!" He pushed me backward, and from behind him I saw a stretch of the northbound road that met up with the main highway a mile or so to the south. "Get back, before anyone drives by." He steered me by my shoulders, back into the dark and primitive recesses of the woods. "Hurry!"

He slipped into the front again, and we ran and leapt and climbed until pain stabbed at my right side, below my ribs. The ankle I'd twisted on the porch steps throbbed. The holster pelted my thigh, and the path ahead of me blurred.

"Joe, I need to stop."

"What?" He turned around, at least twenty feet ahead of me.

"I'm hurting." I dropped his belongings and braced my right hand against a fat red trunk, which was cold to the touch. A beetle scrambled up the bark, away from my hand, upon feet swift and silent.

Joe sauntered back to me through piles of fallen pine needles. "What's wrong?"

"My side. My ankle." I pushed my other hand against the trunk and leaned forward to catch my breath. "My ribs feel like they want to split wide open."

"You must have been breathing wrong."

"How much farther should we go?" I asked. "*Where* should we go?"

"I don't know." He set down his lantern, which had long since blown out, and dropped his bag of clothing beside it.

"What are we even doing, Joe? What the hell are we—?"

"Shh!" Joe put out a hand. "A car."

We both stiffened, even though we no longer stood within sight of the road. I held my breath, and my ribs ached all the more from tightening my muscles.

The automobile in question neared us, no more than fifty yards beyond the trees beside us. I heard the *pop-pop-pop* of a motor, and my heart pumped my blood in a staccato rhythm. I imagined the screeching of brakes, car doors opening, bloodhounds barking, Deputy Fortaine charging toward us with a rifle and bared teeth.

We stood as still as the trees surrounding us, not breathing, not flinching. Beyond the wide green firs, the automobile chugged by and rattled off to the south, toward the crossroads where I'd spoken with my father just the night before.

"Come on." Joe picked up the lantern and wheeled back around toward the trail. "Let's keep going and find someplace to sleep overnight, before it gets any darker."

"Am I safe with you?" I asked, not budging.

He glanced at me over his shoulder. "I'm not going to touch you, Hanalee."

"Are you sure? You're not just making up that thing you said about yourself so you can—?"

117

Joe's mouth tautened.

"After those men attacked Mrs. Downs a couple years ago," I said, "I just . . . I want to watch out for myself."

"I'm not going to hurt you. You can sleep with your gun pointing straight at my face if you want, but I'm not planning to attack anyone besides Clyde Koning. Come on." He turned back around to the path ahead of us. "We're wasting time."

He continued onward, this time with steps that made mere whispers of sound against the pine needles that littered the forest floor. I grabbed the basket and blanket and followed.

THE WOODS SLOPED UPWARD IN A DIRECTION THAT I believed to be the north, although the darkness settling over our surroundings proved disorienting. My stomach dipped with the sensation that we were nearing the territory of unkind people.

"How far do you think we are from the road?" I asked. "There are houses up here in the hills. Swanky ones."

"I know." Joe kept walking. "I think we're still far enough away to avoid seeing anyone. I don't hear any dogs or other signs of civilization."

I stopped, set down his belongings, and drew the pistol out of my holster.

Joe spun around, and his shoulders jerked. "Jesus! Why are you bringing *that* out right now?"

"I've got to be honest with you, Joe." I held the derringer by my side, the muzzle pointed toward the ground. "You're not safe at all. Fleur told me that Laurence, the Wittens, and some of the other local fellows want to do terrible things to you because they know . . ." I nodded through the words I didn't know how to say.

Joe leaned back on his left foot. "Who told them about me?"

"I don't know. Fleur suspects Laurence has been hiding you so he can brag about leading the others to you."

Joe tightened his grip on his bag and scanned the forest with his eyes.

"You ever shoot a gun before?" I asked.

He blinked. "No."

"I had to store the pistol in a hiding spot in a log," I said, "instead of sneaking it back to my bedroom. I didn't have time to replace the bullet I shot past your head."

Joe grimaced.

"So there's only one left," I continued. "I'll use it if we're desperate."

He swallowed. "Put that gun back in your holster. I don't want you tripping and shooting me in the back by mistake."

A twig snapped behind me. I flinched and turned and nearly cocked and fired. A deer leapt into view and zigzagged off into the distance, leaves swishing behind its hooves.

"I said, put that gun back into your holster!" snapped Joe. "You almost fired it, didn't you?"

I hiked up my skirt and struggled to fit the pistol back inside the leather casing. My hands trembled from coming so close to shooting that bullet. I couldn't breathe quite right.

"We'll make this work." Joe stepped toward me. "We'll stay safe."

I lowered my skirt. "How?"

"I—" He stopped in front of me and rubbed his left thumb

against the side of his face, while the lantern swung and squeaked from the rest of his fingers. "I don't know just yet. Let's find a place to sleep so we don't have to worry about anyone seeing us walking around. We'll talk about our plans after we've had some time to settle down and think."

I grumbled, but I complied, and the woods turned dark and cold.

A HALF MILE OR SO FARTHER, I CAUGHT SIGHT OF A stretch of water that glistened with moonlight between the trunks of spruces wider than Joe and me and at least two other people put together. In that same direction, hundreds of frogs croaked in a chorus that sounded frantic and urgent and gave me the chills. The world smelled of pines and dampness.

"Is that a lake I see up there," I asked, "shining in the moonlight through the trees?"

Joe ducked down beneath an outstretched branch for a better look. "It's just the widest section of Engle Creek, I think. But . . . wait . . ." He slid beneath the branch and disappeared from view in the blackness ahead. "There's a building of some sort."

I followed him and just barely made out the silhouette of a small log cabin. I inched up behind where Joe stood, and the warmth of his back permeated the chill in the moist night air.

"Do you think anyone's in there?" I asked in a whisper.

"I don't see any lights through the slats. I think it's probably a boathouse. Or maybe a place to store fishing gear, like Mr. Paulissen's shed used to be."

"Or a whiskey still?"

"I doubt it. It's too quiet." He edged down the low embankment, his soles scraping and sliding across the damp earth.

I cupped my hand over the holster against my thigh and followed him. My feet snagged on tree roots and other obstacles I couldn't see without any light.

At the bottom of the slope, I parked the picnic basket and blanket next to a bush. "Let me go ahead of you," I whispered. "I've got the gun."

"I don't want you shooting some poor raccoon."

"I'll be careful."

He snorted. "Like you were with that deer?"

"I didn't shoot that damn deer, did I?" My shoes squished through the soft soil, toward the direction of the door, and I kept my hand pressed against the holster.

The moment I reached the door, my gut told me to act, not to hesitate. I lifted the wooden latch and kicked the door open.

Darkness.

Deep-down-at-the-bottom-of-a-well darkness.

Something moved inside, and I could have sworn I heard my father whisper, "It's not safe here. Go!"

I jumped backward and bumped into Joe, who shrieked, which made me shriek.

"What's in there?" he asked.

"I don't know. I can't see a damn thing."

"Why'd you jump?"

"I thought I heard my father warn it's not safe in there." I rubbed my neck. "Christ, Joe, where are we? What are we doing out here? I'm scared to death."

Joe crouched on the ground and shuffled around in his bag, but I could scarcely see him down there in the pitch-dark.

"What are you doing?" I asked.

"Looking for matches so I can light the lamp."

He struck a match, and a flame hissed to life with a burst of light that illuminated his chin and his hands. I saw that scar on his lip again—the one that looked like a wound that had healed up all wrong. He turned a little apparatus that raised the lantern's glass chimney, and he set the burning end of the match to the flat cotton wick. The lantern awakened and glowed against the side of the cabin, revealing thick logs covered in moss and holes created by either woodpeckers or insects. Joe blew out the match and lowered the chimney.

"I'll go in and see what's there." He rose to his feet.

"Be careful. I could have sworn I heard something."

With cautious footsteps, he sidled his way into the cabin. The lantern's light fluttered against the uneven floorboards within.

"Joe?"

"It's empty," he said. "Just some used-up bottles of booze and French postcards."

I dared to step inside after him, and my eyes widened at the sight of naked white ladies—a half-dozen bare-breasted, bare-bottomed beauties—posing on postcards nailed to the log walls. The lamplight flickered across their smiles and flirty eyes and gave the impression that they were all winking at us. The air inside the cabin stank of whiskey and cigarettes. Fiction magazines and newspapers littered the floor in the far-right corner.

"What is this place?" I asked.

"Don't know. But someone must come here to hide out and drink." Joe wandered over to one of the empty bottles and picked it up for a sniff. "Moonshine—that's for certain." He sniffed again. "Potent moonshine."

I crept over to the pile of reading material to see if the contents would offer any clues about the inhabitants. A few editions of the crime-and-adventure magazine *Black Mask* lay on the floor in front of the toes of my shoes, but my eyes veered straightaway to a copy of a newspaper called the *Western American*. The front page featured illustrations of Klansmen in hoods and robes gazing at the Statue of Liberty. Beside the newspaper rested a pamphlet the color of porridge that bore the words THE TRUTH ABOUT THE JUNIOR ORDER OF KLANSMEN.

My stomach dropped.

I knelt down and picked up the pamphlet with the very tips of my fingers, as if the paper might singe and blister my skin. Down at the bottom of the front page I found a series of handwritten notes, scribbled in pencil.

Konklave, July 2, 1923. New members needed. White, Protestant boys aged twelve to eighteen.

Initiation planned. Necktie party?

The problem of Joe Adder. Moral degenerate.

Pancake breakfast set for Saturday at the Dry Dock. Money raised will repair potholes on Main Street.

"Joe," I said in a suddenly raspy voice. "Look." I stood up and stuck out my hand with the pamphlet.

Joe walked over and took the paper.

"Do you know anything about the Junior Order of Klansmen?" I asked.

His eyes dropped down to the notes penciled in at the bottom. His breathing quickened, which made me breathe twice as fast as usual, and the combined sounds of our panting gave the unsettling impression that a dozen other people crowded around us.

"Did you read it?" I asked.

He plunked the lantern onto the ground and ripped the paper down the middle.

"No!" I clamped a hand around his wrist. "That's evidence."

"Evidence of what?" he asked. "My future beatings? My murder?"

"I don't know, but"—I grabbed the pamphlet and crumpled it down into one of my dress pockets—"I'm keeping it."

"This place makes me sick." He kicked aside a cigarette butt and stumbled out of the cabin with the light from the lantern skittering across the walls.

I followed, and everything outside in the dark—the breeze in the branches, the splash of an animal in the creek, even the damn croaking frogs—spooked me into thinking an entire mob of Elston residents shuffled around in the bushes, spying on us. People our own age. *White, Protestant boys aged twelve to eighteen.*

I blinked to adjust my eyes to the lack of light, and then I grabbed the blanket and basket and trailed Joe and the lantern up the slope. "Where do you think we should go now?"

"How the hell am I supposed to know?" he said. The lantern swung by his side, casting erratic streaks of light that made our surroundings seem to shake and grow.

"Do you think Laurence and the Wittens are in that Junior Order?" I asked.

"Laurence probably is." He veered to his left at the top of the slope and brushed a thick branch out of his way. "He's been speaking highly of the Klan and one hundred percent Americanism."

"Fleur said he's been after her and her mother to spend more time with church groups, to mind how they look in the community." I pushed the branch away, too, and sap smeared across my hand. "He hasn't said a kind word to me in well over a year, not since he befriended those Wittens. Since Uncle Clyde barged his way into our lives."

"You see what I mean?" Joe stopped, for one of his pant legs had gotten snared on a bush. "The local Klan is more than just a group that hosts baseball games and prints anti-Catholic pamphlets. And even if they did just promote anti-Catholicism, what makes you think their hatred would stop with one group?" He shook his leg free of the branch. "I witnessed it in prison, and I'm feeling it out here—there's a powerful movement to cleanse this country of the wrong sorts of people."

I came to a stop near the same bush that had grabbed him. "If they're as hateful as you believe—"

"*Hate* doesn't even begin to describe what's happening." Joe turned back around with the lantern shining across his eyes. "People in this state are controlling who can and can't breed, Hanalee. They're eradicating those of us who aren't white, Protestant, American-born, or sexually normal in their eyes. They're 'purifying' Oregon."

"Oh, God." I dropped the basket to the ground and crouched into a ball, holding my arms around myself.

Joe knelt down in front of me. "I know. I'm scared to death, too." He raised the lantern so we could better see each other's faces. "But if those of us who are being threatened join together and fight back, there will eventually be enough of us to stop them."

I shook my head. "How on earth do we fight a movement like that?"

He lowered his eyes, and the light from the flame streaked across both our faces. Heat nipped at my cheeks.

I rose back up to a standing position. "Do we just keep running? Find other castoffs and build up a ragtag army against people like Uncle Clyde and the rest of the Klan?"

Joe cracked a small smile in the lamplight. "I like that." He stood up, too. "An army of blacks, Catholics, Jews, Japanese, and queers would scare the hell out of the fucking KKK."

I stepped back. "You sure have a foul mouth for a preacher's boy."

"Yeah, well, I haven't been a preacher's boy in a long while." He turned back around to our path. "Come on. Let's find a place to camp."

A mere ten paces farther, we entered a small clearing surrounded by a fortress of trees whose tops disappeared high overhead. We both stopped and inspected the area by the light of the lantern.

"Do you think it's far enough away from the cabin?" asked Joe.

"Well . . ." I cast my eyes toward the darkness that devoured the path back to the building. "It is nice to know the cabin's within running distance, in case rain arrives. Or a bear."

"What?" He gasped. "You think we'll encounter a fucking bear?"

"Jeez, Joe! Stop using that word." I crept over to the outer reaches of the lamp's arc of light and bent down to study the dark outlines of a patch of leaves. "I don't see any poison oak. Or any animal dens."

He set the lantern by his feet and threw his carpetbag onto the grass. "Holy Mother of God, we'd better not get mauled by any bears."

"Stop worrying about the damn bears. They're the least of our problems."

"Why are you getting after me for my language? You swear a lot for a girl."

"I only swear when I'm pushed into situations like this. And my words are tamer." I dropped the picnic basket and shook out the tan blanket.

Joe helped me stretch the bedding across the ground until it covered an area the size of two bodies. Then we both stood back up and stared down at the makeshift bed before us. I heard him swallow—or gulp was more like it. I swallowed, too.

"You can lie on it," he said. "I'll sit against the tree."

"Don't be ridiculous. You'll get a sore back."

"I don't think you'd want me lying beside you."

"I don't hardly care right now." I tucked the holster beneath the right side of the blanket and stretched myself out on the rough surface that scratched like a burlap potato sack. My hair felt lumpy between my head and the ground, but I didn't feel like pulling out all the pins. "As long as you don't mind lying down beside me," I added.

"Why do you say that?" he asked.

"Because of my skin color, of course." I bit down on my lip and then added, "And my sex."

"Now you're just insulting the both of us." He plopped down beside me and pulled out an object from his carpetbag.

I rolled onto my side, away from him. "*Am* I disgusting to you?"

"Hanalee . . ."

"Tell me the truth."

He dropped a woolen garment in front of me. "Here, put this on. You're going to get cold out here."

"What is it?"

"A coat."

I patted the sleeves and the buttons in the dark, verifying that it was, indeed, a jacket. "Won't you get cold?" I asked.

"I'm wearing long sleeves. You've got your arms hanging out. You'll freeze to death without it."

"Well . . ." I tucked the coat over my shoulders like a cape. "Thank you."

He shifted about on the blanket beside me. "I'm blowing out the lantern now."

I shrugged. "That's fine."

He raised the chimney and puffed, and the forest went black. The temperature seemed to drop about thirty degrees, and I found myself shivering in an instant. I slipped my arms inside the sleeves of the coat and buttoned up the garment to my throat. Behind me, Joe wriggled around on the blanket until it sounded as though he faced in my direction. I heard him breathing about a foot away from the back of my neck.

"No," he said, "you're not."

I lifted my head. "Not what?"

"Not disgusting to me." He drew a deep breath that whistled through his nose. "Am I disgusting to you?"

I lay my head back down and tucked my hands inside the warm depths of his coat sleeves. "I haven't yet decided."

He didn't respond.

"It's not because of the boys thing," I chose to add. "Although that's still a bit confusing to me, to be most honest."

Again, he didn't respond.

I cleared my throat. "It's because of the other thing. My original reason for hating you."

"It's still sometimes confusing to me, too."

"What?"

He sighed. "'The boys thing,' as you called it."

"I . . . I suppose that would be."

"Everything would be a hell of a lot easier if . . ."

I nodded in understanding, although I supposed he might not have seen me doing so in the dark.

We lay in silence, the subject of our mutual fear of disgusting each other still taking up space in the air around us. Crickets and frogs called out in their desperate frenzy of chirping and croaking, and I wondered how I could possibly sleep with all the ruckus, never mind the other discomforts and worries. A splash sounded somewhere beyond the trees, and for a moment I thought Joe might have caught the urge to swim around naked again. I still imagined him as a woodland creature, swimming down among the submerged grasses, hiding in the darkest recesses far below the water's surface. Maybe he transformed into a fish when I wasn't looking, like the prince in the Creole story. A sleek coho salmon, or even a swift and frightened minnow.

He scooted closer to me on the blanket—not in a bold and forward way, but in a slow and cautious manner, as though he was trying to come nearer for a smidgen of warmth without sounding like he was doing so.

"Good night, Hanalee," he said, just a few inches away.

A tear leaked out of my right eye and dampened the blanket below my left cheek. I held my breath for a moment, forcing my shoulders not to shake, and then I answered, in as steady a voice as I could muster. "Good night."

OREGON WOODS, CIRCA 1918.

CHAPTER 12

HOW UNWORTHY A THING YOU MAKE OF ME

 IT TOOK A LONG WHILE TO FALL asleep in such a strange and exposed environment. Terrible dreams bothered what little slumber I could snatch, and at one point I woke up in the darkness, huddled against Joe's stomach and chest with my hands balled between our two bodies. My teeth chattered, and I shivered and whimpered and burrowed against him, while he breathed in a steady rhythm beside me. The air on the forest floor felt as bitter cold as December, not at all like the beginning of July.

Joe tucked his arm around my back and pulled me close. He shivered, too, but his shirt heated my cheek and nose.

"Are you all right?" he asked, his voice thick with sleep.

132

"It's freezing out here."

With gentle movements, he scooted the two of us over to my side of the blanket, and then he lifted his arm and wrapped the other side of the covering around us. We had to snuggle close for the blanket to reach around my shoulders, and all I could think was *The world must be mighty atrocious right now if cuddling up with Joe Adder in the middle of the woods seems my most desirable option.*

I DREAMED OF DADDY OPENING UP THE FRONT DOOR to our house. I stood in our gleaming oak entry hall, upon the green and gold rug, and I gaped at the sight of my father pulling his hat off his head of short, tight curls. He reached out his right hand, smiled, and told me in his deep, honey tones, "There's been a mistake, baby doll. I didn't die after all."

A sound awoke me—a crack of a twig or some other minor disturbance that jolted me out of the sweetness of the dream. I grabbed hold of a warm hand that rested near my chest and strove to slip back to the place in which my father walked in from the fields, his coveralls streaked in dirt and flecks of hay, everything smelling fresh and clean and earthy.

A twig cracked again.

"What the hell . . . ?" said a nearby voice that made my heart stop. Cigarette smoke wafted into my nostrils.

My eyes flew open, and I found Robbie and Gil Witten standing over us, gawking, their heads cocked, as though they were viewing a two-headed creature with wings and a beak. Cigarettes burned in their right hands. A bottle of a clear booze that must have been gin dangled from Gil's meaty left fingers. Robbie held a wooden-handled pocketknife with an exposed blade that glinted in the morning sunlight.

I froze beneath Joe's arm.

Robbie closed his mouth and flicked ash from the end of his cigarette toward our feet beneath the blanket. "Hey, jailbird Joe!" he called out.

Joe stirred beside me. He opened his eyes to the faces above us and bolted to a sitting position. "What're you doing here?"

Robbie took a drag from the cigarette and puffed a white cloud of smoke in our direction. "That's precisely what we were about to ask you."

"We were just coming out here for breakfast"—Gil tapped the bottle of gin against his leg—"and heard someone snoring."

"I had no idea," said Robbie, "it would be Elston's most-wanted criminal and sweet Hanalee Denney."

Gil snickered and turned bright red. "I thought for sure Hanalee would be naked under that blanket."

Robbie furrowed his thick eyebrows at me. "What are you doing out here with this ex-convict? I warned you, he's depraved."

"Some breakfast you've got there," said Joe, nodding toward the gin. "Aren't Klan members supposed to be opposed to bootlegging?"

Gil shoved the bottle into a trouser pocket and averted his eyes from mine. "Who said we were in the Ku Klux Klan?"

"What's more important," said Robbie, "is what you and Hanalee Denney are doing wrapped up in a blanket in the middle of our Christian family's property." He sniffed the air. "The whole place reeks of sin."

Gil snorted and slid his cigarette between his wet-looking lips.

All I could do was lie there, paralyzed, with my hand pressed around the outline of the holster beneath the blanket. The Junior Order of Klansmen pamphlet remained tucked inside my pocket.

Joe combed his fingers through his hair. "Hanalee and I are eloping."

I kept my face stoic, despite my urge to shout, *What did you just say?*

"Oregon won't allow us to marry," he continued, "so we're running off to Washington. We just camped here for the night before we set out to cross the hills and the Columbia River."

"*You're* eloping?" Robbie flicked more ash to the ground by our feet.

"That's right." Joe nodded.

Gil reddened again and muttered to his brother, "Jesus. Does Washington really allow fairies to marry mulattoes?"

"What did you just say?" Joe threw off the blanket and jumped to his feet.

"He said," said Robbie, lifting his chin, "you two make a highly peculiar pair. Does your bride-to-be know you were caught diddling some other fellow?"

Joe clenched his hands by his sides. "What pathetic lives you must lead if you have to make up vulgar stories about me."

"It's not true, then?" Robbie wedged his cigarette between his teeth and narrowed his eyes. "You're not a fag?"

"Would you have found me here, wrapped in a blanket with a girl, if I was?"

The twins eyed each other, as if to gauge each other's opinions.

Joe didn't look back at me, but I could tell from the way he rubbed his hands along the sides of his trousers that the Wittens and that pocketknife terrified him. I kept my face and my body still, worried that the wrong expression or word would bring him harm.

"Prove it to us." Robbie stepped closer and picked at the end of his knife. His cigarette hung out of the side of his mouth and desecrated the fragrance of the woods. "Kiss her."

"What?" Joe glanced over his shoulder at me. "No. I'm not giving you a peep show just to prove we love each other."

"What's the matter?" Robbie nudged Joe backward by the fist that held that knife. "Do you feel bile rising to your throat over the idea of kissing a colored girl?"

"I think he feels bile," said Gil, also coming closer, "over the idea of kissing *any* girl."

The twins both chuckled, and Joe kept rubbing the sides of his legs.

I pushed myself to my feet, my knees wobbling, and took hold of Joe's left hand. "Just ignore them, Joey."

"'Joey'?" laughed the twins, reminding me of a skinny version of Tweedledum and Tweedledee, standing there side by side, their shoulders shaking, their cheeks bright red. Even their clothing matched—tweed pants, rolled-up shirtsleeves, floppy plaid caps pulled just above ears as large as abalone shells.

"They're just jealous," I continued, "that no girl would ever want to sleep with them out here in the woods."

Robbie's face sobered, and his laughter ceased. "Is this real, Hanalee?" he asked. "Did you two . . . ?" He gestured with his cigarette toward the blanket on the ground. "Last night . . . did you . . . ?"

I slid my hand across Joe's stomach and felt his muscles stiffen.

Robbie stared me in the eye and squeezed two fingers down upon his cigarette. "I'd sure feel more certain of all of this if I saw you two kiss."

I gritted my teeth. "You don't need—"

"I've had it on pretty good authority"—Robbie toyed with the blade of his knife again—"that your boy here likes men. In fact, I feel like puking just from standing so close to him. I feel like . . ." His green eyes darkened, and the knife and the cigarette shook in his hands.

Joe's arm tensed beside me. I squeezed his hand.

"We just woke up," I said. "I don't have any chewing gum or toothpaste to make my breath nice and sweet for him."

Gil reached inside a coat pocket and drew out his own pocket-knife, as well as a yellow packet of Wrigley's P.K. gum. "Here you go." He stepped forward with one foot and held out his hand with the chewing gum.

Joe and I took a stick apiece, eyeing the knife in Gil's other hand, and then we peeled down the paper wrappers and popped the gum into our mouths. A jolt of peppermint hit my tongue, and my eyes watered from both the taste and the fear of what would happen if I didn't kiss Joe in front of these prying jackasses. Or what would happen if I grabbed up my gun and shot one of the Wittens in the knee with my remaining bullet.

We chewed for a good half minute or so, our chomps the only

sounds in the woods, aside from the pleading calls of a robin and Gil snickering under his breath.

"All right, that should do it," said Robbie. "Spit them out and kiss. I want to be good and certain I'm not sending our sweet little girl into the world with a pervert who'll try sticking his—"

Joe lunged toward Robbie, but before he could take a swing, I grabbed Joe's left arm.

"Come on—let's just show them," I said with a tremor in my voice.

I cupped a hand around the back of Joe's sweating neck and adjusted my footing on the dirt until we faced each other directly. We just stood there for a moment, breathing peppermint on each other, our lips wavering a few mere inches apart, not quite able to touch.

"What do you think, Gil?" asked Robbie. "Does that look like a fellow about to elope with a woman? Or does it look like someone who needs a stern lesson in masculinity?"

At that, I kissed Joe full on the mouth. Our lips just sort of smashed together at first, but then I felt his mouth moving a bit, kissing me back, and he even slid the tip of his tongue against my tongue, which the Wittens must have witnessed, for Gil whispered, "Oh, sweet Jesus." My hand gripped the back of Joe's neck so hard, I must have hurt him; he clung to my waist as though we were withstanding a hurricane. Without realizing what was coming over me, I started to cry, right there, mid-kiss.

Joe pulled his lips away. I dug my forehead into his shoulder and took deep sips of air to try to stop the tears from rolling down my cheeks. I smelled the pond by the Paulissens' shed again and wished us away to anywhere else on earth besides that cold spot of land in front of the Wittens.

"Why is she crying?" asked Gil.

Joe wrapped his arm around me and pulled me against his side. "Because you're threatening us with knives and turning what we have into something dirty. How do you expect her to react?"

Gil scratched his head beneath his cap with the hand that held his knife. Robbie looked the two of us up and down, and my skin chilled in the places touched by his gaze.

"Well, don't just keep gawking at us." Joe brought us both a step backward. "You're not going to see anything else, if that's what you're waiting for."

"I thought I heard a cat yelping outside last night," said Gil, his face reddening again, "but maybe that was just Hanalee, screaming in the throes of passion."

"Shut up, Gil," snapped Robbie. "This whole thing makes me sick to my stomach, to be honest." He tossed his cigarette to the ground and rubbed it out with the toe of his right shoe. "I might have to go tell your mama and stepdaddy about this, Hanalee."

"I don't need the two of you tattling on me, Robbie," I said while coughing up the last of my tears, "so just—"

"Don't worry about it, Hanalee." Joe slid his arm off me but grabbed hold of my left hand. "Come on. Let's get going."

"Well, if God sees fit, then"—Robbie turned around, away from us, yet he peeked over his shoulder and kept his blade exposed by his side—"you two will make it safely across the river to Washington. Let's see how long that marriage lasts until you both wake up and realize how much you repulse each other."

"Go to hell, Robbie," said Joe.

"Oh, I'm not the one who'll be burning for all eternity, Joseph Adder." Robbie pushed his way through the trees.

Gil followed his brother, and their checkered hats disappeared amid leaves and cobwebs shining with dew.

Joe and I stayed still and listened to the sounds of their retreat. Chuckles and derogatory words—words clearly meant for the two of us to hear—traveled past the location of the small log cabin and then off to the west. I flinched at each sickening term directed toward me, while Joe kept his breath held tightly at the insults meant for him. The words pelted my gut like fireballs, and I wished I could think of a phrase dirty and demeaning enough to hurl back at them.

Joe let go of my hand and grabbed up his belongings at our campsite. "Let's pack up and get out of here."

I strapped the holster around my leg and fetched the basket and blanket.

We took off at a brisk pace, toward the east.

A half mile or so later, after hopping over tree roots and ske-daddling down deer paths, Joe took hold of my wrist and pulled us both behind the thick trunk of a fir. I panted to catch my breath, and he put his fingers to his lips and said, "Shh. I want to hear if they're following."

I closed my mouth and attempted to breathe without making a sound, but the air rustling through my nostrils came out as a wind-storm. Some sort of animal with brown fur shook through a bush beside us and made us both gasp.

Joe loosened his grip on my wrist and cursed under his breath.

"I don't hear them," I whispered. "Do you?"

He shook his head.

"Joe," I said in a voice so strained and quiet it hurt my throat. "I'm sorry I started crying."

He wouldn't look me in the eye. "I should have grabbed your gun instead of letting them talk to us that way."

"No, it would have just made things worse if you fired at one of them. And they had knives . . ."

"That cabin was theirs." He swallowed. "I should have known from all the naked pictures and cigarettes. I bet they hide all their vices from their mother out there."

"Uncle Clyde knows their father—he's the pharmacist."

Joe readjusted his hold on the lantern. "I'm sure he knows him for other reasons, as well."

With that, he took off into the hedges. Branches scraped across his sides and tugged at his shirt, and I followed him, running away yet again.

A HALF HOUR OR SO LATER, I REALIZED WE WERE HEADING south, toward Fleur's property . . . and my family's property. My brain had been reeling too much to notice the morning sunlight of the east peeking through the trees to our left.

"Wait!" I dropped the basket in a patch of mushrooms. "You're leading me back home?"

Joe swiveled on his right heel and faced me with the carpetbag and lantern in hand. "I don't want them thinking they chased us out of the state."

"But—"

"We'll starve without food and supplies. And meanwhile, Clyde Koning will be sitting comfortably in your house—alive, healthy, and free."

I brushed my right hand through my hair, which had come loose from the pins I'd slept in all night. "He knows I accused him of murder, Joe. I can't go back to him."

"Put the blame on me for everything. Tell them I seduced you."

"I don't think . . ." I shook my head. "No . . . What if he knows you're not attracted to women?"

"Everyone always assumes this is something I can change. We can use that. Stick with the elopement story, but say you got cold feet and wanted to return to your mother. Apologize."

"But—"

"We're still better off taking care of the doc if you're in the house with him." Joe walked toward me, his ankles brushing through the grasses. "If we stay out here in the woods, we're just going to end up getting scared and fleeing the state."

Without warning, a startling *pop-pop-pop-pop-pop* ricocheted across the tops of the trees.

I ducked and cried out, "What's that?"

"Some early fireworks, probably." Joe looked toward the sky. "I think it's the Fourth of July."

"Oh." I straightened back up. "I forgot about that." I relaxed my shoulders a hair of an inch. "If I go back home, where are you going to stay? You can't go back to the Paulissens' shed."

"I know."

I sighed again. "We have an old stable at the edge of our property.

142

Other than harvesting berries, we don't farm or raise animals anymore, now that Uncle Clyde takes care of us. You can stay in there if you'd like."

He readjusted his grip on the carpetbag. "And do what?"

"Figure out how to make things right."

His mouth twitched in reaction to my words. Using the back of his hand that held the lantern, he nudged away the lock of hair that was always falling over his eyes.

"What's wrong?" I asked.

He lowered the lantern to his side. "You're off the idea of killing him, aren't you?"

"I can't poison him, Joe. I'm considering becoming a lawyer."

"Hmm"—he tapped his bag against the side of his right shin—"I've always heard that unscrupulousness is a prerequisite for becoming a lawyer."

I frowned. "I'm not joking. I want to become a force this state has to reckon with, not a fugitive it's required to kill."

He puffed a frustrated breath out of the corner of his mouth.

I turned toward the path to my house. "I know you said you would need to take your own life directly afterward if you were the one who killed him—"

"I would."

My skin chilled at his lack of hesitancy.

"Hanalee"—he stepped closer—"look at me."

I swallowed and did as he asked.

He stopped two feet in front of me and peered straight at me with eyes as brown as the earth beneath our feet. His peppermint-scented nearness made me remember the kiss, and I didn't know if I should look at his face or the backs of my hands.

"No one else is *ever* going to bring justice to your father," he said, leaning forward on his right foot. "No one else is going to give a damn about us. Those words you just heard those Witten bastards say about people like you and me? That's how most people around here think."

"I don't know. I . . ." I scooted backward an inch. "There's got to be a better way. A legal way."

"A legal way?" He breathed a short laugh. "Oregon's laws are written to work against us. *Eugenics* passed as a law. If they can pass legislation controlling who can and can't have children—"

"If I'm going back home"—I raised my chin—"and getting smacked around or paddled because of running off into the night with you, then you can take the time to come up with a better plan. A solid plan. One that involves justice *and* the two of us leaving Oregon in one piece. You and me and my mother and Fleur. All of us need to get away safely."

Joe swallowed and glanced over his shoulder, toward the path to my house.

"Promise me, Joe. Swear we'll both make it out of this ordeal alive and free. Let's find out if there's someplace out there that would treat us better."

His shoulders tightened, but he nodded. "All right. I'll give the plan some more thought."

"Good. See that you do." I took off the coat he had lent me. "Stay safe out here."

He nodded again.

I set his blanket and the coat on the basket and moved to pass him, but he took hold of my elbow.

"You stay safe with Clyde Koning," he said, his voice low.

My chin trembled. "I'll try."

"Don't let him scare you or intimidate you. Put the entire blame for last night on me."

"All right."

He bent down to pick up the basket.

"Joe?" I said.

He looked up.

I played with the emerald ring on my finger. "Do you want to be an architect?"

He stood up tall and rolled back his shoulders. "Why do you ask that?"

"You built all those card structures in the shed. I just wondered . . . did you do that out of boredom, or do you like to build things in general? Is that your calling?"

He backed away with his bag and the basket and lantern bumping against his sides. "I used to think my calling was to play baseball like Babe Ruth. I planned to sign to the Major Leagues by the age of nineteen, just like he did."

"Oh . . ." I lifted my eyebrows. "Well . . ."

Joe shrugged and kept trekking backward. "Yeah . . . 'Oh, well' just about sums it up."

"That's not what I meant." I swallowed down a tight spot in my throat. "Just so you know . . ."

He slowed his pace a little.

I shoved my hands into my skirt pockets. "I didn't knock that card house down on purpose yesterday. I was just looking at it too closely. Admiring it. It reminded me of a honeycomb."

His lips quirked into a small smile.

"That's all I wanted to say," I said. "I like honeycombs."

He chuckled and swung himself around in the opposite direction, and I turned and cringed over those last words.

I like honeycombs.

After all we'd endured together over the past twelve hours. *I like* blasted *honeycombs.*

His footsteps trailed off into the distance behind me. I shuddered at the absence of his company but told myself it was simply a chill from the shadows.

CHAPTER 13

THE PRIMROSE PATH

 ON THE DIRT DRIVE IN FRONT OF our house stood two empty black automobiles with glass windows and wheels with wooden spokes. They resembled two watchmen, parked at severe angles, facing me, staring me down with unblinking headlights for eyes. I staggered across the yard toward the house, my gaze fixed upon the vehicles. One was a Washington County patrol car; the other, the Adders' Ford Model T—the same car that Joe had crashed into my father on Christmas Eve 1921. The Adders had fixed the dent in the hood and replaced the left headlight even before the county put Joe on trial. I remembered seeing it parked in front of the county courthouse, mended and freshly repainted.

My stomach groaned. If I had eaten any breakfast that morning, I'd probably have thrown it up in the lavender bushes sweetening the air below our back kitchen steps. I tripped on those steps on my climb up them, and I clung to the rail with clammy hands.

Once inside the house, I heard a cacophony of adult voices crashing together in the front living room, including the squeaky tones of Sheriff Rink, who said something about checking the local ponds and lakes.

"Where else can you search?" asked Mama in an octave almost as high as the sheriff's. "For God's sake, it's been over twelve hours now."

A floorboard creaked beneath my right shoe, and the sound reverberated through the house like a peal of thunder. The living room fell silent.

"Hanalee?" asked Mama. "Is that you?"

I wedged my teeth into my bottom lip, sidled around the corner, and came face-to-face with an unsettling tableau: Mama, Uncle Clyde, Reverend and Mrs. Adder, and Sheriff Rink, all gawking at me from our living room furniture. Cups and saucers teetered on their laps, and the smell of coffee filled the air. Everyone blinked and trembled as though their bodies buzzed with caffeine.

"Hanalee!" Mama sprang out of her chair and lunged toward me, her face a red tempest, her hair a tornado of golden tangles. Before I could even think to back away, she grabbed me by my shoulders and shook me with a violence I'd never before experienced from her. My neck popped and cracked, and the room went blurry.

"How could you do that to me?" she cried. "What were you thinking? Where did you go?"

"Let me go."

"Where were you?"

"How could you do that to your mother?" said Uncle Clyde, suddenly next to my mother, his spectacles jumping about before my jostled eyes. "You made her sick with worry."

"Stop shaking me and I'll tell you!"

Mama loosened her grip, but she refused to take her hands off me.

Beyond her, Reverend and Mrs. Adder, their faces pinched and worried, set their cups aside and stood up from our sofa. Mrs. Adder's graying brown curls quivered around her ears, and Reverend Adder—a man taller and much older than his son, with white windswept clouds for hair—wrapped an arm around his wife.

I lifted my face and stood as high as my neck would stretch. "Joe and I were plotting to elope to Washington," I said. "That's why I've been acting so peculiarly lately. That's why I ran off."

No one responded at first. They just stared at me with their eyebrows puckered and their lips parted, as if I'd just uttered, *I've decided to become a Martian.*

Sheriff Rinky-Dink's mouth stretched into a grin that turned his cheeks into round dumplings. "Are you sure you're talking about Joe Adder?"

"Yes." I straightened my posture even farther. "We fell in love and planned to find a place to marry us. But . . . this morning . . . I s-s-started feeling guilty. I decided to return to Mama. And to apologize for my behavior."

The gaping and blinking continued.

"But"—Mama whipped her face toward my stepfather—"last night, you swore to me, Clyde. You said Joe doesn't like . . . that he wouldn't want . . . that he's a . . ."

"You and Joe . . ." Uncle Clyde placed his hands on his hips. "Y-y-you both fell in love with each other? *Mutually*?"

"Maybe he's changed." The reverend stepped forward with clasped hands. "Maybe all that time contemplating his sins in prison has put him on the path to righteousness."

"You sure they didn't operate on him in there?" asked the sheriff with a little less squeak, a little more growl. "Did they . . . *subdue* him already?"

I winced and hunched my shoulders at such questions.

"'Subdue him?'" asked Mama, her voice rising to the sheriff's pitch again. "Dear Lord, is that something that's done?" Her eyes met mine, and I swore I caught a flash of understanding. Of sympathy.

The telephone rang, and we all collectively jumped.

"Maybe that's Joe," said Mrs. Adder, her eyes wide.

My mother arched her eyebrows at me, as if I would know the answer, and I shook my head.

"Excuse me while I answer it." Mama strode out of the room, her thick heels echoing across the walls and the ceiling. Around the corner, in the main hall, she picked up the receiver and offered a curt "Hello."

I smoothed down the right side of my skirt, which now felt flat and limp after I'd tucked the holster back inside the oilcloth in the log before my reluctant return to the house. Everyone else stood about and picked at their buttons and their hair and the wrinkles in

their clothes, while loitering in front of Daddy's fine line drawings mounted on the ivory and yellow wallpaper. We all eavesdropped on my mother's telephone conversation, which primarily consisted of phrases such as "I see" and "Thank you. Thank you for telling me."

She clicked the receiver back onto the telephone's candlestick base and returned to the rest of us. "That was Mr. Witten."

I stiffened.

She wrung her hands together and refused to look at me. "The twins saw Hanalee and Joe on their property this morning and were told the same story about the elopement. He said the boys came upon them . . ." She closed her eyes and swallowed with a pained expression that made me feel bad, as though I were the thing scraping away at the inside of her throat. "They found them wrapped in a blanket together, sleeping on the forest floor near the Wittens' section of Engle Creek."

"So, he *has* changed," murmured the reverend under his breath. "Merciful God, thank you. Thank you for guiding him to the path of male and female unions."

"I beg your pardon?" Mama's eyes flew open. "I don't mean to speak disrespectfully, Reverend Adder, but if your son stole my daughter's virtue—"

"He didn't," I snapped.

"Your son is feeding Hanalee lies about Clyde killing Hank," she continued. "He's luring her out into the woods in the dark—"

"Let's focus on this accusation of murder," squeaked the sheriff with a nervous little laugh, "before we even begin to think about the possibility of an interracial, premarital union. Good heavens." He pulled at his collar. "One crime at a time, please."

Mama, a woman well versed in interracial unions, stepped back at the word *crime*.

"Hanalee"—the sheriff beckoned to me with an index finger—"come here and have a seat on the sofa. We need to have a little talk about the type of information our young Joe has been telling you."

Mrs. Adder pressed her forehead against her husband's chest. The reverend cupped a large hand around the back of her curls, and both members of the couple wilted against each other.

"Come along, Hanalee." The sheriff waved me over to our sofa.

"Go on." Mama nudged me toward him with a little too hard of a push. I tripped over my own feet and proceeded forward, my shoes feeling as ungainly as when I strapped on snowshoes. I stood a mere inch shorter than the sheriff, and I hoped my height intimidated him as I followed him to the sofa.

I noticed that *Babbitt* still sat on the floor next to the armchair—the same spot where I had put it when replacing it with the Bible. I saw my copy of *Noted Negro Women* still parked on the end table next to the sofa from when I'd read about Charlotte E. Ray two nights earlier. I perched on the edge of the sofa and brought *Noted Negro Women* onto my lap.

Sheriff Rink squinted down at the title. "Why did you just grab a book?"

"This is the key that's opened the entire world to me, Sheriff Rink." I laid my right palm across the clothbound cover. "It's taught me that people like me can become lawyers and represent the unprotected."

The sheriff grinned. "A lawyer?"

"That's right."

"You ever even been to a trial?" he asked.

"Of course I have. I sat in the courthouse and watched as two lawyers jabbered on about a boy who'd driven around with gin in his bloodstream." I tilted my head to the right. "But that boy was never allowed to testify. Was he?"

At those words, as if to bulldoze straight over my statement, Uncle Clyde said to the rest of the adults, "Everyone, please, sit down. No need to stand and be uncomfortable. We've all been through enough."

Like a flock of starlings settling over the yard, Joe's parents and my parents descended upon the furniture around me. Mama sidled up beside me on the couch; Uncle Clyde parked himself beside her; Mrs. Adder took the rocking chair; and the reverend stood behind her with his hand propped on the back of the chair, like a man posing for a formal photograph with his wife.

The sheriff plopped his wide backside down in Daddy's armchair.

I fought off the urge to pitch *Noted Negro Women* at his forehead for sitting in that particular chair.

"If Joe were to have testified"—the sheriff clasped his hands together between his knees—"what do you think he would have said?"

I wiggled myself to a more upright position. "What do *you* think he would have said?"

"Hanalee, no." Mama sucked in her breath, her teeth bared. "Don't turn the questions back around on other people, as you did yesterday with Deputy Fortaine."

The sheriff shifted in his seat toward Mama. "Ben's already questioned the girl?"

"He, um . . ." Uncle Clyde coughed into his right fist. "Deputy Fortaine came over for coffee yesterday morning. He asked Hanalee if she knew of Joe's whereabouts."

I noted the sheriff's tension concerning the deputy. "Where's Deputy Fortaine now?" I asked.

The sheriff swiveled back in my direction with a *whoosh* of his rump against the maroon satin. "He's out looking for you and Joe."

"Oh." I tried not to gulp, but the reaction occurred as an involuntary swallow.

"Where is Joe, Hanalee?" asked the sheriff.

"Heading up to Washington without me."

The sheriff's small gray eyes scrutinized me. "Are you certain about that?"

"Yes. No one wants him here in Oregon."

"That's not true," said Mrs. Adder with a break in her voice. "We want him home and safe."

"You want him sterilized—castrated," I said, and the bluntness of my voice smacked against the walls with a thud.

Another hush fell over the room, a silence cold and savage that made everyone's eyes glisten and their lips shiver.

"Hanalee," said Mama in a near whisper. "What did you just say?"

Uncle Clyde ran a hand through his hair and leaned his elbows on his thighs. "She's referring to the eugenics movement."

"We just . . ." The reverend's fingers slipped off the rocking chair. "We just want the boy to make the right choices. None of this has been easy for any of us."

I sank my head into my hands and swallowed down a bitter taste. The weight and shape of a missing person impressed itself upon the room. Instead of my mother, I wished Fleur sat beside me. Or Joe. Or my father. All the wrong people were gathered around me.

"Are you all right, Hanalee?" wheezed the sheriff.

"I'm not feeling well right now. I don't want to talk about this anymore."

No one responded at first, so I stared through my fingers at my black-trimmed Keds. Mud streaked the white canvas. Leaves in the shape of dead moths caked the sides.

"Dr. Koning told me," said the sheriff, "he worries that you and Joe have gotten the wrong idea about him. He fears Joe might want to hurt him."

"*Does* he want to hurt me, Hanalee?" asked Uncle Clyde. "Is Joe armed?"

My head remained lowered, and I lied through clenched teeth. "Joe is on his way to Washington. He doesn't want to be here anymore. Just let him go—*please*. Leave him alone."

"What do you think we should do about her?" asked Mama. "I can't determine if she's telling the truth."

"Bring her to the Fourth of July picnic this afternoon," said the sheriff. "Let's see if Joe decides to show up."

Mama squeezed my right leg. "I don't want her running off again."

"She won't run off," said Uncle Clyde. "Will you, Hanalee?"

I bit down on my bottom lip until all I could feel was the spiked pressure of teeth stabbing my flesh.

"Hanalee?" asked my stepfather again.

I lifted my face to my right and met Uncle Clyde's bespectacled eyes for the first time since he'd chased me out to the woods.

My stepfather held his jaw and his shoulders stiff. "It's sweet of you to continue to mourn your father, but it's time to put his death in the past."

The reverend piped up: "That's wise advice, Hanalee. His death was simply a tragic accident. Nothing more. Allow your father to rest in peace."

I released my lip from my teeth and felt my throat thicken, the muscles in my back tighten. "Well, that's precisely the problem." I swallowed. "My father isn't resting in peace."

CHAPTER 14

CAST THY NIGHTED COLOR OFF

 WHEN A PERSON SPEAKS OF HER father's ghost, I discovered that other people in the room tend to agree that she might, indeed, require an end to her interrogation. Sheriff Rink released me from the questioning, and Mama allowed me to disappear upstairs to my room with a glass of water and a slice of raspberry strudel, although she refused to look at me when she handed me my food and my glass, and her fingers quivered.

"We'll talk more later" was all that she said.

As I made my way upstairs, the gathering of adults in the living room ceased talking, but once I closed my bedroom door, their voices rose and fell with incoherent rumblings down below the soles of my feet. I sat on my bed and devoured the strudel, and I downed the water so quickly, I choked. Then I felt guilty. I wondered if Joe had anything to eat inside that picnic basket that I'd lugged around the woods. I also fretted over the idea of Fleur sitting at her kitchen table with her mother and brother, picking at her breakfast with her fork, not knowing whether I'd been found.

The discussions rumbled on downstairs. I set the dish and the cup down on the floor and heard the crinkling of the Klan pamphlet tucked inside my pocket. I pulled out the crumpled piece of paper and read the penciled notes again.

Konklave, July 2, 1923. New members needed. White, Protestant boys aged twelve to eighteen.

Initiation planned. Necktie party?

The problem of Joe Adder. Moral degenerate.

Pancake breakfast set for Saturday at the Dry Dock. Money raised will repair potholes on Main Street.

A headache erupted between my eyes. I massaged the bridge of my nose and chewed upon the idea of the Junior Order of Klansmen meeting only two days earlier, right after Joe showed up back in Elston. Young local Klan members, aged twelve to eighteen, had discussed the "problem" of Joe's presence the same night I had wandered down the unlit highway with Necromancer's Nectar burning through my veins. The car that had passed me after I dove onto my belly may have very well contained Klan members—young men and their adult supervisors, driving home from talks of initiations and pancake breakfasts and the reverend's wayward son.

My eyes strayed down to the last lines of the notes:

Pancake breakfast set for Saturday at the Dry Dock. Money raised will repair potholes on Main Street.

The nape of my neck tingled. Something didn't feel right about those lines, even though the sentences appeared to be the most benevolent of them all. I reread the sentences, my heart rate doubling, and then I saw it—the word that unsettled me.

Dock.

I shook my head. "No, that wouldn't make sense." I closed my eyes and rubbed my temples and tried to think back to Joe's account of my father's last words to him. My mind went blank, but I knew the word *doc*—or *Dock*—was involved. I dropped to my knees on the floor, slid the basket of toys out from beneath my bed, and yanked out the newsprint containing my note.

I put full blame on the doc.

Or, perhaps I should have written . . .

I put full blame on the Dock.

The Dry Dock.
Doc.
Dock.

Dr. Koning.

The Dry Dock restaurant.

"Oh, God." My brain spun. "Which is it?"

Down below the floor of my bedroom, the front door closed, and voices trailed outside the house. I sprang over to my window and watched the Adders and Sheriff Rink mosey over to their respective automobiles, and my eyes smarted from the glare of the sun hitting the black metal of the vehicles. Uncle Clyde wandered behind them with his hands on his hips. He imparted a few last thoughts to the sheriff and Joe's parents, but my window remained closed, and I couldn't discern the words. The cars sparked to life with swift cranks of the handles below the grilles. The sheriff and the reverend climbed into their vehicles and steered them out of our driveway.

Mama's footsteps sounded on the staircase beyond my closed door; still, I watched my stepfather shade his eyes from the sun and turn from the road toward the barrier of Douglas firs marking the entrance to the woods. My throat went dry.

"Don't go looking for him," I whispered against the glass pane. "Please . . . leave him alone."

Another automobile pulled into our driveway from the highway—a second patrol car, helmed by Deputy Fortaine. The deputy turned off his motor and stepped out of the car while removing his cap. The short waves of his raven-black hair rippled in the wind.

Uncle Clyde headed over to him, and they both spoke with their arms folded across their chests. I wondered if the deputy's last name truly was Fishstein. At the moment, he didn't strike me as being Jewish or Catholic, for a person like that—someone caught outside the circle of normalcy in Elston—would certainly possess more sympathy for a boy in Joe's predicament. He wouldn't want to hunt him down the way he seemed to be doing, unless he was trying with all his might to overcompensate for his own differences.

From the wall behind the head of my bed emerged the sound of crying. I left my window and grabbed the box of toys and bullets from underneath the bed and crammed the Klan pamphlet down the right side.

The weeping continued.

I left my room with caution, unsure if my mother cried out of sorrow or anger, fearful of the fine line between sobbing and smacking. The floorboards of that old house of ours whined and sagged with my every step across the hallway, no matter how much I tried to make my feet move as though they were composed of feathers and air. I sidled over to the open doorway of the bedroom that my mother now shared with Uncle Clyde—a room larger than mine, wallpapered in a royal shade of blue, with a mahogany four-poster bed hogging most of the space. On the edge of the bed sat Mama, crying into a handkerchief. I eyed the wrinkled sheets and forbade myself envisioning her sleeping there with Uncle Clyde.

She lifted her face, revealing bloodshot eyes and a red-rimmed nose, all of which leaked. Her loose hair hung down to her waist like sheaves of dried wheat.

"I don't want to ever again hear you telling a ghost tale about your father," she said in a tone that socked me in the chest.

I clenched my teeth.

"And I want honesty, Hanalee. What did Joe tell you about Uncle Clyde and your father's death?" Fear glinted in her eyes.

The wall of love and support for her new husband must have weakened—I could hear the barrier thinning in the timbre of her voice.

"He said"—I shut the bedroom door behind me and willed my stepfather to stay outside with the deputy—"that aside from a busted leg and a sore arm, Daddy seemed just fine after he hit him with the car." I tiptoed closer to her, still fearful of getting smacked. "When Uncle Clyde arrived, he made Joe stay out in the front room, and the next time Joe saw my father, Daddy was . . . *gone* . . . as if . . ." My lips shook, and the word I wanted to utter slipped back down my throat.

"As if what?" asked Mama.

I covered my mouth with my hand and spoke from behind my fingers. "Poisoned."

My mother's face whitened. Complex highways of green-blue veins manifested beneath her skin.

"Everyone shut Joe up at his trial," I continued, "which led Joe to believe that people got paid to stop him from testifying. He believes that Uncle Clyde might be part of the KKK."

A crooked little line cleaved the skin between Mama's eyebrows. "Joe doesn't know what the devil he's talking about," she said. "Uncle Clyde has promised me over and over that he'd do anything he could—even risk his own life—to keep you safe."

"Yes, well"—I glanced again at their bed—"I've heard a man will promise just about anything in order to bed the woman he wants."

Without warning, Mama jumped to her feet and slapped me across the face with a force that stung with a shock of heat. I reeled back and cradled my cheek in my hand.

"For the last time, did Joe Adder take away your virtue?" she asked. "Is that why you're talking so filthy?"

"No."

"Are you certain? You slept beside him—"

"I slept beside him in the woods, bundled in a blanket to keep from freezing, but that's all. He kept me comfortable and warm because I didn't want to sleep under the same roof as Clyde Koning."

Mama's hand dropped to her side. "You understand what I mean about your virtue, don't you?"

"Joe Adder didn't take away my virginity, Mama. I grew up around farm animals, for heaven's sake. I know what you're talking about, and Joe doesn't want to do that sort of thing with me."

"Then why did he try to elope with you?"

"Because no one else understands an outsider better than I."

She closed her mouth and swallowed. "You're not . . . you're not going to run back into the woods and try to find him?"

"No! I keep telling everyone, he's heading up to Washington." I'd told the fib so often, I began to believe the lie myself. I even stared my mother straight in the eye when I said it.

Mama blinked, and her hazel eyes moistened again.

I switched my attention to the oak wardrobe that housed Uncle Clyde's suits and dress shirts. "Will you help me look through Uncle Clyde's belongings?"

She recoiled. "For what?"

"Klan regalia. A membership card."

"Uncle Clyde is not a part of that organization. Even if he were, the Klan isn't concerned about Negroes here in Oregon. For the most part they're improving schools and roads."

"Are you afraid to look?"

She raised her right hand to slap me again, and I closed my eyes and hunched my shoulders, bracing for pain.

Nothing struck me.

I peeled one eye open and found Mama's outstretched palm frozen in midair. Her chin twitched.

"If I look"—she lowered her hand to her chest—"will you swear to never again speak of your stepfather this way?"

I rubbed the tender skin of my face and sorted out a suitable response.

"Hanalee?"

"All right. I'll stop wanting to raid his belongings if I see for certain he's not hiding anything that links him to that group."

Mama trod to the closed bedroom door and put her ear to the wood.

"I last saw him outside," I said, "speaking to Deputy Fortaine."

"Deputy Fortaine?"

I nodded. "He pulled into our driveway shortly after the sheriff and the Adders left."

She turned the lock with a solid click that seemed to echo through the house. "Stay right here"—she let go of the brass knob—"and let me know if you hear him."

My chest warmed with gratitude over my mother's helpfulness. I felt like a child again, when she and I were two peas in a pod. *Daddy's girls.*

She snuck up to the wardrobe and, after inhaling a deep breath, opened the mighty oak doors with both hands. I stood upon restless legs and watched her rifle through dark trousers and white shirtsleeves with silent movements.

"May I help?" I asked.

"No." She slid open his bottom drawer, filled with socks and undergarments folded in neat piles, which she lifted with the care of a person trying not to wake a sleeping baby.

"What about that hatbox?" I pointed to a black-and-white box sitting on the flat surface on top of the wardrobe.

Mama lifted her face upward. "I honestly don't think he could fit anything so large in that small of a container."

"The box sits high enough that neither of us can reach it, though. What if he's at least storing the hood in there? Or paperwork?"

"I'd need a stepladder, Hanalee."

"How about the chair from your dressing table?" I jogged over to the padded ivory stool tucked beneath the vanity, where she powdered her face and arranged her hair every morning.

She came over to help me, and together we scooted the small piece of furniture below the wardrobe. The cabinet smelled like the doc—Mennen Shaving Cream combined with Lysol.

With cautious movements, Mama held the side of the cabinet for support, climbed atop the stool, and grabbed the hatbox. After both her feet landed safely back on the floor, I lifted the lid and peeked inside.

A hat sat within. A Pendleton wool cap, suitable for wintertime.

I sifted through the protective paper surrounding the plaid fabric.

"What are you looking for?" asked Mama.

"I don't know—a membership card, a list of names, *anything*."

A knock on the door startled the box out of our hands. The hat dropped onto my toes, and the paper flitted to the ground like an autumn leaf.

"Greta?" Uncle Clyde rattled the knob and shook the door. "Why is this door locked?"

"I'm . . ." Mama blanched. "Hanalee's in here. We're talking. Just . . . wait downstairs for a few minutes."

She picked up the box from the floor, and I grabbed the overturned cap, finding nothing but a receipt from the Meier & Frank department store in downtown Portland.

"What's that?" whispered Mama.

"Just a receipt."

"See? There's nothing here."

"Is everything all right in there?" called Uncle Clyde.

Mama shoved the cap into the box and covered the lid. "We're just talking, Clyde. Go downstairs."

We both held our breath. Beyond the door, Uncle Clyde's feet descended the staircase, the steps groaning.

"Does anything strike you as dangerous about the Dry Dock?" I asked in the quietest voice I could muster.

Mama straightened her neck. "The Dock?"

I shrank back. "Why'd you call it that?"

"That was the restaurant's original name, before the state went dry and the Franklins stopped selling liquor there." Mama climbed back up on the stool and shoved the hatbox into place. Dust filtered down from the top of the wardrobe, tickling my nose.

I sneezed twice in a row and had to take a breath. "They're

166

hosting a pancake breakfast"—I rubbed the tip of my nose—"for a group called the Junior Order of Klansmen."

"I told you"—she climbed off the stool—"you don't need to worry about the Klan around here. If I sensed danger, I'd be the first to warn you."

"Are you positive Uncle Clyde's not a part of them?"

"I swear, he's not." She clasped my hands and pulled me toward her. "Stop doubting him, Hanalee. He loves you, and I love you."

I curled my lips inside my mouth and squished them hard together, fighting down the urge for tears.

"Go get washed up." She squeezed my fingers. "Change into fresh clothes. I'll take you to that picnic, if only to try to bring some regularity back into our lives."

"All right." I sniffed.

"And wear something bright. Nothing dark and mournful." She brushed a curl out of my eyes. "It is time to move onward, as the reverend and Uncle Clyde said." She kissed my cheek, and her breath caught near my ear. "I know it's hard, Hanalee. I know you miss your father more than anything. I understand why you might have thought you saw his ghost. But we have to let him go."

"All right," I said again.

She lowered her hand from my head, and I left the room, the smell of the pines and the earth—and Joe and *escape*—still lingering in my hair.

METHODIST YOUTH PICNIC,
WASHINGTON COUNTY, OREGON,
CIRCA 1920s

CHAPTER 15

WHO IS'T THAT CAN INFORM ME?

 DRESSED IN A YELLOW SKIRT AND WHITE blouse that spoke of sunshine and innocence, I rode behind my mother and Uncle Clyde in the back of my stepfather's four-door Buick sedan.

My straw hat sat beside me on the plush seat, and my emerald ring sparkled in the rays of light shining through the open windows. I looked nothing at all like a girl who had slept on a blanket in the forest with a young man no one wanted around.

Mama kept turning in her seat and checking on me, as though she feared she'd find me gone again.

"I'm fine, I'm fine," I said over and over, and I steeled myself against potholes in the road and the sight of Uncle Clyde's head bobbing about on his neck in front of me.

On the way into town, we passed Elston's two restaurants—the Dry Dock and Ginger's—which were separated by an oak tree with a sturdy trunk and crooked branches covered in leaves. The establishments flashed by as blurs of wood-paneled walls and redbrick chimneys, and a stab of dread, as quick as lightning, tore through my stomach.

We reached the strip of brick buildings that made up downtown, the tallest structure being the Lincoln Hotel at the far end, which stood three stories high and boasted a marble statue of "Honest Abe" out front, amid the rhododendrons. The owners claimed to be related to our sixteenth president, but I always wondered if they possessed any verifiable proof of that story. Tall tales and exaggerations seemed to be a staple in Elston.

Just past the heart of the town, we heard the horns of the local brass band blaring "You're a Grand Old Flag." I braced myself for the upcoming barrage of socializing that made my head swim on even normal Julys. Every year Elston held the Independence Day picnic on the lawn in front of our forty-year-old church—the type of church one would find on a Christmas card, complete with a steeple and paint as white as heaven itself, minus a few scuffs from stray baseballs and leaky droppings from the birds that nested in the eaves. Even the townsfolk who attended the church over in Bentley, plus the folks who dared to declare themselves Catholics or atheists, migrated to our Fourth of July festivities. If any actual Jewish folks resided in Elston or Bentley, aside from the aforementioned deputy, they'd probably come puttering over in their automobiles, too.

Uncle Clyde pulled the Buick next to a line of parked cars that gleamed in the sunlight in a patch of dirt. From my backseat window I spied the fair citizens of Elston, clad in red, white, and blue, crowded together on blankets in the lush green grass, hopping about in potato-sack races, and stuffing their mouths full of food. The brass band—all men in white linen suits—trumpeted away on the steps of the church, their cheeks puffed wide, their faces flushed and shiny. They looked as though they might already smell a bit sour.

Uncle Clyde popped his car door open and hurried around to Mama's side to help her with her door. Mama handed my stepfather a basketful of roasted ham, fresh fruit, and sugar cookies and stepped out of the vehicle.

"Thank you, Clyde." She brushed her left hand across the sleeve of his coat, and they leaned in close to each other, as if about to kiss, but Uncle Clyde stopped and turned his sights to me.

"Aren't you getting out?" he asked. He stepped toward me and opened my door.

I folded the rim of my hat with a satisfying crunch of the straw, and I remembered how the sheriff had asked Uncle Clyde and Mama to take me to the picnic to serve as bait for Joe.

In the Creole story about the prince whom a wizard turned into a fish, the girl's father killed the fish to keep his daughter from visiting him by the river. He forced her to cook the fish. And then he ate him.

"Hanalee." Mama set her hand on the crook of Uncle Clyde's arm again. "Are you all right?"

I shoved my hat onto my head and slid off the seat. The soles of my sandals thudded against the dirt, and the ground coughed up a cloud of dust. "I'm just dandy."

Mama frowned.

The three of us entered the picnic grounds, my mother walking in the middle and Uncle Clyde on her right side, still carrying the basket. From beneath the brim of my hat, I glanced around for signs of Fleur but didn't see her or her mother and brother.

"Greta . . . Dr. Koning," called Mrs. Adder, coming our way with two glasses of lemonade. "Oh, I'm so glad you came, despite all." She squinted into the sunlight and stopped a few feet in front of us. "There's no sign of Joe yet."

Mama and Uncle Clyde glanced at each other with weary eyes, as if they had both tired of speaking about the preacher's son for the day.

"I'm sorry." Uncle Clyde placed his hand on Mama's back. "I hope he's safe."

"Thank you. I do, too." Mrs. Adder's gaze flitted toward me for the briefest of moments. She gave a strained smile and then continued onward, toward an area occupied by Joe's six brothers and sisters—all well-dressed children, younger than he, with hair ranging from caramel-brown to Joe's darker walnut shade. The weight of an absence settled over me again. The Adders struck me as a jigsaw puzzle with a missing piece. A multi-angled, not-quite-the-same-shape-as-the-others piece that they tried to cover by squishing closer together on their picnic blanket.

Mama and Uncle Clyde walked faster than me, so I ended up trekking behind them through the obstacles of blankets and families, including the Witten twins' parents, who were dressed in Sunday-best attire and didn't seem at all like people with sons who carried around knives and gin. Faces shifted my way. Glances settled upon me, no doubt because of the inevitable spread of rumors about Joe and me, but also due to the fact that most people stopped and stared whenever I made an appearance in town.

"Will I ever stop sticking out like a sore thumb?" I remembered asking Daddy one morning on our walk home from buying seeds at the farm-supply store. I only came up to his ribs at the time, so I must not have been much more than seven or eight.

Daddy's smile had faded at my question, yet the light from his eyes never dimmed. "Probably not, baby doll," he said. "Not when you're the only one who looks like you. Just lift your head and show them who you are deep inside. Look them in the eye and smile, and the kind ones will see that brown is a beautiful color."

I did my best to lift my head on those church grounds, and I tried to ignore all the eyes, although I noted that some of the faces smiled with expressions of understanding, or maybe pity, as if they didn't blame me for running off with another Elston misfit. No one whispered unpleasant words about me—no hisses of "slut" or "floozy" or even worse. I pressed forward to the patch of grass Mama had selected for our picnic blanket. I helped my mother and stepfather spread the checkered blue cloth over the ground and thought of Joe flapping his brown blanket over us on the forest floor in the dark. I knelt down and stretched out a corner of Mama's blanket and had to stop and rub my hands over my eyes.

"Hanalee?" asked Mama. "Are you sure you're all right?"

The lingering dew on the grass bled through both the blanket and my skirt, moistening my knees. I sat there for a moment and wondered how the universe had seen fit to throw me together with a person I was supposed to hate. A person who wouldn't ever want to be with me, even if my skin was whiter than his. I imagined someone from up above—certainly not God, I hoped—devising all the various stumbling blocks he could place in front of me, all the barriers to love and freedom and simple happiness, just to see how I'd react. Just for a laugh.

Before I could answer my mother, someone called my name. I raised my head and found Mildred Marks plodding toward me, dodging through a three-legged race that was claiming more victims than victors. She wore her usual fedora and filthy brown boots and looked like a cross between a gangster and a farmhand—a furious one at that, with her hands balled into fists by her sides. She plowed straight toward me, her mouth clamped shut in an ugly scowl.

"I . . ." I jumped to my feet from our blanket. "I think I might need to step away for a spell and talk to Mildred."

Mama stopped pulling dishes out of the picnic basket and raised her head. "I don't want you stepping too far away from us."

"Joe's not going to come anywhere near the church grounds, Greta," said Uncle Clyde, leaning back on his hands. "I can guarantee he won't show up within a mile of this crowd."

"I need to speak to you, Hanalee." Mildred stopped right in front of me, smelling a little tangy and pungent, like the grains distilling inside that back room in her house. "Do you have a moment to spare?"

I glanced down at Mama, who then glanced at Uncle Clyde.

"Just as long as you stay on church property," said my stepfather. "No wandering out of sight."

"It'll only take a moment." Mildred grabbed me by an elbow

and yanked me through the maze of picnickers until we reached a row of birches on the edge of the church grounds. She then threw my arm back at me as if it were a stick.

"He's still coming to our house," she said with a hiss. "Why in hell aren't you using the Necromancer's Nectar?"

"But I did."

"When?"

I counted in my head. "Two nights ago. I did exactly what you said—the spoonful, the crossroads, the circle on the ground—and I spoke to him."

"Well, he's still barging through our front door, still looking lost and desperate, giving us all a fright. Even Mama saw him last night. She's planning to hire a Spiritualist to exorcise him."

"No!" I waved my hands in her face. "Don't do anything to hurt him. Please."

She swatted my fingers away. "We don't want him in our house."

"I'll speak to him again. I'll see what he wants. I'll . . ." I turned my head and looked beyond the other townsfolk, spotting Mama and Uncle Clyde nestled together on the blanket, their heads tipped close together, their arms touching. "I'll do whatever it takes to set things right."

"I hope you do."

"I'll speak to him tonight, in fact. Just"—I rubbed the back of my neck—"please, don't do anything that might cause him any harm. Don't send him away just yet."

"All right." She pushed her hat farther down on her head, shadowing her face with the short brim. "I'll tell my mother you're taking care of him tonight, but if he—"

"Wait a minute." I dropped my hand to my side. "Tell me again why you think my father is heading to your particular house all the time, looking so upset."

"We're sensitive, that's why."

My jaw hardened.

Mildred stepped back on her left foot. "What's that look for?"

"Are you sure there's no other reason?"

"Cheese and crust, Hanalee. Why are you glaring like you suspect me of murder?"

"There's a troubling undercurrent rumbling beneath the surface of this town," I said. "I don't trust much of anyone these days."

"I'm prone to seeing ghosts. That's all. And I find myself overcome with premonitory sensations whenever something awful is about to happen." She tipped her fedora out of her eyes. "In fact, I experienced one of those sensations that Christmas Eve, right after your father left our house."

My head jerked back. *What?*

"I . . ." She inched backward. "What? I just said—"

"Why on earth was my father at your house that Christmas Eve?"

Mildred scratched at her elbow, and her lips sputtered as if she didn't know what to say.

I edged toward her. "Don't you dare tell me my father was seeing your mama."

"No! That's not it at all. He was picking up whiskey for a bootlegging run."

"He . . . No!" I darted a quick peek in Mama's direction again. "My father was most certainly not a bootlegger."

"Yes, he was. He hadn't been doing it long, and he seemed nervous about it."

"No, my father simply wasn't feeling well that night. We believe he decided to walk to the Christmas Eve service after he felt better, and—"

"Bootlegging is nothing to be ashamed about, Hanalee," said Mildred, and her eyes softened. "We all know the farms have been suffering since the war ended. He came by that night and picked up a crate of hooch, and directly afterward I trembled with one of my premonitions so violently, I dropped to my knees on the floor."

I grabbed hold of a nearby tree trunk and found it difficult to stand without doubling over.

"I tried to help him, though, I swear." Mildred also braced a hand against the birch. "After I found the strength to get to my feet, I hopped onto my bicycle and rode after him. I tried my best to stop him from going any farther with that crate, but he must have been walking through the trees and the fields instead of the road."

"Where was he taking the whiskey?"

"I don't remember him saying."

"The Dry Dock?"

She shrugged. "I honestly don't remember. So much happened that night."

"Did Joe hit him when he was carrying that crate, then?"

"Joe wasn't driving back to his house just yet."

"How do you know?"

She scratched at her elbow again and rocked a little from side to side.

I nudged her left arm. "How do you know Joe wasn't driving home just yet, Mildred? Tell me."

"B-b-because . . ." Her eyes shifted about. "When I was riding my bicycle in the dark, I saw a car pulling off the side of the road up ahead of me. By the time I pedaled farther, I heard"—she blinked—"*sounds* . . . coming from behind the trees on the drive to that old abandoned vineyard. Not the Paulissens' vineyard; that other one that's been closed and overgrown for years."

I furrowed my brow. "What types of sounds?"

Her face reddened, to the point where the blush blended in with her freckles and rendered the spots invisible. "Love sounds," she said, and she grimaced.

"Oh." I swallowed.

"I know I shouldn't have stopped—I should have kept bicycling after your father." She removed her fedora and fanned her face. "But I did stop. I parked my bicycle on the road and crept through the bushes, and I saw the reverend's Model T—I knew it was his, because the first three numbers of the license plate are one-three-zero, like my father's birthday, January thirtieth."

"And Joe was . . ." I cleared my throat. "He was in the car?"

"I didn't know who was in there at first, but then the deputy's car came driving around the bend—he must have seen my bicycle sitting there and worried. His headlights shone against the Model T, and I saw Joe's head pop up from the driver's side. The next thing I knew, some other fellow was jumping out of the car, pulling up his pants, and running off into the trees, while the deputy was yelling at Joe to get out of the vehicle."

"All right, all right." I readjusted my own hat on my head with a crinkle of the straw. "That's all I need to know about that."

"I've felt guilty about Joe ever since." She pursed her lips and sniffed.

I squinted at her. "Why do you feel guilty about him?"

Again, she braced herself against the trunk of the birch. "I watched as he stumbled out of the car while buttoning up his own trousers. He dropped to his knees and begged Deputy Fortaine to keep quiet about what he saw, for the sake of his father. 'He's a man of the cloth,' he kept saying over and over with tears rolling down his cheeks. 'People will run him out of town for raising a boy like me.'"

"But the deputy didn't care," I huffed. "Did he?"

"Oh, but he did." Mildred nodded. "He took pity on Joe and let him go. He said he was going to pretend he didn't see anything there, and he told Joe to drive straight home."

"Even though Joe had been drinking?"

"I don't know if he'd been drinking. He sure sounded sober when he was caught in those headlights and was begging for his freedom."

I squeezed my head between my hands, pressing the heels of my palms against the bones of my temples. "Then . . . then how did other people find out about Joe? Joe said he thinks he was put in jail mainly because of what he was caught doing with that boy, not because of my father's death."

Mildred flopped her fedora back over her head.

"Did they find the boy he was with?" I asked. "The boy from the party?"

"I blabbed about Joe," she said, ignoring my question, her eyes cast downward. "Sheriff Rink was over at our house the next day and told us about Joe running the car into your father."

"You told Sheriff Rink what you saw?"

She nodded. "I always enjoyed Joe's good looks, but what I found him doing . . ." She shook her head, as if she still didn't understand what she'd witnessed that Christmas Eve. "And then the idea of him killing your father . . . I blurted out, 'I hope Deputy Fortaine told you he found Joe and some other fellow with their pants down together.'"

She wrapped her arms around herself and fell silent with an abruptness that made me again aware of the band and the picnic. All the Fourth of July noises rushed back into my ears.

"I bet they treated Joe worse than they treat most people arrested for manslaughter," said Mildred. "He was just sixteen at the time of his arrest, I think, and I probably made his life hell."

I slid my hands down my face to my cheeks, and a damp chill rose to the surface of my skin. I thought of the bruises I'd seen on Joe's ribs, and the scar near his eye, the healed wound on his lip.

"Maybe . . ." She sniffed again, her eyes rimmed in red. "Maybe I should have just kept riding my bicycle after your father. Maybe it's my fault that he died. I got so distracted with Joe, I didn't warn your father about that terrible, premonitory pain. And if Joe would have just stayed with that boy without my bicycle attracting the deputy . . . Maybe that's why your father's storming into my house these past few nights. Maybe it is because of me, not you."

I struggled to find my voice. "H-h-how long did it take you to recover from that premonition pain before you hopped onto your bicycle?"

"I don't remember," she said. "A little while."

"Do you think my father made his delivery before he encountered Joe?"

"Why does that even matter, Hanalee? Who cares about that delivery?"

"I just want to fill in all the missing pieces. There's talk of a doc being involved, and I don't know if my father means 'Dr. Koning' or 'the Dry Dock.'"

"*Ask* your father."

I nodded. "I will. Tonight."

"If he's not gone by tomorrow, I swear, Mama will summon that Spiritualist—"

"I said, I'll ask him tonight," I said with a sting to my voice.

"Good. See as you do." Mildred wiped her eyes with the tips of her fingers and staggered back over to the festivities.

CHAPTER 16

NOBLE DUST

 UP AHEAD, TO THE RIGHT OF THE church, stood the wrought-iron archway that marked the entrance to the cemetery in which we'd buried my father two days after Christmas 1921. Joe had sat behind bars in the local jail while his father presided over the memorial service with a voice that cracked with emotion. Uncle Clyde and Fleur's mama, both friends with my mother since they were all children, had to revive my mother when she fainted by the graveside, and I remembered Uncle Clyde lifting Mama's head, whisking smelling salts beneath her nose, and murmuring, "I'm here, Greta. I'm here. You're not alone."

I peeked again across the grassy grounds, toward my mother and stepfather's picnic spot. I found them chatting with other members of our congregation. Mama glanced once my way, but then she returned to her socializing, neatening a lock of hair that had fallen out of her chignon.

I wandered into the graveyard with the horns and the drums of "The Yankee Doodle Boy" ringing in my ears and vibrating up the bones and muscles in my calves. The grounds grew cooler. Or, at least, the chill of silent graves spooked me into imagining a drop in the temperature.

We treated our dead in grand style in Elston, with polished gray obelisks and thick marble headstones marking the names of the deceased, from our Oregon Trail pioneers to those who died in recent years from the Spanish flu and other calamities. The conjoined graves of our former reverend and his wife lay to my right, no more than ten feet beyond the iron archway. I saw their surname, York, carved in block letters that felt smooth and solid beneath my hand, as well as the matching date of their deaths: October 8, 1918. The flu had snatched them both in the middle of the night when the pandemic ambushed Elston. Those two gentle souls—people who could have counseled and comforted me at the moment—had turned to dust, while the physician who couldn't save them still roamed the earth.

Tears burned in my eyes, for I remembered Mrs. York pulling my parents aside after church one Sunday morning during my second year at the schoolhouse. Her face was lined in soft wrinkles, and she had kind blue-green eyes shaded by a homespun bonnet.

She stood no more than four foot ten, and yet she possessed a sturdiness to her voice that made her appear six feet tall.

"I've heard about Hanalee's troubles in school," she had said to my parents. "I know Mrs. Corning ignores her whenever she raises her hand."

My parents couldn't disagree, so Mrs. York wrapped her arm around my bony shoulders and told them, "Bring Hanalee to our house one afternoon each week. I used to be employed as a schoolteacher myself. I'll ensure she's as least as smart as the other children in that school, if not smarter."

The Yorks' names on the gravestone blurred from view. I tucked my chin against my chest and allowed myself to cry—a good, shoulder-shaking bawl that other people might have heard if the brass band wasn't now blasting "The Star-Spangled Banner" across the church grounds. I couldn't even bring myself to venture farther inside the cemetery and visit Daddy's grave. I just stood there and sobbed, tears dripping to my chest, and I missed everyone with all my heart: the Yorks, my father, my mother, Laurence, Joe, Fleur, even me—the former me who never would have lingered in a church cemetery, pondering if she should dare put Clyde Koning into one of those graves.

"Hanalee?" said a voice I knew to be Fleur's.

I raised my head and found my friend standing at the entrance of the graveyard, dressed all in white. A breeze played with the airy sleeves below her shoulders, making the fabric flutter up and down. Red geraniums encircled the crown of her straw hat, and I knew she would smell as sweet as the petals.

"You're back," she said, stepping toward me.

I wiped my eyes with a knuckle. "Yeah, I'm back." I gave a sharp cough and cleared my throat with grunts that resembled the thumps of Mildred's whiskey still.

Fleur crossed her arms over her chest and walked toward me through the grass in her white Mary Janes. "Why'd you run off with Joe like that? Why'd you tell everyone you were eloping?"

"Uncle Clyde . . ." I took a breath, unsure where to begin. "We had a terrible falling out. I took off toward the woods, and I kept on running . . . with Joe."

She stopped in front of me and laced her fingers through mine. I, indeed, smelled the perfume of geraniums.

"I need to tell you something," she said, her voice small.

I swallowed. "What is it?"

"Laurence . . . he warned me that if you . . . if you came back . . ." She sighed and looked up toward the sky, stretching her eyes wide, which I knew to be her way of stopping herself from crying.

I squeezed her hand. "What did Laurence say?"

"He told me . . . I could never . . ." She blinked. "I could never see you again."

"What?"

"He said, you and Joe . . . what you did was so wrong. A boy—a boy like him . . ." She held my hand tighter. "A girl like you . . . together." She puckered her lips, as though her words tasted sour. "The Wittens came over this morning and told him they found you two together, sleeping on their property, and—"

"It was only sleeping, Fleur. Uncle Clyde got mad because

I insinuated that he killed my father. I ran off with Joe so Clyde wouldn't hurt either of us."

She rubbed the inner corner of her right eye and looked up at the sky again. "They want to kill him so badly now. Robbie hates himself for not hurting Joe this morning when they found you. He said that if either of you came back . . ." She cupped a hand around her chin to keep it from quivering. "Laurence grabbed me so hard and made me swear I wouldn't see you again. He left bruises on my arm."

"Where?"

She lifted the butterfly wings of her sleeves and showed me purple marks the size of two thumbs, one per arm.

"Oh, Fleur!" I took hold of her elbows with the softest touch I could muster.

"I'm so scared of losing you, Hanalee." She tipped her forehead against mine. "You're the only person here who's worried about what will happen to me, and I'm terrified of what's going to happen to you."

I pulled her close and held her against my chest, my arms locked around her back. Boisterous slides of trombones and the loud belches of tubas ricocheted over the headstones around us, but I squeezed my eyes shut and pushed the picnic away.

"I think something unspeakable happened to my father that Christmas Eve," I said against her shoulder. "Something more damaging than Joe's car. Something related to the boys' desire to hunt down Joe." I lifted my head so that we stood face-to-face again. "Have you ever heard anything about the Dry Dock being dangerous for nonwhites?"

She knitted her sunshine-blond eyebrows. "I don't think so."

"Have you heard anything about the owners' ties to the Klan?"

"I . . ." She grimaced. "Well . . . they do have that sign out front."

"What sign?"

"Do you ever eat at the Dry Dock?"

"No." I shook my head. "We tend to avoid it, but I've always thought it's because Mama doesn't like their food."

She rubbed her lips together. "Well, they have a sign on the door that says, 'We reserve the right to serve whom we please,' but I always thought it was a nice sign. I thought they were saying they didn't want their customers making a fuss over any of their clientele."

My stomach tightened. "I'm not so sure that's a nice sign, Fleur."

"Fleur!" called a male voice to my right. "What're you doing with her?"

I turned my head and found Laurence standing just outside the cemetery entrance, hand in hand with Opal Rickert, a brunette with bobbed hair and a red dress that showed off her skinny knees.

"You stay away from my sister, Hanalee Denney." He let go of Opal and ran toward me.

I took my hands off Fleur and shuffled backward, tripping over my feet.

Laurence grabbed hold of both my arms, and the next thing I knew, my back slammed against an obelisk, and Laurence shoved his face into mine.

"Why'd you have to go and run off with Joe?" He squeezed my arms by my sides and shook me against the stone. "That was the stupidest thing you could have done."

"What are you doing, Laurence?" asked Opal from behind him

with a lift of her plucked and painted eyebrows. "Picking a fight with a girl?"

"Go back to the picnic," he called over his shoulder. "Take Fleur with you."

"Let go of her," said Fleur, running her hands through her hair, and I again saw the bruises beneath her sleeves.

"Go back to the picnic!" he shouted. "Go! Before I hurt her. I swear, I'll hurt her if you don't leave immediately."

The girls retreated, for Laurence's tone carried a rage that chilled me to my core and would have sent me running, too, if he didn't have me pinned against a dead man's marker.

He returned his blue eyes to me and spoke so close to my face, his hot breath blew into my mouth. "You two should have just kept running. Why'd you come back?"

"Joe . . ." My teeth chattered; it took all the courage I possessed to find my voice. "He didn't want . . . we didn't have . . ."

"I want you both gone and far from here. Do you hear me?" He shook me again. "Get out of this state, and take him with you. You're going to get yourselves killed. We're planning a necktie party for him. Do you know what that is?"

"No."

"It's when a person gets raised by a rope from the branch of a tree—not long enough to die, but enough to get scared into running out of town for good."

I froze. "W-w-what do you mean 'we,' Laurence? What are you a part of?"

He loosened his grip and stepped back a foot. The sun shone down on his golden hair and skin, brightening the soft smattering of freckles on the bridge of his nose, just as the rays used to set his skin and his eyelashes aglow whenever we climbed stacks of hay in my parents' field.

"Why do you hate me so much, Laurence?" I asked.

"My family comes first." He placed his hands on his hips, looking tall and sturdy and strong—or at least like a boy pretending to be all those things. "To keep us all safe, we can't afford to associate with a mulatto any longer."

I sank back against the stone and felt my vertebrae become no stronger than blades of river grass.

Don't ever let them hurt you, Hanalee, Laurence had told me himself when he held his arms around me and taught me to shoot his father's gun. *Don't ever let them make you feel small.*

I stepped forward and spat in his face—right beneath his right eye, with those sun-streaked lashes I used to want to kiss—and I walked away from the cemetery.

CHAPTER 17

THE WEEPING BROOK

 SOMETHING HAD CHANGED IN THE air by the time I came around the side of the church and rejoined the Fourth of July picnic. The music had stopped, and an unnatural stillness hung over the grounds. Everyone shaded their eyes with their hands and faced the main highway, where Sheriff Rink's black patrol car reflected the afternoon sun.

In front of the vehicle stood the sheriff, tightly holding the belt surrounding his thick waist. He spoke with Reverend Adder, who stooped as if carrying a great weight on his upper back. Mrs. Adder clung to her husband's right arm and, without warning, howled like an injured dog—the wail of a woman in the throes of early grief. I knew that sound all too well from the night my father died.

My stomach dropped to my toes. I ran toward Mama through the other picnickers, who turned into streaks of red and white clothing.

"What's happening?" I called out. "What happened?"

Mama turned to me with a worried brow. "I don't know. There are murmurings of a death."

Uncle Clyde sauntered our way from the highway, his face wan, his mouth drawn. His arms hung by his sides.

"They found . . ." He slowed to a stop in front of our blanket and tugged a handkerchief out of the breast pocket of his coat. "This afternoon, in St. Johns, along the northernmost stretch of the Willamette River, the body of a young man . . . a young man meeting Joe's description . . . washed ashore."

I dropped down to a crouched position on the grass. No air entered my lungs; I completely forgot how to inhale.

"Breathe, Hanalee." Mama knelt beside me and patted my back. "Come on—take a deep breath."

I dug my fingers into Mama's arm. The world around me turned bright and blurry and distorted, and all I could do was squeeze my mother's flesh and wonder how a boy—a boy alive in our woods just that morning—could have ended up in a body of water miles and miles over the forested hills.

Uncle Clyde took off his coat and flapped the garment in front of my face, which at first caused me more panic, but somehow the air blowing into my nose reminded me how to take a breath. My lungs expanded, and after more gasping and coat-flapping and clinging to Mama, I lay back on our blanket with my knees bent and breathed in a shallow rhythm.

Uncle Clyde rubbed my arms and asked if I could hear him, but he looked so strange and far away, with the glare of the sun shining against the lenses of his spectacles. My brain flitted to an image of him sitting beside my father on a bed, a needle full of morphine at the ready.

"How f-f-far is the r-r-river from our house?" I somehow managed to ask, still seeing the world as shiny and fuzzy, still imagining Uncle Clyde positioned beside my father in Joe's bedroom on a Christmas Eve.

Uncle Clyde made responses I only half heard: "At least sixteen miles . . . Tualatin Mountains . . . he could have gotten a ride . . ." I closed my eyes and pushed his voice into the distance and let the world slip away into darkness.

UNCLE CLYDE CARRIED ME TOWARD HIS CAR. I HAD vague memories of townspeople in red ribbons and white suits staring, gaping, as the man who presumably killed my father lugged my limp body toward the family of a boy who might lie dead on a riverbank—a boy who might have died because of the man who carried me, or at least because of people like him. I heard the reverend murmur something about going to identify the body, and the next thing I knew, my head was jostling against the half-opened window in the backseat of Uncle Clyde's automobile. My stepfather and mother sat in silence in the front seat, and the wind from their open windows screamed past my ears. I stared out at the passing fields and farmhouses and the white clouds smeared across the sky.

We neared a brown-skinned man in a dark suit and a derby hat who lumbered down the highway with a limp. My jaw dropped, and I sat up straighter, and I saw him—my father—right there in broad daylight, wandering in the direction of our house. Daddy raised his head and met my eyes, but the car sailed past him and drifted around a bend, stealing him from view.

"Are you all right?" asked Mama, turning toward me. "I heard you gasp."

I slumped back down in the seat and closed my eyes.

BACK AT HOME, MAMA TOOK HOLD OF MY RIGHT ARM in the driveway and steered me straight toward the front door.

"I want to look for Joe," I said, pulling away.

"No." She pulled back, refusing to let go. "You're not going anywhere by yourself."

"Wait," said Uncle Clyde from the stone walkway behind us. "I want to speak to Hanalee in private."

"About what?" asked Mama, gripping my shoulders.

"I just . . . I need a few words with her"—he readjusted his spectacles on his nose—"to clear up the trouble between us. Help her get seated on the porch here."

I didn't possess the strength or the clarity of mind to keep fighting to run off, so I allowed Mama to guide me up the porch steps and sit me down on our wooden swing built for three.

"Everything will be all right." She kissed the top of my head and patted my shoulder. "Just stay here. Recover. Behave. I'll be inside if you need me."

I nodded and rested my head in my hands, my elbows digging into the tops of my thighs. I focused on all the splinters sticking out from the worn boards of the porch and saw, out of the tops of my eyes, Uncle Clyde's black oxfords clomping up the steps. Then the shiny shoes came to a stop.

"I don't think he's dead, Hanalee," he said, his voice so calm it made me shudder.

"Hmm," I said in a low murmur. "You must be like Mildred, then. Gifted with premonitory senses."

"The northern Willamette River's too far. I was thinking about the logistics on the car ride home. If you were with him in the woods just this morning, he couldn't have hiked over the hills that quickly."

I raised my head. "Unless someone fetched him and threw him into the river."

"If someone wanted him dead, they'd have killed him in the woods instead of going to the trouble of driving him seventeen miles away."

I sat back against the swing and couldn't decide if that statement comforted or troubled me.

Uncle Clyde took hold of one of the white posts that supported the porch overhang. "The Adders and I asked the sheriff to make telephone calls to try to find the two of you. He contacted ports at both major rivers. Some other poor body likely washed ashore and made for a terrible coincidence." He rubbed his left temple, ruffling the short hair that came to a stop above his ear. "I'm sure the mistake is killing the Adders right now."

"They don't care about Joe."

"Don't make such quick assumptions about what parents feel for their children. Including stepparents."

I folded my arms over my chest.

"I want you to know," he said in a voice that quavered with emotion, "that I've made a great many sacrifices for your safety, Hanalee. I've even sacrificed the safety of others to keep you alive."

I narrowed my eyes.

"Don't glare at me." He let go of the post. "Everything I've done since the death of your father has been with the primary intention of keeping you and your mother alive and unharmed."

I blinked at him. "Are you trying to tell me that you married my mother to keep me safe?"

"In some ways, yes. I love your mother dearly, of course, but my reasons for becoming her husband included protecting the two of you."

I sat there, stiff and silent, while he tucked his thumbs into his coat pockets and seemed to wait for my response.

"Well?" he asked. "Do you have anything to say to that?"

"Yes." I pushed my feet against the floorboards and rocked myself on the swing. "What—or *who*, as you put it—did you sacrifice to keep me safe?"

He tapped his fingers against his sides. "I'd rather not say."

"Why not?"

He exhaled a short breath and shifted his face toward the highway. "Because we're living in corrupt times, Hanalee. Even the best intentions can sound cruel when spoken aloud."

I kept rocking and glowering.

"If Joe shows up here," said Uncle Clyde, "if he didn't actually run off to Washington as you claim, I'd like to tell him that I have a friend in Seattle, an old medical-school classmate of mine, who could use an assistant to help with filing and other organizational tasks in his office."

I brought the swing to a stop. "What on earth are you talking about?"

"I want to help Joe find work. I know his time spent in prison will keep him from acquiring the type of position he once aspired to." Uncle Clyde removed his spectacles and used the hem of his coat to wipe a smudge from the left lens. "This friend of mine . . . he has a brother who's like Joe. He'll be compassionate toward the boy. Joe would be safe and well cared for. There's some tolerance in my friend's community."

"Why?" In spite of myself, I looked toward the opening to the woods between the firs on the edge of our property. "Why do you want to help him?"

A swallow bobbed down Uncle Clyde's throat. He placed his specs back upon his nose. "To make amends."

My lips parted, but no words formed.

"If he shows up in this area again . . ." Uncle Clyde wrapped his arms around himself and swiveled in the direction of the woods, as if he, too, sensed Joe's presence there. "Tell him, if he sets aside his anger toward me, I'll do whatever I can to make sure no one puts him back in that prison. I'm well aware of the state's push for sterilization of homosexuals, and I don't agree with the practice in the slightest." He swallowed again. "It'll only cause more anguish."

"Why do you need to make amends, Uncle Clyde?" I cocked my head at him. My heart pounded, but I kept talking. "What did you do?"

My stepfather returned his gaze to me. "Joe was the sacrifice."

I gripped the bottom edge of the swing.

He shifted his weight between his legs and failed to elaborate.

"Are you admitting to me," I asked, my heart thumping faster, my palms slick with sweat, "that you allowed an innocent sixteen-year-old boy to head to prison . . . and not a guilty one?"

"You don't—"

"Is that what you mean by a 'sacrifice'?"

"It's not . . ."

"Not what?" I asked. "Not as bad as it sounds?"

"It's not what you think," said Uncle Clyde. "Just . . . just know I'm on Joe's side. I want him to be all right."

I stared up at my stepfather without blinking.

He nodded toward the front door. "Now go inside and drink a couple of glasses of water. And eat. You're probably dehydrated and hungry."

I refused to tear my eyes away from him.

"Go on now." He opened the door for me. "I don't want you getting sick."

"I'm going to look for him."

"You'll do no such thing. You tore your mother's heart to pieces last night. I know you don't care for me in the slightest right now, but show the woman who raised you and loves you some respect." He pulled the door farther open. "Come inside. For her. *Now.*"

With a deep groan from the bottom of my throat, I pushed myself off the swing and did as he asked, for the sake of my mother, but not without one last glare at him, and one last peek at the woods.

CHAPTER 18

DESPERATE UNDERTAKINGS

 RESTING ALL AFTERNOON ALLOWED me to stay wide-awake and alert at night when Mama and Uncle Clyde retired to their bedroom. They closed their door, and through the wall I heard murmurings and the squeaks of dresser drawers—and then private sounds I didn't care to hear. I pushed my hands over my ears and told myself, *Drink it, drink it, drink it . . .*

I slid out the box of toys and Klan notes and derringer ammunition from beneath my bed and dug around for the bottle of Necromancer's Nectar.

Another fiery spoonful.

Another rush of heat exploded through my chest, my stomach, my head, my extremities.

This time around, I remembered to screw the cap back on and tuck the bottle into its hiding place, and as soon as I pushed the box back beneath my bed, my hair, too, seemed to catch fire. Flames scalded my cheeks and my neck, and I couldn't stand the heat of my burning curls against my back a moment longer.

Time jumped forward again. I found myself in the hall. Then the middle of the staircase. The kitchen. I fetched silver scissors from Mama's worktable and cut my hair until my skin cooled and the fire died. Dark locks coiled around my feet like a pile of lifeless snakes.

Lifeless adders.

The front door.

The front yard.

The highway.

The crossroads.

A fog that smelled of briny ocean air veiled the patch of road that lay before me. The compulsion to seek more answers propelled my feet forward.

Using the toe of my right shoe, I drew a circle in the dirt. The mist dampened the skin of my now-bare neck and kissed the tip of my nose. I stepped inside the marking and peered ahead at an undulating mass of gray that blocked the view ten feet ahead. The fog seemed a living creature . . . waiting . . . listening . . . silent.

"Daddy," I called, and my voice splattered against the haze and the flat stretch of land without the slightest quiver of an echo. "Daddy, I need to talk to you. I need to find out which doc you

200

meant. Come here." I clasped my hands beneath my chin and trembled. "Please . . . come. Talk to me."

I bowed my head and sniffled and shook. I heard no owls, no bats, no barking hounds. No patrol cars puttered through the night, searching for boys who sinned with other boys or for girls with brown skin who ran off with such boys. Fleur rested in her bed, safe, I hoped, from her brother and the Wittens. Joe lay in some unknown place—alive or dead, I still didn't know.

And there I stood, alone, waiting. Ready for a ghost to tell me whether I should kill.

A sound started up ahead in the fog.

I lifted my chin and held my breath.

Footsteps thumped my way. One sturdy leg and one leg busted by a Model T limped beyond the wall of fog and shadows, and all the hairs on my neck and arms bristled. I stood on tiptoe, as though the act of rising up tall would better allow me to see my father approach.

The silhouette of his hat and his body emerged first. A shadow— a well-dressed shadow—wandered toward me and transformed into a familiar face and a derby hat and a suit with shining buttons. Once he walked more fully into view, Daddy smiled a sad smile and removed his hat.

I settled back down on my heels and forgot how to speak.

"Are you staying safe, honey?" he asked, holding his derby by his side, above his right hip. "You look distressed. No one's hurting you, I hope."

"I'm . . ." I tore my eyes away from his and peered out at the dark fields beside me. "I'm tempted to commit a murder."

"I beg your pardon?" He pushed forward another two steps. "What in tarnation are you talking about, Hanalee? Who on God's green earth would you want to murder?"

I swallowed and shook with shame and terror. "When you said you blamed the doc for your death, did you . . . d-d-did you mean Dr. Koning?"

He stepped back on his good leg. "Oh, sweet Jesus, no, Hanalee. Don't you dare kill the doctor."

"But . . . is it the Dry Dock, then? The restaurant?"

"Yes, the Dry Dock. If I'd just stayed away from that place that night, if I'd been a stronger man, I'd still be alive today."

I wrapped my arms around myself. "W-w-what happened to you there?"

"Don't you dare go to that place by yourself. Don't even get close to it."

"What happened? Tell me."

"I—" His eyes welled with tears, and he turned his face away. His chin quaked, and his left hand clenched and unclenched by his side.

I inched forward inside my circle and heard my soles scraping across bits of gravel—a sound that made the surfaces of my teeth buzz. "You've got to tell me, Daddy. I've got to know."

"It was supposed to have been a peaceful night. Christmas Eve." He rubbed his neck with the hand that didn't hold his hat, and a tear rolled down his left cheek, landing on his lips. "People should have been in church, or at home with their loved ones, but hate won out that night."

"Oh . . . Daddy . . . what did they . . . ?" I covered my mouth and muffled my own tears. "What did someone do to you?"

"Go far away from Elston, darling." He put his hat back on his head. "Get yourself educated. Come back with weapons of justice and truth that will kill off the ignorance and fear. Help the innocent live in peace." He shook his head with a look of warning in his eyes. "But don't you dare murder anyone. Don't become like one of them."

I nodded. "Yes, sir."

"You understand me?"

"Yes. I do."

"Don't forget me, Hanalee."

"I won't." I pressed my hot hands against my cheeks. "Of course I won't."

"But don't kill for me, either."

I nodded again. "All right."

"Now go home. It's not safe out here. Stop coming out to find me all by yourself."

"Haven't you been trying to find me? Isn't that why you've been wandering this road?"

"I've been trying to . . ." He swallowed and cast his eyes toward the stretch of highway behind me, while the fog spilled over his shoulders. "To make it back home. To protect your home from those boys."

"Which boys?"

"I'm not entirely sure," he said, and the fog closed around him like a fist.

All I saw were his legs and his shoes.

"Daddy?"

"There's nothing worse," he said from within the haze, "than luring boys who aren't yet even men into a life of hatred."

The mist snaked around his legs and swallowed him up entirely, robbing me of my view of him. I stood alone on the road, in the devil's circle, racking my brain to remember if Laurence had been sitting in the Paulissens' pew that Christmas Eve that Daddy died. As hard as I tried, as much as I strained to remember Fleur seated beside both her mother and her brother, I couldn't help but think Laurence wasn't there.

"Was Laurence at the Dry Dock?" I asked into the darkness. "Was he one of the boys?"

"Maybe," I heard my father say in a voice grown distant and hushed. "They covered their faces in those ungodly hoods. I'm sorry. I should have been stronger."

CHAPTER 19

NEVER DOUBT I LOVE

 I TORE THROUGH THE WOODS TO the Paulissens' shed, intent on telling Joe what I'd gleaned from my encounter. I'd forgotten all about the body in the river and Mrs. Adder howling with grief against her husband's side. I'd even forgotten that Joe had had to leave the shack.

I threw open the door, and a cold streak of remembrance shot through my veins. The little building sat in darkness. A small strip of moonlight showed me the cot, empty and bare, parked against the right wall. The rectangular card house still stood on the floor by the foot of the bed, but nothing else—no books nor blankets nor carpetbags—indicated signs of a recent habitation.

"Oh, Joe." I covered my face with my hands. "I forgot. Oh, God."

I turned and whisked myself back over the creek and through the trees and hedges to my family's property. The white sliver of a moon ducked behind treetops and the traveling fog, which rolled across the land, blanketing the world in a mist that chilled and smothered. To find my way, I relied on my memories of the pathways, as well as the strange golden luminescence of the woods that Mildred's potion always offered. Gray-green moss dangled like fringe-covered sleeves from the arms of the branches overhead.

I pushed down my fears and pressed onward.

On the easternmost edge of our land stood the weather-beaten stable I'd mentioned to Joe. I sprinted toward its dark silhouette, my feet clapping across the ground and hope surging through my blood. The roof sat crooked; the boards of the walls had warped from summer suns and nine long months of rain each year. Yet the structure remained upright, intact enough to hide Joe.

I grabbed the handle and hoisted open the door with a whine of rusted hinges. The scent of horse manure hit my nose, despite the animals' long absence. Mama had sold off our mare and stallion the summer before, to make ends meet, before Uncle Clyde proposed to her last fall.

"Joe?" I asked into the dark void in front of me.

Something moved from within—a rustle in the hay.

I jumped back and asked, "Who's there?"

"It's me."

Joe's voice.

"Holy hell!" I grabbed my throat. "Are—oh, God. Oh, Christ." I sank to my knees in the all-consuming blackness. "You're not a ghost now, too, are you?"

Joe struck a match and set his kerosene lantern aglow in a far corner, brightening his face and a blue button-down shirt.

"What are you talking about?" he asked.

"They found a body—one that looked like you—up by the river, by St. Johns."

"Well"—he shook out the match—"it's not me."

"You're not a ghost?"

"If I were, don't you think I'd find a better place to haunt than a rickety old stable that reeks of horse shit?"

I shoved the door closed and stumbled toward him across hay. A floorboard buckled under my weight, tripping me, and I had to hold my arms out to my sides to keep from falling.

Joe pushed himself off the ground. "Are you all right?"

"I took that Necromancer's Nectar again."

"Oh, jeez, Hanalee." He tramped toward me on bare feet. "Why'd you do that to yourself again? You already got your answer the other night."

I tipped too far to my right, and my hip and shoulder slammed against the floor. No pain registered within my bones or my nerves, so I kept right on talking.

"I needed to speak to my father again," I said from down on the ground—a roiling sea of wood and stale hay. "I had more questions."

Joe leaned down and hooked his fingers into my armpits.

"Hey!" I called out. "What are you doing?"

He dragged me around in the opposite direction. The dark rafters above whirled in a half circle, and my brain and stomach spun.

"Where are you taking me?" I asked.

"I'm bringing you over to my blanket so you don't kill yourself. There's some rusted old farm equipment stored in here, and you could smack your head on it if you're not careful." He pulled me over to the same blanket we had shared in the woods and draped me across the coarse fabric. The floorboards beneath dug against my spine and tailbone. The blanket scratched my bare neck.

"What's this?" Joe uncoiled one of my curls. "You chopped off your hair?"

"I got too hot after drinking that potion. I think the rest of my curls might still be lying all over the kitchen floor."

"Your mother's going to kill you."

"Better her than someone else."

Joe plopped himself down beside me with a sigh that sounded like the hiss of one of his matches. He set the lantern between us and leaned his shoulder blades against the wall. The light of the flame danced up and down his face, showing me the brown of his eyes and the soft curve of his lips, as if to verify he still existed as a person made of flesh and bone. I liked the way he looked—liked it so much, my chest ached—but I forced myself to stay quiet about that particular sensation.

"Well," I said with a sigh myself, "I'm awfully sorry for whoever that was who ended up in the river. Your poor father drove up to St. Johns with Sheriff Rink to identify the body."

"I'm sure my pop was praying that body was mine."

"I don't know about that. I spoke to him this morning."

He tilted his head. "You spoke to my father?"

"When I got back this morning, your parents and Sheriff Rinky-Dink were at my house with my parents, waiting to pounce."

"Oh." He shrank back against the wall. "Sorry about that."

"You should be. You tossed me smack-dab into the middle of the Spanish Inquisition, Joe. I'll have you know I both defended your honor and mourned your death, all in one day."

He breathed out a curt laugh. "I doubt you mourned me with too many tears."

"Stop saying things like that."

"Like what?"

"Stop saying people would be glad about you dying. I stopped breathing when I heard about the body in the river. Dr. Koning had to help to bring air back into my lungs."

Joe shifted his legs but didn't say anything in reply.

"You're welcome," I snapped.

"Thank you. For worrying."

I covered my eyes with my right hand and settled my breathing.

"Do you believe you spoke to your father just now?" he asked.

I nodded, my hand still cupping my face. "Yes. I do."

"And what did he say?"

"He said . . ." I swallowed. "You're not going to like this at all when I tell you."

"What did he say?"

I lowered my fingers to my right cheek and peered up at the dark rafters, expecting to see the yellow eyes of a rat or a bat staring down at me. "He said he meant the Dry Dock, not Dr. Koning."

Joe lifted his head off the wall. "*What?*"

"Mildred told me that my father had just become a bootlegger. He picked up a crate of whiskey from her house that Christmas Eve, and I'm willing to bet my life he delivered it to the Dry Dock."

Joe ran his fingers through the shorter strands of hair toward the back of his head. "Are you sure this is genuinely your father's spirit you're seeing?"

"Jeez, you didn't ask me that question the other night, when you thought Daddy meant Uncle Clyde."

He grumbled and kept mussing up his hair.

"He said something about boys being there," I continued. "Boys in 'ungodly hoods,' as he called them. And today at the picnic, Laurence told me—"

"Why were you talking to Laurence?"

"He came after me when I was speaking to Fleur, and he told me what was meant by the 'necktie party' line on those Junior Order of Klansmen notes. He said a person gets hoisted off the ground with a rope around his neck—not long enough to kill him, but enough to scare him out of town."

Joe didn't respond. I craned my neck to better see him and found his eyes haunted, his breathing shallow.

"Are you all right?" I asked.

He blinked. "Did Laurence say that's what people are planning to do to me?"

I nodded and exhaled an erratic breath that made the lamp's flame jump. Shadows streaked across Joe's face.

"What about Dr. Koning?" he asked. "What about the medicine he shot into Hank Denney's veins in my bedroom?"

"I don't think there was any medicine, Joe. Daddy told me not to blame Uncle Clyde—or to murder him. He begged me not to kill anyone and insisted I leave town and better myself. He said to come back to Elston when I've got the tools to change things."

Joe's brow creased. He curled his lips and slammed the back of his head against the wall, jangling a harness hanging above him. "How the hell would something that occurred before I hit your father have caused his death?"

"The other night, my father said that his heart wasn't strong enough that Christmas Eve. I think the Klan might have terrorized him. Do you remember what he looked like when you saw him walking down the road? Was he holding a crate of whiskey?"

"No, there weren't any crates."

"Did he walk strangely, like he was hurt? Or scared?"

"I didn't even see him until I hit him." Joe rubbed his face with the palms of his hands, stretching his cheeks and his eyes in the flickering light. "He just sort of sprang out from nowhere in the dark. I was already out of sorts."

"Because Deputy Fortaine caught you in your father's car with that boy."

Joe's hands froze on his face. His eyes turned a liquid shade of brown, and I sobered up enough to realize I had trod into delicate territory. I pressed the heels of my palms against my eyes to dull an awakening pain.

"If Clyde Koning didn't kill your father," said Joe, sounding out of breath, "then even if something did scare him before I saw him that night . . ."

I waited for him to continue. My hands stayed shoved against my eye sockets.

He sniffed. "If Dr. Koning didn't kill your father, then that would mean that I did, after all."

My palms slid down to my temples. "I don't entirely believe that to be the case."

"My mind has always insisted that Koning killed him behind the closed bedroom door," he said, his voice cracking, "but what if I've only been lying to myself? What if I caused your father more than a busted leg and a sore arm? I drove home after drinking, for Christ's sake."

"I know you did, and I still hate you for that, to tell you the truth." I smacked my hands against the floorboards and wiggled myself up to a seated position against the wall. "But Uncle Clyde said some things that made me feel absolutely certain that something more occurred that night. He told me that you were a sacrifice back then. He also spoke of sending you off to a better life—up to a job in Seattle—to appease his guilt."

"When did he say all of that?" asked Joe.

"Today, right after the Fourth of July picnic—after I thought you'd died, and he was trying to reassure me you hadn't." I shifted myself in Joe's direction and braced my palms against the floor in front of me. "Somehow, Uncle Clyde was still involved, even if he didn't administer poison. I'm certain the Klan was involved, too, including the Junior Order of Klansmen. I don't think it was ever a simple case of a white boy hitting a black man with a car."

"That's what I've been telling you all along."

"I know. But I don't think you had the details quite right." The muscles in my neck stiffened. I grabbed my left shoulder and massaged a spot that ached. "I feel I should go to the Dry Dock. There's that big old tree sitting between it and Ginger's . . ."

"You can't just wander into a restaurant and ask if anyone there tried to lynch your father."

"What else am I supposed to do? Sit around and wait for someone to finally tell me the truth about what happened that night? No one is ever going to explain it to me. You've hidden parts of the night from me yourself."

"What parts?"

"The part about Deputy Fortaine letting you drive off with just a warning. Why didn't you tell me he helped you?"

Joe squished his lips together and scratched at his knee through a hole in his trousers. "He didn't help me. He still ended up blabbing about what he saw to Sheriff Rink. The sheriff came marching up to my holding cell the next morning and called me a . . ." He winced as though the sheriff had just struck him. "He called me every vicious word he knew. And he talked the judge into raising my bail. I couldn't go home before my trial because of them. I just sat there in that cell with local drunks and thieves who liked to run their fingers through my hair."

I sank against the wall and remembered what Mildred had said about telling the sheriff about Joe and the boy from the party. I even opened my mouth to say it wasn't the deputy who'd blabbed, but I soon closed it, not wanting any more hate passing between people.

Joe tilted his face toward the ceiling, his jaw tight. His outstretched throat looked vulnerable and pale in the light of the flame, and I experienced the terrible image of a knife slicing across it.

"People hurt you, didn't they?" I asked. "You've got those scars above your eye and on your lip . . . and those bruises on your ribs."

"I haven't been touched by kind hands since I was with that boy on Christmas Eve 1921—let's put it that way." He lowered his eyelids. "I'm just glad they let me out on good behavior before anyone in that prison got wise to how I am."

"Did you know anyone who went through the"—I softened my voice—"procedure?"

Joe nodded. "A fellow not as young as me, but still pretty young for a prisoner. A college student. They put him in jail specifically because he got caught with another man in a Portland hotel." Joe opened his eyes and blinked in the direction of the ceiling. "The guards and a doctor took him out of his cell one day. They promised to relieve him of his urges. They spoke of eugenics saving the country from all its problems. 'Sterilization for the good of all,' they said. 'The purification of America.'" Joe rubbed a knuckle against the inner corner of his right eye. "Then they brought him back in pain . . . all the life in him, gone. Just"—he shook his head—"gone."

I slid my hand across the dusty floorboards that divided us. "I'm sorry."

Joe cleared his throat and pushed himself up higher against the wall. "That's when I straightened up and made sure I didn't make a peep of complaint or get pushed into any fights. People beat on me and humiliated me, but I just let them—I just took it—because I wanted to get the hell out of that place before anyone took a scalpel to me."

"And then you came home to your father calling you terrible words . . . and me, shooting a bullet past your ear."

"I probably would have shot at me, too, if I were in your shoes." He turned his face toward mine. "We've got to be very, very careful about putting you in situations like that, though—ones that could get you arrested. They're operating on women, too, and the fact that your skin is dark will only make them want to stop you from having children all the more."

I drew my knees to my chest and sank my chin against my right wrist. "People are really doing that sort of thing? Stopping other races from procreating?"

"There's rumors that's a major part of eugenics. Cleansing the country of anyone who isn't white, middle- or upper-class, and fit enough to perpetuate the 'master race.'"

"Are you sure?"

His voice dropped to a frightened whisper. "Yes. I'm sorry, but . . . yes."

I tucked my chin against my chest and shivered. "I don't want my life to end in tragedy, Joe."

"I don't want it to end that way for you, either."

"And I don't think it should."

"No, it shouldn't."

"What's wrong with people out there," I asked, "deciding who gets to have children and who has to be stopped from living the type of life that feels right to them? What's wrong with them?"

"Hanalee . . ."

I glanced his way when he didn't continue, realizing he wanted me to look him in the eye. "What?"

"Have you ever gotten the chance to love someone?"

My face warmed, and my hair burned white-hot again, despite its shorn length. "H-h-how do you mean?"

"Have you had the chance to experience what it's like, despite all the obstacles against you?"

I squirmed and felt my mouth go dry, but I didn't avert my face from his.

"I don't know." My voice sounded small and naked in that empty horse stall. "A boy and I used to kiss when we were younger. A white boy, of course. I've never even seen a black boy my own age in Elston."

"Who'd you kiss?"

I turned away.

He snickered. "Oh, come on—tell me. You're not going to find me running out and gossiping."

I sighed against my wrist and warmed my flesh with my breath. "It doesn't even matter. We were just kids playing fairy-tale games. It didn't mean anything."

I heard a piece of wood creak and I jumped, but I quickly realized the sound came from Joe leaning his head farther back against the wall.

"Do you hope to get married someday?" he asked.

"As long as I don't fall in love with a man the wrong color."

He exhaled a steady stream of air through his nostrils. "I think *love* and *wrong* are two deeply unrelated words that should never be thrown into the same sentence together. Like *dessert* and *broccoli*."

I laughed.

Joe moved the lamp to the other side of himself and scooted toward me. The sides of our arms and legs bumped against each other.

"No matter what happened the night your father died, Hanalee," he said, "you need to go to a place that will treat you better."

"I know."

"Elston's got nothing to offer you."

"I can't go anywhere before I know the full truth about my father. I don't care if I get hurt in the process. I've got to find out what happened and learn who was there with him. Otherwise . . . I know he'll keep wandering that road." I relaxed my shoulders against the wall. "*I'll* keep wandering."

Joe closed his mouth and nodded. "All right. I'm still not entirely convinced Dr. Koning doesn't own the largest share of responsibility, though. I don't trust him in the slightest."

"We can't kill him, Joe. Not until I find out what happened at the Dry Dock."

"I know." He picked at the hole in the knee of his trousers. "What am I supposed to do, then? Just sit here and pretend to be dead?"

"I'll see if I can get my mother to take me to the restaurant tomorrow morning. I know she doesn't want to let me out of her sight, so I'll see if she'll help me. And then I'll find you and tell you what I learned. Where do you think you'll be late tomorrow morning?"

"Here, maybe." His eyes shifted toward the shadows surrounding the front door. "Or at the pond."

"Bathing again?"

"I just can't seem to get the stink of that prison off me," he said with a chuckle that carried a weight to it.

I pushed my arm close against his. "You don't smell like prison. You smell of these woods. You smell nice."

He lifted his face to mine with a startled look in his eyes, and I worried I'd accidentally just sounded as though I loved him.

"I like honeycombs," I said with a wiggle of my feet, and a second later I burst out laughing.

"What?" he asked with a smile that seemed confused.

I shook my head. "Nothing. Just proving that it might not be my skin color alone that's a hindrance to relationships." My face sobered. I stretched out my legs in front of me and let his arm warm mine.

We both turned our gazes toward the empty stable in front of us, and we just sat there, side by side, until the oil burned out and the lamplight died without even a sigh of warning. The sudden darkness made a small knot tighten in my lower back. I couldn't see my own hands and legs in front of me.

"I'll bring you some oil and food tomorrow," I said, scooting up to a kneeling position, my knees slipping on hay. "Stay as hidden as you can. I don't want anyone finding and hurting you."

He nodded. I couldn't see him in the slightest, but something about the way he breathed showed me the movement of his head.

I reached my hands into the blackness and found the sturdy slope of his shoulders, and then his neck and the line of his jaw.

"What are you doing?" he asked with a nervous snicker, pulling away a little. "You're tickling me."

I leaned forward and kissed his forehead, grazing part of an eyebrow with my lips.

His snickering stopped. He went still below me. I let my mouth linger a moment longer before I pulled away and sat back on my heels.

"What was that for?" he asked in a whisper.

"Christmas Eve 1921 is far too long a time to go without a kind touch, Joe." I cupped his cheek in my hand, and then I slipped away into the darkness and found my way home.

CHAPTER 20

BE EVEN AND DIRECT WITH ME

 MAMA WOKE ME UP THE NEXT MORN-
ing by shaking my right shoulder.

"What's this?" she asked.

I opened my eyes to find her dangling one of
the clipped locks of my hair in front of my face.

"When and why did you cut off your hair, Hanalee?"

I shrugged. "I just . . . I got too warm last night."

"Hanalee Denney!" She squeezed her fist around the curl.
"Every night it's some new cause for alarm with you."

"I spent most of yesterday thinking Joe Adder had been murdered. What do you expect from me?"

"Stop worrying about Joe Adder."

"Everyone in this town who's different seems to die."

"Joe's not dead. Reverend Adder called this morning to tell us the body wasn't his. The authorities in St. Johns now believe it was the body of a young rumrunner who fell off a boat."

I pushed myself up to a seated position and didn't make a peep about spending time with Joe in the shed the night before. "Well . . . I'm relieved it wasn't him."

"I know you must be"—she sat down on the edge of my bed—"*confused* about how you're supposed to feel about Joe."

"I'm just worried about him. A shocking number of people seem so passionate about wanting to hurt him."

"After all that talk of an elopement, though . . . I don't want you to get your heart broken."

I picked at the edge of my quilted bedspread.

She stretched my brown curl across the width of her right thigh. "I know how it feels to be told you're not supposed to love a certain person."

I swallowed down a thickness in my throat and changed the subject. "Why didn't you ever tell me Daddy was a bootlegger?"

She lifted her head. "What?"

"You heard me."

"Who told you that?"

"Mildred said Daddy picked up a crate of whiskey from their house that Christmas Eve."

She swiveled to her right and faced me directly. "Why must we keep dwelling on that night, Hanalee? It was just a terrible, tragic accident, for heaven's sake."

"But some parts about it still don't feel right." I wrapped my hand around her left wrist. "Be honest with me, Mama. Was Daddy a bootlegger?"

She clenched her teeth, and then she nodded. "We had trouble making ends meet after the war. Europe didn't need our crops anymore. Prices fell."

"And that's what he was doing Christmas Eve?"

"Yes." Mama closed her eyes. "He received a telephone call for a moonshine delivery, right before we were to head out to church. He was already dressed and ready to go with us, but he insisted he needed to make that delivery because the money would be good. It would pay for Christmas."

I lowered my head. "He risked his life, just to make sure we celebrated a nice Christmas?"

"That's how your father was. I never met a man with a bigger heart. That's why I loved him so dearly."

"Who called him?" I asked.

"He wouldn't say." Mama's shoulders fell. "He wouldn't tell me where he was going. He simply said he'd earn us a nice bit of money and be home by the time we returned from church."

"Have you ever wondered"—I scooted closer to her across the mattress—"if something happened to him during that delivery that would have made him stumble into the road in front of Joe's car?"

"No, not at all." She pulled her wrist out of my fingers. "Fate simply didn't work in the favor of Joe and your father that night. No matter what Joe might have told you, Daddy's death was nothing more than a matter of terrible timing and the mistakes people make when it comes to liquor."

"Then why does Uncle Clyde feel guilty about Joe's imprisonment?"

Mama's face hardened. "Your stepfather does not feel guilty, Hanalee. Stop saying such things."

"Uncle Clyde told me he wants to send Joe to work with a colleague up in Seattle who would be kind to Joe—to appease his own guilt over what happened that night. He called Joe a 'sacrifice.' A sacrifice he made to protect me."

My mother leaned away from me, and her mouth twisted into that difficult-to-watch grimace people make before they're about to either scream or cry—but she did neither. She simply stared at me with that about-to-explode expression, her lips trembling, her eyes crinkled and bloodshot. "When did he tell you that?"

"Yesterday, when he spoke with me in private on the front porch." I glanced toward my open doorway. "Where is Uncle Clyde?"

"He went to work early. Joe's potential drowning troubled him, so he didn't sleep much last night, and he wanted to—"

"You see what I mean?" I leaned forward. "Joe makes him feel guilty."

Mama stood up from my bed and pressed a hand to her stomach. "No. I will not let you lead me down this road of suspicion again."

"Do you think Daddy went to the Dry Dock on Christmas Eve?"

She blinked as if startled. "The Dock?"

I nodded. "Do you think the owners were the ones who made the request for moonshine?"

"I already told you, the Franklins haven't sold alcohol since

Oregon first banned the sale of liquor, back when you were just a child."

"Fleur says they have a sign on the door that reads 'We reserve the right to serve whom we please.' Do you know anything about that?"

"I'm aware of that sign." She brushed hair out of her eyes. "That's why I avoid the restaurant."

"In case they order me to leave?"

She rubbed her right arm, the same way Mildred scratched at her elbow when avoiding prickly subjects. "Hanalee, it's true, some people around here have a problem with your skin color. I'm not going to deny that fact. It wouldn't be fair to you if I pretended otherwise."

"Like the ladies from church who urge you to bleach my skin."

"Those older ladies are harmless and don't know any better. Just ignore them. For the most part"—she stopped rubbing—"people embrace you. It's only an obnoxious few spreading words of hate and bigotry."

I crossed my legs in front of me and pulled at the edges of my quilt again. "Doesn't it seem awfully strange, though, that a mysterious someone telephoned Daddy, and just a short while later he stumbled in front of Joe's car in the dark . . . and then suddenly died from a busted leg and a sore arm? *After* the crate had been delivered?"

Mama clamped her arms around herself and gave a shudder. "I don't even want to imagine people in this town deliberately hurting your father."

"I don't, either, but I would like to go to that restaurant and see what the Franklins have to say."

"No, absolutely not. You are not going to the Dry Dock when they have that sign hanging on their door."

"Do you know them?"

"The Franklins are a couple from the church in Bentley. I've never actually met them."

I raked my hands through my short hair, digging at my scalp, knowing what difficult question would need to be asked next. "Do you believe in ghosts, Mama?"

She frowned and stiffened. "Don't you dare mention *that* again."

"Not only have I seen Daddy during the past few nights, but I've spoken to him."

She stepped back.

"He looked me in the eye," I said, "and he told me—"

"You did not see your father."

"He said, 'I put full blame on the Dock'—meaning the Dry Dock. And then he told me, 'If I'd just stayed away from that place that night, if I'd been a stronger man, I'd still be alive today.'"

"No," said Mama. "Your father did not speak to you."

"Yes, he did, Mama." I rose to my feet. "I'm going to that restaurant this morning. I don't know what I'm looking for exactly, but I've got to head there, or I won't rest."

Mama's face shifted from me to my window, as if she could see the restaurant from two miles away, beyond all the trees and the farms. "You can't go to the Dry Dock on your own."

"Then come with me."

Her throat rippled with a swallow.

"Please, come with me." I held out my hand to her, my fingers shaking. "I'm never going to be able to sleep another night until I learn what happened to Daddy before he and Joe crossed paths on that road. And I don't think Daddy will rest until then, either. Please. Come."

She hesitated. I watched as gooseflesh dotted her arms, and her chest rose and fell with breaths that looked labored. But then she straightened her back and reached behind her.

She grabbed hold of my hand and held it as fiercely as if she were saving me from drowning.

POURING WHISKEY INTO
A SEWER, PROHIBITION-ERA
UNITED STATES.

CHAPTER 21

MOST UNNATURAL MURDER

 MAMA AND I WALKED THE NEARLY two-mile stretch into town and stopped to catch our breath beneath the shade of a pine tree. Mama wiped her forehead with a hand-kerchief, and I peered through the needles at the restaurants up ahead.

Ginger's was an old brown shack—a former watering hole for local farmers, loggers, and railway men. The Dry Dock, on the other hand, sat in a fine white clapboard building with fancy gables and dormer windows and two brick chimneys that rose from the roof's black shingles. Wicker rocking chairs welcomed visitors for a moment of respite on the low front porch, and a wreath of dried flowers hung on the door, above a handwritten sign I'd always mistaken for a list of the hours of operation. The two establishments sat uphill from a creek, separated by that monstrous old oak tree with branches thicker than any I'd ever swung from as a child. Fleur, Laurence, and I could have wrapped our arms and legs around the limbs and pretended to be tigers if we'd ever played downtown instead of in the woods.

"I want to go inside," I said.

"You can't." Mama mopped her flushed cheeks with the white cloth. "And don't you dare try."

"Would they throw me out?"

"Yes, I'm sure they would."

I took a step closer, and my nose filled up with the sweet scent of pine sap. The tips of my fingers felt sticky, even though I hadn't touched the tree. "Doesn't it make you fighting mad," I said, "that everyone else's daughters can step inside the place, but not yours?"

My mother lowered the handkerchief from her face. "Of course it does, Hanalee. Why do you even have to ask?"

"Then take me inside." I snapped a clump of dry needles off the branch dangling in front of my face. "I don't want to sit down at one of their tables or take one bite of their food. I just want to speak to the owners."

"You can't just walk up to people and accuse them of hurting your father a year and a half ago."

I eyed the Dry Dock.

It would take no more than twenty long strides to get myself to the front door.

I glanced at Mama.

I eyed the Dry Dock again.

"Hanalee . . ."

"I'm sorry, Mama." I dashed off to the front door upon legs grown strong and swift from running through the woods with Joe.

The black-lettered sign greeted me on the door:

WE RESERVE THE RIGHT TO SERVE WHOM WE PLEASE.

I flinched, for the phrase, up close, stung like a slap across my face. I grabbed the iron handle and pulled the door open.

Mama ran up behind me and caught the door, but not before I slipped inside. She followed me, and a little gold bell tinkled above our heads.

The dining area before us consisted of one large room with square tables draped in ivory cloths amid pale green walls adorned with paintings of canoes and kayaks drifting down the local creeks and rivers. Only one set of customers—a mother, a grandmother, and three golden-haired children, all regulars at our church—dined in the place on that quiet Thursday morning. The air carried the aromas of eggs and maple syrup and freshly brewed coffee, and I almost worried I'd walked into a private family home.

An embroidered poem, stitched in periwinkle-blue thread, hung on the wall beside my right elbow.

Kind hearts are the gardens,
Kind thoughts are the roots,
Kind words are the blossoms,
Kind deeds are the fruits.

A slender woman with gray-streaked hair—hair pulled tightly enough off her face to stretch out her eyes—rounded a corner from the far end of the dining room. She wiped her hands on her white apron and smiled at first, but then she caught sight of me, and her hands fell still; the smile wilted.

"No." She pointed straight at me. "She cannot be inside this establishment. Didn't you see our sign on the door?"

"But I know these customers," I said, looking toward the family at the table who held their forks frozen in midair between their plates and their mouths. "They go to our church. They're not afraid of me . . . or disgusted by me. Are you?"

"No!" The restaurant woman pointed to the door. "You need to leave these premises immediately."

"What's wrong, Esther?" A bug-eyed man in his forties or fifties sauntered around the corner behind her, a spatula in hand, a white chef's hat sitting cockeyed on his head.

The woman—his wife, I presumed—crossed her arms over her bosom. "The Denney widow brought her mulatto daughter in here."

"No, no, no, no, no." The man puffed up his chest and put his hands on his hips with the blade of the spatula pointing upward. "I don't know what you think that sign on the door means, but we refuse service to mulattoes and Negroes. This state opposes miscegenation, I hope you know."

"Oh, I know all about the state's marriage laws all too well," said Mama. She clutched my right shoulder and pulled me back. "Come on, Hanalee."

I pulled away from my mother's grip. "I don't want to sit down and eat your food in this filthy Klan restaurant. I just want to ask you a question."

The couple exchanged a look with their mouths drawn tight, and the women at the table fished for money in their handbags. No one denied that the restaurant supported the Ku Klux Klan.

"Should I telephone Sheriff Rink?" Esther asked her husband.

"Only if this woman doesn't remove her girl within five seconds."

"Did you summon my father, Hank Denney, here the night he died?" I asked, pulling forward, for Mama tried to tug me backward with all her might. "Did you ask him to deliver moonshine that Christmas Eve of 1921?"

"Get out of this restaurant now," said the man, pointing toward the door with his spatula.

"We tolerate bootleggers as little as we tolerate the likes of you," said Esther behind him, squeezing her apron into a ball between her hands.

"Just answer my question!" I shouted. "Was my father here Christmas Eve 1921, like his restless spirit told me he was?"

The man paled. His wife grabbed a little gold crucifix she wore around her neck and rubbed it with one of her thumbs. The little family from our church gathered up their belongings and scrambled out of the restaurant with a slam of the door behind them.

"Hanalee, please." Mama snatched my hand. "Let's just get out of this place and forget about these people."

"Listen to your mother, girl," said the mister. "Go!"

"I'll have you know"—Mama thrust out her chest and glowered at the man—"I intend to speak to the reverend about this establishment and let him know you don't practice the love of good Christians."

"Don't talk to me about being a good Christian." The man held up his spatula, as if unsheathing a sword. "You're a whore with an illegitimate child, as far as the law of this state is concerned. You ought to be ashamed of yourself and thankful you're free of your bootlegging Negro." He raised the spatula above his head, as though he intended to lunge and strike us with it, which was both ludicrous and terrifying at the same time. "Now get out of here."

"Are you in the Klan?" I asked, backing up with Mama's hand clamped down on my wrist.

"I am, indeed." The man lifted his round chin. "A proud, card-carrying member, and I'm not ashamed to say so."

"Was my father here the night he died?"

"You come inside my establishment one more time"—he nodded toward the window, toward the shadow of the oak tree stretched across the glass—"and I'll show you exactly what happened to your daddy that Christmas Eve."

My skin went cold. The shadows of the branches bobbed across the window—the ugliest sight I'd ever encountered.

"Get out!" barked his wife. "You've ruined our breakfast shift, you no-good black and white trash."

Mama wrenched me away, and we stumbled out the door into the glaring light of day.

I pushed her fingers off me and staggered through the tall grasses surrounding the oak, whose weighty boughs blocked the sun and made me colder still. I braced my hands against the trunk and panted through a painful stitch in my side. Just above my eyes hovered the shapes of letters, carved in the grayish bark. I assumed they were the names of local sweethearts.

"Let's go, Hanalee." Mama hooked her hand around my elbow.

"Wait a minute." I lowered my head. "Let me catch my breath."

My vision blurred. I stared at the trunk and watched the rippling stripes in the wood sharpen into focus. A carved name caught my eye, to my right: *Delia Downs*.

I leaned toward the words, my eyes narrowed, for Mrs. Downs was the black war widow who had been attacked in her home in Bentley—a woman scared into moving out of the county. Someone had scratched a line across her name.

"What is this?" I asked.

"What is what?" asked Mama.

I ran my hands over the bark, and a splinter stabbed my thumb. A slew of other names emerged in the jagged pieces, seemingly rising to the surface, the same way I spotted multiple crawdads in the creek whenever I first thought there were none.

Hank Denney—scratched out.

Joseph Adder.

Benjamin Fortaine.

Greta Koning.

Clyde Koning.

Hanalee Denney.

"L-l-look." I pounded my palm against the names. "Look what they've done."

Mama rested her hands on the trunk, and her eyes widened and darted back and forth over the letters in the bark. She rubbed her right palm across my name, as though she could erase the etchings

234

with her hand, and she breathed with a bleat of panic I'd never heard from her before—a wounded sound, a desperate sound.

"Who did this?" Her nails tore at the bark that contained the *H* and the *a* of my name. "What's happening here?"

"It's the Klan. They're not just anti-Catholic, Mama. They're threatening to hang Joe. I saw one of their pamphlets, and Laurence told me himself . . . they'll hang him."

"Oh, God." Her fingernails tore at Daddy's name, chipping away the letters—letters that someone had crossed off as though a task had been completed.

"I want to talk to Uncle Clyde," I said.

"Uncle Clyde is not a part of them! Don't you see his name on this tree?" She slammed her palm against the name *Koning*. "They want to get rid of him, too. And the deputy. Oh, God." Her knees buckled. "What's happened to this town?"

"Please, Mama . . ." I wrapped my arms around her waist and shouldered her weight, tasting her hair on my lips. "Let's go talk to him in his office right now. Let's tell him it's all right to speak the truth. I want to know what happened to Daddy that night. I've got to know, or I'll end up exactly like him."

CHAPTER 22

O HEAVY BURDEN

 HAND IN HAND, PETRIFIED OF LET-
ting each other go and allowing the world to
topple entirely off its axis, Mama and I marched
up the cement front path to the forest-green
Queen Anne house that served as the home of
Uncle Clyde's medical practice, one block north of the main highway. The building had once housed the doctor, too, before his
marriage to Mama brought him inside our own walls.

The front parlor sat empty, with only my stepfather's stiff brown
furniture and potted ferns greeting us. An ugly gold clock ticked
away the seconds upon the mantel of the brick fireplace, next to a
framed photograph of Mama.

"Clyde!" My mother slammed the front door closed behind us. "Where are you?"

"Greta?" Uncle Clyde slunk out of his office from around the corner, carrying paperwork of some sort. He looked like a tall frightened mouse, tiptoeing into view that way. I imagined a tail tucked between his legs. "What's happened?"

"Do you have any patients in here?" asked Mama.

He straightened his posture. "No."

My mother locked the door with a loud click.

"What happened?" My stepfather's forehead creased.

Mama turned back toward him and covered her eyes with one hand.

"Greta?" He stepped closer. "Talk to me."

I slipped my right hand into my mother's left one and took a breath. "All three of our names are carved on that tree next to the Dry Dock," I said, "along with Joe's, Deputy Fortaine's, Daddy's, and Mrs. Downs's."

Uncle Clyde's face froze, and he gasped the word "What?"

"Someone crossed off the names of Daddy and Mrs. Downs," I continued, "but the rest of our names are just sitting there"—my voice faltered—"waiting for us to . . . to disappear."

"I know that the . . ." Mama moved her hand to her mouth and made a burbling noise. Tears washed down her cheeks and slid across her knuckles. "As much as it sickens me, I'm aware of the prejudices against Hanalee and me, and even Joe, and I've heard the rumors about Deputy Fortaine being a Jewish man. But why you? What's happening here? Why aren't any of us safe?"

Uncle Clyde inhaled with a force that brought a flash of pain into his eyes. He put a hand on his side and glanced over his shoulder at his office around the corner. "Come . . . sit down." He waved us over with fingers that looked as though they weighed too much. "We have some things to discuss."

Mama drew a short breath, and I squeezed her fingers again. We followed my stepfather into his little octagonal office that fit into the house's front tower. A second fireplace hibernated in one corner of the room, swept of all ashes, a log sitting on the grate, awaiting the first snap of cold in the fall. Upon the mantel stood a photograph of all three of us—Mama, me, and Uncle Clyde—from their January wedding. I stood in the middle of them, in front of Joe's father's church steps, the stair rails damp from a recent rain.

Uncle Clyde seated himself behind his desk, a wide worktable with a deep cherry hue, topped with a wooden pencil holder, a lamp, a set of medical books, and a tidy pile of papers. Mama and I took the two chairs with rounded backs directly across from him, below a copy of the Hippocratic oath and a framed degree from the University of Oregon Medical School.

With a whine of his chair, my stepfather leaned forward on his elbows and rubbed his right fingers across his lips, which paled to the same bone shade of white as his hand. "I committed a crime, Greta."

All the blood left my face. The room tipped to the left, but I clutched the cold armrests and fought to keep my senses about me.

"What crime?" asked Mama in a voice that sounded as though it strained her throat.

Uncle Clyde's eyes flitted down toward the grains of wood

squiggling across his desk. A clock in the room—a plain, round wall clock with a no-nonsense frame and large Roman numerals—ticked with fidgety beats of the second hand.

"Clyde?"

"Perjury." My stepfather cleared his throat. "I lied in court about the severity of the injuries Joe Adder caused Hank with that Model T."

Mama stared at her husband with eyes moist and unblinking.

"Did you kill him?" I asked, squirming in my chair. "After you told Joe to wait in the front room, did you hurt my father?"

"No." He shook his head and folded his hands on his desk. "I did not kill Hank Denney, Hanalee. Nor did I ever want to. I genuinely liked your father and mourned his death as a good friend."

"Then who did kill him?" asked Mama, scooting forward in her chair. "Why did you lie? Why did you court me and marry me and move into our house, knowing you'd lied?"

"I tried to do the right thing—I went straight to the sheriff and told him what I learned from Hank before he died."

"What did you learn?" asked Mama. "What have you kept from me this past year and a half?"

"Hank's neck . . ." Uncle Clyde licked his lips and placed his hands around his throat. "When I examined him, I saw bruising . . . redness . . . encircling his neck. I asked him what happened, and he seemed"—he removed his hands from his throat—"*distressed*. Terribly distressed. He wouldn't talk to me about it at first, not until I said that the marks looked like rope burns."

"A mock lynching?" I asked before Uncle Clyde could speak the words himself. "A-a-a necktie party?"

"What?" asked Mama. "H-h-how do you know about something like that, Hanalee? How do . . . why would—?"

"Laurence taught me about that just yesterday." I cleared my throat. "And I saw it written on a Klan pamphlet. Laurence said that a group called the Junior Order of Klansmen is planning to do the same thing to Joe."

"'Junior Order'?" asked Mama, looking to Uncle Clyde. "They've recruited youths into performing this violence?"

"Their violence is limited." Uncle Clyde removed his spectacles and rubbed his eyelids so hard, I could swear I heard them squeak. "But apparently it does, indeed, happen, more often than what's reported."

"So . . . you're saying . . ." Mama shook. "Th-th-they hanged him? My Hank? They hanged him?"

Uncle Clyde lowered his hand to his lap and nodded. "I'm sorry."

"At the Dry Dock?" I asked.

"Yes." Uncle Clyde's voice dropped to a tone that creaked from the depths of his chest. "According to Hank, Mr. Franklin, the owner of the Dock, telephoned him that night and asked him to deliver a case of whiskey. When Hank arrived, a party of Klansmen awaited with a burning cross and a rope slung around that oak tree."

Mama's chin sank against her chest, and she broke into tears that made her shoulders convulse.

Uncle Clyde drew a handkerchief from his breast pocket and handed it to Mama.

I rubbed my mother's arm but kept my eyes on my stepfather. "What did they say to my father?"

"Hank said they told him"—Uncle Clyde swallowed—"that they didn't tolerate bootleggers. They fastened a rope around his neck, and they raised him a few feet off the ground . . . to scare him." His jaw stiffened. "To scare him out of town."

"Who were the Klansmen?" I moved my hands to the armrests. "Did Daddy say? Were they boys?"

"Young men were, indeed, in attendance." Uncle Clyde peeked at the doorway of the office, as though worried someone might be eavesdropping.

I craned my neck and checked behind me but found no one there.

"The Kleagle—that's what they call their local recruiting officer," he continued, and I turned back to him. "He was initiating members into the Junior Order. That part seemed to make Hank the saddest of all. Boys his own daughter's age fastened that noose around his neck."

"But they didn't kill him?" asked Mama, lifting her face with the handkerchief pressed against her nose.

"No, they sent him on his way with a warning of a full lynching if he didn't leave the state immediately. Hank said his left arm hurt like the dickens after that. He walked down the highway toward your house, and the pain grew so blinding, he ended up tripping into the road"—Uncle Clyde folded his hands on his desk, and his knuckles quaked against the wood like a telegrapher tapping a line of Morse code—"in front of Joe's car, as you already know."

"But the car injured him." Mama scooted to the edge of the chair and grabbed hold of Uncle Clyde's desk. "Joe still caused his death, didn't he?"

"The Model T broke Hank's leg," said Uncle Clyde, "that's for certain. But the arm pain and the breathing difficulty started at the Dry Dock. Hank said he hadn't been able to catch his breath since the Klan let him go." Uncle Clyde slid his glasses back over his ears. "Joe hitting him with the car certainly didn't help matters, but Hank died because his heart was giving out after that mock lynching. I've observed other men with failing hearts who experienced that same arm pain, and I'm ninety-five percent certain his heart would have stopped beating that night even if Joe never drove down the road."

I raised my chin. "Why did you lie in court?"

"The sheriff threatened to harm you if I spoke of what I'd learned." He looked me in the eye. "I couldn't risk them hanging you, too."

I bowed my head—not to pray, but to absorb the density of those words, which bore down on my spine like a slab of stone. Beside me, Mama covered her eyes, and all three of us sat in silence.

"What do we do now, Clyde?" asked Mama, still pressing her palms to her eyelids. "What do we do?"

"I don't know." Uncle Clyde shook his head, his eyebrows puckered behind the top rims of his glasses. "I honestly don't know if it would be better to stay and fight or to take Hanalee somewhere else. Somewhere where she won't be threatened, and where she's free to marry whomever she wants and live wherever she wants."

"I'm attending law school as soon as I'm able," I said, pushing myself upright in my chair. "Get me out of this place so I can obtain a solid education and come back with the tools to fight these high-

and-mighty bigots. I don't want to hear about people deciding who can live and breathe—and breed—another minute longer."

"Oh . . . sweetie . . ." Mama reached over to my wrist. "I don't even know if many law schools are accepting female students, let alone students who'd be considered 'colored.'"

Uncle Clyde nodded in agreement. "It would be an awfully difficult path, Hanalee, but not an impossible one."

"I'm already on a difficult path," I said with a wheeze of exasperation, my palms raised toward the ceiling on the armrests. "What do you think this is?"

Neither of them responded, so I sank back in the chair, feeling quite old and weathered and exhausted—and sick with dread that my old friend Laurence had helped hoist my father into the air with a lynching rope when he was just sixteen.

CHAPTER 23

THE DEVIL TAKE THY SOUL

 OUR NERVES FELT RAW AND SEARED.

We rode back home in Uncle Clyde's car, for he insisted upon driving us. The anonymity of the Klan's hooded guises obliterated my trust of *everyone* in Elston. When the postman waved at Uncle Clyde in front of the central mailbox, I couldn't help but think the man's smile seemed forced and his eyes lacked warmth. Twelve-year-old boys with bicycles gawked at the glass display windows of the candy store, and the sight of their caps and short pants caused me to shrink back against my seat. They reminded me that the KKK recruited the young, to sink the organization's influence deep into the soil of our community. Poisonous rivulets of hate and fear spread beneath the town's sidewalks and buildings and strangled the beauty that had once bloomed throughout Elston.

Or . . . maybe I had always been fooled into believing the town possessed beauty.

Uncle Clyde's Buick tore through the sunlit countryside. I stared out my backseat window at the blur of hayfields and woods, and I thought once again of the golden-haired boy who used to run ahead of his sister and me as we hurried into the forest after chores. I could still hear Laurence's childhood laughter, the low, mischievous chuckles, the teasing cry of "I bet you can't keep up with me, Hanalee."

I blinked into the breeze and called to Mama in the front seat, "Do you remember Laurence being in church on Christmas Eve when Daddy died?"

She tamed down strands of her hair flying about in the wind, and with a heavy sigh, she said over her shoulder to me, "I can't remember a detail like that, Hanalee. That whole night turned into a fog, and it's feeling even more distorted and upsetting now."

"I think I remember Fleur telling me he was sick that night." I leaned my elbow against the side of the car, on the curved ridge below the window. "Yes . . ." I nodded toward the train tracks we passed, as if the church sat beside them, opened and arranged just as it had looked in December 1921. "I'm positive he wasn't there. I remember Fleur and me discussing how empty the church seemed without both her brother and my father there at the service that night." I pulled on the back of the front seat, hard enough to make

Uncle Clyde's shoulders move. "Did Daddy say he heard Laurence's voice at the Dry Dock?"

"No," said Uncle Clyde, "he didn't mention specific names."

"Laurence wouldn't hurt your father." Mama twisted toward me. "You two grew up together. His mother and I grew up together."

"I'm certain Laurence is in the Klan, Mama."

She frowned. "How do you know that?"

"He's friends with those Wittens, and the Wittens are in the Klan. Joe and I stumbled upon their family's shed the other night, and that's where I found the pamphlet with notes about an initiation involving a necktie party." I sank down in the car seat and chewed the nail of my right pinkie.

Mama put her hand on Uncle Clyde's forearm. "Will you drive us to the Paulissens' house?"

His face whipped toward hers. "Why?"

"I don't want anything dividing our families, especially not the Ku Klux Klan. Polly and I have always been too close of friends for anything to come between us." Mama crossed her arms and shifted in the seat.

Just up ahead, the dirt driveway leading to our own house came into view, beyond the trees with wine-colored leaves. Uncle Clyde slowed his speed and positioned the gears and his foot in such a way that the Buick chugged and jerked like a horse about to buck us into the street.

"Please, Clyde." Mama sat up straight and built up her voice into a brick wall. "Take us to the Paulissens."

Uncle Clyde stiffened his back and shifted the clutch and

the throttle until the car rumbled down the road, toward Fleur's house at a steady pace. I watched the trees alongside the road bend and rustle from the wind, and I thought their trunks looked darker and thicker than I remembered, their leaves less plentiful, more ragged. Everything suddenly appeared different. Unfamiliar. Inhospitable.

My stepfather steered the sedan around the bend, through the thicket of elms that led up to the front of the Paulissens' property. I saw the Ford truck, parked in front of the white house with all its blooming flower boxes, and my stomach churned at the sight of what surrounded the vehicle: local boys, a whole pack of them, gathered about like feral dogs. Laurence. Robbie and Gil. Other fellows from our school—Harry Cornelius, Al Voltman, Oscar and Chester Klein. They wore their caps pulled down over their eyebrows and were dressed in either overalls or shirts with the sleeves rolled up. Half of them smoked cigarettes. Robbie drank openly from a bottle of booze. Laurence clutched one of his father's Colt pistols in his right hand.

Uncle Clyde's shoulders inched toward his ears, and Mama breathed so rapidly, I worried she might faint.

The boys turned our way and watched us roll to a stop, the tires scraping across stones in the dirt. The engine popped and coughed with an obnoxious, hacking commotion that made us stand out even more than we already did.

Laurence looked to Robbie, who gave him a firm nod, and then my former childhood friend drew in his breath and strutted our way, the pistol by his side.

Laurence stopped in front of Uncle Clyde's window and leaned down. "What can I help you with, Dr. Koning?"

"Mrs. Koning would like to pay a visit to your mother."

Laurence glanced at Robbie again and received a cockeyed grin.

"I'm sorry, Dr. Koning." He rested his free hand on top of the car, right above Uncle Clyde's head. "Our house is now supporting the principles of a white homeland for Oregon. Your family isn't welcome here anymore."

"Laurie Paulissen," hissed Mama, leaning across Uncle Clyde. "What despicable lies are you learning from those delinquents over there?"

"They're not lies, ma'am."

"I helped raise you, for heaven's sake, and your mother helped raise Hanalee. I changed your diapers and wiped your snotty little nose, so don't you dare stand there and tell me I'm banned from your house."

"None of that matters anymore, Mrs. Koning." Laurence scratched the side of his leg with his pistol. "I don't want Hanalee coming anywhere near my sister. Not only is her skin color muddying this community, but we all know that she slept with a sexual deviant who's threatening the moral integrity of Elston."

I turned my face away from Laurence's and discovered Mrs. Paulissen observing the scene through the butterscotch curtains of the living room window. From her bedroom window up above, Fleur watched over us with her palms pressed against the glass. My heart dried up into tiny granules of sand that scattered throughout my chest and piled in a sickening lump at the bottom of my stomach.

"Back up this automobile"—Laurence slapped his hand against the roof—"and keep away from this house."

"You're making a terrible mistake, son," said Uncle Clyde, shifting the gears into reverse. "Your father would be appalled to hear the words coming out of your mouth right now."

Laurence scrunched up his face, and without even hesitating, he raised the pistol in the air and cocked the hammer. At that, Uncle Clyde leaned his arm across the back of his seat and shot us backward down the driveway, swearing under his breath—something about "goddamned baby rattlesnakes not knowing when to stop biting."

"WHERE'S JOE, HANALEE?" ASKED MY STEPFATHER AS we rounded the bend to our house.

I fidgeted, nudging the back of the front seat with the toes of my shoes. "Why do you ask?"

"Because those boys will kill him if we don't get him out of Elston."

I closed my eyes and forced myself not to feel a single thing—not anguish, not anger, not terror. A wicked pain bore down on my chest, squeezing a fist around my heart; if I wasn't careful, the pressure would suffocate me. My heart would fail to keep beating, like my father's.

"I don't know where he is," I said. Something about the tone of Uncle Clyde's voice triggered an uneasy twinge in my gut. Trust had turned into a precious commodity that I'd only hand out with great care.

"If you do hear from him"—he glanced back at me for the breadth of a second—"if he comes to the house, looking for your help, hide him out in the stable, and then let me know he's there."

The fear of forgetting how to breathe again gripped me. I hooked my fingers around the bottom of my seat and thrust my nose into the air streaming through the windows until oxygen expanded my lungs.

CHAPTER 24

THAT IT SHOULD COME TO THIS

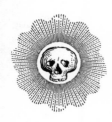 UNCLE CLYDE INSTRUCTED MAMA and me to remain inside the house, behind locked doors, while he honored appointments with two late-morning patients who required his attention. He drove away with the promise of returning by lunchtime.

Mama and I paced the entry hall.

My mother kneaded her scalp and tousled her hair with her fingers. "I'm going to start sorting through all the boxes in the basement. I don't think we'll stay here much longer. Go look through your belongings. Set aside anything you don't absolutely need."

"All right." I gulped down a bout of nausea and trudged up the staircase.

"And at some point I should fix your poor, bobbed hair," she called up after me. "Good Lord, it's uneven as heck."

"I don't care about my damn hair right now, Mama."

"Mind your mouth, Hanalee."

"I don't care!"

I slammed my bedroom door shut, slid the box of toys out from beneath my bed, and plucked a spare bullet from the cardboard container of ammunition.

I MADE MY EXIT WHILE MAMA SCOOTED BOXES AND trunks around in the basement. The racket of crates screeching across the basement floor, the hullabaloo of Mama swearing and tossing about our belongings down in the musty hollow beneath the house, allowed me to click open the front door and close it behind me without interrupting her task. I brought my key along so I could lock her in and keep her safe. To keep her from fretting too badly, I even left a note on my bed:

Mama,
I'll be back within the hour. I'm not far, and I'm safe, but I fear Joe isn't.
All my love,
Hanalee

My search for Joe commenced in the stable. I found a peach pit lying in the stall where I'd sat with him the night before, but all other traces of him had vanished. A lump filled my throat. I gathered up my courage and ventured into the forest, but not without first stopping by the log that concealed the derringer inside the oilcloth. I emptied the gun of the used cartridge case, loaded the pistol with the second bullet, and strapped the holster to my right thigh. Once my legs firmed up and a wave of dizziness passed, I carried the weapon into the shadows of the forest, my eyes and ears alert for all movements. My back refused to straighten to a fully upright position; I prowled across the deer trail, hunched and wide-eyed. I held the gun with both hands, the barrel cradled in my left fingers, my right hand clutching the grip, and my feet sounding too loud to my ears.

The shed at the edge of the Paulissens' property lay empty as well.

A jay screeched above my head and soared over the shed with outstretched wings darker than sapphires. Something moved in the water beyond the little white building—a slight ripple of sound, scarcely a murmur. I kept the pistol out in the open, gripped with all my might in my sweating hands, and in near imitation of the manner in which I had stalked toward the pond the first time I hunted down Joe, just four long days earlier, I tiptoed through the rushes and made my way around the shed.

"Joe," I said in the quietest voice I could muster without actually whispering.

Another ripple.

"Joe?"

"Hanalee?" he asked from somewhere unseen.

I approached the pond's bank. "Where are you?"

"Back over here, around the bend."

"Bathing?"

"Yes."

Whether he wanted me to see him or not, I hustled down the slope to the pond and maneuvered myself around the trunk of a wide fir. Around the bend, I reached a small inlet, sheltered and shadowed by trees cloaked in moss an electric shade of green.

Joe's head and neck stuck out of the water from among a cluster of lily pads.

I lifted my skirt past my right knee and shoved the pistol into the holster. "Get out of there!" I yelled in a whispered shout. "Laurence is at his house right now, carrying one of his guns, surrounded by the Wittens, the Kleins, and Harry and Al."

Joe stiffened. "You saw them?"

"Yes! Uncle Clyde drove Mama and me over there, and—"

"Why were you going there?"

"I'm not going to explain anything right now." I stepped into the pond, shoes and all, and squished my feet through muck I couldn't see down below the murky surface. "Get out of there. Now!"

"Don't panic. I'm coming."

"Hurry!" I waded two feet farther, soaking the hem of my dress.

Joe swam backward, away from me, but he got hung up in the lily pads.

I grabbed my head in frustration. "Get out of the damn lily pads!"

"Stop panicking."

"Where are your clothes?"

"Over here." He rolled onto his stomach and swam to an area where his feet must have touched the ground, for he stopped treading water and started walking.

"Jesus, Joe! You're as slow as a turtle."

"Stop snapping at me. It doesn't help." He climbed out of the water and onto the bank without a stitch of clothing on his body.

I cupped a hand over my eyes, but my absence of sight made me feel as though I stood in an open field in the middle of a lightning storm. I dropped my hand from my face and hustled around the edge of the pond, my pulse drumming in my ears. Joe moved about in the rushes, facing away from me. I saw him turning the legs of his cotton drawers right-side out.

"Hurry—please!" I said, shading my eyes with one hand to avoid looking at him. "Put your drawers on backward if you need to. Just move faster."

"Haven't you heard of privacy?" He shoved a foot through one pant leg. "Jesus Christ, Hanalee."

"They hanged my father, Joe." The hand cupping my eyes wavered. I lowered my fingers to my jaw. "They hanged him from the oak tree at the Dry Dock that Christmas Eve."

Joe slid his other leg into the drawers and pulled the waistband up to his navel. He turned around and faced me, and his eyes softened. "They hanged him?"

I nodded. "They got to him before you even drove down that road. They raised him off the ground by his neck—a mock lynching. A 'necktie party.' They told him to get out of town. His left arm hurt badly afterward, and he could scarcely breathe, and that's why he tripped into the road in front of your car."

Joe picked up his trousers from the ground. "He came out of nowhere."

"You shouldn't have been driving after drinking, Joe. Uncle Clyde said he's ninety-five percent sure Daddy was already dying before you reached him—his heart was failing. But you shouldn't have been out there like that."

"I know."

"It was stupid. You could have killed people."

"I know."

"I hate you for that."

"I'm sorry."

"I hate you."

"I'm really sorry."

"I can't fully forgive you."

"I know."

"But I don't want you to die." I wiped my hands on the sides of my dress. "Put your trousers on. We are *not* going to let a bunch of bigots put us in graves in the prime of our youth."

Without a word, he bent over and stepped into his pant legs.

I picked up his shirt. "Where are the rest of your belongings?"

"I hid them inside your stable." He buttoned up the pants.

"Come on." I tossed his shirt at him. "Throw the sleeves over your arms, and let's get going. You can button up later."

He did as I asked, sliding his hands through the openings in the sleeves and shrugging his shoulders into the shirt.

We circled back around the inlet. My flooded shoes squeaked and slipped on dirt and mud, but I didn't care. I just wanted to get out of those woods. I grabbed hold of a low branch and swung myself around the fir that marked the entrance to the shore of the main pond.

"Joe?" asked someone up ahead, from the opposite side of the shed.

I froze. Joe edged closer, but I put up a hand to stop him.

"Is that you?" asked the voice again—a familiar voice. A boy's voice I'd known all my life, although it had deepened over time. Deepened and hardened.

I peeked back at Joe, and he mouthed the name *Laurence*.

Before I could duck back behind the fir, Laurence stepped around from the front of the shed.

His shoulders jerked when he saw me. "Hanalee?"

"Go back, go back!" I said to Joe, and we turned and dashed back around the inlet with our feet squelching through the mud.

Joe reached behind himself and grabbed my hand, and he hoisted me to higher ground above the slippery bank.

"Stop running!" called Laurence.

I glanced over my shoulder and spotted him brushing through the leaves no more than twenty feet behind us.

With my hand still in his, Joe darted us down another slope and around a bend. We circled so fast, my head spun, and before I knew what was happening, Joe was pulling me by his side on the ground behind a downed spruce, amid a patch of ferns that towered above us. We lay there and panted with our hands cupped over our mouths.

Laurence ran across a cluster of nearby leaves, and his feet came to a stop not far beyond our log.

"Joe?" he called out, and he sounded as though he were turning around a full three hundred and sixty degrees.

Joe lay behind me, his heart beating against my back. He tucked his arm around my waist, as though creating an extra barrier between Laurence and me.

"Hanalee?" called Laurence. "I don't have a gun. You don't have to hide."

I willed every muscle in my body to remain still. Silent breaths escaped my nose, and I kept my mouth clamped shut out of fear of releasing an unintended gasp.

"Come on." Laurence's shoes trampled through the undergrowth beyond the log. "Stop hiding. I need to talk to you both."

With a slow and cautious movement, Joe lifted his arm off my middle and eased his hand down the side of my thigh. I stiffened at first, then tried not to laugh, for his fingers tickled.

I peeked over my shoulder at him, my eyebrows raised, but he just shook his head and mouthed, *Shh.*

"You've got to get out of here—*now*," said Laurence, still rustling through the nearby leaves and grasses. "The plan is to torture and terrify you, Joe."

Joe grabbed hold of my skirt and lifted the hem past my knee, exposing the leather of my holster and the bulge of the pistol inside.

I nodded and reached down for the gun beneath the flap, but Joe took hold of the wooden grip first.

"Let me take care of this," he whispered into my ear.

"You don't know how to shoot," I mouthed to him over my shoulder.

"He's my problem. Let me take care of him."

"No," I squeaked, louder than I'd intended.

"Joe?" asked Laurence.

Joe flinched, and I managed to slide my hand under his and grab the pistol.

"Joe?" Laurence hopped on top of our log and gave a start when he saw us lying down in the ferns.

I jumped to my feet and pointed the pistol straight at him.

"Whoa, whoa, whoa!" Laurence raised his hands and stumbled backward off the log. "Put that down, Hanalee."

Something ugly snapped inside me when he said my name. I climbed after him with the derringer aimed at his chest, and my finger hungered for the feel of a pulled trigger.

"Put the gun down." Laurence backed into the base of a fir. "Put it down!"

"No! Not before you answer a question."

"What question?"

My right thumb hesitated on the hammer. "Were you at the Dry Dock the night the Junior Order of Klansmen lynched my father?"

"Stop pointing the gun at me!"

"Were you there?"

Laurence looked away from me. "No."

"Don't lie to me." I raised the pistol toward the center of his forehead, seeing the shine of perspiration there.

"C-c-come on." Laurence's hands trembled in the air. "P-p-put down the gun, Hanalee."

"You taught me how to use this gun, Laurence. You taught me how to shoot with my aim dead-on, and you told me, 'Don't ever let them hurt you, Hanalee. Don't ever let them make you feel small.' Do you remember that?"

His lips turned a grayish shade of blue, but he managed a meager nod.

"Do you remember how you swore you wouldn't let anyone hurt me or belittle me?"

"P-p-put—"

"Were you part of the group that tied a rope around my father's neck and raised him off the ground?"

"No!" cried Laurence. "I swear, I wasn't there."

"I sure don't remember seeing you in church that Christmas Eve."

"I wasn't there."

"I don't believe you; I didn't see you." I stepped two feet closer to my former friend—my beloved, blue-eyed boy who resembled Fleur so much it hurt my chest—and I shoved the gun against the skin above his eyes.

"Oh, God." Laurence burst into tears and lowered his elbows.

"Hanalee, don't!" yelled Joe behind me. "He's telling the truth. He wasn't part of the Klan that night."

"I don't believe that. I *know* I didn't see him in church."

"He wasn't there," said Joe. "I know—because he was with me."

The pistol quaked, Laurence shook, and the entire world seemed to quiver and rumble and brace for a volcanic eruption. Joe's words changed and re-formed and replayed in my brain before they made any sense.

He was with me.

The boy.

The other boy in the car.

Laurence.

I glanced back at Joe, my aim still centered on Laurence's head. "He was with you that Christmas Eve? In the Model T?"

"Yes." Joe nodded.

"But . . . the boy . . ." I shook my head, confused. "The boy from the party?"

"I never went to any party." Joe took a step forward. "It was just him and me, sharing a drink, finding a moment to spend together."

"That's a goddamned lie," said Laurence, spitting as he spoke. "I know what you're implying, Joe, but that wasn't me. I've got a girl right now—Opal. Voluptuous, eager-to-please Opal."

"You want to die by Hanalee's hand, Laurie?" asked Joe, planting his right foot against a log with a fern growing out of the middle. "Or do you want to speak the truth?"

"I don't engage in hanky-panky with other boys. I'm not some goddamned fairy."

"You mean you don't get *caught* engaging in hanky-panky with boys," said Joe, "but you sure were eager to . . ." Joe stepped back and rubbed the back of his arm across his mouth, as if wiping away a remembered kiss. "I kept my mouth shut when the sheriff questioned me, Laurie. I protect the people I love. I don't throw them to the wolves."

My arm vibrated from the force of Laurence shaking on the other side of my gun.

"I don't love boys, Joe," he said. "That's disgusting."

Joe lifted his chin and swallowed, and his eyes filmed over with tears. "You sure didn't act like it was disgusting when you kissed me."

Before I knew what was coming, Laurence shoved me aside. He lunged toward Joe and punched him in the face with a sickening crack that sent birds scattering out of the trees. Joe fell back and slammed to the ground. Laurence groaned and bent over at his waist, his right fist cradled in his left hand. I gasped and stepped closer and found a shock of bright red blood pouring from Joe's nose. He covered his face with his fingers and rolled onto his side with his eyes squeezed shut. Both boys moaned in pain.

"Go home, Laurence." I nodded in the direction of the Paulissens' house. "Go soak your hand and calm down."

"He's a dead man." Laurence backed away, still bent over with his fist tucked against his chest. "I was trying to help you, Joe, but you're a dead man now."

"Stop threatening him, and don't you dare bruise Fleur's arms ever again." I clasped the derringer firmly in my right hand and aimed the barrel toward his brown shoes, debating if I should raise it toward his head again. "Do you hear me, Laurence?"

Laurence attempted to stand up straight. Strands of his blond hair hung down over his eyes, and the hand he cradled swelled and purpled.

"Go!" I cocked the hammer.

Laurence skidded backward through the ferns. "You're crazy, Hanalee."

"Go!"

He turned and hightailed it off into the trees.

262

CHAPTER 25

A VERY PALPABLE HIT

 JOE REMAINED ON HIS SIDE WITH HIS hands clamped over his nose, blood streaming through his fingers. He groaned some more and brought his knees to his stomach.

I uncocked the derringer—my hands shaking, my heart racing—careful not to fire and draw more attention. "We've got to get you back to the stable." I stuffed the pistol back into the holster on my thigh. "We've got to hide you."

"Christ." Joe winced and sucked air through his teeth. "I think he broke my nose." He lifted his hands away from his face.

I cringed at the bleeding purple lump that used to be the bridge of his nose. More blood leaked from his nostrils and ran across his lips and his teeth. Every part of his head seemed to bleed.

"Oh, Joe," I said.

"Is it bad?"

"If you can just get up and walk for a little while, I'll make you comfortable in the stable." I knelt down, wrapped my arm around his back, and brought him partway up to a sitting position. Drops of scarlet rained down on his partially buttoned blue shirt, but I ignored the gore and kept nudging him to stand. "Come on." I gripped both his arms, lifting, hoisting. "It's just a short walk."

He helped lever himself off the ground, and we got him to his feet with his left arm dangling around my shoulders and his weight pressed against my right side. I stiffened my muscles and trudged forward, which inspired him to do the same.

We shuffled through the pine needles and fallen leaves with a swooshing racket. My eyes darted about the trees. I didn't know if I was hearing just our footsteps alone or if Laurence and the other boys also crept across the forest floor. No animals seemed to stir. No birds or buzzing insects. It was simply Joe and me against other human beings.

We made it across the clearing in front of the shed and stood on the precipice of the slope to the creek.

"We've got to head down this embankment," I said. "Do you think you can do it without falling?"

Joe tried to nod, but he ended up coughing up blood that spattered his shirt. "Oh, God!" he said when he saw the mess on his clothing.

"It's probably just because your nose is bleeding. You're swallowing your own blood." I edged us both forward. "Come on."

He fought to keep his balance and grew sturdier the closer we

got to the bottom. My own feet slid on damp soil, but I quickly righted myself to keep from toppling both of us.

"I'm all right," he said at the edge of the creek. He took his arm off me. "I can cross on my own."

I held on to his back to check if he wobbled. "Are you sure?"

He nodded. "My legs are fine. The pain's in my face."

"Let me go before you so I can help." I stepped onto the first boulder and held out my hand for him.

He clasped my fingers and followed me across the path of rocks, while the water trickled and bubbled below our feet.

"You would have shot him, wouldn't you?" he asked when we reached the other side. "If I didn't tell you where he was that night, you would have killed him."

I pulled hard on Joe's hand and sped us past the deer trail leading to the Paulissens' house. "It terrifies me to think how much I wanted to shoot him."

"I think you made him piss his pants."

"I did?"

Joe half snickered, half groaned. "I think so."

"Well, let's hope so. If he's hurrying to change his underwear, that'll give us time to get out of these woods."

We broke into a trot, for the thought of Laurence gathering up his friends infused my legs with power. I kept my pace slow enough for Joe yet fast enough to stay safe.

I squeezed down on his hand. "We're almost there."

Sunlight from beyond the woods shone across the pinecones and needles scattered on the trail ahead of us. The air warmed. Home awaited just a short way ahead.

"We've got to stay behind the tree line and head to the other end of the yard," I said. "My mother's cleaning out the basement, as far as I know. I don't want her peeking out a window and catching us."

Joe nodded, his teeth clenched against the pain.

We made it through the section of woods that bordered the property behind our open land. I forced us to stop and listen for footsteps, and then we knelt down and darted through the rows of berry bushes to the stable waiting to our left.

Once inside the small outbuilding, I found Joe's belongings stashed beneath his blanket in a dark corner.

"Here, let's get you comfortable." I spread the brown cloth across a pile of hay and helped ease him down to the ground.

The makeshift mattress crunched beneath his back. His head lay at an uncomfortable-looking angle with no pillow behind it, and he closed his eyes and struggled to catch his breath. Blood stained his nose, his lips, his chin, his shirt . . .

"I know this probably isn't helping you feel a whole lot better"—I plumped up the hay under his head—"but I'll fetch you a pillow . . . and some oil for the lantern. I'll take good care of you."

"No." He took hold of my left wrist and opened his eyes. "Go back to the house. Don't come out here again."

I sank back on my heels. "I beg your pardon?"

"Someone will see you. I don't want anyone to know I'm here. I don't want anyone trailing you and hurting you."

"You need ice and bandages. I could get Dr. Koning—"

"No!" He squeezed my wrist. "I still don't trust him, Hanalee."

"Joe . . ." I wrapped my free hand around his cold fingers. "I have to tell you something."

"What?"

"That oak tree at the Dry Dock . . ." My eyes burned. "The one they used . . . for . . ."

Joe nodded in understanding.

"Someone carves the names of certain people on it," I said. "People who don't quite belong. And they seem to cross off the names once a person leaves town. Like Mrs. Downs." I pressed my fingers tighter around him. "And my father."

"Is your name on that tree?" he asked, his voice deep, protective.

"Mine. Mama's. Yours. Deputy Fortaine's." I swallowed. "And Clyde Koning's."

He slipped his fingers out of mine and lowered his hand to his chest.

I dug through the carpetbag and tugged out a white undershirt. "This morning Uncle Clyde admitted to me that he, indeed, lied in court." I dabbed the shirt against Joe's red nostrils with the softest touch I could manage. "When he was in your room with my father, Daddy told him about the near lynching."

Joe maneuvered himself up to a sitting position with his shoulders curled forward. "Here, let me do that," he said, and he took the shirt and swabbed his bloody nose on his own. His eyelids fluttered at each brush of the cloth against his skin.

"I should fetch you ice," I said.

"What did Dr. Koning do with that information?" he asked, still wincing from the dabbing. "How did he go from hearing about a near lynching to accusing me of manslaughter, without one mention of the Ku Klux Klan, in court?"

"Uncle Clyde said he went straight to Sheriff Rink and told him what he saw on my father . . . the marks . . . the marks on his . . ." I held the sides of my throat and crossed my legs beneath me. My mouth refused to utter another syllable, for the words I'd planned to say contained edges sharp and jagged. I closed my eyes and rested my head in the palms of my hands.

Joe stayed beside me without saying a word. He just waited, breathing in a gentle rhythm while he wiped the blood from his lips and chin. A warm breeze nosed through the rafters above our heads.

"Uncle Clyde"—I sniffed—"told the sheriff about the marks from the noose. He reported everything that my father said." I lowered my hands to my lap and watched my fingers hang like unnecessary appendages off the edges of my shins. "It sounds to me as though the Junior Order of Klansmen met at the Dry Dock on Christmas Eve, and, possibly with the help of a few adult leaders, they terrorized my father at that tree, as part of their initiation. They put too much strain on his heart, to the point where it stopped beating entirely in your bedroom." I dragged my thumb across a damp patch of skin that itched below my right eye. "They trapped him into heading to the Dry Dock with the promise that they'd pay him good money for bootlegging."

"And Dr. Koning got paid to keep quiet about the truth."

"No." I wiped both cheeks with the palms of my hands. "People threatened to hurt me if he spoke the truth."

Joe drew his right knee to his chest and leaned his elbow on it, sinking his nose into the undershirt. "You're positive Dr. Koning's telling the God's honest truth?"

"I spoke with the owner of the Dry Dock this morning. He veri-

fied that they used that tree to torture my father. He seemed proud of it, as a matter of fact."

"Christ." Joe closed his eyes. "It's even worse than I imagined. So much worse." He pursed his dark brows. "They've won."

"No." I folded my hands in my lap. "I won't let them win."

"Then what do you propose we do?"

I sat up tall. "We survive."

He looked at me from above his swollen nose, and I saw some fight burning in his eyes, too.

"We're still alive," I said. "Still in one piece. Let's stay that way. Let's go make something of ourselves and show them how much we're thriving."

He breathed a small laugh. "You make it sound simple."

"I didn't say that, but let's do it. Let's become better educated than them—make more money than them—love people more fiercely than they could ever dream of loving."

A smile awakened at the corners of his mouth. His nose had stopped leaking, but it continued to swell and purple. Half circles the same color as his bruises rimmed the skin beneath his eyes.

"But, for now," I said, "I'm going to make sure you get help." I peeked over my shoulder at the closed stable door. "Let me go see if Uncle Clyde came home yet."

"No!"

"You need medical help, Joe."

"I'll rest here for a while." He scooted back down to the ground and propped himself up on his right elbow. "Gather my strength. Eat the last traces of food in that basket. And then I'll sneak out after dark."

"And go where?"

"I'll jump a train."

"Uncle Clyde offered to help you find a job. Let us help you."

He shook his head. "If he knows I'm hiding out in here—"

"I think we can trust him."

"Go back to the house—please. Keep yourself safe. I'll get myself feeling better, and then I'll leave."

I raised the hem of my skirt and opened the flap of the holster. "Let me at least leave you my pistol."

"No, don't do that."

I paused with my hand on the derringer. "Why not?"

Joe wouldn't look me in the eye. "If it's here . . . I might be tempted to use it, especially if the pain gets bad. Or if I start thinking too much about Laurie."

"You'd . . . you'd really do that to yourself?"

"I don't know."

The wooden grip beneath my fingers no longer brought a single shred of comfort.

"I'm not leaving you alone if you're feeling suicidal," I said.

"It's just the pain talking." He stretched out on his back with the shirt cupped around the bottom half of his face.

"Joe . . ."

"What?"

I almost asked him if he truly did love Laurence—if they'd been together for a while—but I bit down on my lip and said instead, "I'm going to check on you tonight, after dark. If you need anything before then—food, medical supplies, company—"

"Your parents would telephone my parents if they knew I was

270

out here. And I can't go home." His eyes drooped closed, and his dark lashes disappeared against the swollen mounds of his skin. "I'll be fine, Hanalee. Just go. Keep yourself safe." He drew a long breath. "That's what your father wanted most of all."

I nodded, my lips pressed tightly together. "All right, then. You know where to find me."

I gave his wrist a squeeze, and my heart crumbled again into a grainy pile of sand, just as when I'd left Fleur behind.

ON MY JOURNEY BACK HOME I STAYED LOW TO THE ground, sticking to concealed pathways through berry bushes and trees. My pistol continued to ride against my leg, its two sturdy bullets packed inside the barrels, and it remained with me when I snuck through the front door and tiptoed up to my bedroom.

I unbuckled the holster and crammed it down inside the box of toys.

After a few steadying breaths, a few prayers, a few swears, I reopened my door and padded back downstairs.

The door that led to the basement from the kitchen stood ajar, and the smells of must and mothballs blasted through the opening. I grabbed hold of the brass knob and called down to my mother, "Are you doing all right down there?"

A bare bulb shone across the trunks and old furniture that had found themselves banished belowground. Some of the items had lived down there ever since my grandparents first built the house in the 1870s. Mama's tan shoes with rubber heels clomped into view from behind a small table, but I couldn't see any part of her above her ankles.

"I'm fine," she said. "Just keep the door locked, and stay away from the windows. Are you going through your belongings?"

"I got distracted, but I'm just about to start."

"Keep your curtains drawn while you do so. Uncle Clyde should be home soon."

"Yes, ma'am."

I returned to my room and embarked upon the task of packing up my life in Elston, Oregon.

UNCLE CLYDE RETURNED HOME SHORTLY AFTER noon, and we ate lunch. We planned. We fretted. I longed to tell both him and Mama about Joe in our stable, his face swelling and aching, but I didn't want to be wrong about placing trust in my stepfather.

During most of the afternoon, I packed and sorted some more, and when the task grew too difficult to bear, I slid my sketch pad out from its hiding spot between my mattress and the box spring. My drawing of Joe in the pond caught my eye first, and above it I found the crossed-out sketch of Fleur, seated in her window seat, telling me of Daddy's ghost.

I parked myself at my red desk and flipped to a fresh new page. While Mama and Uncle Clyde bustled about down below, I leaned over the paper with my elbows pressed against my strawberry-colored worktop, and using my supply of charcoal pencils, I drew the story of the past few days. I sketched Fleur and me, kneeling over a magazine with our heads tipped close together. Joe and me, running through the woods, lantern and blanket and carpetbag in hand, my skin shaded quite a bit darker than his, even though I rarely ever drew myself with much color. Uncle Clyde, standing on our front porch with his thumbs tucked in his pockets, his mouth open, speaking of making amends with Joe. Mama and me, together, hand in hand, beneath the pine tree near the Dry Dock. Laurence, bending over at the waist, his bruised fist balled against his stomach. A fish wearing a crown, diving back into a river after bursting free from his captor's stomach. The Dry Dock's oak tree, standing tall and fierce, with its weight-bearing branches reaching out toward the beholder of the drawing, the ends of its boughs curled like fingers.

I spent the bulk of my time on the oak tree, shaping and shading each leaf, each stripe of bark, until the tree looked precisely as I remembered it. Once I finished fussing over the details, I sat up straight at my desk and studied my creation—forced myself to stare the oak down—as though facing an enemy.

If the tree held on to my etched name, waiting for me to disappear, then I would keep a drawing of it, waiting for its demise.

KU KLUX KLAN MARCH, JACKSON
COUNTY, OREGON, 1920s.

CHAPTER 26

HAD I BUT TIME

 I LAY IN BED IN MY DAY CLOTHES AND stared up at the candlelight twitching across my ceiling. It still didn't seem right, leaving a boy marked for death all by himself, unarmed, injured, behind an unlocked stable door.

"Damn it," I muttered up to the ceiling. "I wish I could have given him my pistol." I sighed and blinked. "What in the world am I supposed to do?"

No one answered. The wind didn't even breathe through my curtains.

I waited for Mama and Uncle Clyde to retire to their bedroom and finish opening and closing drawers and get settled in their bed. And then I waited at least a half hour more. The candle burned down to a nub no bigger than half my thumb, and the world out-side my window lay still and as dark as a pot of ink.

I didn't take Necromancer's Nectar that night, but I did slip out of bed. I grabbed my derringer out of its holster and slid the gun, the lucky sprigs of alfalfa, and my bare feet down inside a pair of big black boots I wore whenever rain soaked the yard. In front of my floor-length mirror, I swiveled my right ankle to make sure the der-ringer didn't bulge like a pork chop beneath the boot's leather, as it did whenever I lugged it around beneath my skirt. If Mama and Uncle Clyde were to catch me prowling around the house, they wouldn't see I was armed.

"Good," I said to the mirror with a nod.

I cracked open my door and descended the staircase upon feet that strained to keep from making a sound inside those bungle-some boots. My arches ached from stepping with such caution. My legs moved with a stiff and heavy gait that seemed to fill my calves with sandbags.

Down in the kitchen, I fetched the block of ice from the icebox and chipped large chunks into a dishcloth. I then grabbed our pic-nic basket—now empty and clean from the day before—and packed it with the ice, an apple, cheese, bread, some bandages and scissors from Uncle Clyde's first-aid kit we kept under the sink, and a metal canteen filled up to the screw-top lid with water. I retrieved some oil for Joe's lantern. Silence reigned over the world outside the window above the sink, and only a hint of the glow of whiskey stills peeked above the tops of the trees. Or maybe I only imagined that faint glimmer of orange. Maybe the world slept uneasily, holding its breath, waiting to see what I would do next.

I ventured outside with the basket and the can of oil and bolted across the grass as though a whole herd of Elston boys were chasing me down. I made it to the stable in well under a minute but forced myself not to scare Joe by bursting inside. Instead, I creaked open the door with the softest of movements and stole into the blackness within.

"Joe?" I whispered, closing the door behind me.

"I hope to God that's just you, Hanalee," he said from over in the corner where I'd left him.

"It's me. I brought you ice for your nose and some food and some oil for the lamp." I attempted to walk in his direction but couldn't see a darn thing. "Can you light a match?"

"Here"—he shifted about—"give me the oil, and I'll light the lantern, but just for a short while. I don't want anyone seeing the flame through the slats in the wood."

I crept over to him in the dark as best as I could and set the basket and the oil beside him. "Can you see at all in here?" I asked. "Have your eyes adjusted to the dark?"

"Sort of."

I held my breath and waited while he fumbled around with the lantern and the oil. After a hiss and a quick whiff of sulfur, a match flared to life. Joe's swollen nose and red-rimmed eyes glowed in the wavering light. My stomach dipped. He lit the lantern and shook out the match. "You shouldn't have come here."

"I know, but it seemed wrong to leave you out here with an unlocked door and no treatment for your pain. I'm sure you're also thirsty and famished." I sat down next to his outstretched legs and pulled the canteen out of the basket. "How are you feeling?"

278

"Well"—he took the container and unscrewed the lid—"I could sure use some hooch right about now. That's not what's in here, is it?"

I smiled. "You're not going to find any liquor in a house occupied by Clyde Koning."

Joe chuckled under his breath. "A boy can dream, can't he?" He tipped back his head and took a swig of water.

I glanced over my shoulder to ensure I had remembered to close the door behind me.

Joe swallowed and came up for a breath. "What is it?"

"I just wanted to make sure I shut the door." I shifted back toward him. "Do you think the boys would truly take the time to head out looking for you? Or would those Wittens be too busy getting drunk in that cabin we found near the creek?"

Joe shook his head. "I honestly don't know. I suppose it depends on how embarrassed Laurence felt over what I told you." He screwed the cap back into place. "He must be pretending awfully hard to be something that he isn't if he's running around with the Klan and a girl like Opal."

"Opal's not as bad as some."

"She's fast, though. I kissed her once, at a party, just to see if I'd like it, and she wanted more from me."

I sat back on my heels. "You've kissed girls?"

"Just her." He moved the canteen and the lantern to the other side of his legs, opening the space between us. "And you."

I lowered my eyes and fussed with the handle of the basket. "I only agreed to that unfortunate kiss because I worried the Wittens would hurt you worse than what Laurence just did."

"A true love's kiss, then." He smirked and wrapped his arms around his knees, peeking at me out of the corner of his eye. "One given to save a life. You must love me dearly."

I snickered through my nose, and my face and neck burned as much as when I'd swallowed down the Necromancer's Nectar. "Come on." I reached into the basket and pulled out the chunks of ice wrapped in the cloth. "Let's get this ice on your nose. That's an ugly shade of purple you've got there."

I held on to his back and set the chilled cloth against his nose. He raised his left hand and helped me hold the ice in place.

"Ahh," he said, and his eyes rolled into the back of his head. He breathed a sigh that warmed my palm, while his eyelids batted closed. "Thank you."

"Better?"

"Uh-huh."

"Joe . . ."

"Uh-huh?"

I kept my fingers below his on the cloth. The sides of our hands touched. His breath fluttered against my skin.

"How long have you loved him?"

His eyes remained closed. "I don't know. Since I first saw him, I guess. Since I first came to Elston."

"Didn't you move here from some little town in the mountains when you were about thirteen years old?"

"Yes." He gave a small nod. "That's when I was certain. Of everything."

I lowered my hand from the frozen cloth, finding my fingers numb. "That's a long old time."

"We weren't much of friends at first," he said, his voice quiet. "We even got into a fight over a game of baseball at one point, not long after I moved here. But we had our eyes on each other from the very beginning." He shifted from side to side, readjusting his weight. "It took a little growing up—a little whiskey one summer night right before we both turned sixteen—before we ever broke through all that tension and kissed each other." He opened his eyes and looked at me from above the cloth on his face. "He's the one you kissed when you were little, wasn't he?"

I sat up straight, and my face warmed again. "H-h-how did you know?"

"Because of how much you yelled at him in the woods. The hurt in your voice." He gulped with a noticeable bob of his Adam's apple. "He always talked about spending his younger years running around with you and Fleur."

"Well"—I picked at a corner of the basket with the tip of one of my nails—"we were just kids. Those hardly count as real kisses."

"That kiss in front of the Wittens"—he lowered the ice to his lap—"that was your first then, wasn't it?"

I shrugged. "It doesn't matter." I shrugged again. "I don't even know if we can genuinely call that a real kiss, either." I continued to pick at the basket, although I drew my hand away when I realized how much the sound of the wicker echoed across the rafters.

"Come here," he said in a whisper.

I raised my eyes to his. "What?"

He lowered the ice to the floor on the other side of him. "I want to give you a real kiss."

I snorted. "You mean a pity kiss?"

"No. A thank-you kiss."

I traced my finger across the edge of a floorboard. "I thought you didn't want girls, Joe."

"It doesn't matter. I want to give you a good kiss that will erase the one in the woods. That shouldn't have been your first." He tugged on my wrist with a gentle pull. "Come here."

I snickered. "Your nose is all swollen. What if I bump it with my nose?"

"Just"—he slid me closer to him—"come here."

I scooted over to his side.

We both smiled and laughed a little, our heads bent close to each other. Then his face sobered. He cupped his right hand behind my neck and pressed his lips against mine with a kiss soft and sweet. Not the kiss of a lover, or a brother, or even just a friend. A kiss that defied explanation. One that eased all the way through me with an unexpected sense of peace.

Our mouths left each other with a gentle sound, and we remained side by side, my legs bent toward his. His hand left my neck and returned to his thigh, and then to the cloth filled with ice, which he pressed against his nose again.

"We should get you some food." I slid myself back over to the basket. "I also brought—"

A twig cracked outside the stable.

Joe and I stiffened, our shoulders squared toward the stable door. I refused to breathe—refused to move even the tiniest muscles in my fingers—and I forgot all about the derringer crammed down inside its new hiding spot in my boot. Wind whistled between the boards in the roof and rattled across splinters and nails in the raf-

282

ters. A chill seeped down my body, starting at the roots of my hair, slicing down the length of my back.

Joe scooted himself toward me.

"It . . . it's funny," he said in a whisper. "I'm finding myself sitting here, p-p-praying that's just your father's ghost out there."

The wind toyed with the door, nudging at the wood, as though a person with weak hands attempted to push it open. I heard a gentle *tap-tap-tap*, and the chill washed all the way down to my feet, until every inch of my skin sweated ice.

"Joe," I said. "I'm frightened to death."

"It's all right." He slid all the way next to me. "It's probably just—"

Footsteps! I distinctly heard footsteps scuffling across the dirt outside.

Joe wrapped his arm around me. "It's probably . . ."

I grabbed hold of him by his waist.

Bursts of yellow light traveled past the slats in the boards, rushing toward the door.

I froze and whimpered in fear. Joe pulled me close, clasped my head to his chest, and cussed under his breath.

The door flew open and banged against the stable wall with a crash as loud as a gunshot, and I screamed and clung to Joe. My greatest fear manifested before my eyes: a half-dozen figures in white hoods and robes—red insignias on their chests, round black holes for eyes—pushed their way into the stable with lanterns burning bright. I flew into a panic and tried to climb up Joe's shoulder, just trying to get away—somewhere, *anywhere*—and then hands clamped down on my arms and tore me away from him. Klan members descended upon him, and although Joe thrashed and kicked, they slammed him down on his stomach, tied a cloth around his mouth, and strapped another around his wrists, which they forced behind his back.

Someone yanked a cloth around my mouth, too. The bindings tore into my lips and my cheeks, and my attackers pulled my hair when they tied the knot behind my head. No one spoke—all I heard were panicked grunts from both Joe and me and the swiftness of feet bustling around us—and I wanted to cry out, *Say something! Show me you're people and not faceless creatures.* My eyes bulged. I tried to keep my head facing Joe, to see what they'd do to him. My knees buckled and banged against the floor, but those hooded devils pulled me to my feet and wrenched me out of the stable. They pulled Joe out, too, and dragged him away, ahead of me.

White cloth surrounded me. White cloth with dark eyes peering out of round holes. Lamplight burned at my corneas. The soles of my boots scraped against dirt and rocks, and only then did I remember the little gun wedged inside, down in the crook of my right foot, below the ankle bone. Up ahead, glimpses of Joe's trousers and bare toes peeked through a wall of white cotton. He was on his knees, and they were dragging him toward the highway beyond a narrow thicket of firs on the east side of our property.

A surge of terror gripped my arms and legs. I acquired a strength that nearly set me free from the hands bearing down on my wrists. One of my captors grabbed the back of my neck and pushed me forward, onward, in the direction of a Ford truck that looked to be the Paulissens', parked beyond the trees on the side of the highway. Nothing seemed real.

The air turned cold, and everyone's feet crackled through pine needles on the dark earth beneath us. A bird of some sort flapped its wings out of nowhere and rushed over my head with a suddenness and swiftness that made me scream into the cloth.

I'm dead, I'm dead, I thought, and my knees sank again to the ground. The Klan members had to drag me; I would not willingly walk to whatever fate they intended for me and Joe. Stones and twigs tore at my legs and stung my skin, but I would not walk. I smelled a citrus-tinged cologne that reminded me of Laurence, but my brain forced me to think of the hooded men as creatures and strangers—not neighbors and childhood companions.

One of the Klansmen pulled down the wooden gate at the back of the truck's bed. Three of the robed figures hoisted Joe into the vehicle. Two of them jumped in after him and dragged him by his pinned-back arms across the floor, toward the back of the cab. Two more Klansmen lifted me in by my arms and legs. I writhed and fought, but they shoved me into the open compartment and climbed right in after me before I could reach for my boot. One of them pulled me down onto my back and held me by my elbows, while the other pinned down my legs by my knees. I prayed my little derringer wouldn't slide into view at the edge of my boot. I prayed the truck would crash and kill our attackers before they yanked us anywhere near a tree and a rope.

Someone closed up the back of the truck, rocking the bed, and the remaining Klansmen must have climbed into the cab, for I heard car doors opening and shutting.

The truck engine grumbled to life, and the vehicle lurched forward and headed down the highway, the floor of the bed rattling against the back of my skull. I heard Joe squirming and grunting behind me, and I realized that one of his feet was thrashing about near my right eye. Mainly, though, I saw hooded faces looming above me, and the wide black sky that stretched overhead, the stars winking down as though it were a regular July night in a regular summer. I closed my eyes and pushed my mind to thoughts of Daddy and me standing side by side in the green waters of the creek. I made myself hear the sound of my father's deep voice singing "Wade in the Water," while the current trickled past the tree roots and branches hanging out from the shore. Cool waters lapped at my stinging knees. Daddy's large, warm hand wrapped around mine. The sun shone hot and sweet on my face, and I no longer tasted the cotton of the cloth that bound my mouth or felt hands forcing down my limbs. I willed Joe to escape, too, to join Laurence in the woods when they weren't yet sixteen; to taste their first kiss and run his fingers through the sunshine in Laurence's hair.

The brakes of the truck squealed to a stop. My body jolted. Car doors opened. I writhed again and arched my back, but hands grabbed me and yanked me forward in the dark. My feet hit the ground with a thump that made the gun jump in my boot, and I thanked God for the safety mechanism.

"Look what we found," said one of the Klansmen who squeezed down on my arm. I recognized his voice as being that of Mr. Franklin from the Dry Dock. "Both of them, huddled in the stable on the girl's family's property."

The man whipped me around toward a scene of bright light, and my breath caught in my throat.

A wooden cross, at least eight feet tall, burned in the patch of tall grasses between the Dry Dock and Ginger's. The inferno crackled and strengthened and reflected off the glass of the Dry Dock's windows, brightening the white of the Klansmen's robes. Beyond the cross stood the oak tree, looking larger and blacker and more monstrous than I remembered, its crooked boughs stretching out to the surrounding darkness. Four more Klan members waited by the tree, and they held torches that illuminated a noose that hung from the thickest branch.

Behind me, Klansmen pulled Joe out of the truck, his mouth and hands still bound. His eyes widened at the cross and the noose, the fire shining against his brown irises, and he dropped to his knees.

"Joseph Adder and Hanalee Denney," called out a wheezy, high-pitched voice that I knew for certain to be Sheriff Rink's. He stood by the noose, a slightly shorter figure than the others, and the black and hollow eyes of his hood stared straight inside me. "We have brought you here because you are both threats to the moral purity of this community. As punishment"—he grabbed hold of the noose dangling beside him—"we will bring you each forward, fasten this rope around your neck, and raise you in the air three times in a row."

I whimpered beneath my gag and bent my arms and knees in a frantic fight to break free. The fire on the cross blurred and jumped about, and all I could see was the color red.

"Afterward," continued the sheriff, "you will leave this community, as well as the white homeland of Oregon, for the rest of your living days. You are not welcome in Elston, nor will you ever be. Boys"—the sheriff waved to the Klansmen holding Joe—"let's start with him. You new recruits will have the honor of slipping the rope over his head and ensuring it's secure."

Four of our original attackers crowded around Joe, and at first I couldn't see any part of him, aside from one of his bare feet sticking out from between the bottoms of the Klansmen's dark trousers below the robes. Two of them reached down and hoisted him to his feet. They steered him toward the noose that the sheriff held in his meaty fingers. Joe's hands remained bound behind his back, but he wiggled his elbows and kicked at his captors and gave one last go at escape. The sheriff grabbed him by the back of his collar and forced the rope around his neck.

"No!" I cried out from beneath the cloth—a muffled sound, but one that startled the two Klansmen who held my wrists. Their grips loosened. I somehow yanked myself free of their hands.

I tore off, darting down the side of the highway like a hunted rabbit.

Mr. Franklin shouted, "Run after her!"

Footsteps pounded the soil in the grasses behind me, and I heard my name, called out in Laurence's voice. Adrenaline soared through my body, allowing me to fly over the ground and run harder than I'd ever run in my life. I pulled the binding off my mouth and allowed my lungs to breathe.

The muscles in my legs carried me through the copse of trees that rose up in my path, several yards south of the Dry Dock. With motions swift and powerful, before my pursuers could even think of catching up, I was down on the ground, pulling off my right boot, knocking my fingertips against the wood and cold metal of the pistol.

"Leave me alone, or I'll shoot!" I cried, and I pointed the double barrel up at two white sheets that came to a skidding stop in front of me. "I swear to God, I'll shoot."

"Put the gun down, Hanalee," said Laurence from beneath the hood on the right.

"Take off your hoods and run to my house for help." I rose to my feet. "Tell my parents there's going to be a murder."

"Hanalee—"

"I know that's you, Laurence. Take your goddamned KKK friend here and go get Dr. Koning. Tell him blood will be spilled at the Dock tonight."

"But—"

"If you don't want the blood to be yours"—I lowered the gun to the direction of his groin, figuring he might value that area even more than his head—"then go now and fetch Dr. Koning—quickly!"

Laurence and his friend remained frozen and hidden beneath their sheets.

I cocked the hammer and fired at the ground next to Laurence's left foot, scattering leaves and dirt in all directions. "Now!"

Both Klansmen jumped into the air and skedaddled in the direction of my house.

"What was that?" a voice shouted in the distance, back where I'd last seen Joe with the noose around his neck.

I ran back with one foot in a boot and the other one bare, and I clutched the pistol in my right hand, contemplating the damage I could do with that last precious bullet. I could kill Sheriff Rink. At the very least, I could shoot him in the kneecap and cause him to moan in pain and distract his cohorts while I released Joe from the rope. I pushed past trees and the blur of the highway and thought of all the possibilities—all the consequences that would follow. A funeral. A trial. Tears. Heartache. Prison. Eugenics. Pain. Regret.

I reached the oak tree and found the Klansmen unsettled. Two of them held on to Joe by his shoulders. The noose remained around his neck, and the rest of the rope dangled over the branch. The other Klansmen paced about, their wide sleeves flapping.

"I don't want my life to end in tragedy!" I shouted with my gun raised, and I cocked the hammer with my thumb.

"Oh, Christ!" said a voice that sounded like Robbie's. "Put the gun down!"

I swept the barrel in the direction of them all—all eight of the remaining Klansmen, along with their victim, Joe Adder.

"I want to live and love and thrive," I said, and a solution entered my head—a way to lessen the tragedy. To appease the pain.

I pointed the gun at Joe's head.

His captors dove away from his sides. Joe's eyes expanded above his gag, and he turned as rigid as stone.

"Stay still, Joe!" I shouted, and I closed one eye. "Don't move!"

I squeezed the trigger with the pad of my index finger, and the blast of that shot exploded inside my head. The bullet soared in his direction with a force that rattled my bones.

Joe collapsed into a thick blanket of tall grasses, and the entire world fell silent.

CHAPTER 27

THE REST IS SILENCE

 I DROPPED TO MY KNEES IN A CLOUD of white smoke and watched as all attention shifted toward me. Hoods came off. Voices shouted amid the brain-piercing ringing inside my ears. To my right, Robbie removed his covering and begged me not to kill anyone else, not paying any mind to the fact that the pistol only possessed two barrels, two bullets. Sheriff Rink yanked off his hood and clamored toward me with his hands in the air, demanding, "Drop the gun! Drop the gun!"

I clutched the grip with both my hands and kept the barrels pointed in the direction where Joe had stood. The weight of the little derringer grew too much to bear, as light as it actually was.

My arm muscles weakened and slackened, and the weapon sank toward the ground.

The sheriff lifted the bottom of his robe and fetched a pair of handcuffs from the belt of his dark uniform underneath. "Everyone, leave the scene immediately." He came over and shoved me down to the ground by my back, pushing me onto my stomach. "None of you were here. Do not leave a trace of yourself behind."

Cold metal clicked around my wrists. I tasted dirt on my lips and felt the earth digging into my scraped knees.

"Hanalee Denney," the sheriff barked into my ear in the deepest voice I'd ever heard from him, "you are under arrest for the murder of Joseph Adder."

Legs swathed in sheets and dark trousers leapt past my head in the mass exodus from the scene. I lifted my face far enough off the ground to see a couple of grown men and several boys my age—the same pack of boys from Laurence's place—fleeing down the dark highway, their robes billowing behind them, hoods tucked under their arms like empty pillowcases. They ran with their torches and lanterns and left the clearing dark and abandoned, save for the sheriff and me, and Joe, lying somewhere in the patch of blackness beneath the oak tree, near the burning cross.

Sheriff Rink lifted me to my feet by the crook of my left arm and dragged me alongside the highway, past Ginger's. I tripped on an uneven patch of dirt and imagined hitting my head on the highway, without my arms to catch me. The sheriff yanked me upright before I smacked against the ground, and he tugged me onward.

"You sure saved me a heap of trouble by killing that boy yourself," said the sheriff with a squeak. "I don't know why you did that—maybe you were trying to spare him the pain of the noose—but I'm happy as hell you did."

"I knew exactly what I was doing when I pointed that gun at Joe's head" was all I said, and I held my chin high.

"Hanalee?" shouted a girl's voice from somewhere behind us.

I swiveled around, which made the sheriff wrench me toward his car all the faster. A strange, chirping sound emerged from the darkness.

Mildred's rickety old bicycle.

"Joe's lying below the branches of the oak tree," I called out to her, even though I couldn't see her. "The sheriff's taking me to his car to—"

Sheriff Rink smacked his hand over my mouth and opened the back door of his vehicle. The sideways grin of the moon spit an anemic haze over the automobile's black paint, and a jolt of doubt struck my heart. The words I'd shouted to Joe—*Stay still, Joe! Don't move!*—replayed in my head, and I kept feeling my arm and my hand aim the gun just so and seeing Joe fall to the ground in the darkness.

The sheriff grabbed a clump of my hair on the back of my head, shoved me into his backseat, and slammed the car door closed, just grazing my heel.

I lifted my head from the dark leather seat and heard him crank the vehicle to a start down below the grille in front of the car. With an obnoxious sigh and a hiss from the upholstery, he plopped down on the front seat and slammed his own door shut.

"It's time for you to take a little journey outside Elston," he said with a quick peek over his shoulder.

I scooted myself up to a seated position, despite the hindrance of the handcuffs, and watched Mildred's bicycle careen to a stop up ahead, in the patch of grass leading to the cross and the oak tree. I thanked the Lord for her bizarre premonitions.

"You do realize, Sheriff Rink," I said, forcing my voice to leave my throat with a deep and confident sound, "my father's spirit roams this highway late at night."

"Hogwash!" He shifted the vehicle into gear. "There's no such thing as ghosts."

"Daddy called such spectral apparitions 'haints,' which always sounded to me like 'hate.'"

The sheriff laughed with a wheezy whistle and sent the vehicle rumbling forward onto the black road ahead of us, lit only by the twin beams of the headlights. We passed the burning cross and Mildred, bending down over Joe.

"I sure hope you see him out here," I said, peering out the windshield beyond the sheriff's round head. The glow of the headlights brightened the outstretched tongue of the highway. "I hope you see Hank Denney's face staring straight into your guilty soul."

The sheriff didn't chuckle at that comment and instead increased our speed, sailing the car past the tree-lined stretch of highway where the Adders and several other Elston residents lived, where Daddy had stumbled into the road. We rode beneath the boughs of trees that arched over the highway like the arms of ancient crones.

"Up ahead," I continued, "in the crossroads—that's where I've seen him myself."

"Stop it," said the sheriff, and he sped us through the junction of the roads. "That's not funny in the slightest."

"And farther along, through that next patch of trees—I'm sure he's been there."

"Hank Denney's body and soul left Oregon back in 1921," said the sheriff with a glance back at me. "We made absolutely certain, when we hoisted him off the ground, that no part of that godforsaken Negro would linger in this state—that's for damn sure." Only he didn't say *Negro*.

The sheriff turned back around in his seat and gave a start, for just ahead, smack-dab in the middle of the road, stood my father in the light of the patrol car's headlights.

"Holy Mother of—" The sheriff steered us off the road, to the right. Brakes screeched. The car reared and bucked. A fir tree rose up ahead. I opened my mouth to scream, but before any sound left my throat, my body slammed against something hard amid a deafening crack of thunder.

"HANALEE," SAID A VOICE RICH AND DEEP. OAK AND honey. Woods and river waters. "We need to get you out of this car before the fire reaches the backseat, darling."

My eyes refused to open. Pain awakened across my body, from the top of my forehead all the way down to the muscles of my legs—a dull ache at first, then a roar of agony. I coughed on smoke and believed my bones to be blazing with fire inside me.

"Hanalee," said the voice again, and I knew it was my father, offering comfort.

I lifted my eyelids and found Daddy poking his head into the open doorway of the backseat of the sheriff's car. His black derby sat far enough back on his head for me to see his big brown eyes, which glistened with concern. My body, wedged between the front seat and the backseat, lay in a tangle of bleeding legs and arms, in a space that seemed too small to be the interior of an automobile. Smoke blackened the nighttime air and stung my eyes, and I heard the sputter of flames.

"Wrap your arms around my shoulders, honey"—Daddy leaned into the vehicle and maneuvered his left arm behind my sore back—"and I'll carry you home."

"Can't," I said with a grunt. "Handcuffs."

Daddy reached his free arm under my legs, and before the fire licked its way across the front seat, he scooped me out of a burning mass of twisted steel that hugged the trunk of a tree that no longer stood upright.

"The sheriff?" I asked, remembering our flight into that trunk. "Sheriff Rink?"

"Don't pay any heed to him." Daddy steered me away from the wreckage, while the flames snapped and sparked into the air with flashes of unnatural light. "Now *he's* the one wandering the highway, looking for redemption."

Out by the road, out of the corner of my eye, I saw the movement of a shadow—the stocky figure of a man who carried a white hood beneath his arm. I closed my eyes, and the orange glow of the flames shone against the backs of my lids.

Though I must have been heavy—a grown sixteen-year-old girl with a body weighed down by pain and fatigue—Daddy held me as though I were still no more than four years old. I pressed my face against the fresh whiskers on his cheeks and the coarse wool of his shoulder, and I fell asleep, thinking of wading in creek water and childhood nights when Daddy told me to love the world, even when it didn't love me back.

CHAPTER 28

REST, PERTURBED SPIRIT

 I OPENED MY EYES TO THE SIGHT OF sunshine streaming through my bedroom window, between the ruffles of my ivory curtains. A robin chirped in one of the trees beyond the panes. A hazy blur of white lingered by my red desk, and I smelled lilacs.

I blinked several times in a row, and the haze brightened and shifted into the shape of a girl with blond hair and a lace dress.

"Hana-Honey?" asked the girl, who sounded an awful lot like Fleur. "Are you awake?"

I blinked some more and lifted my right hand in front of my face, unsure if the appendage would be made of solid flesh.

"Hanalee?" she asked again, and she hurried toward me with

her skirts swooshing, her blue eyes gleaming. "You're awake. You're awake!"

"Am I alive?" I asked with a terrible croak in my voice.

"Yes." Fleur laughed and kissed my cheek, and her touch eased a dull pain that nibbled at my right leg and my back. "You're badly banged up, you poor thing. Your right leg is broken and stuck in a cast, and your left wrist is sprained and wrapped up in bandages. But"—she sat down beside me and stroked my hair with the tips of soft fingers—"you're alive."

"Was I . . ." My mind sped back to Daddy, appearing out of nowhere in the middle of the road, and Sheriff Rink, sending us careering off the pavement. "Was I . . . Did the car . . . D-d-did it—?"

"No one's really quite sure what happened to you. Mildred said she saw the sheriff drive away with you, but Dr. Koning found the wreckage of that car, and he said he doesn't . . ." She lowered her eyes. "He doesn't know how you would have made it out of that pile of metal alive."

"Uncle Clyde carried me home?"

She shook her head. "They don't know how you made it home. Your mother discovered you lying on your front porch when Dr. Koning was getting dressed and telephoning Deputy Fortaine. Laurence and Gil had shown up a short while earlier and claimed you talked about a murder. Your mother thought someone had beaten you badly and left you there."

"Joe!" I tried to sit up, but the muscles in my back and my neck screamed at me to stop.

"No, no, no." Fleur lowered me back to my pillow by my shoulders. "Don't try to get up, sweetie. You don't need to worry about Joe."

"Is he dead?"

"No."

"How is he?"

"He's recovering. Mildred found him, fainted dead away, with a noose tied around his neck. She thought he had been lynched to death, but then he came to and said the last thing he remembered seeing was you and a gun."

"Oh . . . yes . . . the gun," I said with a sigh that sank me deeply into the mattress, and only then did I realize I must have been under the influence of morphine or some other substance that shrank the pain into those tiny nibbles. My eyelids—two thick flaps of lead—pushed with all their might to stay open. "I shot a bullet past Joe's ear to make him . . . to stop them from . . ." I closed my eyes and jumped at the sound of the stable door banging open, while Joe and I cowered in a stall.

"Hanalee?" asked Fleur.

I opened my eyes, and it took a moment before the terror from the night before left my tingling nerves, and for the air to become easier to breathe.

"Where is he?" I asked.

"Joe?"

"Yes."

"He's at his parents' house, recovering from the shock of what happened."

"No, that's not good." I tried to sit up again.

"Lie back down, Hanalee." She wrapped her arms around me and hugged me back to the bed. "Everything's going to be all right."

"They're going to hurt him," I said with my face pressed against her cheek. "They're going to send him off to people—people who'll try to change him."

She let me go and sat up straight. "No one's going to hurt Joe."

"We planned to get out of this place, he and I. I wanted to take you, too, and Mama. I imagined all of us living together, free and peaceful, with nobody bothering us about anything. We could marry who we wanted, be what we wanted to be . . ."

She smiled and pulled on a lock of my bobbed hair.

I reached up and nudged my fingers between hers.

For a brief moment, I saw Joe again—in the dark—dragged across the ground with his wrists tied behind his back. The rustle of feet scraping across twigs in the dirt bothered my ears. The smell of torches burned my nostrils.

I tried to shift my position on the bed, attempting to turn onto my right side, but the nips of pain bit down harder. A shaky breath left my lips. "Is the sheriff dead, Fleur?"

"Yes." She squeezed my hand that held hers. "He is."

"The car?"

"Dr. Koning believes he died as soon as the car hit the tree."

I nodded, and a bitter taste scoured my tongue.

"Joe told Dr. Koning and the deputy that he thought you shot at him on purpose," she said, "to make him faint and look dead. He feels terrible if your injuries came about because of ending up inside that patrol car."

"You've talked to Joe?"

"He and his parents were over here this morning. Mama and I came over, too. Everyone's trying to make sense of what happened."

"Who's running Elston now?"

"Deputy Fortaine is taking over, although not everyone's pleased with that arrangement. His Jewish blood and lack of Klan support . . ." Fleur pressed her lips together and gave a shudder. Strands of fair hair swayed against her face. "I know . . ." She drew a deep breath. "I know Laurence was there last night . . . dressed in Klan attire."

"Yes." I grunted and arched my back, for pain suddenly gnashed into my leg. "He was."

"My mama . . . Sh-sh-she . . ." Fleur shifted away from me.

"What?" I asked, opening my eyes, settling back against the mattress. "What about your mother?"

Fleur withdrew her hand from mine. "She says if Laurence needs to be in the Klan to keep himself looking like an upright young man, then that's simply where he needs to be. Deputy Fortaine isn't going to help our family in the slightest, because he's against both the Klan and bootleggers. He aims to clean up Elston of both problems, but Laurence needs to keep bootlegging in secret so we can keep putting food on the table."

"You're going to stay living in a Klan house, Fleur?"

She kept her face tilted away from mine.

"Mama and Uncle Clyde talked about moving me out of this state," I said, "to somewhere with kinder laws." I cupped my fingers around the slim bones of her wrist. "You should come with us."

"Mama would hate that." She squirmed. "Laurence, too."

302

"I don't care. I want to know you'll be all right. I don't want to think of you getting married off to someone like Robbie Witten. I want you with me."

She brushed at her eyes with the back of her hand. "How did you get out of that burned-up patrol car, Hanalee? How did you make it back home?"

I swallowed and remembered the warmth of my cheek nuzzled against the wool of Daddy's shoulder. "I had that lucky sprig of alfalfa you gave me, tucked inside one of my boots."

She lowered her hand to her lap. "Tell me really. What happened?"

"Well . . ." I licked my lips. "My father . . . my biological father, Hank Denney . . . he . . ." I cleared my throat. "He carried me home."

Fleur met my eyes again and didn't say a word.

"If I made it home last night," I said, "then I suppose that means he finally made it home, too." My head drifted to my right. My eyelids sank halfway shut. "And now . . . perhaps . . . he can rest in peace. That poor spirit can finally rest."

"Are you certain? It was truly him?"

"I was there, in the backseat of the sheriff's burning car, and then Daddy pulled me out of the wreckage and carried me home." My breathing eased into the steady pattern of sleep, even though I remained half awake. "Where are my parents?"

"Talking with the reverend again, downstairs. They told me I could sit with you while you slept."

"As soon as you hear we're moving," I said, although my tongue seemed to swell into a slab of cement, "pack your bags."

"I can't run off with your family."

"Don't think of it as running off with my family." I lifted my eyelids far enough to see the concerned blue of her irises. "Think of it as running off to be with me, in a land like the ones we created as children."

"There's no such place, Hanalee."

"We'll make the place ourselves," I said, and I allowed myself to drift back into sleep.

I AWOKE AGAIN SOMETIME LATER AND FOUND THREE vases of flowers sitting on my red desk. The sharp sweetness of petals and pollen flooded my nose, and I squinted in confusion at the baffling array of roses, carnations, lilies, and hydrangeas.

Instead of Fleur, a fuzzy golden teddy bear now sat beside me on the bed, and both Mama and Uncle Clyde stood over me, one parent on each side of my legs. Uncle Clyde sneezed, no doubt because of the pollen.

Mama moved the teddy bear aside and perched herself on the right edge of the mattress.

"How are you feeling, darling?" she asked.

I breathed through a sudden spike of pain. "I hurt."

"I know." She blinked several times in a row and covered the back of my right hand with one of her palms. "I'm sure you do, but I'm just so grateful you're alive."

"The morphine's wearing off by now, I assume." Uncle Clyde cupped a hand around my forehead, as though to check for a fever. "I'll give you another dose soon."

"What happened, Hanalee?" asked Mama. "How did you and Joe end up out at the Dry Dock? Why weren't you in your room?"

304

I sucked in a deep breath and told them the entire story—Joe hiding in our stable with a broken nose, the Klansmen throwing open the door with a crash I could still hear inside my head, the nooses, the gun, the handcuffs, Daddy's ghost standing in the middle of the road, spooking Sheriff Rink. I didn't know if they believed me, but I told them everything, and they nodded and said, "I see."

I peered across my room at the summer blooms. "Why are there flowers in my room?" I lifted the little bear. "And this teddy bear?"

"The bear is from the Adders." Mama tucked the stuffed animal by my side. "The reverend brought that over when he visited earlier this afternoon. The flowers are from friends who heard how badly you got hurt."

I gaped at the tokens of concern. "People . . . people in Elston . . . were worried about me?"

"Quite worried." Uncle Clyde reached across to my right wrist and checked my pulse. "The reverend called a special town meeting just a couple of hours ago and asked for the residents of this community to take a stand against the Klan. He said it's time we put up a fight instead of ignoring the problem."

"And then the Markses and a few of the younger girls from school and their families showed up at the door," said Mama, "bearing flowers and food to ensure you'd feel better. Mildred tried to hand me some sort of questionable cure-all for broken-bone pain, but that particular gift I turned away."

A smile tugged at the corners of my mouth.

"Mildred also told me to thank you for taking care of the matter she requested you to," added Mama. "Although she wouldn't say what that matter was."

I nodded, and a tear slid down my right cheek with the burn of salt.

My mother brushed my face with the back of her right hand. "Not everyone's a part of that group, Hanalee. As I said before, it's just a small, obnoxious percentage of residents causing the trouble."

"We're going to move, though, aren't we?" I asked.

"The Klan, and even the eugenics movement"—Uncle Clyde swallowed—"they aren't problems exclusive to Oregon, unfortunately." He laid my wrist back down on the bed. "But we are strongly considering a move, perhaps up to Washington, where you wouldn't be faced with interracial marriage laws. The physician friend of mine who offered to help Joe said he'd also help me if things turned ugly down here."

I nuzzled the fuzz of the teddy bear's head against my chin and thought I smelled the scent of pond water. "Is Joe going up there?"

"More than likely." Uncle Clyde sat down on the opposite side of my legs from Mama, and the mattress squeaked beneath me. "His father still doesn't know what to do about him."

"Don't worry so much about everyone else right now." Mama stroked my right arm, below my elbow. "You just rest and heal. Your body's been through a great deal of trauma, and it needs sleep and care."

I nodded again, and my brain wobbled from the movement. "I am awfully tired," I said, "but I don't think I can quite stop worrying about everyone just yet."

CHAPTER 29

TO THINE OWN SELF BE TRUE

ON A MONDAY AFTERNOON, FOUR days after I'd seen Joe collapse into the grasses in front of the old oak tree, I heard the distinctive *chug-chug-chug* of a Model T pulling into the drive in front of our house. Uncle Clyde had carried me downstairs for the afternoon, for the heat in my bedroom roasted me good, and my right leg itched from sweating inside my cast. I reclined on the sofa with my broken leg stretched out in front of me and my left wrist propped on a pillow. A sizable percentage of my body remained bruised and sore.

I heard the car pulling up outside while I was in the midst of attempting a pencil sketch of the trees outside our window—the type of sketch my father liked to draw. If we were to leave the state, I wanted a visual record of my woods.

"Is someone here?" I called to Mama upstairs and Uncle Clyde in his little study in the back of the house. An unsettled feeling, equal parts dread and curiosity, brewed inside my chest. The world outside still didn't feel safe enough to expect every visitor to be a benevolent one.

Uncle Clyde—too protective to yet return to full-time office hours—hustled into the living room and veered straight toward the front window. "It's Joe."

"Really?" I set the paper and pencil aside. "Did he drive over? Does his nose look all right?"

"I bandaged him up to ensure it would heal properly. It looks like he hasn't picked off the wrappings, which is good." Uncle Clyde strode out of the living room and to the front door around the corner.

Joe knocked, and I heard my stepfather open the door for him just as Mama's feet traveled down the staircase.

"Hello, Joseph," said Uncle Clyde from around the bend.

"Hello, sir," said Joe, although I couldn't yet see him. His voice sounded so formal, I almost didn't recognize it—I almost even laughed. "How's Hanalee?"

"I'm in here, downstairs." I scooted myself farther up on the sofa's cushions. "Please come in, Joe."

"It looks like the bruising beneath your eyes has gone down," said Mama.

"It's getting there, ma'am."

I smiled at his use of "ma'am."

Flanked by my parents, Joe meandered around the bend, smoothing down his hair, which shone a bit from water or pomade. F. Scott Fitzgerald would have called him a "slicker," with a jazzy, combed-down coiffure such as that. Bandages crisscrossed his nose. He wore clean white shirtsleeves and gray trousers with a shiny black belt.

He stopped when he saw me and drew a short breath. "H-h-how are you?"

"Well"—I cocked an eyebrow—"I must be atrocious if I made you halt in your tracks and gasp."

"No, it's just . . ." He rubbed his hands against the sides of his pants. "I think I was hoping, since I heard you so miraculously survived, that you'd look unscathed."

"She's recovering remarkably well," said Uncle Clyde, bracing a hand on the rocking chair. "She'll need to spend several more weeks in that cast, and the bruising and muscle strain will take time to heal. Yet considering all she endured, we're feeling quite lucky and grateful at the moment."

Joe tucked his hands into his pockets. "I didn't ever mean for you to get hurt, Hanalee. You shouldn't be sitting there in a cast and bandages."

"I'd much rather be sitting here like this," I said, "than to say that the KKK strung us up from a tree."

The world skidded to a stop after I spoke those words. Joe's eyes met mine, and for a moment we both shot back to the woods in the blackness of midnight. Klansmen and torches. Ropes and dirt and the taste of cotton pulled across my mouth. The explosion of gunpowder vibrating against my hand.

Mama appeared behind the sofa without my even realizing she had walked across the room.

"How are your parents, Joe?" she asked, which seemed a forced and meaningless question, akin to asking his thoughts about the weather.

"They're fine, I guess." He took his hands out of his pockets and rubbed his sides again. "I actually came here because I have a gift for Hanalee. But it's something that will require her traveling in a car to see." He inched toward me, the heels of his shoes making a squishing sound against the living room rug. "Are you . . . are you able to take a short ride?"

"I don't know." I peeked at my stepfather. "Am I?"

"That's entirely up to you, Hanalee," said Uncle Clyde. "Do you feel well enough to be jostled about on Elston roads?"

"I think I might." I slid my good foot to the floor. "Especially if it involves a surprise."

Mama placed a hand upon my shoulder. "Were you planning to drive her, Joe?"

"Yes, ma'am. My father let me borrow his car this afternoon, specifically so I could take Hanalee to the surprise." He shifted his weight between his legs. "I know it's a car . . . I know"—he cleared his throat and shoved his hands back inside his pockets—"it holds a dark memory, but I'm leaving town for good this evening. If I could just give Hanalee this gift before I go, I think it would help set things right."

Mama and Uncle Clyde eyed each other. I did my best to shift my gaze between the two of them, to gauge their reactions, without aggravating the stiffness in my neck.

"Well, I want to go," I said. "If Joe's leaving tonight . . ."

"All right." Uncle Clyde nodded. "I'll help carry you to the car."

BOTH JOE AND MY STEPFATHER LUGGED ME OUT TO the black Model T that had struck my father that December night. Uncle Clyde carried the bulk of me, and Joe helped with my legs, including that massive plaster cast that felt like a small child clinging to my calf. Somehow they managed to cram both me and the cast into the front seat of the automobile.

Mama paced behind the two of them, her arms crossed, her forehead wrinkled. "Are you sure about this, Clyde?"

Uncle Clyde stepped back while Joe maneuvered around him to crank the engine to a start down below the car's hood.

"It'll just be a short drive, right, Joe?" asked my stepfather over the roar of the awakening engine. "Just into town?"

Joe popped up his head from the front of the car. "Do you know what the gift is?"

"I remember you mentioning something you wanted to do when you were here the day after the accident." Uncle Clyde straightened his glasses on his nose and squeezed his lips together to suppress what I believed to be a smile. "If it's what I think it might be, just be careful. Don't linger too long in front of it."

"I won't, sir." Joe climbed into the car beside me and shut his door. "Are you ready?" he asked me.

I scooted myself two inches closer to him, to better fit my cast into the small space in front of me. "Yes."

"We'll be back soon." Joe nodded at Uncle Clyde, then at Mama. "Don't you worry."

"Be careful," said Mama.

"We will." Joe pushed the clutch lever forward and drove the Model T down our front drive, toward the highway. I inhaled whiffs of gasoline that reminded me of the sheriff's patrol car, but I clamped my hands around my upper legs and told myself this ride would be different.

Joe turned his face toward me. "How are you, really?"

"I don't know for sure." I swallowed. "How are you?"

"Well, just to be clear"—he steered us onto the highway—"you weren't trying to actually shoot me in the head that night, were you?"

"You know why I fired that gun." I pinched a wrinkle in my skirt. "You know I've had practice with a feat like that."

"What did they do afterward?"

"What I wanted them to do: they turned all their attention to me and left you alone."

He nodded and drove us past Mildred's family's house. "Well, thank you."

"You're welcome."

We approached the patch of trees where the patrol car had sailed off the highway.

"I have a story to tell you, Hanalee," said Joe, keeping his eyes on the road ahead.

"Oh, yeah?"

"It involves a religious experience."

I lifted my eyebrows. "Oh?"

"My father asked me this morning what it would take to get me to believe in God again." He held his breath and drove us through the section of the road where he had encountered my living father in the dark. The shadows of trees cooled my face and filtered sunshine across the highway in a stained-glass pattern of light and darkness. A crow cawed overhead, and I saw the green sheen of its black feathers in a branch that ran as straight as the yardarm of a sailing ship.

"Now"—Joe blew a puff of air through his lips—"I never said that I don't believe in God, but Pop seems to think that doing what I do—loving whom I love—has made me godless. So I said, 'I'll believe in God if he strikes down that oak tree at the Dry Dock.'"

I craned my neck toward him as best as I could. "And what did your father say to that?"

"He told me, 'Let's pray for a lightning strike or a windstorm to smite down that tree, then, for I would like to see that oak destroyed, too.'"

I sputtered a laugh. "I haven't heard any windstorms over the past few days."

"This was just yesterday, when the Dry Dock was closed on account of it being Sunday." Joe adjusted the lever for the throttle on the steering column and sent the Model T roaring toward the brick buildings of town. "So, I went out to his toolshed and grabbed his father's old two-man crosscut saw—his father was a logger, you see. And I strolled up to Pop and said, 'I prayed to God to get rid of that tree, and I believe he led me to find this old saw of yours. What do you think?'"

I smiled. "Don't tell me your father honestly believed that fetching that saw was an act of God."

"He nodded when he witnessed the saw in my hands, and he

said, 'Sometimes the Lord works in mysterious ways, doesn't He?' And the next thing I knew, Pop, the saw, and I were on this road, walking to town."

Joe rolled the Model T to a stop across the street from the Dry Dock and Ginger's. "And without a word," he continued, turning his head to his left, "we went to work, and the tree crashed down."

I leaned forward and saw a mere stump of a tree, no more than four feet high. Beyond it lay the felled trunk and a forest of downed branches.

I gasped. "You and your father . . . ?"

"It's gone now, Hanalee." Joe gazed out at the wreckage of limbs and leaves. "The lynching tree is gone."

I covered my mouth and blinked. My throat tightened. "As much as I love seeing trees standing upright and healthy . . ." I grabbed my chin and rubbed the bottom half of my face. "Oh, Jesus, Joe. That toppled oak is the most beautiful sight I've ever witnessed."

Joe swallowed and nodded, and before anyone from the Dry Dock could come out and yell about the tree, or him, or me, he adjusted the clutch lever and cruised the car to the farthest end of town, slowing down to a stop at a shady spot along the curb in front of the Lincoln Hotel.

He set the brake and leaned back against the seat. We both sighed and stared ahead out the front windshield. A boy with a nose wrapped in bandages. A girl stuck in a cast. Both of us bruised and sore and uncomfortable. The statue of Honest Abe watched us from the rhododendrons to our right.

"Just look at us, Hanalee," said Joe with another sigh. "We look like war casualties."

"We look like survivors."

"Hmm." He slipped his hands off the steering wheel. "I suppose that's true."

I scratched at my leg through my skirt, just above the opening of the cast. "Is it true? You're really leaving town tonight?"

"Yep." He lowered his face. "I'm catching a train to Seattle this evening."

"Are you heading to work in that doctor's office?"

He played with the lower buttons of his starched white shirt. "I'm going to give that job a try. See what it's like."

"What does your father think about that?"

Joe shrugged. "If I stay here, I'll have to change my ways."

"Even after helping you chop down that tree yesterday . . . ?" I asked. "Even after saying the Lord works in mysterious ways . . . ?"

"The tree was for you and your father. Not for me."

I stopped scratching at my leg. "Uncle Clyde and Mama think Washington might be a fine destination for us, too." I tipped my head to the left and squinted at him through a glare of sunlight winking through the leaves of the cherry trees across the street. "Would you be upset if we followed you up there?"

He snorted and leaned back. "Not at all. I don't know a soul up in Washington."

"You sure you'd be all right seeing me again?"

"Of course I'm sure. I'll take you to jazz clubs on Jackson Street."

I grinned. "Is that the place to be?"

"That's what your stepfather claimed, anyway. He said the area's interracial. Tolerant."

"Really?"

He nodded and swiveled toward me in his half of the seat. He picked at a scratch at the top of the upholstery, below his right thumb. "Are you taking Fleur up there, too?"

"I don't know. She's worried about upsetting her mother and Laurence if she comes with us."

"Tell her to just head up there for the rest of the summer. Get her out of Elston while everything's still settling down here. If she likes Washington and her mother's happy to have her safe with you, maybe it could become a permanent arrangement."

"That's a good idea." I gave a small nod. "I hadn't thought of that."

"Give it a try."

"I will."

Across the street, on top of the barbershop, a man crouched on the roof and hammered loose boards into place. A car drove past us, another black Model T, but I didn't recognize its occupants—a couple, young and white and handsome.

I cocked my head at Joe, and he lifted his chin and looked me in the eye. For a moment, neither of us said a word, and I nearly found myself asking, *What are we, Joe? What do we mean to each other? Why did our paths end up crossing?*

"I forgive you," I said instead. "I know in the woods, when I was hurrying you to get dressed, I said I didn't. But I do."

He stiffened his jaw and gulped with a swallow I was able to hear. With a voice that came out as a sigh of relief, he breathed the words "Thank you."

I laid the palm of my left hand on the leatherette seat between us. The man across the street hammered away, and another car whooshed by, whizzing a hot gust of air past my face.

"You swear you'll take me to jazz clubs?" I asked.

"I swear." He spread his hand over mine. "We'll have a rollicking good time."

"That would . . ." My voice caught in my throat. "That would be the bee's knees."

We both snickered at my use of goofy modern slang, and then Joe slid across the seat and wrapped both his arms around me. I pressed my cheek against his shoulder and closed my eyes, and we sat like that in his Model T for a good long while, out in the open where anyone who hated us could have seen us, but we just didn't care.

I breathed in the clean scent of his shirt, and he cupped a hand around the back of my head, and I relived it all—our plotting in the woods, our escape through the darkening trees, the encounter with the Wittens, the Klan, the cross, the torches, the noose. He squeezed me close against him, nestling his face in the crook of my neck, and I passed through all that darkness and came out to a place warm and safe and bright with sunlight. A place in which I sat in a car with a friend, with the sun shining down on my head and loving arms clasped around me.

JOE DROVE US PAST THAT FALLEN OAK AGAIN AND steered us through the sites of both his accident with Daddy and mine with Sheriff Rink. We didn't say one word to each other; we just blasted through the ghosts of the wreckage.

He and Uncle Clyde helped carry me back into the house and parked me on the sofa with my half-drawn pencil sketch still waiting for me.

Joe leaned down and kissed the top of my head. "I'll see you in Seattle."

I grabbed his hand. "Stay true to yourself, Joe. Always. No matter what happens. Please, promise me that."

He opened his mouth, as though about to say something in response, but then he nodded and stood upright.

He left our house, and an empty hollow spread throughout my chest, even though, deep down, I knew I'd see him again. Our tale did not end in tragedy.

TWO WEEKS LATER, MAMA AND UNCLE CLYDE PACKED as many of our belongings as possible in the Buick, and we locked up Mama's family's beautiful yellow house. Uncle Clyde would be back in less than a week to arrange for the transportation of the furniture, as well as to try to rent out the place so we wouldn't need to sell it just yet—in case the laws changed and the Klan died down in the near future. No burning crosses sprang up in our yard, and no one bothered us in the middle of the night, but at church we heard rumors of continued Klan congregations.

I sat in the backseat of the car, crammed between the heat of the traveling bags and the bulk of our bedding, with my cast sticking out at an awkward angle over pillows and blankets. In the front seat, Mama held a crate of kitchen supplies in her lap, with other dishes and toiletries rattling around her ankles. After cranking the engine to a start, Uncle Clyde wedged himself in, beside a pile of winter coats, in front of the steering wheel. He drove us down the driveway, past leaves the shade of banned Paulissen wine.

Over my shoulder, the house's canary-colored siding and my bedroom window disappeared behind the trees. I no longer saw the porch where I had lounged on the swing and the rails and sipped lemonade with Laurence and Fleur in the afterglow of our adventures. My throat thickened.

"Can we please hurry to Fleur's?" I asked Uncle Clyde before he turned onto the highway. "Just to see for sure?"

"I telephoned her mother once more last night," said Mama over the hum of the engine. "Polly still wasn't sure she wanted Fleur heading up there."

"I don't want her stuck in this place if Elston doesn't get any better. Please"—I grabbed hold of the seat in front of me—"let's at least stop by to check. I didn't even get a chance to say good-bye."

Uncle Clyde steered us up the drive to Fleur's house, and this time we didn't see any gangs of armed and glowering boys huddled around the old Ford truck. My stepfather pulled the sedan beside the parked and empty vehicle, and we all turned our faces toward the house.

"I'll get out and talk to Polly," said Mama, shifting toward her door.

"No"—Uncle Clyde grabbed her arm—"wait."

A second later, Laurence pushed open the screen door and blew out to the porch with the metal thwacking shut behind him. He leaned his elbows against the porch rail and rubbed his chin against his left shoulder, as though his face itched. He didn't look any one of us in the eye.

I shook my head, confused. Fear shot though my gut. Paranoia of another Klan ambush turned my breathing shallow.

A moment later, the screen door whisked open again, and Fleur traipsed outside, lugging two canvas suitcases and a bouquet of flowers the pale pink of spun sugar. I sat up straight and watched her skip down the steps of the porch with a cherry-red cloche covering her yellow hair.

Her mama came out behind her and called out, "Just through August, and then you're to come back home."

"Yes, Mama, of course." Fleur smiled and hustled up to the car door on the opposite side of the seat from me. "Is there room for me in here?"

"We'll make room," said Uncle Clyde, and he and Mama got out to rearrange our belongings, while Fleur squeezed into the backseat beside me.

She scooted over and tucked herself right next to me, minding my cast, and my parents crammed her bags and our bags between her and the door. She smelled of lilacs again, and she slipped one of her hands into one of my hands.

"I brought flowering almonds for you," she said, and she handed me the flowers, which she had wrapped in a white handkerchief and secured with a ribbon the same pink as the petals.

"Are these for luck, too," I asked, "like the alfalfa?"

"No, for hope." She squeezed my hand. "An entire bouquet full of hope."

My parents climbed back into the winter coats and the pots and the pans up front, and Uncle Clyde maneuvered the car around in the opposite direction and steered us out of the Paulissens' driveway. Just as I had watched our house disappear from view behind me, I peeked over my shoulder and observed the trees swallowing up Laurence's blond hair, his blue eyes, his lanky figure—his sorrow—until all that I saw were leaves and branches and sparrows flitting across the boughs.

Yet Fleur remained, sitting right there beside me, with her fingers laced through mine and the pink bouquet spread across both of our laps.

Uncle Clyde drove us past the sweet-smelling fields and rolling hills of northwestern Oregon, and we traveled through the growing metropolis of Portland until the bridge crossing the Columbia River to Washington rose into view. We left the state of my birth behind and entered a new world, with different laws, different adventures and challenges; a state in which I'd taste even more of love and heartbreak, hate and triumphs; where I'd dance with Joe in jazz clubs, grow into a woman with Fleur, sharpen my brain, start a career, and meet people with skin colors similar to mine. A state in which I would eventually marry and give birth to children with their own beautiful colors.

For me, the rest was not silence.

It was loud and powerful and melodic.

The Fourteenth Amendment

to the constitution of the United States section I

All persons born or naturalized in the United States, and subject to the jurisdiction thereof, are citizens of the United States and of State wherein they reside. No State shall make or enforce any law which shall abridge the privileges or immunities of citizens of the United States; nor shall any State deprive any person of life liberty, or property, without due process of law; nor deny any person within its jurisdiction the equal protection of the laws.

POST-1923 CHANGES TO OREGON LAWS

1925: The Supreme Court overturned the Ku Klux Klan–sponsored 1922 Compulsory Education Act, which would have required children in Oregon between the ages of eight and sixteen to attend public schools—and *only* public schools. The KKK had pushed for the law in an attempt to close down private Catholic schools. The overturning of the act came at a time when internal struggles and public opinion against the organization ended the KKK's brief control over Oregon and its politics.

1926: Oregonians voted to repeal the "exclusion laws" from the state constitution. The laws, first enacted in 1844 and written into the original 1857 state constitution, were aimed at preventing African Americans from settling in Oregon. Though not rigorously enforced, the laws deterred African Americans from entering the state in the latter half of the nineteenth century and kept the state predominantly white.

1927: Oregonians removed a clause in the state constitution that denied African Americans the right to vote. They also removed restrictions that discriminated against African American and Chinese American voters.

1951: The federal government repealed all legislation banning interracial marriages in Oregon. In 1967, the United States government lifted the nationwide ban on interracial marriages, after the landmark case of *Loving v. Virginia.*

1953: Governor Paul L. Patterson signed Oregon's Civil Rights Bill, outlawing "any distinction, discrimination, or restriction on account of race, religion, color, or national origin" in public places.

1972: Oregon repealed laws that criminalized same-sex sexual activity.

1983: Legislation abolished the Oregon State Board of Eugenics, called at that time the Oregon State Board of Social Protection, responsible for 2,648 forced sterilizations on children, teens, and adults from 1923 to 1981. Nineteen years later, in 2002, Governor John Kitzhaber issued a formal apology for Oregon's use of eugenics. Between 1900 and 1925, thirty-two other states enacted eugenics laws in an effort to prevent the birth of "unfit" Americans.

2002: Oregon removed racist language from the state constitution.

2014: A U.S. federal district court legalized same-sex marriages in Oregon. In 2015, the Supreme Court of the United States lifted a nationwide ban on same-sex marriages.

2015: Oregon became the third state to ban "conversion therapy" on minors. The practice was used in an attempt to change sexual orientation or gender identity.

AUTHOR'S NOTE

LIKE MOST OF MY NOVELS, *THE STEEP AND THORNY Way* grew out of a series of different story ideas that one day, without warning, exploded into a full-fledged book plot that gripped me by the shoulders and refused to let me go. In fact, I had to put this particular novel aside to write another contracted book, but the story called out to me the entire time and begged for me not to forget it.

Inspired by the HBO TV series *Boardwalk Empire* and my interest in World War I history, I at first thought about writing a novel focused on female bootleggers trying to survive with their war-widowed mothers in the 1920s. I also envisioned a completely separate novel involving a teen boy who's hiding the fact that he's gay in early-twentieth-century America. Those two threads eventually worked their way into the fabric of *The Steep and Thorny Way* in the forms of the Paulissens, the Markses, and Joe Adder.

The central plot of the book—Hanalee's story—emerged after I researched Oregon's nineteenth- and twentieth-century interracial marriage laws for one of my other novels. When I dug deeper into the history of the state's prejudices and restrictions, I unearthed the troubling exclusion laws and unofficial "sundown laws," the latter of which kept African Americans from passing through certain towns after dark. I also discovered the widespread use of eugenics in Oregon and the Ku Klux Klan's takeover of the state in the early 1920s—including the KKK's control over the 1922 gubernatorial election. As a lifelong resident of the typically open-minded West Coast, and a resident of Oregon itself since 2006, the lesser-known histories of the area shocked and saddened me. Whenever I experience a passionate reaction to a controversial piece of history, I find myself compelled to write a book about it—not to dig up old wounds and tarnish a region's reputation, but to pay tribute to those who endured and overcame the forgotten injustices of the past. I've always been in awe of fighters and survivors.

For some reason, the idea of using *Hamlet* as the template for such a book entered my head in the summer of 2013, and that's when the entire plot of this novel burst into life. I don't remember the exact moment the *Hamlet* concept possessed me, but I do remember telling my daughter about my early thoughts for the book as we walked between aisles of novels at Powell's Books in downtown Portland, Oregon. She said, "Mom, your eyes look so excited!"

Before I submitted my proposal for *The Steep and Thorny Way* to my agent, Barbara Poelle, I, admittedly, got cold feet, despite my extreme passion for the book. I worried that people would be uncomfortable with the fact that I'm a white woman writing about a biracial character. I got nervous about the controversial nature of my chosen subject matters. I nearly even changed my main character to a half-Jewish girl, because my husband is Jewish and I was raised Protestant, and we witnessed some of the prejudices against interfaith marriages when we married in the mid-1990s. Changing Hanalee's race didn't feel honest, though. That wasn't the story that wanted to be told.

I conferred with my agent and my early readers, all of whom urged me to go forward with the novel. It was important to me to consult with readers of different backgrounds, but I also understood that the opinions of a few people would not necessarily reflect the reactions of all readers.

I approached the creation of my characters the same way I do with all my novels: through intense, detailed research. Thanks to the Oregon Black Pioneers, the Oregon Historical Society, and the Washington County Museum, I found a wealth of information about the first decades of the 1900s in Oregon—everything from photographs to letters and personal items from the time period, as well as oral histories and museum exhibits, such as the wonderful "A Community on the Move," presented by both the Oregon Black Pioneers and the Oregon Historical Society in 2015. I also dove into 1920s Harlem Renaissance literature, exploring the works of such writers as Nella Larsen, Zora Neale Hurston, and Wallace

Thurman, who wrote about the varying experiences of African Americans and biracial individuals during the era. I do not claim to have gotten everything right. However, I made every attempt to portray Hanalee's experiences, as well as Joe's, with accuracy, honesty, and respect. Any mistakes made in this regard are entirely my own.

For Joe's character, I conducted research using such sources as *Same-Sex Affairs: Constructing and Controlling Homosexuality in the Pacific Northwest*, by Peter Boag (University of California Press, 2003), and the Gay and Lesbian Archives of the Pacific Northwest (www.glapn.org). I first learned about the eugenics movement when I read the book *Mad in America: Bad Science, Bad Medicine, and the Enduring Mistreatment of the Mentally Ill*, by Robert Whitaker (Basic Books, 2001). Interestingly, the University of Vermont's website (www.uvm.edu) contains a highly detailed page covering the history of the eugenics movement in Oregon, including a lengthy list of links to historical documents, photographs, and institutions related to the use of eugenics in the state.

When writing a novel about the prejudices of the past, a writer must inevitably tread a delicate line when deciding whether to incorporate terms and labels now considered offensive. If I chose to completely strip *The Steep and Thorny Way* of such words, I felt I'd be sanitizing history—cleaning it up and pretending that modern political correctness actually existed in the past. I strove to study the language of the 1920s to reflect how people in that era would have described both Hanalee and Joe and to learn how the two of them would have identified themselves, to make their characters and social interactions as authentic as possible. There are some words, however, whose power to hurt and belittle goes beyond the need for historical accuracy, and I chose not to use them. No offense is intended by the inclusion of any derogatory and/or outdated words within this book.

As I mentioned before, William Shakespeare's *Hamlet* served as the template for the main plot structure of the novel, as well as the inspiration for the characters and the source of the chapter titles. I also wanted to incorporate an African American story to reflect Hanalee's father's influence upon her. I turned to the 1996 Coretta Scott King Award–winning story collection *Her Stories: African American Folktales, Fairy Tales, and True Tales*, by Virginia Hamilton (Blue Sky Press, 1995)—a book I highly recommend. The Creole-based tale "Marie and Redfish" particularly caught my eye. I did a little digging and also found an 1889 retelling of the same story, titled "Posson [sic] Doré," or "The Golden Fish," in *The Journal of American Folklore* (Vol. 2, No. 4, pp. 36–40, American Folklore Society, Jan.–Mar., 1889). I strove to make Hanalee aware of stories and songs from her father's Southern heritage, as well as from his years of working at the Portland Hotel, in which he would have met other employees transplanted from various regions of the South. To me, "The Golden Fish" also wonderfully represented Hanalee's growing connection to Joe and his fears of getting caught and butchered. The folktale is one of violence, yet also one of survival and love. I hope readers will find the same to be true of *The Steep and Thorny Way*.

I'm extremely grateful that Amulet Books has allowed me to share this novel with the world. If the pages of this book bring hope and inspiration to even one person who's found himself or herself on a steep and thorny path in life, then I'll feel I have done my job as its writer.

ACKNOWLEDGMENTS

MY DEEPEST GRATITUDE GOES TO THE FOLLOWING:

To Barbara Poelle, my tireless agent, for her continued ability to boost my confidence in my work. Thank you from the bottom of my heart for urging me to press forward with this book.

To Maggie Lehrman, my talented editor, for sitting across a restaurant table from me in Philadelphia and saying, "I'm sold," after I'd merely uttered the words "I'm working on a retelling of *Hamlet* set in the 1920s." Thank you for editing this novel while also launching your own writing career. I'm incredibly grateful that I've had the opportunity to work with you on three of my novels.

To the entire team at Amulet Books, for their thorough and

beautiful work on all my young-adult novels. Special thanks to Erica Finkel, Jason Wells, Susan Van Metre, Tamar Brazis, Maria T. Middleton, Emily Dowdell, Tina Mories in the U.K., my diligent copy editor, proofreaders, and everyone else who played a role in the creation and promotion of this book.

To my sister, Carrie Raleigh, the very first reader of all of my books and one of the most special people in my life. She called me up in tears after finishing the last chapters of this novel and made me feel I was on the right track. Thank you!

To Francesca Miller, for her passionate belief in this book and for sharing her insights as a woman who grew up in an interracial home. And to Kim Murphy, for always digging deep into my manuscripts and letting me know exactly what they need.

To Katrina Sarson, producer of the OPB TV series *Oregon Art Beat*, for featuring me in a 2014 episode. To the Oregon Historical Society, especially library director Geoff Wexler, for being so patient while the OPB crew filmed me in the archives, and for providing me with a treasure trove of 1920s documents and photographs to peruse. Thanks to Scott Rook for assistance with the use of OHS images in this book.

To the Oregon Black Pioneers for keeping the history of African Americans in the region so wonderfully alive. And to the Library of Congress and Karen Lange and Pam Madaus of the Washington County Museum in Hillsboro, Oregon, for the generous use of archival images.

To my team of supportive writer friends, both in person and online: Miriam Forster (who came up with the David-and-Bathsheba connection, as well as the idea of using Hanalee's boot as a hiding place), Teri Brown, Kelly Garrett, Amber Keyser, Laura Byrd, Heidi Schulz, Lauren DeStefano, Susan Adrian, Ara Burklund, April Genevieve Tucholke, Megan Shepherd, A. G. Howard, Sarah Skilton, Elisabeth Dahl, April Henry, Jenn Reese, Sarah Bromley, and all the amazing kid-lit authors in Portland, Oregon, and around the world. Thanks, also, to the close friends in my life who've been cheering me on for decades, with special nods to Regena Orr, Cindy Bullock, Susanne Brookens, Jarret Lovell, Marianne Pitterle, Sarah Eishen, Laura Ponto, and Heather Hoffman.

To my parents, Richard and Jennifer Proeschel; my cousin Marie Rourke; my aunts, Carol Hacker and Mary Ward; Jack and Lois Karp; and Tim and Kim Karp, for all the years of love and encouragement.

To my daughter, Meggie, for listening to the entire plot of this book before I'd even written it and telling me she was looking forward to this novel more than anything else I'd written. To my husband, Adam, who has loved and stood by me ever since we were nineteen-year-old college kids. And to my son, Ethan, for his infectious excitement for my books, even though he hasn't yet been old enough to read them. That will change soon.

This book is for my cousin Jimmy Hacker, who passed away while I was revising the novel in February 2015. When we were kids, he helped inspire my imagination. As an adult, he showed me what courage looks like when he made a new life for himself in a place that accepted him for who he was. I hope the dedication of this novel will help keep his memory alive and bring some comfort to his mother, sister, and longtime partner.

IMAGE
CREDITS
....

ABOUT THE AUTHOR

CAT WINTERS is the author of *In the Shadow of Blackbirds*, which collected three starred reviews and was a finalist for the William C. Morris Award for debut YA fiction, and *The Cure for Dreaming*. She lives in Portland, Oregon. www.catwinters.com.

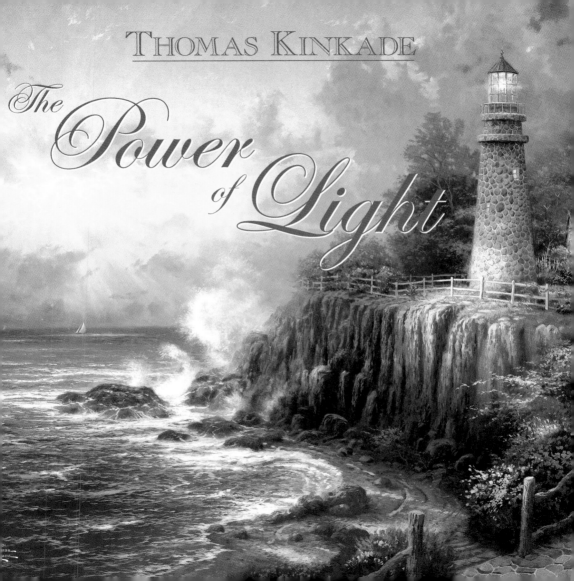

Thomas Kinkade

The Power of Light

Thomas Kinkade

The Power of Light

Thomas Kinkade

ISBN-13: 978-0-7407-7819-3
ISBN-10: 0-7407-7819-6

www.thomaskinkade.com
www.andrewsmcmeel.com

Beacons of Light compiled by Patrick Regan; *Family Traditions* and *A Book of Joy* compiled by Kathleen Blease.

Section I

Beacons
of Light

Light truly has the POWER *to* ILLUMINATE *our* LIVES *and* GUIDE *us home.*

$\mathcal{M}$any's the sea captain who has rejoiced at the sight of an illuminated lighthouse on a distant shore. For hundreds of years, such stoic, reliable beacons have led wayward travelers to sanctuary.

$\mathcal{E}$ven if we never see the world's vast oceans, each of us faces times in life when we feel adrift. In those times when we're weary and sailing on unkind waters, we seek out a safe harbor.

$\mathcal{B}$ut we need not drift on rough waters forever—for even in times of darkness and doubt, there are always bastions of hope and beacons of light to guide us. For some, the light is a powerful friendship, for others, a strong family, and for many, the guiding light comes from an unshakable faith in God.

$\mathcal{A}$s a painter and as a person, I believe in the overwhelming power of light. Whether the strong lighthouse beam cutting through thick fog or the warm glow of firelight emanating from a cottage window, light fills us with hope, warmth, and serenity. Light truly has the power to illuminate our lives and guide us home.

THOMAS KINKADE

Truth

*L*ight
is the
SYMBOL of
TRUTH.

—James Russell Lowell

THE *Foundations*
of a PERSON *are not*
IN *matter*
but in SPIRIT.

—Ralph Waldo Emerson

With every CREATIVE ACT, *you* LIGHT *a fresh candle for a* DARKENED WORLD—*and that in itself is a* POWERFUL *source of joy for your* LIFE.

—Thomas Kinkade

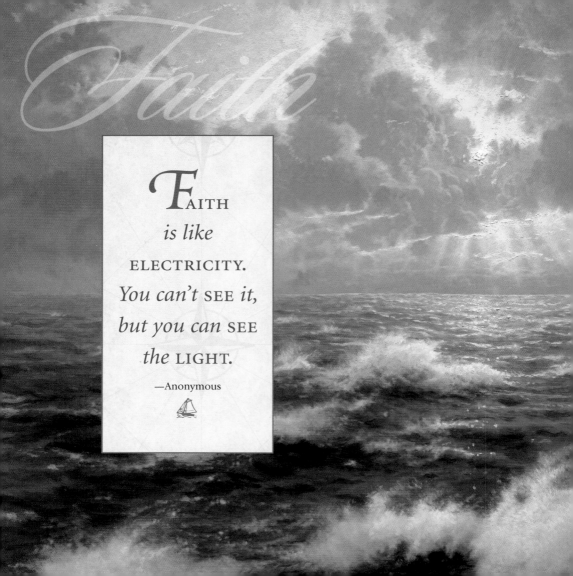

Faith

FAITH
is like
ELECTRICITY.
You can't SEE *it,*
but you can SEE
the LIGHT.
—Anonymous

$\mathcal{M}$an is
so MADE *that*
when
anything
FIRES *his*
SOUL,
impossibilities
vanish.

—Jean de La Fontaine

Your life can

RADIATE

the kind of light that truly makes a

DIFFERENCE

in the

WORLD.

—Thomas Kinkade

*I*t is TRULY said: It does not take much STRENGTH *to* do things, but it REQUIRES great strength to decide what to DO.

—Chow Ching

*M*ost of us, swimming

AGAINST *the tides of* TROUBLE

the world knows nothing about,

need only a bit of PRAISE *or*

ENCOURAGEMENT—*and we will*

make the GOAL.

—Jerome P. Fleishman

When you LIVE *in the* LIGHT *of unfolding* MIRACLES, *there is always a* FUTURE, *always a* HOPE.

—Thomas Kinkade

Thomas Kinkade

*N*o WINTER *lasts forever; no* SPRING *skips its turn.*

—Hal Borland

Appreciation of LIFE itself, becoming suddenly aware of the MIRACLE of being ALIVE, on this planet, can TURN what we call ORDINARY life into a MIRACLE. We come AWAKE to such a REALIZATION when we recognize our CONNECTION to a SPIRITUAL dimension.

—Dan Wakefield

When I see my LIFE *as a series of unfolding* MIRACLES, *I'll always sail forth with* HOPE, TRANQUILLITY, *and* JOY *in my heart.*

—Thomas Kinkade

Not FARE *well,* *but fare* FORWARD, *voyagers.*

—T. S. Eliot

*C*herish your VISIONS;
cherish your IDEALS;
cherish the music
that stirs in your heart,
the BEAUTY that forms in your MIND,
the LOVELINESS that drapes your
purest THOUGHTS . . .
if you but remain true to them,
your world will at last be built.

—James Allen

trust

Faith is the CHOICE *to sail* FORWARD *before you are sure why you are going through what you are going through . . . before you are* CONFIDENT *you can* TRUST *the final outcome.*

—Thomas Kinkade

Beautiful
LIGHT *is born*
of DARKNESS,
so the FAITH
that springs
from conflict is
often the
STRONGEST
and the BEST.

—R. Turnbull

The power in which we must have faith if we would be well, is the

CREATIVE

and

CURATIVE

power which exists in every living thing.

—John Kellogg

power

Thomas Kinkade

HOPE

will HELP *you find your way*

through DARK *and* STORMY

nights . . . through FOGGY *and*

CONFUSING *days.*

—Thomas Kinkade

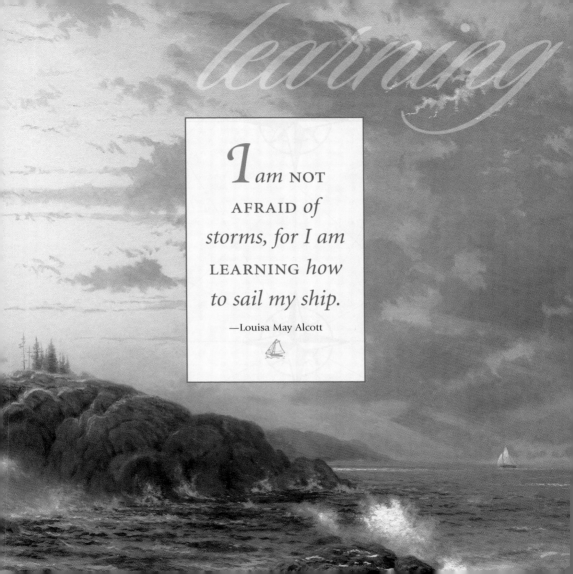

learning

I *am* NOT AFRAID *of* storms, for I am LEARNING *how* to sail my ship.

—Louisa May Alcott

treasure

Thomas
Kinkade

Your treasure house is within; it contains all you'll ever need.

—Hui-Hai

Once we
DISCOVER *how*
to appreciate
the timeless
VALUES *in*
our daily
EXPERIENCES,
we can enjoy
the best things
in LIFE.

—Harry Hepner

MAKE
Time
IN YOUR *Life*
FOR
Wonder.

—Thomas Kinkade

Thomas
Kinkade

*S*pirit is
MATTER *seen*
in a stronger
LIGHT.

—L. P. Jacks

believe

I BELIEVE *though I do not* COMPREHEND, *and I hold by* FAITH *what I cannot* GRASP *with the* MIND.

—St. Bernard

*There are two ways
of spreading light:
to be the candle
or the mirror
that reflects it.*

—Edith Wharton

*C*herish the
PEOPLE *who make*
up your HOME,
and you'll notice
the hearth
FIRES *burn*
BRIGHTER *than*
ever before.

—Thomas Kinkade

home

I have come back again to *where I* BELONG; *not an* ENCHANTED *place, but the* walls are STRONG.

—Dorothy H. Rath

Thomas Kinkade

The WISEST *keeps something of the* VISION *of a child. Though he may* UNDERSTAND *a thousand things that a child could not* UNDERSTAND, *he is always a beginner, close to the* ORIGINAL MEANING *of life.*

—John Macy

Path

You will RECOGNIZE
your own PATH *when you come*
upon it, because you will suddenly
have all the

ENERGY

and

IMAGINATION

you will ever need.

—Jerry Gillies

*Y*our home:
the place
where love and
joy and
tranquillity
burn the
brightest.

—Thomas Kinkade

Love

Thomas Kinkade

The STRENGTH
of a nation
derives from the
INTEGRITY *of*
the HOME.

—Confucius

Hope

*H*ope
*is the parent
of faith.*

—Cyrus A. Bartol

When you cannot make up your mind which of two evenly BALANCED *courses of* ACTION *you should take—choose the* BOLDER.

—William Joseph Slim

Reason

The way to see by Faith is to shut the Eye of Reason.

—Benjamin Franklin

If you find that JOY *is fading in* your HEART, *you might pay attention to your* PASSIONS, *your* PURPOSES, *and* your PURSUITS.

—Thomas Kinkade

passion

glory

I see
heaven's
glories shine
and faith
shines equal.

—Emily Brontë

C REATIVITY, *as has been said,*
consists largely of REARRANGING
what we KNOW *in order to find out*
what we do not know. Hence, to
think CREATIVELY, *we must be able*
to look afresh at what we normally
take for granted.

—George Kneller

Thomas Kinkade

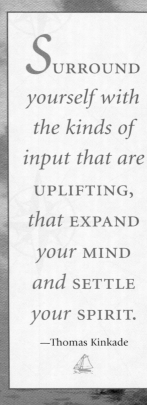

*S*URROUND
yourself with
the kinds of
input that are
UPLIFTING,
that EXPAND
your MIND
and SETTLE
your SPIRIT.

—Thomas Kinkade

*B*elief
consists in
ACCEPTING *the*
affirmations of
the SOUL;
UNBELIEF, *in*
DENYING *them.*

—Ralph Waldo Emerson

WHAT YOU KEEP TO
YOURSELF YOU LOSE;
WHAT YOU
GIVE
AWAY, YOU
KEEP
FOREVER.

—Axel Munthe

*O*nly *let the moving waters* CALM *down, and the sun and moon will be* REFLECTED *on the surface of your* BEING.

—Jal'al al-D'in Rumi

world

*I*t's the highest CALLING *any of us
have in life: making the* WORLD *a little*
BRIGHTER *because of the way we
paint our* DAYS *and* HOURS *and*
MONTHS *and* YEARS.

—Thomas Kinkade

We are
what we
BELIEVE we are.

—Benjamin N. Cardozo

give

The most satisfying thing in life is to have been able to give a large part of oneself to others.

—Pierre Teilhard de Chardin

Your life has meaning and
beauty, and you are not in it alone.

—Thomas Kinkade

Section II

A Book
of Joy

joy

Thomas Kinkade

Beauty enters your heart through all the senses, and the beauty grows stronger when more than one of the senses is involved.

—Thomas Kinkade

*Keeping a glow book
or joy journal is something
I would highly recommend
if you find yourself a little rusty
at recognizing the joy gifts that come your way.*

—Thomas Kinkade

Close your eyes,
and *picture* a place
you're *yearning* to be.
A place that *is beautiful*
and *comforting*,
where *everything*
is hopeful and alive.

—Thomas Kinkade

Thomas
Kinkade

Not many sounds in life,

and I include all urban

and all rural sounds,

exceed in interest

a knock at the door.

—Charles Lamb

life

Harmony

is pure love,

for love

is complete agreement.

—Lope de Vega

He that has light within his own clear breast may sit i' th' centre and enjoy a bright day.

—John Milton

Consistent and durable joy
is generated
when we pursue a passion
that is strong enough
to carry us past pain,
something so meaningful
and absorbing
that we can ignore
unhappy circumstances.

—Thomas Kinkade

Our joys

as winged dreams

do fly.

—Anonymous

Just as the body grows
and flourishes
on a healthy diet,
our joy can grow
and flourish
when fed a steady diet
of beauty.

—Thomas Kinkade

The supreme happiness

of life

is the conviction

that we are loved.

—Victor Hugo

The harvest

of a quiet eye.

—William Wordsworth

*The first beauty
the world has to offer
is in nature.*

—Thomas Kinkade

*A Garden
is a lovesome thing!*

—Thomas Edward Brown

beauty

beauty

Why is beauty so important?
Because we derive energy and
motivation from beautiful sights,
beautiful sounds, beautiful words
and ideas, and beautiful environments.

—Thomas Kinkade

What a piece of work is a man!

how noble in reason! how infinite in faculty!

in form and moving how express and admirable!

in action how like an angel!

in apprehension how like a god!

the beauty of the world!

the paragon of animals!

—William Shakespeare

heart

Decide that joy is the hue
you want your heart to be.

Then start making

the little and large choices that

over time will paint your heart happy.

— Thomas Kinkade

A thing of beauty is a joy forever;

Its loveliness increases; it will never

Pass into nothingness; but still will keep

A bower quiet for us, and a sleep

Full of sweet dreams,

and health, and quiet breathing.

—John Keats

For love is heaven,

and heaven is love.

—Sir Walter Scott

Give love,

   and love to your life will flow,

      A strength in your utmost need;

Have faith, and a score of hearts will show

      Their faith in your work and deed.

—Madeline S. Bridges (aka Mary Ainge de Vere)

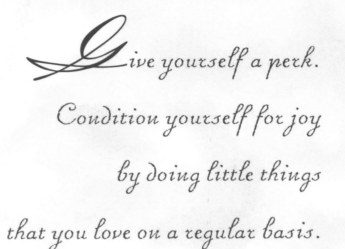

Give yourself a perk.

Condition yourself for joy

by doing little things

that you love on a regular basis.

— Thomas Kinkade

Surely goodness
and mercy
shall follow me
all the days of my life;
and I will dwell
in the house of the Lord
for ever.

—Psalms 23:6, King James version

The art of being happy

lies in the power

of extracting happiness

from common things.

— Henry Ward Beecher

You don't *need* to travel long distances to *revel* in *natural* beauty. All *you* have to *do*, most of the *time*, is go *outside* and *look* at the sky.

— Thomas Kinkade

The greatest pleasure

I know

is to do a good action

by stealth

and have it found out

by accident.

—Charles Lamb

pleasure

Once you begin looking,
you may be surprised to discover
just how much joy
your world has to offer.

— Thomas Kinkade

Grief

can take care of itself,

but to get the full value

of a joy

you must have somebody

to divide it with.

—Mark Twain

Growth itself

contains the germ of happiness.

—Pearl S. Buck

Heather's Hutch

Thomas Kinkade

Happiness is a butterfly

which when pursued

is just out of grasp . . . .

But if you will

sit down quietly,

may alight upon you.

—Nathaniel Hawthorne

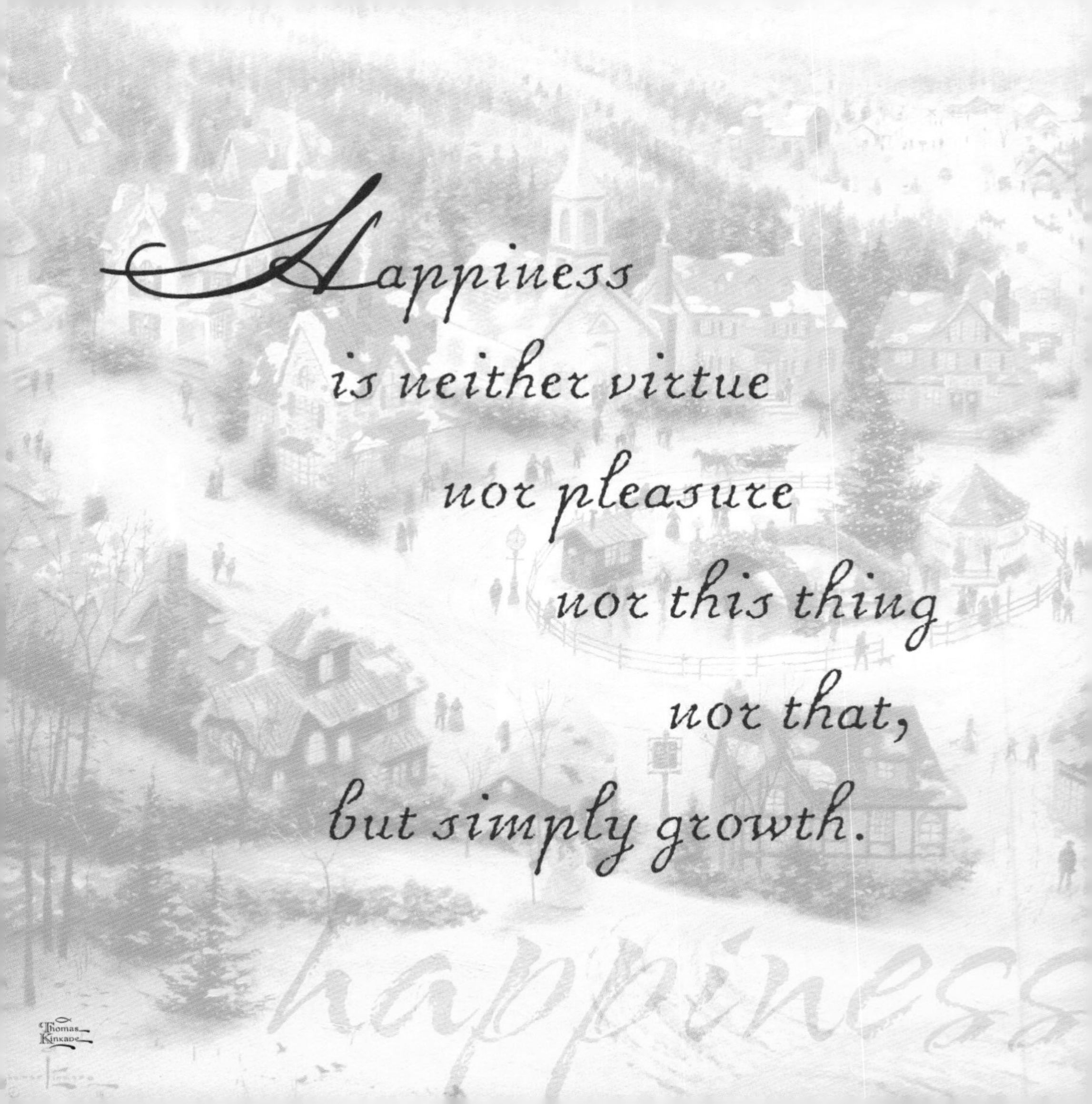

Happiness
is neither virtue
nor pleasure
nor this thing
nor that,
but simply growth.

We are happy when we are growing.

—William Butler Yeats

*Deep, abiding joy
is available to anyone
who learns the secret
of pursuing every task
with energy and dedication,
as though it were a calling.*

—Thomas Kinkade

dedication

*Happiness is the realization
of God in the heart.
Happiness is the result
of praise and thanksgiving,
of faith, of acceptance;
a quiet tranquil realization
of the love of God.*

—White Eagle

First,
keep peace
within yourself,
then you can also
bring peace to others.

—Thomas à Kempis

It really is possible
to color a dark canvas golden,
even with the tiniest of brushes.
You just keep on dabbing the paint,
and sooner or later you transform
the surface with brightness.

*In the same way,
if you keep on making joy choices,
small and large, your heart
will eventually display
a joyful tint that is more durable
than you ever imagined.*

— Thomas Kinkade

*The happiness of life
is made up of minute fractions —
the little, soon-forgotten charities
of a kiss or smile,
a kind look
or heartfelt compliment.*

—Samuel Taylor Coleridge

If you want happiness
for an hour, take a nap.
If you want happiness
for a day, go fishing.
If you want happiness
for a year, inherit a fortune.
If you want happiness
for a lifetime, help somebody.

—Chinese proverb

I've learned from experience
that the greater part
of our happiness or misery
depends on our dispositions
and not on our circumstances.

— Martha Washington

Joy is the happiness of love —

love aware of its own inner happiness.

Pleasure comes from without,
and joy comes from within,
and it is, therefore,
within reach of everyone in the world.

—Bishop Fulton J. Sheen

Many persons have a wrong idea
of what constitutes true happiness.
It is not attained
        through self-gratification
but through fidelity
    to a worthy purpose.

—Helen Keller

May there always be work
for your hands to do,
May your purse always hold a coin or two.
May the sun always shine
warm on your windowpane,
May a rainbow be certain to follow each rain.
May the hand of a friend always be near you,
And may God fill your heart
with gladness to cheer you.

—Anonymous

Somehow not only for Christmas
But all the long year through,
The joy that you give to others
Is the joy that comes back to you.

Thomas Kinkade

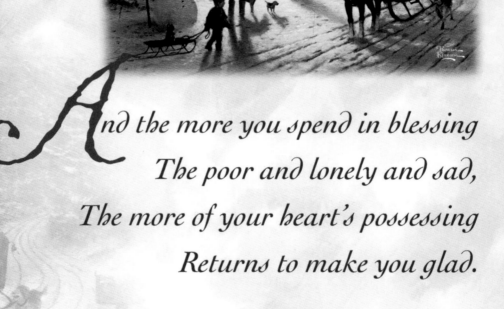

And the more you spend in blessing
The poor and lonely and sad,
The more of your heart's possessing
Returns to make you glad.

—John Greenleaf Whittier

The sun does not shine

for a few trees and flowers,

but for the wide world's joy.

—Henry Ward Beecher

shine

There is no value in life except what you choose to place upon it and no happiness in any place except what you bring to it yourself.

—Henry David Thoreau

There is only one way
to happiness and that is
to cease worrying about things
which are beyond
the power of our will.

—Epictetus

*Twenty years from now
you will be more disappointed
by the things that you didn't do
than the ones you did do.*

sail away

So throw off the bowlines. Sail away from the harbor. Catch the trade winds in your sails. Explore. Dream. Discover.

— Mark Twain

To strive with difficulties, and to conquer them, is the highest human felicity.

—Samuel Johnson

Section III

Family
Traditions

It was once said that no man is an island. Just imagine how life would be without the comforts and strengths of a family. What would happen if they were suddenly taken away? Without them, you wouldn't have a place to learn about life. Here, within the family, is where we (children *and* adults) try on new wings, stretch the mind, hang new hopes, and live out dreams— even before tackling the real world.

There's no greater comfort to a young child than a family. And there's no greater joy to a parent than building a family that is sustaining and nurturing. Family is a funny word. The dictionary defines it as a group of people who share a blood lineage. But so many strong, healthy families are made of people who are not related at all—those who are bonded by joys! Whatever your family tree looks like, whoever you consider your family to be, without them life would be a steep cliff. Family is the tether and the spikes that keep our feet safely planted while we look out over the glorious world. What a blessing family is! A remarkable invention: wings *and* roots, inseparable! Created by God and given to us as His gift.

Home.

Is there a more
evocative word
in all the
English language?

—*Thomas Kinkade*

Picture a world
the way it was meant to be.
Where work and leisure
take their proper place,
where faith and hope
and love abide,
and new possibilities
forever bloom.

—Thomas Kinkade

No matter how many communes

the family

anybody invents,
always creeps back.

　　　　　—*Margaret Mead*

Fill your home with beautiful aromas.
Have you ever noticed how
a single whiff of a familiar fragrance
has the power to carry you instantly
back to your childhood?

— *Thomas Kinkade*

He is rich or poor according to what he is, not according to what he has.

—Henry Ward Beecher

THOMASTON BROOK

WALK YOUR
HORSES

EL. 528

Make home a priority in life. Invest time and energy in creating a warm refuge for yourself and your family, a place where everyone can feel nurtured and cared for, safe and protected, free to be exactly who you are.

—Thomas Kinkade

Ever since I was a boy, my dreams
of travel and adventure have been
balanced with a powerful sense
of home, the vision of a warm
center for all my roamings,
the notion of a glowing hearth
where I could retire after a
hard day's journey to rest,
to be renewed, to remind myself
of who I am and what I love.

—*Thomas Kinkade*

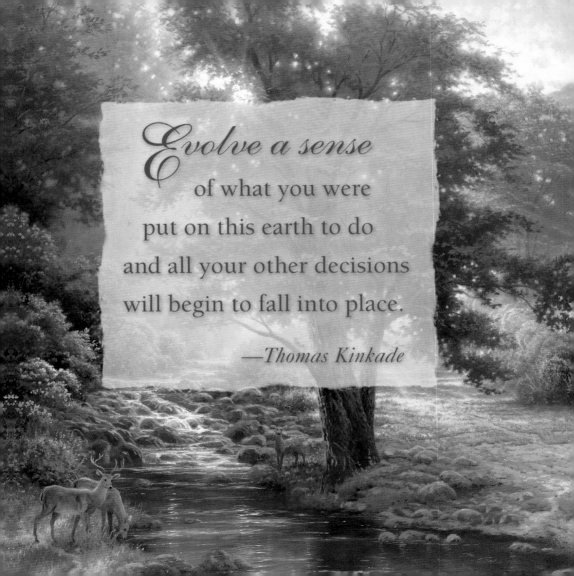

Thomas Kinkade

He that raises a large family does, indeed, while he lives to observe them, stand a broader mark for sorrow; but then he stands a broader mark for pleasure too.

—Benjamin Franklin

When thinking about composing your life, begin by making some foundational decisions about how you'll spend your time, where you'll invest your energy, and why you are

doing it all in the first place.

—Thomas Kinkade

Anyone can spare
fifteen minutes a day
for the practice
of conscious joy.

—Thomas Kinkade

joy

A happy family

is but an

earlier heaven.

— *Sir John Bowring*

Watch for surprises.
A tree full of butterflies...
a fresh breeze on a hot day...
a simple unexpected sense
that all is well.

—*Thomas Kinkade*

It is the security that comes from truly being at home that gives one the courage and freedom to travel, to seek adventure.

—Thomas Kinkade

Thomas Kinkade

Such is the patriot's boast,
His first, best

where'er we roam,
country ever is at home.

— Oliver Goldsmith

I can still picture

the floor plan of the house
where I lived as an older child;
even today I could find my way
around it in the dark.
(Couldn't you do the same?)

—*Thomas Kinkade*

*Passion and joy
are intimately connected.*

—Thomas Kinkade

Sit down with a sheet of paper and try to feel is the primary focus of your life, what you were born to do.

capture, in about ten words, what you
what is important to you,

—*Thomas Kinkade*

*There is history
in all men's lives.*

—William Shakespeare

$\mathcal{R}$EMEMBER *lazy summer days of sipping lemonade and skipping stones or just sitting, being bored? Re-creating that feeling for even a short time can nurture the childlike spirit inside your heart.*

—Thomas Kinkade

Simple comforts—from the warmth of a woolly afghan to

can reinforce your sense that all

*the reassuring glow of a nightlight in the hall—
is well.*
　　　　　　　—Thomas Kinkade

If we want to discover a childlike joy, we need to practice looking at the opportunities of the moment and saying, "Let's do it now!"

—*Thomas Kinkade*

We need to surround ourselves
and our families with objects
and ideas and activities that
please and excite our senses,
that make us smile, that provide
a soothing balm of comfort
for our days.

—Thomas Kinkade

Backward, turn backward,

O Time, in our flight,

Make me a child again

Just for tonight.

—Elizabeth Akers Allen

We live far more joyfully
when we allow ourselves
a playful spirit
in our work
and when we inject
meaning and purpose
into our play.

—Thomas Kinkade

A funny remark from a child, a spectacular
a fresh breeze on a hot day, or just a simple
that all is well—any of these experiences
if you let yourself receive it.

cloud formation, a tree full of butterflies,
unexpected sense
can be a gift of joy

—*Thomas Kinkade*

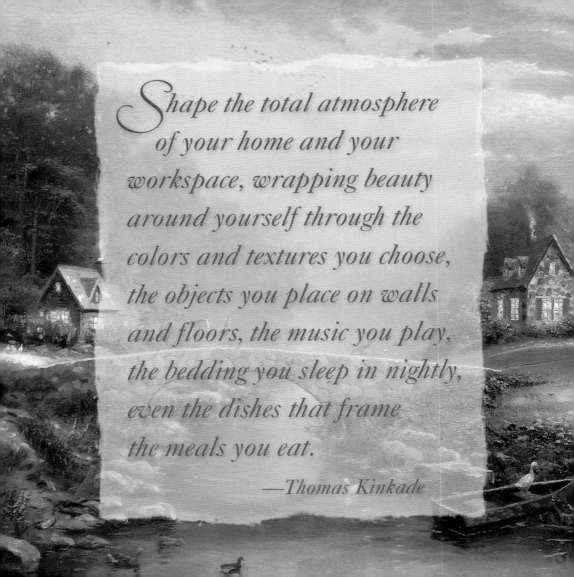

Shape the total atmosphere of your home and your workspace, wrapping beauty around yourself through the colors and textures you choose, the objects you place on walls and floors, the music you play, the bedding you sleep in nightly, even the dishes that frame the meals you eat.

—Thomas Kinkade

Thomas Kinkade

But every house where Love abides

And Friendship is a guest,

Is surely home, and home-sweet-home;

For there the heart can rest.

—Henry Van Dyke

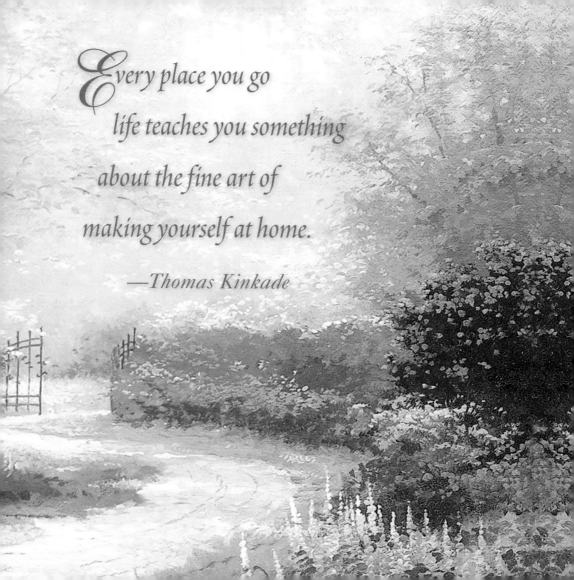

Every place you go
life teaches you something
about the fine art of
making yourself at home.

—*Thomas Kinkade*

One good way to foster the awareness
of all the good in your home
is actually to plan a house blessing—
a time when you and your family
and friends walk through the rooms
of the home and offer special prayers
of thanksgiving and benediction.

—*Thomas Kinkade*

Offer it all,

even the walls and floors

and ceiling, to God's care.

I believe you'll find that this time

of blessing provides you with a

heightened awareness and a deeper

love of the gift that is your home.

—Thomas Kinkade

One of the most meaningful ways we have found to shape our home and make it uniquely ours is to establish and uphold family rituals. We have found that these deliberately repeated experiences are especially effective ways of building a shared history and nurturing our family relationships.

—*Thomas Kinkade*

relationships

Nurturing

Having someplace to go is home.
Having someone

to love is family.
Having both is a blessing.

—*Unknown*

There are only two lasting bequests
we can hope to give our children.
One of these is roots, the other, wings.

—Hodding Carter

The little world of childhood with its familiar surroundings is a model of the greater world.

— Carl Jung

Feelings of worth can flourish only in an atmosphere where individual differences are appreciated, mistakes are tolerated, communication is open, and rules are flexible— the kind of atmosphere that is found in a nurturing family.

—Virginia Satir

Whether a biological family or an extended family of people attracted to each other based on heart resonance and mutual support, the word "family" implies warmth, a place where the core feelings of the heart are nurtured.

— Thomas Kinkade

There is always one moment

in childhood when the door opens

and lets the future in.

—Graham Greene

In the rush of schedules and responsibilities
and even recreational pursuits, it becomes
far too easy to go through life
with blinders on, oblivious to
(and far too busy for)
the joyful surprises waiting
to be discovered at any given moment.
If you want these little gifts of joy
in your life, you may actually have to
train yourself to notice them.

—Thomas Kinkade

My heart is happy, my mind is free

I had a father who talked with me.

—Hilda Bigelow

We find delight in the beauty and happiness of children that makes the heart too big for the body.

—Ralph Waldo Emerson

When voices of childhood
are heard on the green
And laughing is heard on the hill,
My heart is at rest within my breast
And everything else is still.

—William Blake

On the basis of experience
I wholeheartedly offer this prescription
for remaining a child at heart:
Have children.

—Thomas Kinkade